A PLUME

RASHI'S DAU

BOOK I: JOHEVED

MAGGIE ANTON was born Margaret Antonofsky in Los Angeles, California. Raised in a secular, socialist household, she reached adulthood with little knowledge of her Jewish religion. All that changed when Dave Parkhurst entered her life, and they discovered Judaism as adults. That was the start of a lifetime of adult Jewish education, synagogue involvement, and ritual observance. This was in addition to raising their children, Emily and Ari, and working full-time as a clinical chemist.

In 1997, as her nest was emptying and her mother was declining with Alzheimer's disease, Anton became intrigued with the idea that Rashi, one of Judaism's greatest scholars, had no sons, only three daughters. Using techniques developed doing her family's genealogy, she began to research Rashi's family, and the idea of a book about them was born.

Eight years later, the first volume of *Rashi's Daughters* was finally complete, making Maggie Anton a Talmud maven and an authority on medieval French Jewish women. She retired from the lab and spent the next two years researching and writing *Book Two: Miriam*, in addition to lecturing at more than a hundred synagogues, JCCs, and Jewish women's organizations.

Maggie lives with her husband, Dave, of thirty-six years, in Glendale, California, where she is working on *Rashi's Daughters, Book Three: Rachel*, as well as a translation of *Machzor Vitry.* You can follow her blog and contact her at her website: www.rashisdaughters.com.

Praise for

Rashi's Daughters, Book I: Joheved

"*Rashi's Daughters* offers readers a glimpse into a fascinating world . . . and explores the lives of a famous scholar and his (unfortunately) not-so-famous daughters . . . realistic and captivating."

—Dvora Weisberg, PhD, Associate Professor of Rabbinics and Director of the Beit Midrash, Hebrew Union College Jewish Institute of Religion in Los Angeles

"Anton painted a wonderful scene of Jewish life in medieval France; I loved the characters—can't wait to read about Miriam."

—Devorah Zlochower, Director of Full-Time Programs, Drisha Institute, New York

"No one who reads this novel will ever read Rashi's writings in the same way."

—Dr. Neil Gillman, Professor of Jewish Philosophy, Jewish Theological Seminary of America, and author of *Sacred Fragments: Recovering Theology for the Modern Jew*

"Rashi and his entire community spring to life in this intriguing novel. Maggie Anton's combination of history, imagination, and feminist readings of classical Talmudic texts is impressive."

—Rabbi Laura Geller, Senior Rabbi, Temple Emanuel, Beverly Hills

"Maggie Anton does the world a great service in giving us such an accessible picture of Jewish life in Western Europe of the eleventh century."

—Rabbi Tracee Rosen, Congregation Kol Ami, Salt Lake City

"Well written and carries the reader along nicely."

—Emily Taitz, coauthor of the *JPS Guide to Jewish Women: 600 B.C.E.–1900 C.E., Remarkable Jewish Women: Rebels Rabbis and Other Women from Biblical Times until the Present*

"The amount of learning Maggie Anton weaves into her vividly imagined romantic story is amazing. The reader plunges into the world of medieval Ashkenazic tradition, truly becoming the student of the great Salomon ben Isaac."

—Sylvie Weil, Professor Emerita, Hunter College, CUNY, and author of *Les Vendanges de Rachi* and *My Guardian Angel*

"*Rashi's Daughters* brings to life a very different time in the history of the Jewish people . . . focusing on the women who, from the perspective of a traditional account of the period, would be invisible."

—Rabbi Carla Freedman, Jewish Family Congregation, South Salem, New York

"Anton has re-imagined the life and world of the famed eleventh-century biblical teacher Rashi through the lives of his three daughters . . . giving readers a glimpse into everyday medieval family life without detracting from the historical backdrop or a powerful story. Readers will definitely be hooked on this series."

—*Romantic Times*

"The immersion into the world of eleventh-century Troyes, France, is complete . . . I am particularly grateful for Anton's vivid and careful research, which throws a fascinating light on the everyday life of Rashi and his family . . . a wedding-night scene worthy of *The Red Tent.*"

—*World Jewish Digest* by Ruchama King Feuerman, author of *Seven Blessings*

"Impressive work . . . fine storyteller . . . absorbing, detailed account."

—*Jewish Journal*

"The writing successfully captures the pace of medieval life and pulls the reader into the details of the characters' lives."

—*Jewish Times News*

"*Rashi's Daughters* is a wonderful, richly textured yarn incorporating all the sights, sounds, and impressions of an eleventh-century Jewish community."

—*Bookpleasures*

"A forceful novel of the power of learning, faith, and the two sides of love."

—*Midwest Book Review*

Rashi's Daughters

Book I: Joheved

MAGGIE ANTON

A PLUME BOOK

PLUME
Published by Penguin Group
Penguin Group (USA) Inc., 375 Hudson Street, New York, New York 10014, U.S.A. • Penguin Group (Canada), 90 Eglinton Avenue East, Suite 700, Toronto, Ontario, Canada M4P 2Y3 (a division of Pearson Penguin Canada Inc.) • Penguin Books Ltd., 80 Strand, London WC2R 0RL, England • Penguin Ireland, 25 St. Stephen's Green, Dublin 2, Ireland (a division of Penguin Books Ltd.) • Penguin Group (Australia), 250 Camberwell Road, Camberwell, Victoria 3124, Australia (a division of Pearson Australia Group Pty. Ltd.) • Penguin Books India Pvt. Ltd., 11 Community Centre, Panchsheel Park, New Delhi – 110 017, India • Penguin Group (NZ), 67 Apollo Drive, Rosedale, North Shore 0745, Auckland, New Zealand (a division of Pearson New Zealand Ltd.) • Penguin Books (South Africa) (Pty.) Ltd., 24 Sturdee Avenue, Rosebank, Johannesburg 2196, South Africa

Penguin Books Ltd., Registered Offices: 80 Strand, London WC2R 0RL, England

Published by Plume, a member of Penguin Group (USA) Inc. Originally published by Banot Press.

First Plume Printing, August 2007
10 9 8 7 6 5

The Library of Congress has catalogued the Banot Press edition as follows:

Anton, Maggie.
Rashi's Daughters : Book One—Joheved / Maggie Anton.
p. cm.
ISBN: 978-0-9763050-5-7 (Banot)
ISBN: 978-0-452-28862-1 (Plume)
1. Jewish women—Fiction. 2. Rashi, 1040-1105—Fiction. 3. Troyes (France)—Fiction. 4. Jews—France—Fiction. 5. Jews—France—History—to 1500—Fiction. I. Title.
PS3551.N765 R3 2005
813.54—dd22 2005920049

Printed in the United States of America

PUBLISHER'S NOTE
This is a work of fiction. Names, characters, places, and incidents are either the product of the author's imagination or are used fictitiously, and any resemblance to actual persons, living or dead, business establishments, events, or locales is entirely coincidental.

In loving memory of my mother

ANNE S. ANTON EINSTEIN

Like Rashi,

A teacher of teachers

preface

AT THE BEGINNING OF most novels, you come across a statement that says something like, "All characters in this book are fictional and any resemblance to actual persons, living or dead, is purely coincidental." In *Rashi's Daughters,* however, most of the characters are actual persons, and I've made every effort to ensure that their fictional lives resemble reality as accurately as possible.

To this end I have spent much of the last seven years poring over books and journal articles in English, French and Hebrew, as well as visiting Troyes and consulting with medieval and Jewish scholars. Naturally much of my attention centered on women, and I read everything I could find to document how my gender, so often neglected in historical studies, fared during the Middle Ages. I'm lucky that I had access to excellent libraries in the Los Angeles area, including the University of California, the University of Southern California, Hebrew Union College, the University of Judaism, and the Los Angeles and Glendale public libraries.

Of course I must mention the subject that started me on the journey of writing this book—Talmud. I'm proud that over the years I've managed to study with so many wonderful female Talmud scholars: Rachel Adler, Judith Hauptman, Benay Lappe, Janet Sternfeld Davis, Dvora Weisberg. I am also deeply indebted to Rabbi Aaron J. Katz, my friend and study partner, without whose knowledge and encouragement this book would not exist.

I want to thank my editor, Beth Lieberman, for help that went far beyond her job description. Last, but certainly not least, I offer my thanks and love to my husband, David, who listened patiently to countless stories about Rashi and his daughters, who read and critiqued countless drafts, always giving me excellent advice, and to my children, Emily and Ari, who for the most part cheerfully tolerated their mother's obsession.

timeline

1020 (4780) Steel-rimmed plough, capable of making deep furrows in heavy soil, is now in general use in Northern Europe.

1030 Henry I becomes King of France.

Rabbenu Gershom (Light of the Exile) dies in Mayence, Germany.

1030–32 Great famine occurs in France.

1032 Benedict IX becomes pope, reigns until 1045.

1037 Count Eudes II of Blois dies; his son Thibault inherits Blois, son Etienne becomes Count of Champagne.

1040 (4800) Salomon ben Isaac (Rashi) is born in Troyes, France, on February 22.

1047 Count Etienne dies; his son Eudes III inherits Brie and Champagne. Eudes III opposes King Henry; Uncle Thibault is king's loyal vassal.

1050 Invention of horseshoes enables horses to plow fields much more efficiently than oxen.

1054 Salomon goes to Mayence to study with Uncle Simon haZaken.

Under Pope Leo IX, split develops between Byzantine/eastern and Roman/western church.

1057 Salomon marries Rivka, goes to Worms to study under Jacob ben Yakar.

1059 King Henry consecrates son Philip as next king of France in Rheims; Count Eudes III does not attend.

Joheved is born to Salomon and Rivka in Troyes.

1060 Philip I becomes king of France; Henry IV is emperor of Germany. Nicholas II is pope, Benedict X is antipope.

1062 Count Eudes III is found guilty of nobleman's murder; Uncle Thibault takes over Champagne and forces Eudes to flee and take refuge with his cousin, Duke William of Normandy.

Miriam is born to Salomon and Rivka in Troyes.

1064 Jacob ben Yakar of Worms dies; Salomon continues studies in Worms under Isaac ben Eliezer haLevi.

1065 Crusade to expel Moors from Spain begins.

1066 Salomon studies in Mayence with Isaac ben Judah. William (the Conqueror) becomes king of England.

1068 Salomon returns to Troyes.

1069 Rachel/Belle is born to Salomon and Rivka in Troyes.

1070 **(4830)** Count Thibault marries second wife, Adelaide de Bar, a young widow.

Salomon founds Yeshiva in Troyes.

1071 Count Thibault and Adelaide's first son, Eudes IV, is born in Troyes. King Philip I marries Bertha.

1073 Hildebrand, a Cluniac monk, is elected Pope Gregory XII.

1075 Salomon's teacher, Isaac haLevi, dies in Worms.

Robert founds the monastic order of Molesme.

Pope Gregory announces excommunication of married priests, suspends German bishops opposed to clerical celibacy and threatens to excommunicate King Philip.

1076 Thibault and Adelaide's third son, Hugues, is born.
Pope Gregory excommunicates German King Henry.
Winter '76–'77 is coldest in century.

1077 Drought occurs in Champagne.
Pope Gregory appoints Rudolph as new king of Germany.

1078 Daughter Constance is born to King Philip I and Bertha.
Civil war begins in Germany.

1080 Archbishop Manasse of Rheims is deposed by Pope Gregory, a blow to King Philip.
King Henry of Germany appoints Clement III antipope.

1081 Prince Louis VI is born to King Philip and Bertha.

1083 King Henry attacks Rome; Pope Gregory flees.

1084 (4844) Fire in Mayence is attributed to Jews; many move to Speyer.
Count Etienne-Henry marries Adele, daughter of William the Conqueror.
Normans expel Germans from Rome, then sack city.

1085 Pope Gregory dies in Salerno.

1088 Cardinal Otto is elected Pope Urban II.

1089 Epidemic occurs in Champagne, Count Thibault dies. Champagne goes to Eudes IV, Blois to Etienne-Henry.

1092 King Philip repudiates Queen Bertha to marry Bertrada, wife of Count Fulk of Anjou, enraging Pope Urban.

1093 Eudes IV dies; Thibault's son, Hugues, becomes Count of Champagne.
Count Erard of Brienne starts war with Hugues.

1094 Pope Urban excommunicates King Philip over Bertrada.
Terrible drought in Champagne occurs that summer.

1095 Hugues marries Constance, daughter of King Philip.
Spectacular meteor showers occur in April.

1096 (4856) Crusades start. Four major Jewish communities in Rhineland are attacked between Passover and Shavuot: May 3, Speye; May 18, Worms; May 27, Mayence; May 30, Cologne. Over 10,000 Jews die.
Lunar eclipse occurs in early August.

1097 Jews converted during Crusades are permitted to return to Judaism.
Comet is seen for seven nights in October.

1098 Robert of Molesme founds Citeaux Abbey and Cistercian Order.

1099 Crusaders take Jerusalem.

1100 Louis VI becomes king-elect of France.
Paschal II is pope, Theodoric is antipope.
Jews return to Mayence.
Discovery of alcohol by distillation is made in Salerno medical school.

1104 Assassination attempt is made on Count Hugues.

1105 (4865) Salomon ben Isaac dies on July 17.

If the Christians educate their sons, they do so not for God, but for gain, in order that one brother, if he be a cleric, may help his father and mother and his other brothers . . . But the Jews, out of zeal for God and love of the law, put as many sons as they have to letters, that each may understand God's law . . . and not only his sons, but his daughters.

—Anonymous student of Peter Abelard,
twelfth-century Paris

Declared Ben Azzai: "A man must teach his daughter Torah so that if she drinks she will know that her merit will suspend her punishment." Rav Eliezer said: "Whoever teaches his daughter Torah teaches her lechery."

—Babylonian Talmud, Tractate Sotah 20a

Rashi's Daughters

Book I: Joheved

prologue

STUDENTS OF JEWISH HISTORY are aware that medieval Spanish Jewry enjoyed a golden age for five hundred years prior to the Inquisition. It is less well known that the Jews of Northern France possessed at least a silver age for approximately two hundred years at the beginning of the second millennium, in the peace that existed between the final Norse invasion and the start of the One Hundred Years War. Ironically it was through the efforts of two unknown inventors that this period of prosperity, tolerance and intellectual accomplishment was set in motion.

Midway through the eleventh century, the ideas of covering both a plough's wooden nose and a horse's delicate hooves with metal precipitated a revolution in agriculture. With the power of a horse hitched to his sturdy steel-plated plough, a peasant was able to work the heavy soil deeper and faster. Productivity skyrocketed and for the first time in its history, the land of Northern France yielded more food than its inhabitants could eat.

Eager to trade their surplus produce for luxuries, the French lords found the Jews, who had lived among them since the days of the Romans, a perfect partner. The Jewish merchant knew that, no matter how far away he traveled, he'd always find other Jews who shared the Hebrew language, who would shelter him in their midst, and who trusted him implicitly. They also provided invaluable information, such as which goods could be acquired cheaply and which were in demand, as well as which routes were safe and which were dangerous. Thus Jews enjoyed a great advantage in commerce.

In the feudal system, the Jews' social status was high, equal to that of knights. The Jewish trader was a welcome visitor to French estates, buying their surfeit produce and selling them imported goods. Money-lending, the frequently perceived source of Jewish income during the Middle Ages, was not yet a common livelihood among the Jews, only becoming widespread centuries later when other professions became restricted.

Another misconception about the Middle Ages is that Jews suffered greatly from anti-Semitism. While there was no love lost between most Jews and their Christian neighbors prior to the First Crusade, relations between them were cordial and occasional friendships flourished. The Jews and their fellow citizens dressed the same, spoke the same language, and shared the same interest in local politics.

The Catholic Church preached tolerance, with sanctioned persecution still years away. The split between Roman and Byzantium Christians was recent enough that much of the Church's attention was focused on attempts to heal it, and besides, the Church was too busy consolidating its own power and purging France of heretical Christian sects to take much notice of the Jews. In addition, there were still pagans in Europe, and the Church saw them as a higher priority for conversion than the Jews.

Times were good. Commerce increased. Cities sprang up where trade routes crossed. The cities organized fairs where many merchants could buy and sell together, and the rulers who encouraged these fairs grew rich by taxing the transactions that took place at them. And the greatest of these fairs were the two that were held in Troyes, the capital of the French province whose ruler was the Count of Champagne.

Here our chronicle begins. In 1068 Salomon ben Isaac is unknown, but in one hundred years, he will be considered one of the greatest Jewish scholars who ever lived. The first Hebrew book printed will be his Bible commentary, and when the Talmud is printed in the fifteenth century, his extraordinarily clear and concise commentary will fill the inside column of every page. Then he will be known as "Rashi," a Hebrew acronym for Rabbi Shlomo ha Yitzhaki.

Even today, no Talmud is printed without his comments in that same spot, and the words of his grandsons and disciples, known as the Tosaphists, are found on the outside column. But our tale is not really about him or about his grandsons. It is the story of the forgotten generation between them, Rashi's daughters.

one

Troyes, France
Spring 4829 (1069 C.E.)

The cold slowly forced Joheved awake. Sure that Miriam, her younger sister, was comfortably wrapped in more than her share of bedding, Joheved reached out for the covers, only to find them still in their proper place, topped by the rough blanket that Mama had woven from their first clumsy attempts to spin thread from raw wool. There wasn't a hint of morning light, so Joheved snuggled under the covers, determined to ignore her discomfort and find sleep again. Her feet were freezing, but getting up to find her hose would just make them worse. If only she and Miriam could have a charcoal brazier in their room at night. She sighed.

Why did Mama and Papa have to be so secretive about being poor? Did they think they could protect her from poverty by never mentioning it, by telling her that only babies and old people needed their rooms heated once Passover was finished? A girl in her twelfth year was old enough to be told the truth. Joheved rubbed her feet against each other to warm them and bumped into something small lying at the edge of the bed. The room's silence was broken by purring.

People might think it odd that cats slept in Joheved's house at night, but Papa was a scholar who owned valuable manuscripts made of parchment. It was his cats' responsibility to keep mice from nibbling on them, and three cats seemed to be sufficient to protect his treasured collection. Papa once joked that he was merely a three-cat chacham, while his old teacher, Jacob ben Yakar of Worms, had been a seven-cat chacham, and Rabbenu Gershom—Light of the Exile, who died before Papa was even born, surely he had been a ten-cat *talmid chacham.*

Joheved nudged the cat and moved her feet onto the warm spot the creature had vacated. Pleased at this solution, she listened to the small noises outside as she waited for sleep to overtake her. Every so often, the clip-clop of horses' hooves or crunch of cartwheels echoed on a nearby road. What errands kept someone away from home at this hour, when the demon Agrat bat Machlat and her eighteen myriads stalked the night outside?

Joheved shivered and pulled the blankets tighter around her. She had just about drifted off when a low-pitched moan, like someone in pain, jerked her back to consciousness. But this noise wasn't from outside; it was coming from just beyond the bedroom door. Terrified of what had to be an approaching demon, Joheved dived under the covers and grabbed for Miriam.

And felt no one.

A frantic search proved that she was alone in their bed. Convinced that the demon who had somehow taken Miriam was coming for her, she recited the words she'd been taught to say if evil spirits ever threatened her.

"Be split, be accursed, broken and banned, you son of mud, son of clay, like Shamgaz, Merigaz and Istemaah," Joheved whispered through chattering teeth, and then, because incantations said three times were the most powerful, she repeated it twice more. Heart pounding, she waited.

And waited. The cat, still purring, nosed its head under her hand, eager to be scratched. Her fear slowly dissipating, Joheved began to feel both relieved and foolish. How often had she watched the cats chase their invisible prey? Surely no cat would lie so contentedly in her bed if demons lurked nearby.

The world was plagued with evil spirits: from Ashmadia, King of Demons, and Shibeta, who strangles children with croup or whooping cough, to the *cauchmares,* who bring on bad dreams, and little Feltrech, responsible for tangling a sleeper's long hair at night. There were more demons than there were people. Most feared of all was Lillit, whose prey was women in childbirth and their newborn babies. And Mama was due to give birth any day now.

Mon Dieu, what if Mama was in labor right now? Was that where Miriam had gone? It would be just like her little sister too, leaving her to miss out on all the excitement. The cold forgotten, Joheved jumped out of bed. She groped her way along the wall to the pole holding their clothes where, in fact, only her own were hanging. She hurriedly slipped her long linen chemise over her head, making for the doorway at the same time.

Across the landing from where she stood, the door to her parents' room was ajar, and sure enough, a lamp was lit within. Light came from downstairs as well. Joheved tiptoed towards the brightness before her. She had almost reached her parents' doorway when she heard the moaning again, this time followed by a familiar voice, low and melodic, a voice identical to Mama's, except for a slight German accent.

"Miriam, it would be a great help to me if you could keep counting between your mama's pains." The voice belonged to Aunt Sarah, Mama's widowed older sister. "We can tell how soon the baby will come as the number you count gets smaller."

Mama was having the baby! And Miriam was in there as well. Joheved was filled with a whirl of feelings—happiness and excitement, anxiety and fear, plus some righteous indignation that everyone had been quite ready to let her sleep through it.

She stepped boldly into the room and then stopped short. "Oh, what's that smell?" The air was pungent with a strange odor, not unpleasant, but sweet and spicy. It made Joheved's nose want to sneeze.

Mama lay in bed, her eyes closed and her right hand clutching the protective amulet she always wore around her neck. Her long, dark hair was disheveled, spread loosely on the pillow. She appeared to be sleeping, except that she opened her eyes after hearing Joheved's voice and gave her older daughter a wan smile.

Joheved stared at her mother. "How come Mama's hair is spread out like that?" Mama was fastidious about her appearance, her hair always kept out of sight under her veil.

"Aunt Sarah says that it's important to have nothing tight or constricted near the childbed, especially not the mother's hair," Miriam said, proud of her newly acquired knowledge. "It makes it easier for the baby to come out."

Sarah turned around and said firmly, "Hush. Your mama needs to rest between pains, and I don't want you disturbing her. Joheved, you can sit next to Miriam and keep count with her." Her voice softened to the gentle tone Joheved was accustomed to, as she continued, "What you smell is the fennel I've scattered around the floor. It sweetens the air and wards off evil spirits."

A chastened Joheved edged towards the chest where Miriam was sitting. When her sister slid only a handbreadth to the side, Joheved shoved Miriam over, forcing Aunt Sarah to give her nieces a quick frown of reproach. They had barely settled down when Rivka began to breathe faster and clutch at the bedclothes. A groan escaped her lips. Then, as suddenly as it began, whatever had disturbed her was gone. Her grimace faded and she reached for the amulet at her throat.

Aunt Sarah looked at Miriam questioningly, and Miriam replied, "Five hundred. I counted to five hundred that time."

The dread that gripped Joheved was fading now that Mama seemed calm again, but her heart was racing and her stomach felt funny. She had completely forgotten about the counting.

"Don't worry, Joheved, Mama always does that when the pains come, but then they stop right away." Miriam gave her older sister a reassuring hug. "What's the matter? You look like you're going to be sick."

Joheved did feel ill. Was having a baby always like this, one agonizing pain after another? And when the time came, would it be like that for her too? "Miriam, is it . . . ?"

"You two go outside and chat," Aunt Sarah interrupted, motioning them towards the door. "We don't need a count between every contraction." Sympathetic grey eyes focused on Joheved's pale face. "Don't worry. Your mama is doing fine. By the time the sun is up, you'll have a new brother—may the Holy One bless us—or sister."

They went out into the hall, their bare feet moving quietly over the rushes on the floor, and Miriam leaned casually against the wall.

"How long have you been in there?" Joheved asked her little sister, whose confident posture and calm demeanor made her seem quite grown up.

"Not very long. I only did a few counts, all over five hundred, and Aunt Sarah wasn't interested if I counted more than that. She says that things won't begin to happen until I get below two hundred, that Mama's birth pangs will get stronger and last longer, until finally she's in pain most of the time." Miriam straightened up and began gesturing with her hands. "Then we get her out of bed, onto the birthing stool, and she pushes the baby out. Isn't it exciting? I can't wait for the baby to come!"

Joheved's nose wrinkled in distaste. "How can you stand it?"

"You mean how can I stand Mama having a baby?" Miriam recalled how her sister preferred to pluck a chicken rather than gut one, even though it took a lot more time. "Well, probably because I'm not squeamish like you."

"I mean doesn't it bother you to see Mama in pain?" Joheved said. "Besides, you're not doing much except counting."

"I think it's wonderful, and Aunt Sarah let me make up Mama's special drink. It's got the most amazing ingredients in it: myrrh, cinnamon and savin, all mixed together in wine with honey." This was a rare opportunity for Miriam to outshine her sister.

"When the baby's about to come, I'll be able to do more. Aunt Sarah says I can even be her assistant. A laboring woman shouldn't be left alone, on account of demons, so I can run downstairs to fetch things, or I can tend to Mama if Aunt Sarah has to go do something. I might even be a midwife like Aunt Sarah when I grow up." Thank goodness she wasn't a coward like Joheved.

Joheved didn't need to be reminded that Mama was in danger. She wanted to ask if Aunt Sarah had said anything else about demons, particularly about Lillit, but she didn't like her little sister thinking she was ignorant or scared. Besides, it was best to speak of demons as little as possible.

"If you're a midwife, you won't have to worry about money. It's not like making wine, where you never know if you're going to have a good harvest or not. Women are always having babies."

"Aunt Sarah probably does all right." Miriam lowered her voice, loath to provoke the Evil Eye. "She's the only Jewish midwife in Troyes, and she only has herself to support."

Joheved matched her sister's furtive tone and whispered, "I hope Mama has another girl, not a boy baby."

Miriam had also been hoping for a baby sister, but all the same, it was shocking to hear the words from Joheved's mouth. She peered down the hall, not wanting to be overheard. "I've been praying: please don't let Mama die in childbirth and please, make the baby a girl."

There, it was out in the open. Miriam felt guilty about praying that second part; she was pretty sure that Papa, and Mama too, were praying for a boy. "I don't think Papa would pay us any attention if he had a son."

"Not that he pays that much attention to us now." Joheved agreed with her sister, but she didn't want to tempt any evil spirits to harm the baby, no matter what its gender. "Let's go see how Mama is doing," she said. She didn't really want to watch her mother's painful progress, but her parents' room was warm.

They returned to find Aunt Sarah wiping Mama's face with a small cloth. "Rivka, your daughters are here." She motioned for them to stand on either side of the large bed.

Mama took hold of their hands and gave each a gentle squeeze. "Now I have my guardian angels watching over me." She smiled up at them. "This is a woman's greatest blessing, when she can bring forth new life. This is what the Holy One created us to do. I pray that I may live to see you two give me grandchildren."

Perhaps she wanted to say more, but she stopped and began to grip their hands tighter. Right then Joheved wanted nothing more than to get away from the bedside, but Mama held her fast. Joheved shut her eyes rather than watch up close as Mama went through another contraction, clenching her hand tighter and tighter until it was all Joheved could do not to cry out herself. Yet Mama just moaned softly, and suddenly the pressure on Joheved's hand relaxed.

Joheved opened her eyes to see the room starting to spin around her. She felt Aunt Sarah's strong arms supporting her just as her legs began to fail, then helping her over to the storage chest. She could hear Miriam counting, "Five, six, seven, eight," and she felt awful, not only because of her head, which was starting to feel less dizzy, but also because she realized that she was more of a hindrance than a help.

"Joheved, we don't really need two people up here to count," Aunt Sarah said gently. "Why don't you go downstairs and keep your papa company. He must be lonely and worried down there by himself. We'll call you when the baby's been born."

Feeling rejected and useless, Joheved slowly made her way down the circular staircase. Only a faint light came from below, and she took each step carefully. Her father was seated at the dining table facing the hearth, staring into the fire. In the dimness, his brown hair looked black and his grey eyes were hooded under dark brows. Papa was stroking his beard like he always did when he wanted to think, and it seemed as if he was looking at something far away.

Uncertainty stopped Joheved's descent. She didn't dare interrupt him, but she couldn't return to Mama's room; she'd just been expelled. Maybe she should go back to bed?

The room's walls and furnishings had disappeared into the night. Illuminated solely by the flickering flames and an oil lamp on the table, Rabbi

Salomon ben Isaac sat alone in a vast darkness, manuscripts spread before him. In isolated monasteries across the continent, a few monks laboriously copied ancient texts, but Europe had lost the knowledge of Greek philosophy and science. Yet the Jews, despite the bleak intellectual atmosphere of the time, kept the light of their forbearers' wisdom burning bright. Salomon himself had spent the last fifteen years studying at the elite Talmud academies in Allemagne.

As his sister-in-law had intuited, at this moment Salomon was feeling both lonely and worried. It was the first time he'd been present when Rivka was giving birth, and it was a terrible, solitary vigil. In Mayence when a chacham's wife was in labor, his students gathered at the scholar's house. To protect her from demons, they brought a Torah scroll with them and chanted Psalms until the baby arrived, all night if need be. But Salomon had been back in Troyes less than a year, and when Rivka went into labor, he felt reluctant to ask any local men to keep him company.

So he sat at the table, trying to keep his attention focused on the Torah commentary he was writing. Several times he had fought the urge to stand up and pace the room. It was so quiet upstairs. Hearing Rivka's cries earlier had been bad, but this silence was worse. He tried to calm himself and get back to his studies. His sister-in-law was an excellent and experienced midwife; she'd warn him if things were going badly.

If only he were still in Mayence, surrounded by students. But no, he was trapped in Troyes, his mother no longer competent to manage the family's vineyard. He returned to his manuscripts with a sigh. He would have to be satisfied teaching invisible students, the ones he imagined might someday read his *kuntres* (commentaries) and learn from them.

Salomon heard someone coming down the stairs and jumped up to receive the news she brought him, sending the cat that had been asleep at his feet scurrying off in a huff. But rather than the midwife, it was his elder daughter, Joheved, standing timidly at the bottom of the stairs. Her two long braids were coming undone and she was barefoot. Dressed in a rather threadbare chemise that barely covered her knees, her arms hugging herself, she seemed a forlorn figure. He recalled that a girl's chemise ought to be ankle length and felt a pang of remorse. His daughter had probably been wearing this one for years.

Three times a day, as part of the prescribed liturgy, Salomon prayed for the year's produce to be blessed with abundance. If the Holy One blessed him with a good wine harvest this fall, he might finally be able to afford new clothes for his family at Rosh Hashanah, the Jewish New Year. Especially for his older daughter, who appeared to be growing out of her old ones before his eyes. She was already taller than Rivka, on the very threshold of womanhood. Sadness came over him again. How was he ever going to afford a dowry for her and her sister, when he scarcely had the money for food and parchment? And now another mouth to feed.

His immediate worries suppressed his future ones. "So, *ma fille,* what news do you have for me?"

"Everything is fine, Papa. Aunt Sarah says the baby should come before dawn." Joheved shivered in her thin chemise. It was much colder downstairs than in Mama's cozy bedroom.

"Come closer to the hearth," Salomon beckoned to her. "We don't want you to catch cold."

Joheved approached the fireplace, but feeling shy, she stopped at the far side of the table. She could feel, rather than see, his deep-set eyes scrutinizing her. What was he thinking, this stranger who was her father? She was still getting used to his being home. Except for Passover, Shavuot, and Rosh Hashanah, when Papa returned for a few weeks at a time, their household had been completely female.

Even now, except for meals, they hardly spent any time together. Papa went to synagogue in the morning, labored all day in the vineyard, and worked on his manuscripts after *souper.* Maybe she could ask him about demons. He was a scholar.

"Papa, why does Lillit hate newborn babies so much?"

Surprised by her question, yet hungry to be teaching again, Salomon chose to answer his daughter exactly as he would have for one of the young students at the *yeshiva.* She has a right to know about Lillit, he told himself. She'd be a mother herself one day, Le Bon Dieu willing.

"Lillit was Adam's first wife. Because she too was created from the dust of the ground, Lillit insisted on equality with her husband. They quarreled, and she left him." Joheved's rapt expression encouraged Salomon to continue. "Three angels were sent to capture her, but when they did, she refused to return. They threatened her, yet Lillit preferred being punished to living with Adam. Now she takes her revenge by harming new mothers and their babies, boys before their circumcision and girls until they're twenty days old."

Joheved was appalled. She had vague memories of Mama having other babies who died, and she recalled a neighbor woman who had died in childbirth last year. She grabbed her father's arm and appealed to him, "What can we do to protect Mama and the baby, to keep Lillit away?"

Tears were forming in his daughter's blue eyes and Salomon felt ashamed for frightening her. He should know better; a good teacher gives lessons appropriate for his student's level.

"The Almighty has given us powerful tools of protection, ma fille. Your mama is wearing the amulet her mother gave her, my *tefillin* are wrapped around the top of our bed, and as soon as the baby is born, he will be given an amulet with those three angels' names on it. In addition, I am here praying and studying Torah. Don't worry—the Merciful One will guard our pious household."

Papa's calm words reassured her. He was home now and that would make the difference. Joheved didn't want to jeopardize the closeness that had suddenly developed between them, but she had to ask another question. "Papa, you called the baby 'he.' Are you praying for a son?"

Salomon hesitated as he considered how best to answer his daughter. He did not see how he could give an honest explanation, one that did not compromise his integrity as a teacher, without using the Talmud as its source. But teaching Talmud to a girl?

He began to argue with himself: I can't teach Joheved from the Talmud; women aren't allowed to study Talmud. *Yes, you can. You know it isn't actually forbidden. And didn't you yourself take notes at the yeshiva even though all study is supposed to be oral?* Women certainly don't study at the yeshiva. *Yet the Talmud itself mentions learned women, often the daughters of scholars.* She won't understand Talmud; women are light-headed. *Joheved might understand; she knows the Bible, both in Hebrew and Aramaic. Your mother saw to that.* If only I had a son to teach. *Well, you don't have one, and if you want to teach your children, you'll have to make do with her.* But a father's obligated to teach Torah to his sons, not to his daughters. *It doesn't matter that you're not obligated to teach her; you want to teach her; don't deny it.*

Watching his daughter's chin begin to quiver with rejection, Salomon realized that he wouldn't disappoint Joheved or himself. He could no more refuse to teach an eager student than he could stop breathing, and if it was sinful to teach his daughter Talmud, then let the sin be on his head.

He smiled down at Joheved and said, "Just when I was sighing over not having any students, the Merciful One has provided me with one. Tell me, do you know what Talmud is?"

Her father's long silence had worried Joheved. But he didn't look angry. She had no idea why he was asking her about Talmud, but she answered, "*Oui,* Papa, it's the Oral Law."

Salomon nodded his head. "That's right. When Moses, our teacher, received the Law on Mount Sinai, it was in two forms, the Written Law, which we read in the synagogue—and the Oral Law, which was taught in person from teacher to student. Moses taught it to Joshua, and so on down to the earliest rabbis. After the Holy Temple in Jerusalem was destroyed, Rabbi Judah the Prince worried that too many scholars who knew the Oral Law had been killed, that it might be forgotten. So he ordered the Oral Law, called the Talmud, to be recorded. Do you understand?"

"Oui, Papa. Grandmama taught me and Miriam all about it."

"That's right, she wrote me about what good students you were." He paused and stroked his beard before continuing. "Talmud has two parts, Mishnah and Gemara. Suppose you wanted to find all the laws in the Torah concerning a certain subject, let's say the Sabbath. Judah the Prince knew that was difficult, so he wrote the Mishnah, which takes the laws from all over the Torah and arranges them by topic."

Joheved nodded as he spoke, so he continued, "But Mishnah is only a small part of the Talmud. Most of Talmud is Gemara, which records the sages' discussions about the meaning of the Mishnah. Don't worry; you'll understand better when you see it."

When you see it! Joheved couldn't believe her ears. Papa was going to teach her, a girl, Talmud! Terrified, yet fascinated, she didn't dare do anything to interrupt him, to give him a chance to reconsider what he was doing.

She nodded her head and squeaked out, "Oui, Papa."

Salomon got up from the chest he was sitting on and rummaged around inside it. He pulled out a large volume, bound in leather, which had seen much wear, and he thumbed through it until he reached nearly the end. Joheved could see that the pages were covered with Hebrew script. She was almost sure she'd be able to read it, if only the light was brighter. She leaned forward to get a better look.

Chuckling at her eagerness, he said, "This book, the Talmud's first tractate, is called Berachot, 'Blessings.' It concerns, as you might surmise, the laws of prayer. Here in the ninth chapter, we have a Mishnah that answers your question. See if you can read it to me. It shouldn't be much different from reading scripture."

He pointed to where the characters were written slightly larger than the rest of the text. Joheved was afraid that she wouldn't be able to understand it, that Papa would realize it was a mistake to try to teach a girl Talmud, yet she was excited and curious too. She sighed in relief when she saw that she could read the words, which were written in Papa's own handwriting, like the occasional letters he had written home to them.

two

Troyes
Spring 4829 (1069 C.E.)

eart racing, Joheved began reading the Mishnah aloud.

> If a man cries out (to God) over what is past, his prayer is in vain. If his wife is with child and he says, "May it be Your will that my wife bear a male," this prayer is in vain.

Salomon gave an inward sigh of relief; Joheved had read the text without difficulty. "And you understand why these prayers are in vain, for no purpose?" he asked her.

Joheved gulped. Had she and Miriam sinned when they prayed for a sister? "If the wife is with child, then it is already either a boy or a girl, and no prayer can change that," she said slowly.

"Oui, ma fille." Salomon was even more pleased with his daughter. "But while it is true that these prayers are empty or useless, they are not forbidden, because it is man's nature to pray these things."

Joheved sighed with relief and he continued, "Let's look at the Gemara and see what the rabbis say about this Mishnah." He took her hand and placed her finger on the text. "See, first they discuss the pregnant wife and conclude,

> These prayers will not help.

But then Rav Joseph objects and questions the part in Genesis about Leah's children:

> And afterwards she bore a daughter. But what is meant by afterwards?"

Salomon could see his daughter blinking in confusion, so he paused.

This part about Leah and Dinah baffled her. Papa was obviously waiting for her and she didn't want to sit there dumbly. So she asked, "Why does Rav Joseph care about the word 'afterwards'?"

Salomon loved this part of teaching, when he enabled the perplexed student to understand the lesson. "When Leah has each of her sons, it says simply, 'She bore a son.' But when Leah bears a daughter, it says 'afterwards.' Why?"

He smiled and gave the answer. "It says 'afterwards' because the Holy One wants us to ask: After what?"

Joheved stared at the text open mouthed. She considered herself learned because she knew scripture, but this was a different, deeper kind of learning. The fire of her curiosity stoked, she looked up at her father and asked, "So what was it after?"

The pleasure Salomon felt in watching his daughter's demeanor change from confused and frustrated to excited and eager to learn was almost physical in its intensity. "Be patient, ma fille. The very next thing we read in the Gemara is Rav Joseph's answer: After pregnant Leah prayed, saying,

> 'Twelve tribes will descend from my husband, Jacob. Six have come from me and four from his concubines, making ten. If this child is a male, my sister Rachel will not be equal to even one of the concubines.' Immediately the child was turned into a girl, as it is written: And afterwards she bore a daughter."

Joheved thought for a while and then asked him, "So Rav Joseph says that prayer *can* change the sex of a pregnant woman's child. Does this mean the Mishnah is wrong?"

He smiled and motioned Joheved to read on.

> We cannot cite a miracle to refute the Mishnah. Only those righteous like Leah may pray for miracles and have their prayers answered.

Joheved sighed. "I see, Papa, regular people like us shouldn't expect miracles."

"Exactly," Salomon said.

She continued reading.

> From the third to 40th day, he should pray that it will be a male. From the 40th day to three months, he should pray that it not be deformed. From three months to six months, he should pray that it not be a stillborn. From six months to nine months, he should pray for a safe delivery.

Salomon reached over and closed the book. "According to this view, the baby's sex is not determined until forty days, so one may pray for a boy until then. Of course," he quickly added, "if the parents desire a daughter instead of a son, they may also ask during this time. And praying for a safe delivery at nine months is what we should both be doing right now."

Joheved closed her eyes and tried to concentrate on Mama in the room upstairs. But she couldn't stop thinking about what had just happened. Papa had taught her Talmud and she had understood it! And there were so many tractates of Talmud. Who knew what amazing things were written in them? As fervently as Joheved prayed for her mother's safety, she also prayed that today would be the first of many such study sessions with her father.

Salomon closed his eyes as well, but he was thinking about the Gemara that followed the text they had studied. There it said that the sex of the embryo was determined at conception. If the woman is so aroused that she emits seed first, she bears a male, but if the man emits his seed first, she bears a female. It was just as well that he had closed the book quickly; satisfaction in marital relations was not a subject he wanted to discuss with his young daughter. Especially since he felt certain that this baby, like the others, would be female because he lacked the ability to give his wife sufficient pleasure in their marriage bed.

Would he have spent so much time away if he'd known the cost would be having no sons? It was a foolish question. Nobody can change the past. Hadn't he just studied that very subject in the Talmud with his daughter? And he intended to keep teaching her too, no matter what others might think. He would teach Joheved any Mishnah and Gemara she wanted to learn. And not just Joheved; he would teach Miriam and this young one too!

Salomon knew he had made the right decision when Joheved turned to him with anxious eyes and asked, "When will you teach me more Talmud, Papa? I want to learn what the rabbis say about everything, not just about prayers."

"Ma fille, we can study together every night. We'll start with blessings and see how things go after that."

It would have been difficult at that moment to say which of them felt happier. Their joy was shattered by Rivka's scream, followed by the thin wail of a newborn baby. Father and daughter stared at each other for a moment, then Joheved raced for the stairs and almost collided with Miriam coming out of the bedroom.

"A girl, the baby is a big, healthy, girl!" Miriam was so excited, she was almost dancing. "Mama is fine too," she added before disappearing back into the bedroom.

When Salomon and Joheved were finally allowed to enter, Rivka, her hair neatly tucked under her veil, was soothing the baby with a mother's own best remedy. The room smelled different now; something sweet was smoking in the charcoal brazier.

"A pleasant smell encourages the baby to come out quickly, so Aunt Sarah burned some rosemary," Miriam explained before Joheved could ask.

Obviously all was well, and Salomon began the traditional Shehecheyanu prayer of thanksgiving, said on those happy occasions when something is done for the first time. "*Baruch ata Adonai* (Blessed are You, Lord) our God, King of the World, Who has kept us alive, sustained us, and brought us to this season."

Aunt Sarah's dawn estimate for the baby's arrival had been accurate, for no sooner had Salomon finished the blessing for seeing his youngest daughter for the first time, than Troyes' many church bells began their daily cacophony. When all was silent, Rivka began giving her daughters the necessary instructions to keep her household running smoothly.

"Go downstairs and tell Marie that the baby has come. She'll know what to do. While she's helping Grandmama Leah get dressed, you two stoke the fire and get breakfast ready." Rivka paused and shifted the baby to her other breast. "There should be some oatmeal stirabout that just needs to be heated, as well as some stewed fruit. And for heaven's sake, put some clothes on."

"Don't you worry about breakfast," Aunt Sarah told her nieces once they were out in the hall. "I'll prepare it myself." Anticipating the early morning birth, she had bought some special foods for what she hoped would be a celebration. And celebrate they would, even if the baby was another girl.

After all, Rivka had come through the birth safely. And not only that, which, the Merciful One be blessed, was plenty to be happy about, but Miriam had also shown unexpected promise as an apprentice midwife.

Sarah was even more pleased when she reached the kitchen and found that Marie, the young maidservant, already had a fire burning in the fireplace. Two kettles hung on the hearth from a toothed iron rack, the large copper one full of water. There were some smaller pots standing on tripods above the flames, their warm contents giving off enticing smells.

"When I heard the babe crying, I knew I'd better get things ready down here right away," Marie said, her high voice both happy and excited. "I've heated up a kettle of ale for the mistress, the best thing for getting her milk flowing. Is it all right for me to bring her some on my way up to dress Mistress Leah?"

Sarah smiled at the servant's eagerness to see the new baby. "You're a great help to this family, Marie. Warm ale is just what my sister needs. Take your time with Mistress Leah; the girls and I will see to breakfast."

Once their hair was braided, Joheved and Miriam accompanied their aunt to her house on the other side of their shared courtyard. There Sarah filled their arms with fern fronds. "Ferns have a certain force such that evil spirits avoid it. So when a woman gives birth, we place its fronds around her bed and the infant's cradle."

When they returned to the kitchen, they heard Grandmama Leah's voice screeching upstairs, "You robber, you stole my favorite brooch. You should be ashamed of yourself, stealing from the hand that feeds you. You ungrateful wretch, you thief."

"You're mistaken, Mistress. I never took your brooch. I've never taken anything of yours."

In a few moments everyone except Rivka had assembled in Leah's room. The grey-haired matriarch surveyed her audience with satisfaction. "Salomon, I insist that you fire this thieving girl at once." Leah pointed at Marie. "She's stolen my brooch and probably lots more besides that." Leah addressed her son with the authority of one who brooks no arguments.

Without waiting for his assent, she gave her orders to the sobbing maid. "Pack your things and leave my house this instant. I won't share my roof with somebody who steals. For all we know, you're in league with a band of rogues just waiting to cut our throats in the night and take away everything."

Marie broke into tears and tried to run from the room, but Salomon caught hold of her arm and led her into the hall.

"Don't worry, Marie. We know you didn't steal anything." He then addressed the distraught girl in a softer voice, "My wife and child must not be left alone. Please keep them company while I sort this out."

But it was too late. Rivka was limping down the hall towards him, the baby in her arms, her eyebrows knit with trepidation. Before she could speak, Leah began a new tirade, this time directed at Sarah.

"What are you doing here? How dare you enter my bedroom!" Grandmama Leah pointed her bony finger at the midwife. "Don't think for a moment that I don't know what you're up to. You've been putting a curse on Rivka for years to keep her from having any more children, so she'll be barren like you."

This was so patently absurd that the family stood paralyzed, uncertain how to respond to Leah's indictment. Arguments were futile, but Miriam realized that her grandmother's latest grievance might be the key to distracting her.

"Grandmama, Aunt Sarah's here because Mama had the new baby last night." Miriam made her voice sound as cheerful as possible. "She had a baby girl. Don't you want to see her?"

"What baby?" Grandmama Leah looked warily around the room, suspecting a conspiracy to keep this important information from her. "Nobody told me anything about a baby."

Miriam took Leah by the hand. "Aren't you lucky, Grandmama? Now you have three granddaughters instead of two. After all, odd numbers are good luck and even numbers are bad luck."

"A boy would have been luckier," Leah muttered, but she took the baby in her arms and allowed herself to be led from the room.

"I guess I'll be leaving too," Aunt Sarah said, giving her sister a quick hug. "I'll check on you after breakfast, when everyone's gone to synagogue."

His mother and sister-in-law gone, Salomon sighed and surveyed the scene. Near the door, his diminutive wife was patting the distraught maidservant who towered over her. Rivka looked close to tears herself.

He'd deal with Marie first, then they could look for the brooch. "Marie, please calm yourself. You mustn't even think of leaving us, not now when we need you so much. Not with both the new baby and my mother to take care of." He tried to keep the anxiety out of his voice. "How long will it be until your fiancé finishes his cobbler's apprenticeship?"

"Just a few more years, Master Salomon, not more than three."

"Surely, you can remain with us for that small amount of time. It would hardly be worth it for you to start again somewhere else when you'd be leaving in a couple of years anyway."

Marie nodded and headed for the stairs. Salomon turned to Rivka and asked, "Now where do you suppose my mother put that brooch? I suppose we'll have to search her usual hiding places."

He had hoped that such clear confidence in Marie's innocence would cheer those left in the room, but the mood only became more somber. Rivka and Joheved looked at each other apprehensively, as if each expected the other to save her. Salomon waited for a response, but the nervous silence continued and neither one would meet his gaze. His wife and daughter were hiding something.

He fought to control his temper; if he frightened them he'd never discover their guilty secret. He held out his hands and appealed to Joheved. "Ma fille, please tell me what's the matter. It can't be that bad." At least, he hoped it wouldn't be.

Joheved couldn't refuse her father's direct request. "Papa, Grandmama's brooch isn't lost." She took a deep breath and spoke quickly, her eyes fixed on the floor. "Grandmama took it to the goldsmith last spring, before you came home. He loaned us enough money to make a nice Passover."

Salomon stepped backwards as if he'd been punched in the stomach. "I see," he said slowly. "Is the goldsmith the only one in Troyes we owe money to, or are there more?"

Rivka shook her head, too mortified to speak. Tears filled her eyes and began to slide down her cheeks.

"Now, now. Let's not be so glum. What's done is done." Salomon gave his wife an encouraging smile. At least they weren't too badly in debt. "We should be celebrating the birth of our new daughter."

When they got downstairs, Miriam and Grandmama Leah were waiting for them at the breakfast table. Contentedly cooing at the sleeping baby in her lap, the old woman showed no signs of ill will towards Marie, who was ladling out the stirabout.

Leah turned and admonished the latecomers, "You'd better come and eat, or we'll be late for services this morning."

The sun was clearing the city walls as Grandmama Leah and Salomon set off for weekday services, Miriam and Joheved following behind them. Rivka and the new baby wouldn't leave home for at least two weeks, not until the child had been safely named in the synagogue. From her kitchen window Sarah watched her nieces close the courtyard gate behind them, and then she slipped back to her sister's house.

"Oh, Sarah, what am I going to do about Leah?" Rivka put her head down on the table and wept. "After what she said here about you and Marie, I can't bear to think of the things she might tell others about us."

"Don't worry, Mistress," Marie said. "Mistress Leah would never air her dirty laundry in public."

"And I'm sure I would have heard if people were gossiping about your family." Sarah gave her sister a reassuring hug.

Rivka allowed the two women to lead her upstairs. "But what about the shopping?" She let Marie take the baby while Sarah helped her use the chamber pot. "The grocers will cheat Leah if she can't remember any prices."

"No they won't," Marie said proudly. "Mistress Leah may be forgetful, but she can tell right away if somebody is trying to cheat her. Besides, Joheved remembers all the prices for her . . . She's a clever one, your Joheved is."

"Rivka, let your husband worry about Leah." Sarah tucked her sister in bed and adjusted the fern fronds. "You need to relax or your milk won't come in properly. Get some sleep now."

But Rivka wasn't tired. She looked down at the sleeping baby and then up at her sister. "Who do you think she looks like?"

Sarah couldn't help but smile. "With that curly hair and her cute little nose, I think she'll grow up to be pretty like you."

"Joheved and Miriam may be plain, but they're good girls, pious and hardworking—may the Holy One protect them." Rivka's voice was filled with pride. Then she lowered her voice so Marie couldn't hear. "I am glad that they take after Salomon rather than me."

Both girls clearly had their father's high forehead, strong jaw and thick brown hair. They also had his deep-set, intelligent eyes, but Joheved's were blue like Rivka's while Miriam's were more hazel.

Sarah looked at her in surprise and Rivka said, "That way no one will ever doubt that he's their father, no matter how much time he spent away from home."

"Rivka, how can you possibly worry about such a thing?" Sarah shook her head in disbelief. "You're one of the most virtuous women in Troyes."

"It doesn't matter how chaste a woman is; people will still gossip about her," Rivka said, covering a yawn with her hand.

Sarah yawned herself, then strode over to the shutters and closed them tight. "That's enough talk. You should be sleeping while the baby is asleep, and I want to catch up on my rest too."

Salomon's family didn't have to walk far to reach the Old Synagogue, as opposed to the New Synagogue in the market district that had been built during Grandmama Leah's lifetime. Located on Rue de Giourie in the oldest part of Troyes, the Old Synagogue was constructed of stone, like the count's castle, the cathedral and the Abbey of Saint Loup, all built before Charlemagne.

As they hurried past the abbey, Miriam babbled excitedly about the birth she'd just witnessed, but her sister scarcely heard her. Grandmama Leah's missing brooch was forgotten as Joheved remembered herself in front of the hearth, studying Talmud with Papa. She basked in her new knowledge, like a miser admiring a chest of gold.

"Joheved, what's the matter with you? Haven't you heard a single word I've said?" Miriam was seething with indignation. Here she was, trying to tell her older sister all the amazing things that happened when a woman gave birth, and Joheved wasn't paying the slightest attention. "You just don't want to admit that there's something I know that you don't."

In fact, the few words Joheved did hear had convinced her that the less she knew about childbirth the better. Let Miriam prattle on about how babies were born; she knew something better. "You're not the only one exciting things happened to last night."

"What are you talking about?" Miriam grew suspicious of her sister's self-satisfied smirk.

"Miriam, you'll never guess. While you were helping Aunt Sarah deliver Mama's baby, Papa was teaching me Talmud!" Joheved took a deep breath and waited for Miriam's response.

"What? Papa wouldn't teach you Talmud; nobody teaches Talmud to girls. Girls aren't supposed to learn Talmud!"

Joheved reveled in her sister's agitation. "He did too teach me Talmud. We studied the ninth chapter of Tractate Berachot, about prayers you say when a woman is pregnant. I read it myself and didn't have any trouble at all. Papa even said he would teach us, both of us, more of Berachot, a little each night. So there!"

Miriam was torn between admiration for her sister and shock at how their father had broken tradition. But no matter how scandalized she might feel, if Joheved was going to study Talmud, then she would too. Before she could say anything else, they reached the synagogue doorway. Under their grandmother's watchful eye, Joheved and Miriam tried to adopt the proper attitude of reverence and thankfulness. And that meant no more talking.

They entered into a small anteroom, which offered a view of the sanctuary a few steps below. The focal point of the room was the *bimah,* a raised area along the eastern wall. Here stood the ornate carved wooden cabinet that held the Torah scrolls, as well as a table on which the scroll was opened to read that week's portion of scripture. A row of tall windows facing the central courtyard provided illumination.

Stairs from the entry, their banister worn smooth by the hands of women climbing them for generations, led to the women's gallery, a deep balcony along the width of the sanctuary opposite the *bimah.* As usual, the other girls had spread themselves over the back benches so that Joheved and Miriam would have to sit by themselves in the front row.

"Just ignore them," Grandmama Leah had advised her granddaughters when the other girls snubbed them. "You don't want to associate with such ignorant people anyway. They'll just distract you from important matters like learning to make wine and manage a scholar's household."

That was easy for Grandmama Leah to say. Leah was learned enough to lead the women in prayer; she ran her own vineyard, and her son was a chacham. Well, let the silly girls gossip and giggle in the back. Joheved liked sitting in the first row, right at the balcony's edge; then she could watch the services below.

Word of Salomon's newborn daughter swept through the congregation. Never acknowledged aloud, giving birth was a risky undertaking. Of the roughly one hundred Jewish families in Troyes, nearly every one had lost a baby, and many had a mother or sister who'd succumbed in childbirth.

After services Salomon found himself surrounded by men he barely knew inquiring about Rivka and the baby's health, while upstairs the women listened eagerly as Miriam related her experience at the birth. Eventually the crowd thinned as people began to return home for *disner,* the midday meal.

Grandmama Leah kept tapping her foot and saying, "We really need to get going," or "It's time to leave." But she refused to leave without Salomon, who was deep in conversation with Isaac haParnas and his son, Joseph.

The Parnas, leader of the Jewish community, was probably the most important Jew in Troyes, and definitely one of the richest. He was responsible for paying the communal taxes to Count Thibault and for making sure that every Jewish family contributed their fair share. He also headed the committee that administered the community charity fund.

Watching the three men in earnest conversation, Joheved didn't dare disturb them. Perhaps her family's financial circumstances were so dire that Papa had been forced to apply to the Parnas for assistance. Yet Grandmama Leah was growing increasingly agitated.

It seemed like ages before Salomon finally noticed his daughters' desperate glances and excused himself for a moment. "You can leave now and tell Rivka that I'll be along shortly."

With this dismissal, Leah allowed Joheved and Miriam to walk her home. Along with other Jews in Troyes, their family lived in the Broce-aux-Juifs district, located at the center of a triangle formed by the Abbey of Saint Loup to the east, the count's palace to the south, and his castle to the north. The Jews' houses, like others in town, were timber post-and-beam structures surrounding a central courtyard. Each story jutted out above the other, and because they had a tendency to lean as they aged, it was sometimes possible for a woman on the third floor of one house to hand an item to her neighbor in the house across the street.

The narrow alleyways below were graded like a V with the highest level immediately next to the houses and the lowest point in the center. Garbage of all sorts was thrown into the middle of the road, with the hope that a rainstorm would soon wash it into the nearest waterway. Pedestrians tried to walk as close to the buildings as possible, leaving the vile median to those on carts or horseback. Shopkeepers found this arrangement convenient since it forced passersby close to their open windows, from which they called to the potential customers to advertise their wares. Joheved and Miriam were used to ignoring the clamor.

"Do you really think it will be all right for Papa to teach us Talmud?" Miriam was trying to recall exactly why girls weren't taught such things, but she couldn't think of anything except that it just wasn't done. "What if somebody finds out?"

"Who could possibly find out? I doubt Papa will tell anyone, and if we don't say anything either . . ."

Miriam was not reassured. "Grandmama?" She pulled on Leah's sleeve. "What happens to women who study Talmud?"

Even knowing this conversation would be forgotten before they got home, Joheved was flooded with trepidation. But Grandmama Leah didn't ask Miriam why she wanted to know. She merely wrinkled her nose and replied, "Any such masculine activity will certainly cause a woman's womb to wander, probably so much so that she develops hysteria. Not that anyone teaches Talmud to girls."

Joheved had no idea what hysteria or a wandering womb was, but she was willing to risk them both. Once home she helped Marie prepare some baked fish and vegetable stew for souper that evening, to be eaten with the cheese pies and fruit pastries that a couple of women had dropped off earlier. The family was surely planning to retire early, but if she and Miriam tidied the kitchen quickly, Papa might still have time to teach them Talmud. Joheved steeled herself not to feel too disappointed if he was tired and wanted to put off more study until tomorrow.

But Salomon was not about to skip what he anticipated would be a most gratifying experience. After souper, he surprised Rivka with his offer to put the girls to bed so she could rest, and as soon as she was upstairs, he got out Tractate Berachot. First they reviewed what Salomon and Joheved had done earlier. Then he instructed the two girls to help each other learn the text by heart, just as study partners in the yeshiva did.

"Copies of Talmud are rare," he told them, "and a yeshiva student is not considered proficient in a chapter unless he can recite it by memory."

From that night on, each evening after Rivka and the baby went to sleep, learning Talmud became Joheved and Miriam's secret bedtime ritual. The door to higher Jewish education had been opened for them, and they were eager to enter. That this knowledge was traditionally reserved for males only made it more enticing.

three

For the next two weeks Joheved and Miriam had unprecedented freedom to explore outside the Jewish Quarter. Troyes, with over ten thousand inhabitants, was one of the largest cities in France and there were lots of interesting avenues to investigate. The girls spent most mornings on the bustling Rue de l'Epicerie, home to the various food vendors.

They hurried past the butchers and poulterers, lingered at the pastry shops and bakeries and elbowed their way through the peddlers touting everything from fish and cheese to milk and honey. But they didn't need to buy anything except staples. Thanks to the congregation's generosity, an array of savory dishes awaited them each day when they returned from synagogue.

Today Joheved and Miriam had a different agenda; they were going to the parchment maker's. Salomon used a great deal of parchment to write his kuntres, but full pages were expensive. Most tanneries sold scraps at reduced prices, and one tanner in particular had a daughter, Catharina, who enjoyed the sisters' company and often set aside the best pieces for them. Catharina didn't have any visitors her own age. The tanneries gave off such a dreadful smell that most people chose to stay as far away from their streets as possible.

When the girls arrived at the shop, Catharina jumped up from her work to greet them. "I'm so glad to see you. Foxes attacked the sheepfold at a manor near Ervy. The lord wants to salvage what he can, which means we'll be getting a wagon load of sheepskins, and, wouldn't you know it, my brother won't be home for days.

"So here we are, with all these skins coming in together, and just me and my father to work them," Catharina said as they collected the scraps she had set aside for them. "If you help us, you can have some of the parchment when it's ready."

"I suppose so," Joheved said slowly. She had no idea what it took to make vellum, except that it was sure to be a smelly process. "Will it take long?"

"Oh no, only a few days. Especially if you both come."

"We'll have to ask Papa's permission, of course," Miriam added, a bit more enthusiastic than Joheved. "But I expect he'll be eager for more parchment."

"And you won't be getting odds and ends," Catharina called out as they began walking back. "You'll have lots of full pages."

"Just think of it. We'll be able to bring home folios of parchment," Joheved said, walking faster. Papa would be so surprised with their good luck.

But their news had to wait.

Papa was waiting for them when they got home. He put the parchment away without a glance and announced, "Isaac haParnas has offered me a business partnership, and he wants to discuss the details over disner. If your mother feels well enough, we'll go a week from Thursday."

Isaac haParnas was a widower who lived with his son's family on Rue de Vielle-Rome. An invitation to dine with him was an honor; the prospect of a business partnership was incredible.

Before the girls could say anything, Grandmama Leah declared, "I'm too tired; you go without me."

Salomon rolled his eyes in frustration. There was no point in telling his mother that the meal wasn't today; she was stubborn as a mule when it came to doing anything beyond her usual routine. He sighed in resignation; it was probably best for her to stay home anyway.

Joheved and Miriam, so excited by thoughts of disner at the Parnas's house that they forgot all about making parchment, wished they were going immediately. But Monday and Wednesday were unlucky for new undertakings, and Tuesday, under the influence of Mars, was associated with enmity and destruction.

Finally the day arrived. Rivka had changed clothes three times before finally settling on wearing her newest weekday *bliaut,* or tunic, over her embroidered Shabbat chemise. Miriam and Joheved, dressed in their best, were nervous too.

"Mama, are you sure it's all right for you and the baby to go out?" Miriam asked as they passed the Old Synagogue. "It's barely been two weeks since she was born."

"I'm sure your new sister, Rachel, will be fine." Rivka looked down at the sleeping baby and fingered the amulet around her neck. "I fed her before we left, and I'm perfectly capable of sitting and eating at somebody else's house instead of my own."

As they walked along Rue de Vielle-Rome, the breeze brought an occasional whiff of some mouth-watering odor. Joheved's stomach growled, and she hugged her belly in embarrassment. She'd eaten a good breakfast, but now she was starving.

"I see that we are just in time," Salomon said, giving her a quick hug. "Here is the house with the blue door, just as Isaac haParnas directed me."

"Remember your manners, girls." Rivka straightened their clothes and tidied their braids. "Don't speak until you're spoken to and don't talk with your mouths full."

The door was opened by a hulking manservant, as much a guard as a butler. Joheved scarcely noticed the man as she surveyed her surroundings. The linen wall hangings in the main room, or *salle,* were dyed a sunny golden yellow, unlike those at home, which were left in their natural undyed state. Everyone except peasants used wall hangings to shut out drafts, but how extravagant to expend costly dyes on them.

Several people at once could have walked through the massive fireplace at the far end of the *salle.* A large trestle table was set up on a raised floor in front of the hearth, all the better to show off the intricate carvings on its legs. Their hosts sat in matching high-back chairs. Joheved could not have described any of this elegance; she was overwhelmed by the delicious smells coming from the kitchen. Her stomach growled again, and she pressed her arms into her belly even harder to silence it.

Isaac haParnas and his son rose to greet them. Even with her small knowledge of clothes, Joheved could tell that they were as well dressed as they were well fed. Isaac's bliaut fell nearly to the floor in luxurious blue velvet folds, while Joseph's, made of similar material, was knee length. Despite the rich fabric and jeweled belts they wore, both men were so plump that Joheved was reminded of two bulging sacks of flour, each tied loosely in the middle. Both men had neatly trimmed beards and bushy eyebrows, so bushy that they appeared to be two fat caterpillars above their eyes. Each man had a large emerald ring on his left hand—the green stone of Zebulun was reputed to increase good will and bring success in trade to those who wore it.

"Length of days and years of life and well-being shall they bestow on you," Salomon addressed his hosts with the traditional visitor's greeting from Proverbs.

"Rav Salomon, I greatly enjoyed this morning's Talmud lesson." Isaac took Salomon's arm and led his guests towards the table. "Your explanations brought out several points I hadn't considered before." He inclined his head to Rivka and continued, "I'm particularly honored that you, Mistress, would rise from your childbed to dine with us. My daughter-in-law will be delighted to have feminine companions at the table for a change."

At that moment, an even stouter woman entered from the kitchen, followed by two young boys giggling and jostling each other. Joheved recognized Joseph's wife, Johanna. If her husband's torso resembled a sack of flour, Johanna's ample hips and bosom made her look more like a sack of pumpkins tied in the middle. Her round face broke into a grin when she saw them and she hurried forward, her bulky frame moving with surprising grace.

"I'm so glad you could come. I apologize for not visiting yet, but I hope your family enjoyed the fish pies I sent over." She embraced Rivka and cooed at the infant in her arms. "Your baby is adorable—may the Holy One protect her. I can't wait to hear all about her."

"These are my twin grandsons, Menachem and Ephraim, boys who never slow down, except when they're asleep." Isaac patted each of their heads affectionately. "I'm sure you're all hungry. Come, let's eat."

He led them to a stand containing several wooden and metal basins, where they were to wash their hands. Joheved and Miriam hung back; they disliked the gooey soft soap made of mutton fat. Youngsters were always the last to wash, and at home the towel was inevitably clammy and slimy with leftover soap by the time the final girl used it. Joheved and Miriam constantly bickered over who got to go first.

Today, under their father's stern gaze, they reluctantly made their way to the washbasin. But there was no greasy soap container in sight. Instead there was a small, cream-colored ball, sitting on a wooden tray. They watched, fascinated, as Mama turned the ball this way and that in her wetted hands, then rinsed them off and dried them on one of two large towels.

"It's made in Italy, from olive oil," Isaac haParnas explained proudly. "It's called Jew's soap."

"Why do they call it that?" Salomon asked. "Do the Italian Jews make it?"

"I don't know who makes it," Isaac said. "But Jews in the south won't use other soaps because they're made from pork."

"There's perfume in it, too," Johanna added, bringing her hand to her nose. "So your hands smell nice when they're clean."

Joheved followed their mother's lead, using a separate towel from Miriam, and sniffed her hands appreciatively when she was done. This fancy Jew's soap had to be very expensive.

The men and women sat down at opposite ends of the table. Joheved's mouth watered with anticipation to see each place set with a *trencher,* a thick slice of day-old bread; this meant sliced meats were sure to be served upon it. Once everyone was seated, Isaac led the blessings, which the servants recognized as their signal to begin serving the meal.

First came a poultry and vegetable stew, served in small two-handled bowls. Joheved knew her mother was watching, so, despite her hunger, she broke off some bread, then slowly and deliberately mopped up her stew from the bowl she shared with Miriam. The twins were fidgeting, tearing up their bread into small pieces, but not eating much of the stew.

As Johanna admonished them to stop playing with their food, Miriam whispered to her sister, "They can't be full already; maybe they're waiting for something better . . ."

Her voice trailed off in awe as a servant brought a roasted leg of lamb, still on the spit, before their host, who began slicing pieces onto the *trencher* in front of Salomon. Another servant laid a tray of roasted onions and turnips on the table, while a third refilled the adults' wine goblets from a large jug.

All except Rivka's, who indicated that she preferred the well-watered wine that the children were drinking. At the women's end of the table, Johanna was eager to hear Rivka's description of her recent confinement, and retell, in turn, the difficulties she had experienced with the birth of her twin sons. Miriam plied Johanna with questions, while Joheved, who had begun salivating the moment she smelled the roast lamb, was losing her appetite.

Not babies again. Ever since Rachel's birth, they'd been inundated with female visitors who brought gifts of food and a great desire to share their own childbirth experiences. All she'd ever hear about was babies if it weren't for Papa teaching her Talmud. Maybe that's what the men were discussing now. Without taking her eyes off her mother, Joheved turned her attention to the head of the table, but the men were talking politics.

"I don't understand how can you trust Count Thibault, Papa." Joseph's black caterpillars creased together in exasperation. "Look how he stole Champagne away from Eudes, his own nephew."

Isaac turned to face his son. "I never said that I trusted Thibault. If Eudes was fool enough to fall into his uncle's trap, then it's just as well that he's not Count of Troyes anymore."

Salomon held up his hands to interrupt them. "Please, gentlemen, I was in Mayence when Thibault took over Champagne, and I only heard rumors about what happened. Please enlighten me."

When she heard her father's request, Joheved gave up even the pretence of listening to the women. Isaac allowed a sly smile to play on his lips and Joheved thought he looked exactly like the women in synagogue before they shared a choice piece of gossip.

"Very well," he said, leaning forward in his seat. "After Count Etienne died, his brother, Thibault of Blois, became young Eudes' guardian. There was trouble from the beginning. Thibault tried to keep his nephew under his thumb once the boy reached majority, so what did Eudes do? When Thibault allied himself with the Duke of Aquitane, Eudes supported King Philippe instead."

Joseph waved his knife to get Salomon's attention. "Somehow Eudes arranged for Thibault to be captured, and I can tell you it cost the Jews of Blois a pretty penny in taxes to pay his ransom."

Joheved couldn't believe her ears. Eudes had betrayed his own uncle. Despite her mother's warning, she spoke up. "But why did he . . . ?" She stopped and covered her mouth with her hand.

Isaac's eyes twinkled as he encouraged her to continue. Joheved looked nervously in Rivka's direction, but her mother was completely engrossed in Johanna's description of the twins' birth. She cleared her throat and asked, "Why did they have to fight so much? Why couldn't Thibault be content in Blois and let Eudes rule in Troyes?"

Salomon shook his head and said, "Such men are never content when others have something they want."

Isaac sliced another round of lamb onto the men's *trenchers,* then winked at Joheved and gave her one as well. Thank heaven nobody was chastising her for interrupting their conversation.

"Of course Thibault harbored a grudge," Isaac's words were directed at Papa, but he was looking at her. "And a few years ago, he saw his chance for revenge. He accused Eudes of murdering one of his vassals and ordered his nephew to appear at his high court at Blois." Isaac stabbed his knife into a roasted onion for emphasis. "Where he was sure to be convicted."

"Rumors of that accusation were rather vague," Salomon said.

"Vague? They were completely imaginary." Joseph threw his knife down and wiped his hands on the tablecloth. "Nobody in Troyes could even find out the name of the murdered man, and believe me, we tried. Frankly, I doubt there was a murder."

Joheved was caught up in the tale. "So what happened? What did Thibault do to him?"

"Nothing." Joseph grinned at her. "Instead of showing up in Blois, Eudes joined his cousin, Guillaume the Bastard, when the Normans invaded Angleterre. In gratitude, Guillaume, now the Conqueror instead of the Bastard, made Eudes a duke and gave him his sister in marriage."

Salomon chuckled softly. "So on the other side of the channel, the new Duke Eudes is doing well indeed, and naturally decides to remain there and avoid his troubles in France. Thibault then takes over the lands his nephew has abandoned and gets what he wanted in the first place, lordship over both Blois and Champagne. Surely everybody is happy with this arrangement."

Father and son nodded in agreement, then Isaac smiled wickedly and added, "Not everybody is happy. King Philippe is certainly not happy with Thibault in control of territory on both sides of Paris."

The meal was nearly over but no one appeared in any hurry to get up. Johanna smiled proudly as two servants entered, one with a tray piled high with small pies and the other with bowls of raspberry preserves. Joheved watched as Papa and Mama each dipped a pie in the preserves, and then eagerly followed suit. The flaky pastry was filled with a mixture of spiced meat and raisins in a sweet wine sauce. It was even more delicious than the lamb.

Everyone was wiping their hands on the tablecloth when Isaac got down to business. "Tell me, Salomon the winemaker, what did you think of the wine we had today? Don't worry about hurting my feelings."

Salomon picked up his wine goblet, as if examining its workmanship. "Frankly, the wine was adequate, but by no means up to the high quality of your food. The first wine was inferior to the wine served later, probably made with grapes that had not completely ripened before harvest. The second wine may have been excellent a few seasons ago, but it has aged poorly."

"You know wine as well as you know Talmud," Isaac said, slapping his hand down on the table. "The first wine was from Rheims, the best I could find from last year's harvest. The second was from your own vineyard, a few years back."

Isaac leaned forward and fixed his gaze on Salomon. "A week ago, I asked you how much good wine you could make if you had unlimited resources. It was not an idle question."

The whole table waited in expectant silence, and Joheved suddenly realized that she needed to use the privy. But she couldn't leave the table now and miss Papa's answer.

Salomon didn't need time to consider his reply. "I have often asked myself this very question," he said. "Much of a successful harvest is in the hands of the Almighty. The weather, after all, is not in my control. But to increase the yield of my vineyard, I need people to help me. My family and I were not able to prune the entire property last winter, yet only those vines that were well pruned will produce useful grapes this summer." He shook his head sadly.

"These pruning helpers needn't be Jewish," Salomon began to speak louder and faster. "Anyone can work in the vineyard and the grapes still be made into kosher wine. But once the grapes are harvested, the wine production itself must be done by Jews."

"What about this year?" Isaac raised his voice as well, and he pointed his finger at Salomon. "If you are telling me that you can do nothing to boost your current harvest, then how about getting grapes from another vineyard, perhaps an Edomite's?"

Edom was the name used in Genesis to describe descendants of Esau, and the Talmudic rabbis adopted that name for the Roman rulers of Israel. It was one of the more benign names that Jews called the Christians they lived amongst.

Joheved squirmed in her seat. She desperately wanted to excuse herself from the table, but she had to see if Papa and Isaac could reach an agreement.

"I could doubtless make more wine this fall if I had more grapes and more Jewish workers. But not just anybody's grapes will do!" Salomon shook his finger back at Isaac. "I must first inspect the vineyard. And I will not accept any grapes I haven't tasted." He finished the wine in his cup and set it down firmly on the table.

"Naturally, nobody would expect you to make good wine from bad grapes," Isaac said soothingly. "Now here's my offer." He paused, the eyes of the room upon him. "I'll find a suitable source of grapes and provide all the Jewish workers you need. For my effort I get half the wine made from those grapes. You can keep the other half, as well as any wine coming from your own vineyard."

Salomon's eyes widened and his jaw dropped. "You will assume the entire monetary risk for half the profits?" When Isaac nodded his confirmation, Salomon grinned at the others and joked, "If I had known he was so desperate for good wine, I would have bargained harder."

Joheved couldn't ignore her full bladder any longer. A flustered whisper to Mama and then Johanna was motioning for a maidservant, who quickly led Joheved through the kitchen and past the garden. And not a moment too soon, Joheved thought with relief, as she closed the door and sank onto the privy's seat.

When she was finished, she let out an impressed "Oh." On the seat next to her sat a basket of the softest moss she had ever felt. Johanna must send servants a good distance out along the river to find it so fresh and velvety. At home, Marie didn't have much time to search out moss for the privy, and sometimes the riverbank was picked over already when she arrived. It was even worse in the winter, when all they had was straw. Joheved was sure the Parnas's family never used straw.

She went back into the kitchen to wash her hands. Dark and disgusting places usually harbored evil spirits, and one demon in particular, the Shaydshel Betkisay, was known to inhabit privies. People who neglected to wash after doing their business might inadvertently allow the demon into one of their body's openings. Heaven forbid she should touch her eye and induce blindness or wipe her mouth and bring on the flux.

When Joheved returned to the table, Joseph was speaking, and she helped herself to another pie. "Our entire Jewish community is desperate for good kosher wine and probably most of northern France as well," he said. "If Troyes had such wine for sale, we could entice more merchants to our Champagne fairs."

He glanced nervously at his wife and continued hurriedly, "You know, Count Thibault is so eager to enlarge the fairs that he has offered to completely indemnify anyone who is robbed on his roads. Not only that, anyone waylaid outside of Champagne must be reimbursed by the local lord or else Thibault will forbid that district's merchants from trading in Troyes."

Johanna was frowning at her husband. He swallowed a few times before taking a last look at his wife's stern visage. "Rav Salomon, I have an offer for you as well. I'd like you to tutor Menachem and Ephraim. I would pay you ten *livres* a year."

The twins froze as Salomon stared at them. Joheved shot her mother a worried glance. What was wrong with these boys that Joseph would offer ten times the going rate to teach them?

"My sons are smart, perhaps a little too smart for their own good," Joseph said, almost pleading. "They question and question and question. Their teacher complains that they do not respect him, so he beats them." He turned around and frowned at the boys. "Things have gotten so bad lately that they refuse to go to school at all, and their teacher merely responds 'Good riddance!'"

Salomon smiled to himself as he listened to Joseph's appeal. They didn't need to bribe him. He would have jumped at an opportunity to have students again, even such young, and possibly rebellious, ones. "I accept your offer, Joseph. I'm sure I can turn these two into scholars." He grinned at the twins. "Anyone who asks so many questions is already on the proper path."

When Salomon announced his acceptance, Rivka nearly wept with relief. Ten *livres* would lift them out of poverty, and if the wine business went well, they could hire another servant to help care for Leah. At the very least there would be linen for new chemises and wool to knit new stockings.

Suddenly the baby started to fuss. Rivka tried to rock her youngest daughter to sleep, but this only succeeded in agitating her further. As the baby's cries grew louder, Rivka looked around helplessly, her gaze shifting from Rachel to Salomon and then back to the baby again. At this juncture Johanna earned her distraught guest's eternal gratitude by announcing that she'd like to accompany Rivka home and help her carry back a few gifts of food.

Joheved hoped she and Miriam wouldn't be forced to leave with the women, and when nobody made that suggestion, she remained seated at the table. Miriam was torn; she had enjoyed the women's conversation, and Johanna had answered her questions about the twins' birth without condescension. But if she left now, only Joheved would get to hear whatever the men talked about when the women were absent. Miriam decided to stay as well.

Isaac haParnas was pleased that Salomon's daughters had remained. He had noted how intently Joheved had followed the men's conversation during *disner* and he intended to make her his accomplice for his final proposal to the scholar. His dark eyes met her blue ones and he asked her gently, "Joheved, you are Salomon's oldest child, oui?"

Joheved was so surprised to be addressed by her host that all she could do was nod. "I believe you to be a clever girl," he continued, "so I'd like to tell you a little story, more like a parable, and you can tell me what you think when I'm done."

Joheved swallowed nervously and nodded. What did Isaac want from her?

"Joheved," Isaac began speaking with the same tone of voice parents use when they tell bedtime stories. Mama told her and Miriam tales of Reynard the Fox and his animal associates, while Grandmama told them stories about the people in the Bible, but they both used the same kind of voice.

"Let's say you were a merchant and you came to a new town just before the Sabbath. The inhabitants welcomed you and gave you hospitality. You saw that they were well dressed and had fine homes. What would you think about doing business with them?"

An easy question, thank goodness. "I'd think the town might be a good place to do business. Since the people looked prosperous, they could probably afford to buy things from me."

Isaac beamed his approval and motioned for a servant to refill the wine cups. "The next morning, you went with them to synagogue. But when they removed the Torah scroll from the ark, you saw that the Torah's mantel was not made of fine material with beautiful embroidery, but was torn and shabby." Isaac shook his head disapprovingly. "And there were no silver ornaments to decorate it, no adornment of any kind. Now what would you think about doing business there?"

Joheved smiled. "I'd think that since these people didn't honor the Torah scroll, they might not honor what was in the Torah. They might cheat or steal. I probably wouldn't be so eager to trade with them after all."

Again, the Parnas questioned her. "Let's say you go to a town with a great Torah scholar. You want to study with him, and you also think that you might do some business there. The residents are well dressed, except for the scholar, whose clothes are old and worn." The grey caterpillars that were his eyebrows rose and he nodded slightly at her, urging her to speak quickly.

Joheved knew she'd better answer before her father objected. "I'd think that the townspeople didn't respect Torah scholarship. Otherwise they'd see to it that their scholar had enough business to support himself." Of course, that was why the Parnas had offered Papa a business partnership. She took a gulp of wine and, feeling a little tipsy, grinned boldly at Isaac. "I would especially think this if his wife and children weren't well dressed, because a true scholar might be too absorbed in Torah study to care about his own clothes."

Isaac may have been pleased with her reply, but Salomon was livid. "Now, listen you two. First of all, I am not the great Talmud scholar you believe me to be, and it is an insult to my *maîtres* in Mayence to suggest that I am even remotely their equal. Second, I have every intention of buying my family new clothes in time for Rosh Hashanah. I am not too absorbed in study to care about their looks."

As Joheved shrank back in her seat, Isaac frowned and Salomon apparently realized that he had protested too strongly. He gave a small bow in Isaac's direction and added, "I know your intentions are good, but I am not worthy of such honor."

Isaac saw no point telling Salomon about the many merchants who had attended last year's fairs, stayed after services to study Talmud, and asked him again and again if this new chacham would be there this year. These merchants, the ones he hoped would form the core of a yeshiva in Troyes, would soon be here for the Hot Fair. New clothes at the New Year would be too late.

Despite her father's anger, Joheved thought about how wonderful it was to study Talmud with him. What if some of the Jewish merchants felt the same way? Like her, they couldn't go to a yeshiva. Maybe studying during the fairs was their only chance. She knew what she needed to say, what might make her father see how important he was.

Isaac saw the sudden eagerness in Joheved's eyes, and he hoped that she might safely say to her father what he could not. "What is it, Joheved?"

"Papa, surely there are Jewish merchants who love Talmud but can't go to Mayence to study with your *maîtres* there. At least when they come to our fairs, they can study with you. And wouldn't all that trade be good for Troyes?"

Hearing the passion in her voice reminded Salomon of their study sessions. Joheved was right. Even great scholars left the yeshiva eventually to earn a living. Perhaps he could attract a few intelligent minds to his city; then they would attract more, and soon there might even be a center of learning here, at least during the Hot Fair months of July and August and again for the Cold Fair in November and December.

"Very well, Isaac, I will accept that you and my daughter think I'm a talmid chacham because you don't know any better. And I'll grant that perhaps some merchants who come to the fairs to study Talmud will be disappointed if my family and I are not dressed in the latest fashion."

"Salomon, every Jew in Troyes will thank you." Isaac slapped him on the back. "You see, Thibault forbids any foreign merchant from selling directly to another at his fairs. All transactions must be handled by a local middleman."

"With a portion of the sale going into the count's coffers, as well," Joseph added, winking at Salomon as he drained his cup. Still, if all these learned foreign merchants came to Troyes, there would be plenty of profit to go around.

Isaac lifted his cup in Joheved's direction and drank it down. "Salomon, your daughter has a mind like a jewel," he said. "What a wife she will make for some lucky man."

Isaac was about to suggest that he would be happy to help Salomon find a bridegroom for Joheved among the merchants and their sons at the upcoming Hot Fair, when the air was split by the first note in the clangorous dialogue of bells that kept time in Troyes. The Cathedral of Saint Pierre, the bishop's church, had the right to ring first, then the count's chapel, followed by the Abbey of Saint Loup. Only after these three finished could the bells at the numerous other churches and abbeys chime in. No one could speak over the din.

When the echoes of bells ringing in their heads had finally quieted, Salomon stood up. "Where has the time gone? Here it is midday already and I have work to do in the vineyard."

Isaac took Salomon's arm and walked them to the door. "I'll let you know when I find a source of grapes for your inspection."

Joseph added, "I will bring the boys to you after services on Sunday, while the moon is still waxing." Everyone knew that the waxing moon advanced growth and development, just as the waning moon promoted decay. It went without saying that no student began lessons with a new teacher on a Monday, Tuesday or Wednesday.

Salomon and his two daughters walked home in silence. Like the meal they had just shared, that morning's surprising events needed time to be digested. Just before they reached their street, a whiff of noxious fumes from the tannery district blew past them, and Miriam remembered that they had been asked to help make parchment.

"Joheved, what are we going to do about Catharina?" she whispered. "Now that Papa has a teaching job and a wine partner, he'll probably be able to buy all the parchment he wants."

"I don't know. Did we actually promise to help or did we only say we'd ask Papa?"

"Ask Papa what?" Salomon interrupted her. Embarrassed at being overheard, they had no choice but to explain their dilemma. He made his decision quickly. "You must certainly help make parchment if you said you would."

There was enough distrust between the Jews and Edomites as it was; he didn't want anyone saying that his daughters had made an agreement and then broke it. "I believe I will help as well. The parchment maker has been kind to us, and now I can return the favor. And I am curious to see how the stuff is made. After all, Torah scrolls are made of parchment."

four

That evening, Rivka was still wide awake after feeding the baby, so she decided to kiss her daughters good night. Finding their bed empty, and annoyed at her husband for allowing them to stay up so late, she went downstairs to complain. It took only a few moments of listening to realize what Salomon was discussing with her daughters, and she could not restrain her temper.

"Salomon, are you out of your mind? How can you consider teaching our daughters Talmud? What will everybody think?"

Joheved and Miriam sat in stunned silence as she ranted on. "Once you get them studying Talmud, they won't have any time to learn how to run a household—they won't even want to learn how to run a household." Her voice rose even higher. "Don't you realize that no man will want to marry a girl who is more learned than he is? We'll never find them husbands!" Rivka put her hands on her hips and stared stonily at Salomon. "I won't tolerate it; I tell you, I won't."

At first Salomon was just as shocked as the girls. But whatever misgivings he had about this endeavor, he was not about to be cowed by his wife. "If I want to teach my daughters Talmud, I will teach them Talmud!" he thundered, banging his fist down on the table. "It doesn't matter what anybody else thinks."

Rivka cringed and slowly backed away. "It obviously doesn't matter what I think," she muttered as she stormed off to bed.

Too upset to study any more, Joheved and Miriam quietly let Salomon tuck them in. He admonished them to be sure that their chores were done before they studied, so their mother could find no fault with them. Miriam eventually drifted off to sleep, remembering the wonderful meal they had shared with Isaac haParnas that afternoon, but Joheved lay awake.

It hurt when Papa and Mama argued. Would they get along better now if they hadn't lived apart all those years? She remembered how anxious Mama always became as the festivals approached, and how relieved Mama acted after Papa finally left. Probably she'd feel that way too if her husband spent most of his time at a yeshiva far away and came home only three times a year . . . except she didn't want a marriage like her parents'. But she had to marry somebody, and who else but a scholar would agree to marry a girl who studied Talmud?

CLANG! CRASH! Joheved had just finished braiding her hair the next morning when she heard the violent sounds coming from the kitchen below. Uh oh, Mama was banging the pots around something awful. She must be really angry.

The clanging sounded even louder as Joheved cautiously entered the kitchen. Miriam was already inside, trying to calm the fretful baby, while at the other end of the room, their mother brandished two copper skillets as if they were weapons. Just as Joheved reached her sister's side, Salomon burst in.

He still had on his tefillin, the small boxes containing words of Torah that pious Jewish men wear when they say their morning prayers, and his face was bright red against the black leather box tied to his forehead. Joheved and Miriam shrank from his furious presence.

"Would you mind keeping quiet? I'm trying to pray." He stood stiff as a statue, his fists tightly clenched.

Rivka's reply was defiant. "I'm trying to make breakfast."

Salomon took several steps in his wife's direction and raised his right hand. She in turn held the pans up between them. As his daughters watched in dread, he stopped and stared at the tefillin box tied on his biceps and its leather straps that wound up his arm. Then he lowered his hand and said in a voice as hard as steel, "Woman, you can bang your pots as much as you like, but I will not stop teaching my daughters Talmud!" He pounded his left hand on the table, sending the crockery skittering across it.

Rivka burst into tears. Joheved could barely keep from crying herself. Had her parents been possessed by demons? In desperation she gave the baby a pinch, and the room was immediately filled with the infant's howls.

Salomon could see that he would be surrounded by weeping females if he didn't soften his stance. He inwardly cursed his short temper and remembered a saying from Tractate Taanit:

> When Rabbi Adda bar Ahavah was asked to what he attributed his long life, he replied that he had never lost his temper in the midst of his family.

Salomon watched his wife fumbling at her chemise, trying to quiet little Rachel with her breast, and he felt ashamed. He knew she'd have to calm herself in order to nurse properly, so he waited until the baby was sucking before he spoke again. "Rivka, I can't stop teaching our daughters now that I know how eager they are to learn." He paused and stroked his beard. "How can I explain it to you?

"Ah, I have it." He hurried over to the chest and pulled out a book of Talmud. "This is Tractate Pesachim, and what I want to show you is near the end." Joheved and Miriam craned their necks to look, but Rivka stared stonily down at the baby.

Salomon held out his hands to her. "Even while jailed by the Romans for teaching Torah, Rabbi Akiva continued to instruct his students. When asked why he taught despite the danger,

> 'Rabbi Akiva said to his pupil: More than a calf wishes to suck does the cow desire to suckle.'"

Rivka was a nursing mother herself; surely she would understand.

Rivka sighed in resignation. Was her husband's craving to teach truly that powerful? "I see that your need to teach Talmud is so strong that you cannot resist instructing your wife." She shrugged her shoulders. "Very well then, teach them whatever you think is appropriate, but please try to be discreet." She emphasized the word "discreet."

Did Salomon understand the importance of discretion? Everyone else knew how much the demons hated Torah scholars. Did he realize his selfish need to teach might make Joheved and Miriam their target? As if the world wasn't dangerous enough. Rivka reached up to stroke the amulet around her neck.

"Don't worry, Rivka. Torah study confers divine protection." Salomon leaned down and spoke softly to her, "And I promise to find great scholars to marry our daughters, so they will have husbands more learned than they are."

Rivka rearranged the dishes in their previous position, and the family managed a relatively calm breakfast.

Joheved was still thinking about her parents' fight when they turned onto Rue de la Petite Tannerie. Catharina was waiting for them at the door to her father's shop. "I was afraid you wouldn't come," she said, hugging Joheved, then Miriam. "Papa is already down by the canal, setting up the frames."

Catharina led them down a well-worn path through cattails and rushes towards the Rû Cordé canal. A few years ago, to improve sanitation, Count Thibault had ordered a canal dug off the Seine. Tanners relocated onto two streets near where the canal exited under the town walls, thus sparing Troyes' inhabitants from drinking their effluent. The canal was not without its undesirable effects; city authorities regularly fished out the bodies of careless drunkards.

As far back as she could remember, Joheved had been warned to stay well away from the river's edge. She worried that the ground near the canal might be slippery and muddy, but to her relief, much usage had tamped the trail solid. There were even clumps of fresh green moss growing nearby. Perhaps they could collect some later to take home for the privy.

They reached a clearing where the sheepskins lay in small piles, surrounded by swarms of flies. The stench of decomposing animal remains assaulted them, and Catharina quickly moved them upwind to where her father was fastening one of the raw skins into an open wooden frame. The stink was not so bad there, but Joheved had trouble breathing and began to cough.

"Here, take a deep breath of this." Catharina's father thrust a damp handkerchief at her. The pungent smell of vinegar replaced that of dead sheep and Joheved's head cleared.

"*Merci,* I feel better now."

"Let me explain what we'll be doing today." The parchment maker held up four fingers. "Parchment is made in four stages. The first one is getting the skins attached to these wooden frames and into the river. We also need to scrape the wool from the outsides and the flesh from the insides, but if we can't get it all off today, it can be done later."

"I'm fairly handy with knives," Salomon said. "I've been pruning grapevines for years."

"Excellent. The girls can pin the skins between the frames, then you and I will clean them up and get them into the water."

He was surprised that the Jewish scholar was also a winemaker; the cathedral and abbey scholars who frequented his shop seemed to do nothing except write their manuscripts and pray. And they looked like it, too, all pale and flabby. But Salomon was sinewy and tanned, apparently used to hard work outdoors.

They soon made an efficient team. Joheved and Miriam grabbed opposite ends of a sheepskin and pulled. When they stretched it as far as they could, Catharina slid a frame around the skin and closed it tight. Then the framed skin went to one of the men, who scraped it with his knives until the girls announced that the next frame was ready. At that time, no matter how much or little had been cleaned from the skin, he dropped the frame into a holding area that the parchment maker had prepared in the shallow water.

The day grew steadily warmer. Joheved pushed her vinegar-soaked handkerchief up on her forehead to catch the sweat forming there, and Miriam removed hers entirely. "I can't believe it, but your father was right," she said to Catharina. "I can barely smell the sheepskins any more, even though you'd think they'd really stink now that it's gotten so warm."

Joheved cautiously sniffed the air. "Maybe the vinegar in our noses has stopped us from smelling anything?"

Catharina laughed as they tried to figure out if their noses still worked. "I have an idea. I'll find some flowers and a dead fish, and you see if you can tell the difference between them."

The parchment maker laughed too. Not only was his daughter happy, but the piles of sheepskins were shrinking rapidly. "You probably don't smell the skins because there aren't so many of them. I believe we can get them all into the frames by tomorrow afternoon. And in this heat, that's not a moment too soon."

He added emphasis to his statement by splashing himself after he dropped his latest frame into the canal. Then he grinned at the sweating girls and sent a gentle stream of water in their direction. They rewarded him with squeals and giggles.

Salomon was trying to work efficiently, but he could only manage to scrape the skin three times on each side before a new frame was ready for him. A breeze coming off the river afforded some relief from the heat and smell, but his chemise was drenched with perspiration. He watched with amusement and envy as his daughters got wetter and wetter.

Joheved and Miriam heard a sudden splash as something heavy fell in the water. They anxiously scanned the work area for their father, and just when they were sure the river demons had seized him, he resurfaced and waved to them from the middle of the canal.

"Miriam, look." Joheved grabbed her sister and pointed towards the water. "Papa's all right. He's swimming!"

The parchment maker stared at Salomon in amazement. It never occurred to him to bathe in the river. He knew that Jews went to the public baths regularly, but most Christians avoided immersing themselves in water for fear of the demons who lurked there. The "stews" were also notorious places of assignation for whores, another reason respectable Christian folk avoided them.

Salomon swam gracefully towards the shallow water where his daughters stood waiting for him. "Papa, Papa, I didn't know you could swim." Miriam wanted to hug him, but he was so wet that she just clung to his hand instead.

"I didn't mean to startle you." He pushed his wet hair back off his face. "My father Isaac—may his merit protect us—taught me how to swim in this very river when I was a boy. And on hot days in Mayence, the yeshiva students often go swimming together in the Rhine. You see, there is a Mishnah in Tractate Kiddushin that says that a father is obligated to teach his son to swim."

"Oh, Papa, can you teach us to swim?" Wouldn't it be wonderful, swimming around in the cool water on hot days?

"No, Joheved, a father is only required to teach his sons to swim, not his daughters." Salomon spoke in a voice that brooked no discussion.

Joheved's face fell in disappointment, so he added, "Considering how your mother feels about demons, I can only imagine the fuss she'd make if I took you into the water. She's already angry enough at me for teaching you Talmud."

The afternoon passed swiftly. The next day went just as smoothly, and as the parchment maker predicted, they were able to finish well before sunset. When the girls set off to collect moss to take home, Salomon asked when they should return.

"I don't see any reason to burden you further," the parchment maker replied. "After these skins have sat in the Seine for several days, they'll be soft and fairly clean. I'm sure my son will be home in time for the second stage, when we move the frames into troughs of lime solution."

"But I'd like to see the complete procedure, even if I can't help very much. What happens after the skins sit in the lime? Could you use help with the next part?"

The parchment maker stepped into the water to attach a net over the frames to keep hungry fish away. "After they've spent two weeks in the lime water, we scrape each skin clean of all remaining wool and fat. This is easier than what we did today, because the lime causes most of it to come off in the troughs. Then we rinse the skins in the river and put them back in lime for another two weeks."

"What happens when they're finished with the lime?" As much as Salomon wanted to participate in the entire process, he couldn't make a commitment for months of work. He had new students to instruct and the vineyard to tend.

The parchment maker heard the hesitancy in Salomon's voice and wanted to reassure him. "Next comes the third stage. We let the skins dry, all the while cleaning them with pumice, chalk and water. Then they're ready to be thinned, which is the final step. Sometimes it takes months before we're finished. We take our time and work carefully, until all that remains is to trim the parchment and fold it into sheaves."

Salomon felt around the frames to make sure that the netting covered his side completely. "So when should I come back for the third part?"

"Just wait for a rainy summer day when it's too wet to work in your vineyard. You'll be welcome to join my family in the workroom, thinning and scraping the skins into parchment."

As spring ripened into summer, the weather remained excellent, much to Salomon's consternation. The better the climate and the more luxuriant his plants' growth, the more the vintner fretted over the possible disasters awaiting him. A late May frost would cut down his tender buds before they flowered, and too much rain in early summer could hamper fertilization by washing away the pollen. Then, if midsummer was cool and humid, mildew would destroy the grapes before they'd even begun to grow.

Salomon could only pray for the warm, calm weather that facilitated the critical flowering and fruit-set. And so far this year the Creator obliged him; the young grapes hung heavy on the vines, slowly becoming translucent. But peril still threatened. A sudden hail shower could crash down with a summer storm, and the result would be destruction of leaves, shoots and grapes.

This summer Salomon divided his time between tending his vineyard and tending his new young students. The first thing he had to do was teach Menachem and Ephraim to ask questions, to shower him with their most difficult queries. He did this by asking them questions in return, and not just academic ones.

Why didn't the lions on Noah's ark eat the other animals? What did Abraham say to the Holy One when he was told to sacrifice his son? How did Sarah die? Why did Moses break the tablets containing the Ten Commandments? How did Rachel help her older sister Leah marry Jacob first? Why wasn't Joseph buried in Egypt?

Joheved and Miriam loved this part of studying Torah, when Salomon told them about the people in the Bible. *Midrash* he called them, stories that explained so much more than the original text. And judging from Menachem and Ephraim's rapt expressions, Joheved could see that they loved it too.

She and Miriam would sit near the kitchen, listening carefully as they silently spun thread, embroidered or did mending. They knew their father expected them to question him at bedtime, even more vigorously than the boys did. Still they were careful to give no indication of how closely they followed their father's lectures. Although Rivka no longer spoke of it, the girls were sure there'd be trouble if their studies became public knowledge.

No matter how much Rivka disapproved of her daughters studying, she had to admit that their spinning and needlework had improved greatly. Joheved in particular had become quite adept at spinning flax into thread for weaving linen. The process was tedious, but her hands took on a life of their own as she listened to her father teach Torah.

In the morning Joheved and Miriam attended services, and after disner they crossed the short distance beyond the city walls to the vineyard. From their vantage point atop a small rise, the vines' bright green foliage was easily identified among the golden fields of grain. The road was surrounded by tall stalks of wheat, soon to be cut, and the remains of oat fields already harvested. Here and there livestock grazed on fallow land, which would be enriched with their manure.

Summer was Joheved's favorite time to work in the vineyard. The earth between rows was soft and warm, squishing pleasantly between her bare toes as she and Miriam hoed the ground free of weeds. Under their father's or grandmother's supervision, they lifted some foliage and attached it to the trellis, while other parts they trimmed off altogether. The leafy vines on their trellis were only slightly taller than the girls were, offering excellent conditions for "hide and seek" games.

Despite Grandmama Leah's failing memory, she still knew exactly which leaves should remain and which should be pulled off to allow maximum sunlight to reach the grapes. She lectured them continually on the importance of careful foliage control, as if neglecting to trim leaves properly was a moral failing.

"You must have enough leaves to feed the growing grapes, but shaded branches produce thin, soapy wine." Leah tore off several offending leaves and let them flutter to the ground. "Leaves must also be trimmed to reduce the vine's vigor or else they will grow excessively and smother their own grapes, as well as next season's latent buds."

Grandmama Leah's lessons on viticulture had been interesting the first few times she offered them, but she repeated them so often now that Joheved and Miriam paid attention only out of politeness. They wouldn't dream of telling her that she had already given them the same advice several times that day.

In another part of the vineyard, the men hired by Isaac haParnas were working on the vines that Salomon's family had not been able to prune last winter. These plants were unlikely to produce grapes worth pressing this season, but their leaves still had to be trimmed.

Joheved and Miriam, remembering how their grandmother had antagonized previous workers, tried to keep Grandmama Leah occupied far away from the Parnas's employees.

One day she suddenly started screeching, "Someone's stealing my grapes!" She picked up a discarded branch and, shaking it at the men in the distance, began running towards them. "Keep away from my grapes, you thieves! Get out of my vineyard!"

"Grandmama, stop! Wait for us!" Joheved and Miriam took off after her, but she was amazingly agile for her years and eluded them among the vines. "Nobody's stealing your grapes; those men work for us."

Salomon managed to catch up with her before the workers could make out what she was shouting at them. "It's all right, Mama, it's all right," he repeatedly reassured her, using his most soothing voice. When she grew calmer, he tried to distract her. "Mama, look at those grey clouds. Do you think it will hail?"

Leah stared silently at the darkening sky and then declared, "Don't worry. This storm will only rain gently for a few days, which is just what the vineyard needs."

"Perhaps we ought to be getting back home then." Salomon sighed, unable to hide the sadness he felt whenever he was forced to confront his mother's deterioration. Most of the time he tried not to dwell on her condition; it was too depressing, and there didn't seem to be anything anyone could do to cure her.

When night fell, he was still worrying about his mother. The air was sultry and humid, leaving Troyes' inhabitants feeling damp and poorly rested when the church bells woke them at dawn the next morning. It was drizzling when Salomon's family left for services, and by disner, the rain was coming down so heavily that Salomon announced that they might as well help the parchment maker finish his skins. Joheved and Miriam drew their cloaks tightly around them and set out with their father along the muddy street towards the canal.

They walked carefully along the road, staying as close as possible to the buildings where the jutting second floors offered a narrow shelter for pedestrians below. The girls tried to keep well away from the center of the street, where the running water was moving faster and faster, taking with it all the garbage that had accumulated since the previous rainstorm. As they hurried along, they encountered servants emptying the fetid contents of their masters' waste pits into the small creek that had recently been the road. They grinned at each other to acknowledge that they had managed to avoid that odious chore.

The parchment maker was at home with both his son and daughter, each working on sheepskins stretched out on frames. He greeted Salomon cheerfully and waved them over to dry out in front of the hearth. Then he showed Salomon how to scrape the skin clean with various small knives, to remove even the tiniest blemish on its surface. At the same time, Catharina taught the girls to rub the scraped skin with pumice to make it soft and smooth. Soon they were all busily occupied.

The parchment maker's son announced that he had recently done business with a Jew who raised sheep nearby. "His name is Samuel and he has a small estate near Ramerupt. He was glad to find a tanner who would deal with him regularly because his son's a student who needs a lot of parchment." The youth smiled at Salomon. "I happened to mention that we had a Jewish scholar in town who frequently bought from us, and the man nearly attacked me with questions about you."

"Really now," Salomon said, his eyebrows raised slightly. "What interest could a man who raises sheep have in me?"

"Well, first off, he was curious how long you've lived in Troyes because he couldn't remember any scholars here. I said you'd grown up here but only moved back again last year."

"I don't think I know him." Salomon stroked his beard. "I wonder if his family comes to Troyes for Rosh Hashanah."

"I doubt it. You see, he asked about your family and nearly jumped out of his chair when I mentioned your daughters." The son laid down his knife, grinning widely. "He wanted to know how many unmarried ones you had, how old they were, what they looked like. I told him about your girls and asked why he was so interested. Did he perhaps have an unmarried son himself?"

Joheved felt herself getting warm and moved her chair away from the fire. Catharina and Miriam were looking at her strangely and Salomon gave her a quick glance before encouraging the speaker to continue.

"So Samuel admits that he does have a son yet unmarried, his youngest boy, the very one who needs all the parchment, who is away studying in Mayence." The parchment maker's son leered at Joheved, apparently enjoying her discomfort with the subject. "But I must apologize. I neglected to ask for his son's name."

Joheved was greatly relieved when Salomon ended the conversation by announcing that he needed silence to concentrate on the skin he was scraping. As she smoothed the pumice along her nearly finished parchment, Joheved tried to sort out her disconcerting feelings.

Of course she'd be the first to marry; she was the eldest. And it was her father's job to find her a suitable husband. So why was the subject so embarrassing? Why did it bother her to hear people discussing a prospective match? Joheved had no answer for herself, only the knowledge that the more she considered the question, the more embarrassed she felt. She caught herself continually polishing the same area of parchment far thinner than necessary, and in dread of tearing the precious material, she resolved to stop daydreaming and pay full attention to her work.

The rain continued in fits and starts, sometimes raining so hard that Salomon stopped his knife and listened long enough to ascertain that it was only rain he heard, not hail. Then, with a sigh of relief, he'd begin working the skin again. The end product was indeed parchment, and he was pleased that he could visualize the entire process.

A sudden increase in the room's illumination made the occupants realize that the rain had halted.

"Papa, I think it's stopped raining for a while," Catharina said, laying aside the skin she'd been working. "I need to do some shopping for souper, and it was raining too hard to go out earlier. Maybe I should go now while it's let up some."

Before her father could say anything, her older brother rebuked her. "You should have gone in the morning, rain or no rain. Now the bread won't be fresh and the best meat will be gone. Papa spoils you too much, letting you put off your chores."

The parchment maker scowled at his son. "I don't see why Catharina should catch cold in the rain so you can have fresher bread. She was very useful with all these skins, and I dare say that her pumice work is finer than yours. If you must have the best meat, get up early and go buy it yourself."

Eager to avert any further arguments, Salomon suggested that his daughters could accompany Catharina to the food stalls and then go on home during this lull in the storm. "I'd like to stay a while longer and see the final steps." He attempted to mollify the son by appealing to his expertise. "Can you show me how you trim and fold the parchment?"

The youth took Salomon over to the worktable by the window. "We need good light for this part, folding the parchment into pages and cutting them perfectly straight." He glowered at his sister as she left, and she stuck her tongue out at him in return.

five

Summer 4829 (1069 C.E.)

The three girls made their way to Rue de l'Epicerie, holding their skirts up out of the mud and trying to dodge puddles. The green grocer and butcher shops were open, but to Catharina's dismay, the bakery was shuttered.

"Oh no, they must have sold all their bread this morning. Now what am I going to do?" She looked close to tears. "My father may put up with less than fresh bread for my sake, but he's going to be mad if I come home with no bread at all. And my brother will gloat over my failure for days."

Miriam took her hand and started pulling her towards the bridge. "Come with us to a bakery in the Jewish Quarter. The one near the castle is always open late."

"How do you know they won't be shut too?" If this Jewish bakery were closed, Catharina would have gone all this distance for naught. But she soon received the answer to her question, for the mouth-watering smell of newly baked bread wafted towards them from the direction they were heading.

Joheved took a deep breath of the sweet odor and explained, "This bakery is a partnership, owned by both a Jew and a Notzri. On Sunday, your sabbath, the Jewish partner bakes and sells bread, and on Saturday, our sabbath, the Notzri bakes and sells bread. The same thing during Passover and your holy days. They're never closed, no matter what day it is."

"What's a Notzri?" Catharina's eyes narrowed with suspicion.

"Notzrim are those who worship the one from Nazareth, you know." Not eager to discuss what names the Jews had for the gentiles, Joheved urged her companions to hurry.

The sky had darkened alarmingly, but the bakery was in sight. Like other shops in Troyes, one of the bakery's windows had shutters that opened up and down rather than to the sides. The lower shutter was propped up parallel to the ground by posts, thus forming a large counter. The upper shutter was fastened halfway open to make a roof over the counter, sheltering its contents. Here the baker and his family served their customers. Catharina was not alone in her desire to buy bread during the storm's lull, so the three girls had to wait.

Miriam began to tease her sister. "Joheved's going to be a rich lady when she marries the sheep farmer's son. She'll have all the wool, parchment and lamb roasts she wants."

Catharina joined the good-natured assault. "Did you hear my brother say the boy's father has a manor near Ramerupt? What a life. Bossing servants around and producing wheat, sheep and babies! Lots and lots of servants." She elbowed Joheved suggestively. "And lots and lots of babies."

"I wonder what he looks like. Maybe he'll be tall, dark and handsome." Miriam giggled. "But, if he's still not betrothed, he might be short and ugly."

"I bet he's a hunchback from spending all his time bent over books." Catharina covered her mouth with her hands, trying to repress her laughter.

"If he's a student, he's probably thin and pale. They spend all their time indoors and hardly ever eat." Miriam's tone became serious. "But if he's a scholar in Mayence, he'll be more learned than you, Joheved, just what Papa wants."

All this marriage talk was too much for Joheved. "I don't care if I have a thousand servants. I won't marry a scholar who spends all his time in Mayence and hardly ever comes home." She stared defiantly at Miriam. "I want a husband who lives in the same house as I do every day, not just on holidays."

She hadn't intended to reveal her fears to them, and until she'd spoken, she hadn't even realized what her fears were. But now she knew—she didn't want to sleep with a stranger. And a husband who spent only a few weeks a year at home would always be a stranger, no matter how long they'd been married.

Dismayed at her outburst, Catharina and Miriam tried to offer solace. But they both knew Joheved would have little say over whom she married. Miriam put an arm around her sister's shoulder. "Don't worry, Joheved. Most husbands don't stay away from home as much as Papa did."

Catharina had more practical advice, although it wasn't very comforting. "You're a Jew, which means you're either going to marry a merchant or scholar, and both of them are usually away from home a lot. Besides, maybe you won't like your husband much, and you'll be glad when he's away."

"It wasn't so bad having Papa gone, and I don't think Mama minded it as much as you think you will, Joheved," Miriam said. "Except for being poor, I liked living with just Mama, Grandmama and you. Who needs a man around all the time anyway?"

Joheved had no answer for her, only questions jumping around inside her mind. Did Mama really prefer it when Papa wasn't home? And why didn't Grandmama Leah get married again after Grandpapa Isaac died? Aunt Sarah hadn't remarried either. Maybe there was something bad about marriage that nobody talked about. Yet Mama worried so desperately that her daughters wouldn't find husbands.

"At least you know that you will get married," Catharina said soberly, interrupting Joheved's musings. "All Jews get married, some more than once. No matter how poor you are, even if you're ugly, they make sure you get married. But if my father doesn't save enough money for my dowry, I'll never get a husband. I'll end up an old maid taking care of him forever. And if Papa can't buy me a husband before he dies, my brother will keep the money for himself. I know he will."

Joheved and Miriam were shocked into silence at the thought of Catharina's not being allowed to marry. They knew about monks and nuns, but those people chose that life, and besides, they weren't Jewish. For Jews, to be fruitful and multiply was the Creator's first commandment, and anyone who refused to marry was considered selfish in the extreme, even sinful. Who knows what wonderful scholars would be denied life if their ordained parents didn't wed? Even old people beyond childbearing, like Isaac haParnas, were supposed to marry. Didn't the Holy One create Eve because it was not good for Adam to be alone?

"But you're so pretty, Catharina," Joheved said, her own doubts dissolving in concern for her friend. "Even if your father doesn't leave you a dowry, you can still marry. Our maidservant, Marie, is saving her wages for her own dowry. She's engaged to a cobbler's apprentice, and by the time he's a journeyman, she'll have enough money for them to get married."

Miriam wanted to encourage Catharina, too. "And Marie gets to marry whoever she wants. She earned her dowry herself and chose her own husband."

They reached the counter just as the first few drops of the renewed storm began to fall. The baker's wife recognized the young rabbi's daughters and gave them a misshapen loaf to share on their way home. Joheved thanked her and tore off a piece for Catharina, who quickly took it and waved good-bye.

No sooner had Joheved divided the remaining bread in two, than Miriam whispered to her, "Look at those beggars. They're soaking wet. I bet they've been here all day."

Several paupers, sensing that they were under discussion, stretched out their hands towards the girls.

Miriam started to tear her bread into pieces, but Joheved stepped between her and the beggars. "Surely you don't intend to give your bread away." Joheved's vehemence increased. "They're probably only pretending, to try to gain your sympathy."

The raindrops grew larger and more frequent, and Miriam pulled her cloak close around her. "What about those children?" She pointed to several skinny youngsters, dressed in sopping rags. "I don't care if they are fakers. I'm giving them bread anyway."

Even though Joheved was hungry, it was impossible to eat her own bread while watching the pathetic children wolf down Miriam's. With a sigh, she handed her bread to the small beggars and continued home with her sister in silence. A new worry assailed her and her appetite diminished.

At least Ramerupt was nearby. But what if Papa arranged a match with someone who lived far away and she had to move to another town, like Mama did when she married Papa? She might never see her family again. And if she didn't live near Papa and Miriam, she'd never be able to study Talmud either.

She walked slowly, each foot suddenly heavy as lead, feeling increasingly pessimistic about her chances for a good marriage. There was nothing she could do about it either; her future was in her father's hands, and the Holy One's.

Salomon, walking home slowly through the muddy streets, tried to remember the youngest students in Mayence. Was one of them from Ramerupt or had Salomon returned to Troyes before this particular boy began yeshiva? Parchment was scarce and expensive (and after today's work, he could see why), so Talmudic scholars were trained to develop prodigious memories. An advanced yeshiva student was expected to know scripture by heart, plus all the major tractates of the Talmud. Salomon, who had learned many of the minor tractates as well, was justifiably proud of his memory, and knew if he had ever met such a boy at Mayence he would be able to recall it.

Voilà! He slapped his thigh in triumph. He had it. The more he considered the students whose first year at the yeshiva had coincided with his last, the more he knew he was right. The boy's name was Meir ben Samuel.

Older students like Salomon normally had little contact with their youngest colleagues. They all prayed together in synagogue and attended the same lectures, but contemporaries generally studied with each other. The first year was especially difficult, and boys at this level rarely did more than listen attentively and try to remember as much as possible. They rarely asked questions.

But Salomon remembered this one youth, mainly because they had traveled in the same merchant caravans to and from Mayence. He could picture Meir in his mind; small and thin, rather gangly actually, in the way boys are just before they start growing. Meir's trunk of books and new fur-lined cloak proclaimed him the son of a prosperous man. The boy never mentioned Ramerupt, but Salomon knew he lived nearby. Once, when he'd expressed concern about the youth's going on alone while the others stopped in Troyes, Meir had assured him that home was only a short ride away.

Their first trip together, they'd hardly spoken. Salomon utilized his time expanding the notes he'd taken during the recent session, and Meir was too intimidated to approach the chacham. By the following journey, Meir was so curious about the older man's journals that he couldn't resist asking about them. Salomon remembered that the youth had been both astonished and impressed. Talmud study was an oral tradition and extensive kuntres such as Salomon's were unheard of.

Salomon smiled wistfully. He had explained to Meir that his yeshiva days were limited, that he'd been taking notes all these years so that when the time came, he'd be able to study Talmud by himself. Meir had been sympathetic and offered reassurance that anybody with such excellent records would never forget his studies. After that, the ice was broken and the boy had plied Salomon with questions.

The more Salomon recalled about the youth, the higher his opinion of him. Meir's questions had shown intelligence and enthusiasm for learning. It was possible . . . he might indeed make a proper husband for Joheved. Then financial reality intruded into Salomon's pleasant reverie. The boy's father had an estate, which meant he was some sort of lord. He would expect his son to marry into an equally prominent family, to wed a girl with a substantial dowry. Salomon sighed heavily and continued home. He needed to concentrate on his new students and his grapes this summer; he'd worry about other matters later.

Rain continued for several days, but the July sunshine eventually reasserted its dominance. One afternoon it was so hot that the normally playful new kittens were curled up together under a bush to nap in the shade. According to the Hebrew calendar, it was the month of Av, and Salomon's students, along with other Jews, were beginning the book of Deuteronomy.

Rather than risk his pupils' nodding off in the warm *salle,* Salomon decided to teach in the courtyard under the apple tree. He spread out a blanket for the baby, who wiggled contentedly in the warm air. Rachel was a happy child, a joy to be around. She shook her dark curls and smiled at everyone, rarely crying unless she was hungry.

Salomon's family lived in the middle of three houses built in a U surrounding the courtyard. Sarah's was on the left, closest to the gate, while the right-hand dwelling belonged to two widows who made their living selling eggs and poultry. Many women transacted business with the "chicken ladies," and Joheved tried not to worry what these clients would think if they saw her and Miriam attending their father's lessons.

As usual Joheved had her spindle and distaff, but these days Miriam did embroidery while Salomon taught. Rivka had bought linen to make chemises, and whenever the light was good, Miriam painstakingly decorated the necks and sleeves of the girls' new undergarments. Today Joheved noticed that, besides the Bible, her father had another book with him that she did not recognize.

Menachem and Ephraim had been chanting a few verses each and then translating them when they came to the sixth chapter. Here the text included the Shema, the Jewish affirmation of faith, one of the most important prayers in the Hebrew liturgy. It was Ephraim's turn, and Salomon was watching him intently.

> "Shema Israel, Adonai Eloheinu, Adonai Echad: Hear, O Israel, the Lord is our God, the Lord is One. You shall love the Lord your God with all your heart, with all your soul and with all your . . ."

Ephraim paused and looked up at Salomon for direction. He didn't know how to translate the Hebrew word, *m'odecha,* which meant something like "very much."

"To love God with all your *m'odecha.*" Salomon smiled and began his explanation. "This strange usage means your wealth, your property. We all know people whose possessions seem dearer to them than their bodies or their souls, and it is on their account that this last word is added."

The twins nodded in appreciation. Several, if not many, of their grandfather's business associates were in this category.

Later that night, Salomon showed Joheved and Miriam where the identical subject was discussed in Tractate Berachot's ninth chapter. "You can take turns reading."

> And you shall love the Lord, your God . . . Rav Eliezer says: Since it says, "with all your soul," why does it also say "with all your wealth"? And since it says, "with all your wealth," why does it also say "with all your soul"?

Joheved, eager to read first, was baffled. "Aren't Rav Eliezer's questions the same?"

"But your soul and your property aren't the same thing," Miriam challenged her sister.

The girls started to argue and Salomon chuckled at their impatience. "Hold your tongues, mes filles; the Gemara doesn't end here."

Miriam began to read.

> But rather, if you have a person whose body is more precious to him than his money, then for him it was said, "with all your soul." And if you have a person whose money is more precious to him than his body, then for him it was said, "with all your wealth."

Her voice rose with excitement. "Papa, this is just what you taught us this morning. It's from the Talmud!"

Salomon took the book from her and closed it. "When the Hot Fair starts, I'll be occupied studying Talmud with the merchants after morning services and again at night. It will be difficult finding enough time to teach the twins properly." He sighed. It wasn't easy telling his daughters that he would have no time to teach them Talmud until the fair was over. "I'll need you two to help Grandmama Leah in the vineyard while I'm at synagogue."

Joheved understood at once. "It's all right, Papa. We'll just review our old lessons until you can teach us again."

After she said the bedtime Shema, Joheved lay awake a while longer. What would she do if she had to sacrifice her most precious possession for the love of God? She wasn't sure what her most precious possession was, but she did know that she had sacrificed her mother's approval in order to study Talmud.

All that week Joheved tried to savor the last of her lessons with Papa. At Shabbat services, she felt a special pride when the Torah was read and she remembered what she had learned about the Shema and loving God. But pride in her knowledge was mingled with shame about her appearance. Until Isaac haParnas had encouraged, almost ordered, Papa to buy the family new clothes, Joheved hadn't thought much about how hers compared with other girls'. And on the Sabbath, Jewish women wore their finest clothing.

Joheved tried to concentrate on her prayers, but found herself surreptitiously surveying the occupants of the women's gallery. The other girls had colored bliauts, and like usual, they were chattering together in the back. One of them glanced up, noticed Joheved staring and glared back. Then she whispered something behind her hand, and several of the girls giggled.

Joheved knew what the local girls said about her and Miriam, that the two of them dirtied their hands working outdoors among the vines, that they were no better than peasants. And they dressed like them too. She and Miriam, with their brown bliauts and unadorned chemises, looked like common sparrows in a room full of peacocks. It didn't help to remind herself that she studied Talmud, while the other girls didn't even know Hebrew. Especially since the rest of her family didn't dress very well either.

Grandmama Leah wore a violet silk bliaut, but it had seen better days. Mama had been wearing her dark red wool one for as long as Joheved could remember, but at least it had elaborate trimmings. Yet even Mama's best embroidery could not prevent Papa's clothes from looking old and faded. Still, every year Mama carefully took them apart, cleaned them, and sewed them back together with the inside out to make them last longer.

Thus he managed to make do with the same weekday outfits he had worn as a student, while his Shabbat bliaut was the one he had been married in. Faced with a choice between new clothes and more parchment, Papa bought the parchment. Thank heaven he'd accepted Isaac haParnas's belief that foreign merchants might judge Troyes' Jewish community based on how their family dressed, no matter how unfair that judgment might be.

The Champagne region's six fairs were the most important trading centers in France, some said in Europe, with the Hot Fair of Troyes the most celebrated of all. Throughout the province, brush was cleared back from the roads, which were then patrolled by the count's men. Troyes' streets were clean, or at least cleaner, tavern and hostel keepers laid in supplies for a flood of guests, and an army of officials made sure that all went smoothly.

From the time when Joheved and Miriam first noticed synagogue attendance swelling with unfamiliar men, they could hardly wait to attend the Hot Fair. Years earlier, when she had plenty of wine to sell, they had gone with Grandmama Leah. But then she began to get lost among the stalls and made one excuse after another to avoid the fairgrounds.

Mama never liked the fair; it was crowded and noisy and attracted all sorts of unsavory people. She wouldn't hear of Joheved and Miriam going there alone, saying, "Seeing all those fancy goods will make you greedy and covetous, and knowing that we can't afford to buy them will only make you unhappy."

But now, finally, the opening day of the cloth market, they were not only permitted to attend the fair, but would be escorted there by no less a personage than the Parnas of Troyes and his daughter-in-law. And not just to look, but to buy! Even Joheved woke up early, and at breakfast, Rivka had to remind her and Miriam several times not to bolt down their food. After synagogue, they forced themselves to be patient as Johanna discussed the arrangements with Salomon and Isaac.

Joheved and Miriam tried not to rush their patroness, but she seemed to sense their eagerness and hurried along, chattering to them about the different kinds of fabrics they would find. When they entered the cloth hall, which was actually a large tent, the girls stopped, overwhelmed by the visual feast. The tables were covered with a kaleidoscope of colored bolts, ranging from uncolored and little finished, through green and brown, to the brightest shades of yellow and scarlet. All around was the pleasant hubbub of buying and selling. Mama had been right about the noise level, but her daughters found it exciting, not annoying.

Johanna smiled at their appreciation. "Isn't it beautiful?"

Joheved found her voice first. "Oui, I never imagined there could be so many different colors."

Miriam was quiet a bit longer, and then realized that Johanna was waiting for her reply. "It's like an indoor rainbow. I could just stand here looking and be happy."

Joheved's earlier impatience was replaced with hesitation. "There are so many tables; we can't possibly see them all. How do we know where to start?"

Johanna smiled to herself. It would be fun to teach the girls how to tell the difference between grades of wool, to recognize fine fabric when they felt it. For the first time in her life, she regretted not having any daughters.

"We won't shop at every stall, my dear," she said. "There are certain merchants whom I trust, and we will deal with them. But you can stop and look whenever you like."

Although wool predominated, there were other materials for sale, and they stopped briefly at stalls selling cotton and linen. They lingered longer at the silk merchants, fingering the slippery smoothness and admiring the bright colors. Many of the silk dealers were Jewish, and most of them knew Johanna. Each insisted that he had the most beautiful bolts of silk cloth, exactly what she was looking for.

"Shouldn't we start looking at the woolens?" Miriam asked, turning back the way they'd come. "What if Papa gets here and we haven't found what we like yet?"

"Don't worry." Johanna spoke with an authority the girls had never heard their mother use. "If we haven't found just the right thing when your Papa arrives, we'll send him off to the vineyard and tell him to come back later."

They soon reached the wool dealers' area. There were tables for each of the different towns, and Johanna explained how an expert could recognize at a glance the cloths of Douai, Arras, Bruges or Ypres. The Flemish towns carefully guarded their reputations, so only their finest cloth was exported to the Champagne fairs.

As they wandered among the stalls, the girls stole glances at the exotic foreigners. Many spoke in unknown languages, but to Joheved's surprise, she recognized some Hebrew conversations. Several times, she or Miriam found what they thought was good cloth, but Johanna, while praising their discernment, insisted that they continue their search. It was just as well that something had delayed the men's arrival. Services had been over for some time.

They separated to cover more ground, and Joheved was drawn to a vigorous bargaining session going on a few stalls away. The two men involved were a study in contrast. The seller, standing behind his table of merchandise, was freckled with auburn hair. He was fashionably dressed in a red *côte* with yellow hose. His outfit might be considered striking, except that the buyer's was outright flamboyant, a robe of brilliant green silk, tied with a blue sash. This man had swarthy skin and a short black beard that tapered to a point. His hair was almost completely hidden under a turban of the same material as his robe. Buyer and seller furiously gestured with their hands, heads nodding or shaking, oblivious to those around them. To Joheved, they looked like a sparrow and a raven, involved in some bizarre mating dance.

She stopped short when she realized that, despite the dark man's strange accent, they were speaking Hebrew. Their argument was fierce, but they weren't angry. It was not about the quality of the fabric, only about cost, and somehow both seemed to understand that an agreement would ultimately be reached. Most potential buyers eagerly found fault with the merchandise; the cloth had been stretched, material left out all night in the damp to increase its weight, the wool dyed by the piece rather than by its thread. But this fabric was acknowledged to be exceptionally fine; the dispute was over its price.

Joheved was intrigued—what was this wonderful stuff? She stood quietly nearby, her attention focused on the two men. Soon Miriam noticed her sister standing there transfixed and joined her. When the merchants saw that they had an audience, they increased their theatrics, unable to resist showing off to the little dears who apparently understood everything they said.

"You won't find anything finer at this entire fair, and you know it." Sparrow, the seller, shook his finger at Raven. "These sheep are very rare; they give less wool per animal than most, but require just as much pasture. My supplier is entitled to a fair profit." Actually, Sparrow had already paid the supplier an excellent price. It was his own profit that mattered.

Raven knew this. He had come from the land of the Saracens, carrying rare spices and jewels, on a journey short of miraculous. Pirates had not attacked his ship, highwaymen had not assaulted him on land, and in Provence, he had joined a caravan of Jews who seemed to know somebody in charge at each of the toll places on their route. If his return was anything like that, he stood to make a small fortune. Even if his return trip had the usual amount of expenses, he would still arrive home with a tidy sum.

"I have come a great distance, and I must return a great distance." Raven waved his arm expansively. "I cannot pay you so much that it was not worth my coming here. I have a large family who depend on my support." He thought fondly of his three wives and several daughters who would be thrilled with this beautiful cloth. He had already decided to keep some of it.

Sparrow understood that the strange merchant had a large amount invested in the trip. "All the more reason for you to buy my best woolens. The more expensive the goods you bring back, the more profit you can make."

Back and forth they went, Sparrow extolling his wool, and Raven insisting that he could not afford it. The seller lowered his price, the buyer countered, and the debate continued, to the delight of Joheved and Miriam.

Sparrow was saying something about how special these particular sheep were, when Raven interrupted. "I don't care if your precious sheep shit roses; the price is far too high."

Sparrow was quick with his retort. "Only some of the sheep shit roses; the others shit fleurs-de-lys."

Miriam and Joheved looked at each other and quickly covered their mouths with their hands to hide their smiles, but it was too late. A few giggles escaped, then they dissolved in laughter. Their mirth was contagious. First Raven grinned, then Sparrow chuckled, and soon all four of them were convulsed with laughter. Joheved, bent over and holding her stomach with glee, noticed a familiar bliaut and stood up to see Johanna looking down at them. How long had she been there?

Joheved was too embarrassed to speak, but Miriam piped up, "Johanna, you came just in time. I think we've found the finest wool at the fair."

"If Nissim's sheep are as excellent as he says," she replied with a grin, looking the seller in the eye, "then you are probably right."

"Mistress Johanna, I am overjoyed to see you again." The Sparrow, whose name was now Nissim, bowed low. "And who are these charming young mademoiselles?" He knew she didn't have any daughters, and these girls were dressed too poorly to be members of her family anyway. But they obviously weren't servants.

"The older one is Joheved, and the younger is Miriam. They are daughters of Rav Salomon, the winemaker, Isaac's new business partner. In fact, I expect both men to join us anytime now."

Both merchants made small bows in the girls' direction. Raven coughed delicately, and Nissim remembered his manners. "Pardon me, sir, allow me to introduce Mistress Johanna, wife of Joseph ben Isaac haParnas of Troyes."

"*Shalom aleichem* (peace be to you). I am Hiyya ibn Ezra of Cairo." The Egyptian Jew spoke in halting, heavily accented French. "I am honored to meet you."

"Peace be to you as well, Hiyya ibn Ezra. You are a long way from Egypt," she said, switching easily to Hebrew. "I hope our fair will be worth your lengthy journey." She turned to Nissim. "I myself happen to be in the market for some wool cloth, so I'd very much like to see what your fabulous sheep have produced."

Giving Hiyya a helpless look, Nissim retrieved a covered bolt from under the table and carefully unwrapped it. Miriam couldn't repress an awed exclamation, and the three females leaned forward for a closer examination. The wool was dyed a deep burgundy, yet the color was clear and not the least bit muddy. Johanna caressed the fine cloth and held up a length to the light. She put her face in the material and smelled it.

"This is fine fabric indeed. I'll take enough to make five bliauts, one man's, two women's and two girls', and perhaps some extra for cloaks as well." She turned to the two merchants and asked them, "What was your last asking price and your last offer?"

When she heard their answers, she turned to Nissim and announced that she would pay him exactly halfway between the two amounts. She then turned to Hiyya, "I expect him to give you a better deal, since you're buying much more than I am. But I'll act as your middleman for only half the usual fee, which will make it less painful for him."

If Hiyya was surprised at her boldness, his expression didn't show it. He was a stranger here and this woman was obviously someone important. Hadn't Nissim introduced her as related to the Parnas? And the girls as the rabbi's daughters?

As if to confirm this, Isaac and Salomon strode up and joined them.

Hiyya ibn Ezra greeted Isaac with the respectful politeness expected towards a community leader. Salomon, however, he met with joy. "Rav Salomon, I am so glad to meet you at last." Hiyya pumped his hand vigorously. "Three things induced me to make this journey. That in Troyes I would be able to buy excellent steel swords and fine wool, as well as study Talmud with their talmid chacham. I have not been disappointed in two of the three, and I expect to find the swords soon. Ever since my yeshiva days, I have never understood that difficult section in Tractate Sanhedrin. This week you explained it, and I am in your debt."

"You are too kind," Salomon said, coloring brightly. "It is a complex passage, and I only explained it so well because you and that fellow from Provence questioned me so relentlessly."

Joheved had never seen her father look more pleased or more embarrassed. Isaac winked at her and whispered, "I told you so."

"Papa, Papa, we've found the most wonderful cloth. It's so soft and smooth, almost like silk." Miriam nearly knocked him over with her enthusiastic embrace. "And guess what color it is? The same color as wine!"

Salomon kept his arm around his daughter while Nissim proudly presented the material for inspection. Salomon groaned inwardly. The finest wool at the Hot Fair, and he was obligated to buy it, even if took him years to pay Isaac back. Nissim, expert trader that he was, read Salomon's emotions like an open book, and tried to figure out how he could diplomatically undercharge the scholar while still maintaining his previous price for the Egyptian.

Isaac haParnas bent over and addressed Joheved, "Speaking of wine, the reason we were delayed is that we were visiting the Abbey of Montier-la-Celle. They have an excellent vineyard; even your father was impressed. The monk in charge has a green thumb when it comes to raising grapes, but admits he has no such talent for winemaking." Isaac paused dramatically. "Montier-la-Celle's abbot has agreed to trade us his grapes to make into kosher wine, in exchange for an equal amount of regular wine, which I can easily obtain for him."

Nissim saw his opportunity. "I will take payment for this wine-colored cloth with a cask of your kosher wine, payable at the Troyes Cold Fair." He would even buy additional casks at that price, higher than anyone had paid for Leah's recent vintages.

Hiyya quickly offered to pay 5 percent more for Salomon's wine. To ensure that Jewish scholars had adequate time to study, the community was obligated to see that every avenue of profit was made available to them. This was definitely the time to buy, before the other merchants who studied with Salomon became aware of his profession.

"Gentlemen, please restrain yourselves." Salomon gulped in alarm. "The grapes are still on the vine. I cannot guarantee that I will be able to produce any wine at all this year, let alone wine of the quality your offer requires."

Hiyya ibn Ezra held up his hand to stop Salomon's objections. "I am a merchant who is used to taking risks. The ship carrying my spices may sink in a storm. My caravan may be robbed, my agents captured and held for ransom. If I am willing to expose myself to these dangers and many more, do you think I worry about the possibility that your vineyard will fail, with only a few short weeks left until harvest?"

six

Troyes and Ramerupt, France
Fall 4829 (1069 C.E.)

From that day on, Joheved and Miriam tried to do as many of Mama's chores as possible so she could devote her attention to making the family's new Shabbat bliauts. The days were long, and between doing extra chores, working in the vineyard and not studying Talmud, Joheved was so frustrated and exhausted that she didn't know whether to scream or cry. One night, after a difficult day when Mama had to redo nearly all of her embroidery, she couldn't wait for bedtime.

Making an effort to distribute the blanket evenly, Rivka tucked her daughters in and kissed them goodnight. She had no sooner gotten into her own bed, than the evening's quiet was broken by Joheved and Miriam quarrelling.

"Ouch! You kicked me. When was the last time you trimmed your toenails?"

"Never mind my toenails. If you stayed on your side of the bed, you wouldn't get kicked."

"How can I stay on my side of the bed when you always grab all the covers?"

"That's not true; you're the one who hogs them all."

"No, I don't. You do."

As her daughters' disagreement degenerated into a litany of alternating accusations, Rivka sighed and pondered whether her intervention was necessary. She was so tired; taking care of Rachel and Leah, plus feeding all these guests and making her family's new clothes kept her busy from dawn to dark, even with Marie to help. Joheved and Miriam tried to be useful, but they were more valuable in the vineyard than at home.

There was a sudden holler from Leah's bedroom. "You two girls keep quiet out there. I'm trying to sleep!" Silence resumed, and Salomon found his household asleep when he returned.

Soon the days grew shorter and the Troyes Hot Fair was but a memory. Salomon's family was busy with the grape harvest, but not his family alone. Most of the Troyes Jewish community was stomping on grapes, working the wine press, siphoning wine from one container to another or sealing the casks—all jobs that had to be performed by Jews. Everyone worked furiously to transform the ripe grapes into kosher wine.

Once that task was done, they could turn their attention to the spiritual arena. The holiest days of the year, Yom Kippur and Rosh Hashanah, were almost upon them. The wine would ferment in its casks until winter, when the final result of the year's labor would be known. Every so often, Grandmama Leah adjusted the cellar's temperature by opening or closing its windows a bit, thus controlling the fermentation rate in the casks. No matter how Joheved questioned her, Leah could not explain exactly how she knew; she just announced that it was too warm or too cold.

But Joheved did get Grandmama Leah to explain why she had never remarried. "The purpose of marriage is to have children. I was already past bearing when your grandfather died—may his merit protect us—and I wasn't going to bring up somebody else's brats," Leah declared, wrinkling her nose in distaste.

"Weren't you lonely, Grandmama, living all by yourself?"

Leah shook her head. "Of course not. I was teaching your mother to run a household, there was you and Miriam to raise, and I expected plenty more grandchildren to follow . . ." Leah's voice trailed off as she scowled in the direction of Sarah's house.

"What about before Papa got married, when he was away studying all the time? Were you lonely then?"

"I was too busy to be lonely, what with running the vineyard and selling the wine all by myself," Grandmama Leah replied. "There were always merchants here during the fairs, not to mention all the other folks who stopped in to buy wine." She stared up at the ceiling, as if trying to remember.

"You used to run a tavern? In our house?" Joheved tried to assimilate this new view of her pious grandmother.

There was a momentary silence before Grandmama Leah exploded. "What liar told you that I used to run a tavern? I'm a vintner, and there's a big difference between selling the wine I make myself and running a tavern. Next they'll be saying I ran a brothel," she muttered. Leah wiped her hands on her skirt and Joheved knew the subject was closed.

A few days before Rosh Hashanah, Johanna stayed a while after dropping her sons off for their studies. She had a package with her, a gift for the girls. Joheved and Miriam gathered around the dining table while Johanna unwrapped the most beautiful silk bliaut they had ever seen. It was such a vibrant blue that Joheved knew the color had to come from the rare dye indigo. The embroidery around the neckline and sleeves, a pattern of leafless trees done in silver thread, shimmered in the light. How could such a present be for them? This was clothing for a princess.

"Johanna, thank you, but shouldn't this stay in your family?" Mama asked.

"My father-in-law gave it to me when I became betrothed to Joseph." Johanna smiled softly as she smoothed out the blue silk. "I was Joheved's size then, and, as you can see, it's been a long time since I've been able to wear it. I want to give your girls a Rosh Hashanah present, to bring them a good new year."

Joheved and Miriam stared at Johanna, amazed that she had once been small enough to fit into the beautiful bliaut.

Johanna laughed at their consternation and patted her broad belly. "You can see how much marriage has agreed with me." Then she became serious. "The twins' birth was so difficult that Sarah doubted I'd have any more children." She sighed. "So I thought I'd let Joheved wear it, and then Miriam after her."

"Very well, but we will have to return it if my husband doesn't approve." Rivka reached out to caress the bliaut's softness. When Joheved wore this dress, she would also have to wear a red ribbon, to protect her from the Evil Eye.

On the afternoon before Rosh Hashanah, Joheved found herself dressed in blue silk with a red ribbon tied under each sleeve. It was important to start the year wearing one's best clothes and having eaten a lavish meal since "He who has spent less is given less, and he who has spent more is given more." She could smell the traditional New Year's stew of squash, beets and leeks cooking on the hearth. She wasn't fond of the dish, but because those vegetables grew rapidly, Jews ate them this time of year with hopes that their possessions would also multiply quickly.

This was the Day of Judgment, when the Almighty opened the Book of Life and decided whose names would be inscribed there for the coming year and whose would not. Joheved tried to meditate on her behavior of the previous year, to remember the good deeds and resolve to add to them, to regret the evil deeds and repent of them. For the whole month of Elul, she had not quarreled with Miriam over the bedclothes or whose turn it was to wash first.

For the most part, Joheved was excited and proud of her magnificent new holiday bliaut, but sometimes she felt fraudulent, at best like a little girl dressing up in her mother's clothing, and at worst like the small round pieces of mud mixed into black peppercorns by dishonest merchants. But heaven forbid she should give Satan, the Accuser, an opening, so she tried to concentrate instead on how nice her family looked in their new outfits.

At first Mama insisted on tying the red ribbon around her neck, as protection from such envy, but Joheved had protested so vigorously against such a conspicuous splash of red that Mama finally agreed to let her wear the ribbons more discreetly. Miriam had no such worries. She was thrilled with her own soft wine-colored wool bliaut, expertly embroidered by Rivka with a pattern of vines and grapes, and she thought her sister looked positively royal.

"Joheved, the other girls will be fit to be tied when they see you all dressed up in indigo silk." She grinned as she sewed up the sleeves on her sister's chemise. "They don't dare be envious or covetous on Rosh Hashanah."

"Well, at least we won't be envious or covetous this year," Joheved said seriously. With all their new clothes, she didn't feel quite so ashamed at services anymore.

Miriam was enjoying her musings too much to be serious. "Everyone will have to think generous thoughts, to compliment you on your new outfit and wish you a good year. And if they don't, well, that's why you're wearing red ribbons." She laughed out loud at Joheved's appalled expression.

If anyone was jealous of Salomon's family's sudden splendor, they hid it well. But Salomon was not the only one whose business had done well this year. The entire congregation seemed to be dressed in colorful new wear.

"May you be inscribed and sealed for a good year," they complimented each other. Cheerfulness and good will abounded, to assure the Holy Judge that they were worthy of another year of goodness and blessing.

In fact, the year had been so bountiful that the congregation didn't know what to do about *kapparah.* As long as anyone could remember, Jewish families slaughtered fowl on the eve of Yom Kippur, a cock for a man and a hen for a woman. Each person passed their bird three times overhead while reciting the following declaration: "This fowl is my substitute, this is my surrogate, this is my atonement. May it be designated for death, and I for life." The ritual was completed by presenting the bird to the poor, in accordance with the words from Proverbs, "Charity delivers from death."

As much as she enjoyed eating chicken, Joheved resented getting the rich man's sins along with his bird. Salomon may have felt the same, for when the community found itself with too few poor Jews willing to take its many fowl, he instituted an alternative procedure. This year, after the chickens made the usual progress around their proxies' heads, a family would give their monetary value to charity and then eat them themselves.

Yom Kippur dawned quietly in Salomon's courtyard. Much to Joheved's relief, she and Miriam had to prompt Grandmama Leah only occasionally during the lengthy services for Rosh Hashanah and Yom Kippur. But the best thing about the new year was that, with the harvest finished, Papa had time to study Talmud with them every day.

Several miles north of Troyes, at his family's manor in Ramerupt, the new year had not gotten off to a good start for Meir ben Samuel. His first year in Mayence, he had missed his family terribly, especially his sister, Hannah. The second year wasn't so bad. No longer overwhelmed by the change from child's schoolroom to scholars' yeshiva, he'd begun to enjoy his studies.

This year everything changed. He supposed that things had first become different in June, when he returned to celebrate the festival of Shavuot and his sister's wedding. For years after the marriage of their older brother, Meshullam, Meir and Hannah were the only children at home. Every evening in bed, they shared their day's activities with each other, and on Shabbat, they took long walks in the fields around the manor.

He hadn't had time to be lonely during that previous visit, not with the house crowded with wedding guests. His visit was a whirlwind, and returning to his studies in Mayence was a relief. Meir knew he and Hannah wouldn't have the same relationship after her marriage, but he never imagined how different things would be. Of course, she would sleep in another room with her new husband, Simcha, but he didn't expect to be so bereft when he found himself alone at night.

Meir briefly considered asking his parents to let one of the servants share his room, but he already had enough of Marona, his mother, treating him like a little boy. So he nervously lay in bed the first few nights, noticing for the first time the myriad of sounds that disturbed the evening's silence. Sometimes he could hear Hannah and her new husband whispering in the next room, and he missed her.

The day after Rosh Hashanah, Hannah got up from the dinner table, exchanged an intimate look with Simcha, and announced that she was going for a little walk. When Meir jumped up and offered to join her, she blushed and said it wasn't necessary, that her husband would accompany her. But this was Meir's first chance to be alone with his sister since her wedding, and he would not be dissuaded. Simcha gallantly relinquished his position; the siblings set off on a path along the Aube River, and it was almost like old times.

Hannah gushed on about how happy she was, how kind and gentle her husband was, how she couldn't wait until they were blessed with children. That's why she was going to the river tonight, to immerse there. Jewish communities large enough to build a synagogue always constructed a *mikvah,* the ritual bath, underneath it, but rural Jewish women had to use a local stream.

Jewish men are forbidden to have marital relations with their wives during their menstrual period and for seven clean days afterwards. When that time, during which she is considered *niddah,* has elapsed, the woman immerses herself in the mikvah and is again permitted to her husband. Some say that a Jewish man never grows tired of his wife, because he is not allowed to lie with her whenever he likes.

Meir stood guard while his sister dunked herself in a small pond created where the river turned a bend. Once they returned, Hannah and her husband could scarcely restrain their eagerness to excuse themselves and go to bed. Samuel and Marona smiled benevolently as the newlyweds hurriedly bid everyone goodnight, then Samuel suggested that he and Meir study a bit of Talmud before bedtime. There was a small section of Tractate Berachot he had a question about, and he was curious how his son's teachers had explained it.

Meir had memorized nearly all of Berachot and knew his father would derive immodest pleasure from his erudition. So he obligingly asked what part Samuel had in mind.

"I believe it's in the last chapter, something about several groups of three items each, how they affect a man," Samuel said slowly, scratching his head.

"Oui, Papa. I remember something like that," Meir answered with pride. "Is this it?"

> Three things enter the body, but the body does not enjoy them—cherries, poor dates and unripe dates. Three things do not enter the body, but the body does enjoy them—washing, anointing, and using the bed.

Meir tried to say, "using the bed," a Talmudic euphemism for sexual relations, in the same tone of voice he used for "washing."

"That's the text, all right." Samuel beamed with satisfaction. His son had not failed him. "Please continue."

> Three things resemble the World to Come: the Sabbath, sunshine and usage. Using what?! If you say using the bed, surely not because it weakens the body. Rather it means using one's orifices for defecation.

Samuel waved at Meir to finish the passage.

> Three things restore a man's heart: sound, sight and smell. Three things lift a man's spirit: a beautiful house, a beautiful wife, and beautiful furnishings.

"I've always had misgivings about that section," Samuel said, frowning. "Considering that entire passage enumerates pleasurable activities, I don't see how the 'usage' that resembles the World to Come can mean '*faire caca.*'" He looked hopefully at Meir. "Did your teachers ever mention this inconsistency?"

"I'm sorry, Papa, but we didn't discuss this text in depth." Meir felt ashamed that he couldn't satisfy his father's query. "It seemed straightforward at the time, but I can understand your difficulty now. It does seem incongruous for a line about *caca* to be followed by one about how sight, sound and smell restores a man's heart."

"My point exactly." Samuel paused and put his arm around Meir's shoulder. "*Mon fils,* please don't feel discouraged if Hannah prefers Simcha's company to yours these days. The joys of marriage are new and wonderful for her."

"Well, who wouldn't prefer a semblance of the World to Come to ordinary conversation?" Meir said. He suddenly understood that his father had delayed him to give the newlyweds some privacy. Just then Marona came into view and Meir saw his opportunity for escape. "Is it all right if I go upstairs now? I'd like to use my own bed to get some sleep."

Samuel joined his wife, and the two of them walked upstairs together with an intimacy that disconcerted Meir. He appreciated that his father thought him mature enough to discuss adult subjects, but the notion that his parents actually used the bed discomforted him greatly, and he was relieved to seek solace in his own room. He took off his clothes and hung them on the hooks near his bed. Naked, he slipped between the sheets and recited the evening Shema.

But as soon as he finished his prayers, he heard them, and if Meir found his sister whispering with her husband disturbing, that night he discovered what was worse. At first he tried to ignore their bed's creaky noises, then he covered his head with the pillow. Nothing helped. Meir alternated between fascination and acute embarrassment as their moaning grew louder, and at one point his sister's cries became so intense that Meir had to restrain himself from jumping out of bed to rescue her from her tormenter.

Then, all was quiet. Dreading that they would start up again, it was a long time before he could fall asleep. In the morning, he discovered that a visit from Lillit, the night demon, had caused him to have a nocturnal emission.

And so it continued, with only a break on Yom Kippur when eating, drinking and marital relations are forbidden. During the day, Meir studied Talmud and took long walks through the hills, where views of white sheep dotting the green pasture had always soothed him. He rode his horse far into the forest, to tire himself as much as possible. He considered riding into Troyes to visit the scholar, Salomon, who lived there, but felt awkward about showing up uninvited. Meir even stayed up late talking with his parents, trying to delay his own bedtime until Hannah and her husband finally finished using the bed.

Yet he rarely had an undisturbed night. People said that sleeping alone was dangerous because of demons, and now he knew why. In Mayence, when the other students teased each other about Lillit's visits, how she stole young men's semen at night to produce her demon children, Meir tried to avoid their vulgar conversation. Lillit's visits were exciting, but he felt defiled afterwards, and tried to get to morning services early so he'd have time to immerse himself in the mikvah first.

When his father suggested that they spend a few days in Troyes together before he returned to the yeshiva, Meir jumped at the idea of leaving Ramerupt early.

The night before their departure, Meir was still packing when his parents joined him. This was a normal part of his leave-taking ritual, although his parents usually spoke to him individually. Samuel would say how proud he was of his scholarly son, encourage him in his studies, warn him to be careful on the road, and give him money for expenses. Marona echoed her husband's pride, hugged Meir and told him how much she was going to miss him. And in addition to slipping him money, she also provided some treats to eat on the way.

This time his parents stood together in his room. Samuel shifted from one foot to the other, apparently reluctant to begin the conversation, and Marona looked back and forth from husband to son, nervously waiting to see who was going to speak first. Meir was trying to think of something to say that didn't mention their odd behavior when Samuel broke the silence.

"Meir, you're our youngest son, and we're very proud of how well you're doing at the yeshiva." Samuel cleared his throat before continuing. "It has always been our dream that one of our sons should become a scholar. The Holy One has blessed us and given us sufficient affluence that you may remain in Mayence to study as long as you like."

So far this sounded like the speech Samuel always gave. What was going on? Then his father surprised him with a question about Salomon of Troyes.

"You mentioned wanting to visit a friend of yours in Troyes, a chacham you studied with at the yeshiva. Tell us about him."

"Well, Salomon ben Isaac was one of the finest scholars I've ever known, and we used to travel together to and from Mayence." Meir spoke carefully, unsure what his father wanted to know. "He was very kind and would help me when I had trouble understanding something, even though he was older and I was just a beginner. He could explain the most complicated passages."

His parents seemed pleased with that, and Meir grew more voluble. "It was a terrible loss when he had to leave the yeshiva two years ago to support his family. I think his mother was ill. He had a wife and some children back in Troyes, who depended on him." Meir walked over and embraced his parents. "I'm glad that we're not poor. I mean I appreciate that I can study for as long as I want without it being a hardship for you."

Silence descended on the room again. Samuel cleared his throat a few more times, but Marona spoke first. "Now that Hannah is married and settled, we only have you to worry about. With you being such a good student, we think it would be splendid if we had grandsons who were scholars too." She smiled and waited for this to sink in. "So the best thing would be for you to marry a chacham's daughter."

As the implication of his parents' words dawned on Meir, a blush crept up his face. How wonderful if his parents could arrange a match between him and one of Salomon's daughters. But did Salomon have any daughters? Had he ever met them?

Samuel seemed to find Meir's reaction amusing. "I must say that I'm impressed with your devotion to your old colleague. Your mother and I have been doing some quiet investigating, and we've heard from both my cousin and the parchment maker of Troyes that your Salomon has two daughters, neither of whom is betrothed yet." He grinned fondly at his youngest son, now quite red in the face. "What do you think?"

Meir didn't know what to say. Things were happening so fast. Did his parents know how Hannah's marriage had affected him? He remembered what Rav Hisda said in the Talmud tractate Kiddushin, the Hebrew word for marriage:

> The reason I am superior to my colleagues is that I married at sixteen and my mind is entirely free for study. Had I married at fourteen, I would have said to Satan, "An arrow in your eye."

If he were married, he'd be safe from sinful thoughts too.

His parents were waiting for an answer. "I would, of course, marry whomever you thought was best for me," he stammered. Then he realized that his parents probably wanted a more positive reaction. "I mean that I would very much like to marry one of Salomon's daughters, and I would appreciate it if you could make the arrangements."

"We can meet Salomon and his daughters while we're in Troyes," Samuel said. "If all goes well and you find one of them attractive, then we can open negotiations. If possible, I'd like to have the betrothal arranged before you return to Mayence."

"But I do think Meir must consider the older daughter as his potential bride," Marona added. "Salomon is unlikely to consider a match for a younger girl if the elder is still available."

Meir's heart began to beat faster. Once he joined Salomon's family, he would never lack a study partner, he would live in a home imbued with Torah, and he would be close to his family in Ramerupt. He had visions of his parents enjoying his and Hannah's children playing together. "I'm sure the older daughter will be best; then we can get married sooner."

"Well, since we're all in agreement, we'd better get to bed." Samuel affectionately tousled his son's hair. "We'll need to have an early start tomorrow morning if we expect to arrive in Troyes before morning services are over."

seven

Troyes
Fall 4830 (1070 C.E.)

The next morning Meir could scarcely hide his impatience as his parents consulted with the steward about what supplies the manor needed. Convinced they'd be late, he was greatly relieved when they entered the synagogue just as the Torah reading began.

Upstairs in the women's section, Joheved didn't take any special notice of the unfamiliar latecomer. She was completely engaged in preparing to translate the Hebrew scriptures into French for the women's benefit. Leah had managed Rosh Hashanah without trouble, but the lengthy Yom Kippur service, done while fasting, had been too much for her, and she had asked her surprised granddaughter to translate the afternoon Torah portion in her stead. Since then, Leah had left the daily Torah translations for Joheved, much to the girl's consternation.

Johanna noticed the tall, slender newcomer immediately. This stranger had not been in Troyes for the holidays; Johanna would have remembered the aristocratic brunette. Her demeanor was happy, so she was not here for a funeral or illness, but nobody in town was celebrating a wedding or birth in the near future either.

Johanna moved closer, determined to engage the woman in conversation. "Shalom aleichem, my good mistress; welcome to Troyes. What brings you to our fair city?"

"Johanna, peace be to you as well," the woman sitting next to the stranger answered for her. "Allow me to introduce Marona, the wife of my cousin Samuel. They have an estate near Ramerupt, and are in town to attend to some personal business."

Marona's clothes were of excellent quality, a bit too fine for a weekday, and the longer she watched them, the more peculiar Johanna found the women's behavior. Their conversation seemed skittish, almost clandestine.

"In case your cousin has neglected to inform you," Johanna addressed Marona sternly, "I must remind you that all business conducted in Troyes requires a local agent."

Marona turned red, but her cousin giggled and quickly whispered, "They're not here to transact financial business, Johanna. They're here to negotiate a betrothal. Samuel and their son are downstairs right now."

"Will you be quiet!" Marona hushed her cousin through clenched teeth. "We haven't even approached the girl's family yet, and you're making announcements to total strangers."

Pleased at having discovered the newcomer's intentions, Johanna retreated. Was it her imagination or were they watching Joheved? When Joheved began translating the Torah portion, the women's interest and approval was so manifest that Johanna was convinced she had seen enough. She had to get to Rivka's house, to give her time to prepare for these potentially very important guests. But first she had to speak with Joseph.

Downstairs, Meir wanted to greet Salomon immediately, but Samuel insisted that they not interrupt the Talmud session. Meir couldn't see where Salomon was sitting; the men in front were too tall. An old man at the head of the table began reading from Tractate Bava Metzia, an advanced portion that Meir had never studied. The subject was what transactions constituted charging interest, which is forbidden by Jewish Law. The text described several situations in detail, each more complicated than the last. Meir tried to remember them all, but he was getting confused.

The old man continued reading:

> Rav Nachman said: *Tarsha* is permitted, but Rami bar Hama objected: It is forbidden.

Meir had no idea what "tarsha" was or why Rav Nachman found it acceptable. A few of the men offered suggestions as to what the different Sages meant, but nobody sounded confident in his interpretation. Meir looked anxiously around the room. Where was Salomon? Why wasn't he saying anything? Meir could see his father staring at the ceiling, drumming his fingers on the bench. He had to be disappointed. Maybe their trip to Troyes had been a mistake. Samuel shifted in his seat and Meir's throat tightened as he waited for his father to motion him to get up and leave.

But then someone else began to speak. Meir still couldn't see, but Samuel got a glimpse of a nondescript young man with brown hair and beard, not much older than his older son. The fellow modestly suggested that what he had learned from his teachers might help in understanding this complicated discussion.

"The word 'tarsha' means 'silent' in Aramaic, and refers to a transaction in which the interest is not specifically stated," he began. "Rav Nachman holds that when the surcharge is not explicit, even if both parties understand that it represents an extra payment for credit, we ought to treat it leniently and not cause undue hardship for commerce."

Meir thought the voice might be Salomon's, but he wasn't sure. At least his father had stopped fidgeting. Several men asked questions and all agreed that Jewish Law should not cause them hardship in their business transactions.

The young man waited until the room was quiet before starting the next case.

> Rav Pappa said: My *tarsha* is permitted. Why?—My beer does not spoil, and I am doing a favor for the buyer.

He paused for a moment to let them consider this. "Rav Pappa rejects Rav Nachman's unlimited tarsha, but justifies his own. Because the price of beer was seasonal, low in autumn and high in spring, Rav Pappa would let his buyers take autumn beer immediately and pay for it in spring, provided that they paid the higher spring price. Beer stored easily, so he considered it a favor to sell it in autumn. Of course he saw no reason why he should charge less at that time than he could get later."

This answer seemed to satisfy the group, so he continued.

> Rav Sheshet said to him: If they had the money, they would take it now, but they do not have money so they take it at a higher future price.

"We see that Rav Sheshet objects and says that Rav Pappa's tarsha *is* interest, because, if the buyers had enough money to pay for beer in autumn, they would buy it from somebody else at that season's low price."

The young man waited for questions, but everyone seemed to have understood the case. Meir wanted to stand up and see who was talking, but his father had made it clear that they were to be observers only. It had to be Salomon; it had to be.

> Rav Hama said: My *tarsha* is clearly permitted. What is the reason?—They are pleased that it stays in my possession.

"Now Rav Hama would buy merchandise where it was cheap and sell it in another place where it was expensive. Sometimes he had traders transport the stuff and sell it for him, and when these men returned, they paid Rav Hama the high price at which they had sold it. Thus it appeared as if Rav Hama was charging the men, not the low price that he paid originally, but a higher price for delayed payment, which is prohibited."

"But why would anyone agree to this arrangement?" someone with a nasal twang challenged him. "It doesn't make sense."

The young man wasn't offended. "It makes sense because after selling Rav Hama's goods, the traders used the money to buy things selling cheaply at the new location, which they then brought back to sell for their own profit," he explained.

A deep-voiced man wanted to make sure he understood. "So Rav Hama made his profit from the original goods, while the traders made their profit when they returned?"

"Exactly. Only after they sold his merchandise did the money become a loan from Rav Hama, which they later repaid without any interest," the knowledgeable young man said.

Meir could see looks of comprehension in the men's faces, and several of them sighed in appreciation. Buying things that were cheap in one location and selling them for a profit somewhere else was how most Jews earned their living. Only Samuel didn't look pleased, and Meir's throat began to tighten again.

The old man at the table's head smiled proudly. "Rav Salomon," he addressed the young man, "I'm sorry that you are unable to continue your studies in Mayence, but I am grateful that you are here to study with us in Troyes."

"Rav Zera, your kind words flatter me." The young man, now identified as Rav Salomon, was gracious in his reply. "I also appreciate the opportunity to share what I have learned."

Meir was grinning from ear to ear. He elbowed his father and whispered, "See, I told you Salomon was a talmid chacham."

Samuel stared at the young scholar in shock. All this time, he had been under the mistaken impression that the old man, now identified as Zera, was Salomon. And to think that he had almost walked out. "I agree," he said, nodding vigorously, "and I think it's time to meet him."

Father and son made their way to where the scholar stood, speaking earnestly with those who remained. When Salomon saw Meir, his eyes opened wide and he hurried to embrace the boy. Meir was the first student he'd seen from Mayence since he'd left, and the ache of nostalgia surprised him. He tried to refocus on Meir. How the boy had grown; he was as tall as Salomon now.

Meir saw the tears in Salomon's eyes and almost started crying himself. He quickly turned away to introduce his father, and Salomon's expression became pensive. So here was Meir, and here also was his sheep-raising father, who was looking at Salomon the way he might appraise a ram at the livestock fair.

Salomon stroked his beard as he considered the situation. Joheved could certainly do worse than this young fellow. He had no trouble persuading them to return home with him, and was convinced that his suspicions were correct when Meir introduced his mother, patiently waiting outside.

Sure enough, Samuel enthusiastically linked arms with him and announced, "Let's take the long route there. I have something important to discuss with you on the way."

The calm that Salomon projected was in direct contrast to the whirlwind of activity at his house. Rivka had just finished changing Rachel's swaddling when Johanna rushed in, two servants weighted down with food in her wake. One servant produced several fat capons and had them roasting on the spit in Rivka's hearth before she could say anything. The other proceeded to furiously chop up a variety of vegetables.

Johanna burst into speech. "Rivka, we have to hurry. An out-of-town family is here today, and I'm almost certain that they intend to open negotiations for Joheved's hand. If I'm right, they will be here for disner, and we mustn't disappoint them."

"What?" Rivka gasped. "Who are these people . . . and how do you know they're here about Joheved?" She tried to resist being caught up in her friend's sense of urgency, but it was hopeless. "How much time do we have before they get here?"

Johanna told her what had transpired in synagogue. "Look, I asked Joseph to investigate further. If he tells us it's a false alarm," and her tone of voice made it clear that this was unlikely, "then we'll just have a nice quiet meal here with our two families. By the way, the boy's parents are Samuel and Marona of Ramerupt. Do you have any idea who they are?"

"None at all. Nobody has approached us." Rivka was too shocked to think about such possibilities. (Salomon had never mentioned the parchment maker's gossip to his wife, certain that she would only nag him more about planning for the girls' future.)

Rivka went to the cupboard and began to take down her best linens, while Johanna got the wine cups and dishes. As they set the table, she said to Rivka, "Samuel has a cousin here in Troyes, who happened to mention that he has an estate nearby. And I must say that Marona's clothes were fine indeed." Johanna smiled conspiratorially. "I have a feeling that your daughter may do very well for herself with this match."

"To see Joheved married into a wealthy family would be wonderful, of course, but I know my husband wants a learned son-in-law." Rivka shook her head. Only an ignorant rich man would want to marry a poor chacham's daughter. A wealthy scholar would have his choice of brides.

After Rivka dropped a wooden bowl and knocked over two wine goblets, Johanna decided that talking about something else might calm her friend's anxiety. "Speaking of betrothals, I've heard that Count Thibault is planning to marry Adelaide de Bar. That will give him more land to the south as a buffer against the Duke of Burgundy."

"Perhaps the new countess will want to live here near her own holdings rather than in Blois," Rivka said. Somehow it was easier to discuss the count's marital prospects than her own daughter's.

"I think Thibault plans to leave his lands in Blois to his oldest son, Etienne-Henry." Johanna nodded knowingly. "If I had a son by my first wife, I'd want him far away from my second wife, particularly if she was a lot younger than me."

Rivka walked over to the hearth and stirred several pots cooking in it. "Count Thibault is over fifty now. I wonder if he'll get any children from Adelaide."

"I don't see why not. I believe that she's still less than thirty years old."

"It will be exciting to have a big royal wedding in Troyes," Rivka said, pausing to taste a spoonful of liquid from one of the pots. "It's a good thing we had a big grape harvest this year."

Johanna didn't share Rivka's enthusiasm. "It's also a good thing the Hot Fair was so lucrative, since Thibault will certainly levy extra taxes on us Jews to pay his wedding expenses."

At that moment, the door opened and in came Grandmama Leah, followed by her granddaughters.

"Oh, what smells so good?" Joheved asked.

"Look, we're having capon, and Johanna's here too," Miriam pointed out. "What's the party for?"

Rivka's panic returned and she didn't know what to say, but Johanna was eager to explain the situation. "Joheved, I don't have time to tell you everything now, but I believe some people will be here soon to discuss a betrothal between you and their son. So please go change into your blue silk bliaut."

Joheved was too stunned to speak, but Johanna continued giving instructions. "Miriam, why don't you help your sister get dressed? And you can wear your new bliaut too. Hurry up, now."

The two girls raced upstairs. Miriam insisted that Joheved take time to rebraid her hair. They said little besides the occasional "Mon Dieu," and "I wonder who it could be." Miriam didn't have the heart to tease her sister. She'd never seen Joheved's face this white, and the poor girl's hands were shaking so badly that Miriam had to do her hair for her. If Johanna said people were coming to arrange Joheved's betrothal, then it must be so. But why hadn't Papa or Mama told them about it earlier?

They came downstairs to find that Isaac and Joseph had arrived with some delicacies for dessert. Joheved, her dread mounting, listened as the men confirmed that they had seen Salomon leave the synagogue with a well-dressed couple and a youth whose likeness proved him to be their son.

Joheved wanted to ask questions, but her mouth was too dry. It didn't help that the last thing Miriam said before they joined the company was, "Remember, they can't make you marry this fellow if you don't want to. You have to agree or there's no betrothal." Then Miriam disappeared outside to keep a lookout.

Rivka sensed her daughter's fear and tried to reassure her. "Don't worry, Joheved, you look lovely." She then added, as much to herself as to her daughter, "I'm sure everything will be fine," and gave Joheved a lengthy hug.

"Joheved will make an excellent impression," Isaac haParnas said loudly. Then he turned and whispered to Johanna, "It's a good thing you got us invited, too. Salomon is a scholar with his head in his books, and now I can make sure any negotiations are done under my auspices."

Suddenly Miriam popped back into the room. "They're coming, they're coming," she squealed. "Papa, a grey-bearded man and a tall woman, and their son."

The company arranged themselves around the *salle* as though nothing extraordinary was happening. So when Salomon arrived home with his guests, he was surprised, but not too surprised, to find Joheved and Miriam in their best clothes, a sumptuous meal prepared, and Isaac haParnas's family visiting.

As guests were introduced, Joheved's heart was pounding so hard she was sure that everyone in the room could hear it. The boy's name was Meir, and he had apparently attended yeshiva in Mayence with Papa. Conversation avoided the subject of what these people were doing in Troyes, besides sending their son back to his studies. Salomon had Meir telling him all the latest news from the yeshiva, while Isaac questioned Samuel about his livelihood. Miriam couldn't resist poking her sister when Samuel replied that he had an estate in Ramerupt that produced wheat and sheep.

At the women's end of the table, Marona tried, with Johanna's help, to draw Joheved into conversation, but Leah dominated their discussion. Joheved didn't mind; her emotions were too jumbled for her to say anything worthwhile. Rivka, relieved beyond belief upon hearing that Meir had actually studied with her husband, hoped desperately that Leah wouldn't make up some improbable tale because she could no longer remember what had really happened.

The two young people, on whose account these strangers found themselves eating together, said nothing to each other. They knew better than to stare, but couldn't resist frequent glances in the other's direction. Joheved didn't find Meir especially handsome; he was too skinny and his skin was bad. But he wasn't ugly. His hair was nice, a warm shade of brown that was flattered by his deep gold bliaut and sunny yellow chemise, identical to his father's. He had a pleasant, low-pitched voice, and when she caught him looking at her, he grinned and revealed a fine set of white teeth. She was glad he was taller than her.

And he was a yeshiva student. She could study as much Talmud as she wanted now that Papa had found her a learned husband. Then her heart sank. If she married him, they would spend who knows how many years apart. Meir's father could probably afford to keep him studying in Mayence a long time. She tried to conquer her despair. Maybe his father would pay for both of them to live in Mayence, but then she'd never see her family.

All the grown-ups around the table seemed to be staring at her, and Joheved knew she was trapped. She didn't dare refuse the match, not with all the adults in agreement, not after Papa had made good on his promise to find a scholar for her to marry. Yet she didn't really want to refuse—for some reason this youth appealed to her. Enough! She must stop thinking about potential problems, problems that were out of her control, and start the new year with an optimistic frame of mind.

The first thing Meir noticed about Joheved was that her eyes were exactly the same shade of blue as her bliaut. But she was so young, still only a child. He glanced at her chest and quickly looked away; she hadn't even grown breasts yet. An early marriage was out of the question, and he tried to hide his disappointment. The girl wasn't bad looking—not that it mattered what she looked like, as long as she wasn't ugly. The important thing was she was Rav Salomon's daughter. Their sons would be great scholars.

Gradually the meal came to a close. Grandmama Leah was having trouble sitting still, and Rivka suggested that the girls take her for a walk. To everyone's surprise, including his own, Meir jumped up and offered to accompany them.

But before they could leave, Salomon stood up and addressed his daughter. "Joheved, you know why all these people are here?" he asked gently. When she nodded, he continued, "I will not betroth you without your consent; you must see your bridegroom and accept him."

Salomon glanced back at Joheved, whose gaze was fixed on the plate in front on her. "So here he is, standing in front of you. Do you want Meir ben Samuel for your husband? Shall I work out an agreement with his father?"

Even though she knew what her answer would be, what her answer had to be, Joheved made a point of looking at Meir from head to foot before speaking. Then she took a deep breath and tried to keep her voice from shaking. "Oui, Papa, I will have him. I give my consent." At least her future husband did not shy away, but returned her stare with an equally searching look.

Meir knew that he would be asked for his approval next. He had studied the part in Tractate Kiddushin about betrothals where

> Rav Judah said: A man may not marry a woman until he has first seen her, and Rav Eleazar said: A man may not give his daughter in marriage until she is old enough to say "I want so-and-so."

Meir didn't wait for the question, but said with what he hoped sounded like confidence, "I have seen your daughter and I agree to take her as my bride."

Salomon felt uncomfortable with magical incantations based on scripture, but he had been to enough betrothals to know that it was expected. He stroked his beard and considered what mystic blessing he would invoke for the couple. Then he put his hands on Meir's and Joheved's shoulders, closed his eyes, and began chanting in Aramaic:

> How sweet is your love, my own, my bride. When the wind blows softly and the shadows flee, I will betake me to the mount of myrrh. You have captured my heart, my own, my bride. Drink deep of my love. How much more delightful is your love than wine. Every part of you is fair, my darling, and there is no blemish in you.

Although they had no idea what words Salomon had spoken, Rivka, Marona, and even Johanna had tears in their eyes.

Isaac stood up, raised his wine goblet, and offered his congratulations, "So may joy be with you in the future."

Leah alone seemed unaffected. "We can celebrate when the agreements are signed. And with my granddaughter's *yichus,* you shouldn't need a large dowry. My brother was the talmid chacham, Simon ben Isaac haZaken—may his merit protect us—and Rivka's brother, Isaac ben Judah of Mayence, is also a great scholar."

"Papa," Meir whispered urgently. "Isaac ben Judah is one of my teachers in Mayence. Some say he'll be the next Rosh Yeshiva."

Samuel nodded back with a grin. Content to be aligned with Salomon's family based on the chacham's own worth, he now found that Joheved had an even greater lineage. Isaac haParnas was also smiling; this new information would make negotiations easier.

Leah, oblivious to the effect her announcement was having on the company, had sat long enough. "Right now I need to walk. Who's coming with me?"

The four walkers left the others to work out the financial details. They strolled along the Rû Cordé canal, which marked the western edge of both the old city and its Jewish quarter, past the public baths and the castle at the north end of the canal, where it split off from the Seine, then they walked south again towards Thibault's palace. Joheved's moment of boldness had passed, and she left conversation to her grandmother and sister. Miriam proudly informed Meir that they knew how to make parchment, and he admitted his ignorance on the subject.

It was only as they approached Salomon's courtyard that Joheved found the courage to speak. "Meir, you understood what my father said?" It was more a statement than a question, but he nodded and she continued, "It sounded like the fourth chapter of Song of Songs, except the verses were out of order."

"You're right. I've been to several betrothals in Mayence and somebody always makes an Aramaic incantation from that chapter of Song of Songs. But they never say it like it's written." Meir hesitated a moment as his gaze met hers, and he stared into those incredibly blue eyes. "I mean, sometimes they transpose the words or recite a few of the verses three times. Once I heard it chanted backwards."

"Thank you for explaining it to me," Joheved replied as they approached the house, and Meir felt a rush of pride at being able to demonstrate his esoteric knowledge to her.

It took several days, under Isaac's patient supervision, to negotiate the detailed betrothal agreement. Joheved found spinning thread kept her nervous hands occupied, so Marona got plenty of opportunity to observe her competence with spindle and distaff. Samuel, eager for scholarly grandsons, didn't quibble about the small dowry—one third of Salomon's vineyard and some jewelry from Leah. As a token of his esteem for the chacham, Samuel would begin providing any parchment Salomon needed.

The *nisuin* (wedding) would take place as soon as Joheved was old enough. As was customary, Samuel would provide the wedding banquet, excepting the wine, of course, which would be Salomon's pleasure to supply. With everything finally arranged, the congregation was invited to the *erusin* (betrothal) ceremony. Once the *erusin* documents were signed and witnessed, Joheved and Meir were married according to Jewish Law. Only death or divorce could prevent *nisuin,* and the cohabitation that would finalize their marriage.

When Meir finally left Troyes, groggy and hung over from the previous night's raucous betrothal celebration, he could hardly believe how quickly his life had changed. When his fellows in Mayence asked about his holidays, and he acknowledged that he now had a fiancée waiting for him back home, several more nights of revel followed. By the time Meir was back at his studies, those days in Troyes seemed almost like a dream. It wasn't long before he couldn't quite remember what Joheved looked like, except that she had blue eyes. That she was learned enough to recognize Song of Songs recited at random in Aramaic had escaped him completely.

For Joheved, excepting that Rivka made her cover her hair in public now, life went on much as before. She worked on the vintage, studied Talmud and helped Grandmama Leah lead the women's services. She didn't feel betrothed, whatever that ought to feel like—she didn't think she felt different at all. But in quiet moments, especially at night, she remembered that somewhere to the east was Meir ben Samuel, the young scholar who, Le Bon Dieu willing, would one day be the father of her children, and she wondered what he was studying.

eight

Similar to its summer cousin, the Troyes Cold Fair began with cloth and finished with account settling. The winter livestock market was larger, because sellers hoped to avoid maintaining extra animals through the cold weather. Numerous knights looking to buy warhorses also ensured the presence of merchants selling armor and weapons. For Salomon's family, the Cold Fair was when the new vintage would be ready to taste and sell. The Parisian wine dealers would be there in force, needing only to load their barrels onto barges and float them downriver to market.

As during the Hot Fair, Salomon spent his mornings and evenings studying with the merchant scholars. Determined that all his vines would be properly cut back this year, he spent the short afternoons preparing to prune the vineyard. Joheved, Miriam and Grandmama Leah's job was pulling out the vine-props and stacking them between the rows. As much as the girls disliked all the bending involved, they realized that their father had the truly backbreaking work.

Vineyards were planted on hillsides, and men had the task of transporting back up the slope earth that had gradually slipped downhill during the year. After several years of this, a vintner could truthfully claim to have carried his entire vineyard on his back. Thank heaven Isaac haParnas had found several strapping young fellows willing to work for meals and a few coins at the end of the week, reducing Salomon's toil considerably.

One afternoon, Grandmama Leah announced that she was too cold to continue in the vineyard. So Joheved, sure her grandmother would never be able to find her way back alone, volunteered to take her home.

Marie met them at the door with a look of relief. "Joheved, I'm so glad to see you. Mistress Rivka is out shopping, Rachel is napping, and Isaac haParnas just arrived with a strange man to see Master Salomon."

"It's all right Marie; just help Grandmama get upstairs," Joheved said. "I'll see to Isaac haParnas myself."

Isaac introduced the stranger as Hiyya ibn Ezra's agent.

"I hope that Hiyya is well," Joheved said in Hebrew, not sure how well the man spoke French. "And that he arrived home safely."

"Hiyya had an excellent voyage," the stranger replied, also in Hebrew. His gaze darted around the room. "Will your father be home soon?"

"I don't believe Papa was planning to leave the vineyard until sunset. Perhaps you should come back and see him later."

Isaac broke in before his companion could answer. "I don't think that will be necessary, Joheved. It's nearly sunset now, and I'm sure he'll be home directly. In the meantime, you can show us the wine cellar and explain the different vintages."

Joheved lifted up the trap door and showed the two men the stairs going down into the cellar. The high windows brought daylight into the large room, and when Joheved reached the floor, she took a deep breath and sighed. The wine casks stood protectively around her and the wine cellar smelled pleasantly damp and fruity. Isaac was treating her like a knowledgeable adult. Was it because she was betrothed now, or did he still remember how she'd helped him convince Papa to buy new clothes?

"This year we'll have four different kinds of wine." Joheved hesitated when Hiyya's agent stared at her blankly. How could she make the wine process understandable?

"First," she began again, "or maybe I should say first and second, we have wine made with grapes from our vineyard and wine made with the abbey's grapes. That's two kinds."

The men were cautiously looking around the cellar, with Isaac pointing out identifying marks on the various barrels. He urged Joheved to continue.

"Then with the grapes from each vineyard, there's the free-run wine, which gets drawn off before we use the wine-press, and then there's the additional amount the press produces. That's four kinds. The free-run wine is superior, so it costs more, but we won't know exactly how much more until Hanukkah."

The stranger's eyes narrowed in suspicion. "You don't have any idea what you'll charge until the dealers make their offers?"

Isaac put a reassuring arm around the man's shoulder. "During Hanukkah, after the Sabbath has ended, Salomon and Jewish winemakers throughout France will taste their new vintages for the first time. He, and those of us lucky enough to be in his company, will toast the festival with his new wine." Isaac gave the man a knowing wink. "I expect quite a celebration this year."

"And therefore, quite a profit for Hiyya." The merchant edged his way towards the outside door and said, "Could you please excuse me? I need to find the privy."

Isaac directed him to the back of the courtyard, but made no move to follow. "Joheved, you've impressed me once again." He grinned down at her. "A lord's son and a scholar—I think you have a worthy husband in Meir ben Samuel. Don't you agree?"

Joheved tried to control her emotions, but the sudden change of conversation took her by surprise. Everyone else had been so thrilled with her betrothal that she had kept her fears to herself. But Isaac looked at her with such concern that, tears rolling down her cheeks, she unburdened herself to him.

"Please don't think I'm being finicky or ungrateful," she concluded. "But I don't want to live in Troyes while Meir lives in Mayence, and I don't want to live in Mayence if the rest of my family lives in Troyes." It sounded so selfish; when she actually heard the words out loud, she felt ashamed.

But Isaac didn't admonish her. He smiled and said gently, "But one of the clauses in your betrothal agreement stipulates that part of your dowry will be Meir's board at Troyes from the beginning of the Hot Fair through the end of the Cold Fair. I reminded your father how busy he was last summer and suggested that Meir could help with the younger students."

Joheved blinked and looked at him without comprehension.

"It is one of my foremost goals that your father establish a yeshiva in Troyes," Isaac whispered.

Once they were married, Meir would be living in Troyes at least half the year! Joheved couldn't believe her ears. "Does Papa know about your plans?"

"I haven't told him as directly as I've just told you," he admitted, "but he must realize that he can't go back to Allemagne. Even if he hired the best workers available, the vineyard still needs his supervision."

"That's true," Joheved said. How unhappy Papa must be, stuck here in Troyes teaching his daughters and little boys.

"Don't worry about your father," Isaac said as he helped Joheved close the cellar windows. "Already some of the best scholars in Europe are bringing their business to our fairs in order to study with him. I'm sure it won't be long before they want their sons to study with him as well."

Joheved wanted to believe him; he sounded so confident. She kissed his palm, the way children were taught to show gratitude to adults. "Thank you for telling me all this. I feel much better." Her fears began to melt away as she contemplated this wonderful new possibility.

"If only it were always this easy to change a woman's tears to smiles." Isaac chuckled and headed for the stairs. "Come along now; we'd better see what has become of our new customer."

Joheved wiped her nose and followed Isaac up the stairs. She came into the kitchen and learned that Rivka had invited the merchant to dine with them the first night of Hanukkah.

Because the Cold Fair began on All Saints' Day and didn't end until late December, Troyes was always full of Jewish travelers during the festival of Hanukkah. Each evening at sunset, Salomon's family squeezed into the crowded synagogue and watched as the holiday lamps were lit with blessings and songs during the service. Then, like other local Jews, Salomon's family shared their holiday soupers with guests. Before they ate, he kindled the family's holiday lamp, a beautiful silver menorah that Leah had brought as part of her dowry. After the meal came more singing.

Women refrained from work while the lamp was lit, in memory of one woman's heroism. Salomon explained that, in those days, a virgin about to be married was required to first submit to the king. So when the high priest's daughter was betrothed, the Greek monarch demanded that she lie with him. She went to the king, fed him cheese until he was thirsty, and then gave him enough wine to make him drunk. Once he'd fallen asleep, she severed his head and brought it back to her father in Jerusalem. When the enemy general saw that his king was dead, he and his army fled.

Some women made the entire week a holiday, but Grandmama Leah regarded this as excessive and allowed her granddaughters to rest only on the first and last of the eight days. With all the pruning and digging that needed to be done in the vineyard, they couldn't afford a whole week of idleness. But for Joheved and Miriam, who had helped their father move vineyard soil uphill the previous winter, that the onerous job was being done by somebody else was vacation enough.

As wonderful as the weekdays were during the Festival of Lights, its Sabbath was even better. During services, the Scroll of the Hasmoneans was read aloud, and the congregation listened raptly as the reader recounted the triumphs of Mattathias and his sons over the evil despot Antiochus, intent on destroying them. Grandmama Leah had read this part for so many years that she had no difficulty translating for the women, and Joheved thought she made it sound as if she'd lived through the time herself.

> When the enemy was defeated, and the Hasmoneans entered the sanctuary in Jerusalem, they found only one flask of pure olive oil. Though its quantity seemed sufficient only for one day, it lasted eight days, owing to the blessing of the God of Heaven who established His Name there. Hence, the Jews instituted these eight days as a time of feasting and rejoicing, and of kindling lights to commemorate the victories the Holy One had given them.

On most Saturday nights, Jewish families prolonged their evening meal, reluctant to leave the Sabbath and reenter the regular week. But tonight Isaac's family joined them for a brief souper, and when they went outside to light the Hanukkah lamp at the doorway to the courtyard, Joheved was surprised to see over a dozen people waiting, covered dishes in their hands.

"I see the celebrants have already started to arrive." Isaac laughingly nudged his host. "I wonder how many more we'll have by the time the Compline bells ring."

Salomon and Joseph began to make tables by laying boards on some of the benches outside, and several men came over to assist them. More people continued to enter the courtyard, and Salomon eyed the growing crowd with anxiety. "I hope there's still some of my wine left to sell tomorrow."

"You mean our wine," Isaac said, throwing his arm around Salomon's shoulder. "Consider it an advertising expense. If this vintage is as good as everyone seems to expect, merchants will be lining up at your door, making exorbitant offers."

Musicians soon arrived, and the strains of popular Hanukkah melodies filled the air. Joheved couldn't see who was performing, but she could make out the sounds of string and wind instruments, as well as drums.

"We never used to have parties at our house before, and now we've had two in six months," she said in awe.

"Papa said we'd have a lot of people here to taste the new wine tonight, since so many of them helped make it." Miriam had to shout to be heard. "But I never expected such a mob."

"Do we have to open up every barrel for tasting?" Joheved asked her father. "They won't drink it all, will they?"

"Don't worry," Salomon said. "Most will only fill their cups a couple of times. They know the wine is our livelihood."

"And we'll only let them sample the pressed wine," Isaac declared. "The free-run wine casks remain sealed."

The menorah had nearly burned out, and torches were lit. Grandmama Leah took one look at the noisy bunch of strangers outside and announced that she was too tired to celebrate. Rivka jumped at the opportunity to withdraw, and asked Sarah to see to the guests so she could get Leah to bed. Joheved and Miriam held their breaths, afraid that Mama would make them come inside and miss this marvelous event. But she only admonished them not to make themselves sick by eating too many rich desserts.

The Hanukkah lamp's going out seemed to be a signal. Salomon and Isaac strode to the cellar doors where several men helped them lay down planks for ramps. Cheers rang out each time a cask was rolled out and righted. Then Isaac climbed atop a bench, and those nearby immediately quieted. The hush spread like a ripple in a pond, and soon the courtyard was silent.

"Friends, my partner and I welcome you to our Hanukkah festivities," Isaac boomed, his arms extended wide, and many in the crowd yelled back encouragements.

"We have wine from both Salomon's and the abbey's vineyards. Be sure that you have tasted both." This comment drew more shouts of approval. "But please try to restrain your desire for seconds until everyone has had their first taste." His emphasis on the word "try" brought more guffaws from his listeners. "Now let us fill our cups with new wine and toast the Festival of Lights!"

He jumped down from the bench to loud applause, and the musicians broke into spirited tunes. Circles of dancers began to move in time, their shadows wheeling in the torchlight. Isaac and Joseph stationed themselves at the abbey's casks, while Salomon and his daughters stood behind those from their vineyard. Everyone waited for the owners and their families to have the first tastes.

Salomon took a few bites of bread. Then he filled his wine goblet and recited both the Shehecheyanu and the blessing over wine. When his daughters responded, "Amen," he handed the cup to them. He had waited so long for this moment, but now he couldn't bring himself to take the first taste.

Joheved took a sip and handed the cup to Miriam. The wine seemed quite good to her, but she knew she was no expert.

Miriam took her drink and passed it back to Salomon. It was now or never—Isaac and Joseph were waiting. He held up the goblet and proclaimed, "For life." Then he closed his eyes and took a mouthful.

Salomon kept the liquid on his palate and breathed in the bouquet. He could scarcely believe it. The Holy One had blessed him with an excellent vintage, and this was the press wine! He savored the full-bodied flavor as he swallowed. The free-run wine must be truly sublime. He quickly took another taste to make sure he hadn't imagined that wonderful sensation.

Isaac saw the awe and pleasure in Salomon's eyes and quickly filled his own cup. "For a good life," he toasted his son.

Joseph returned the toast, "For a happy life."

The wine from the abbey's grapes was very good, but it did not merit the same exquisite expression as on Salomon's face. Salomon refilled his goblet and handed it to them, each of whom took a slow swallow and breathed out a very contented "Ah."

The revelers in the courtyard began to whisper excitedly. They could see the pleasure and pride on the vintner's face and crushed forward to get their cups filled. A fine vintage was a blessing for the whole community. Everything Salomon's family bought would be paid for with this wine, and soon it would grace every Jewish table in Troyes.

Salomon had Miriam take some wine inside for Rivka and Leah, while Joseph refilled his cup and asked Joheved to bring it to his wife. She found Johanna deep in conversation with Aunt Sarah, and offered them Joseph's cup. Like the others, Johanna tasted the wine slowly to savor it; then she passed it to Aunt Sarah.

Suddenly Miriam ran up to them. "I need to talk to Papa and Isaac, but I can't get through the crowd." She was almost jumping up and down in her urgency to pull Johanna and Joheved towards the crush at the cellar door. She continued to talk rapidly, as if her speech could somehow propel them faster.

"I gave some wine to Mama and Grandmama, and she, that is Grandmama, got very excited. She said that with wine this good, we have to hide it or sell it right away. She said that the count's men would be here any moment to take away his share, and we'd be left with nothing for all our work." Miriam was almost crying with frustration. "I've got to tell Papa what she said, but I can't even see him."

"I doubt that tithes will be collected tonight," Johanna reassured her. Then she stood up and announced loudly, "We need to speak with Salomon and Isaac at once!" A path opened for them, and they soon reached the men, where Miriam poured out her story.

"Do you think we really need to move the best wine out tonight?" Salomon asked the small group surrounding him. He had thought his worries about the vintage were finally over.

"Did your grandmother tell you that the count's men had taken her best wine before?" Sarah asked Miriam. While Leah had become more distrustful as her memory declined, what she did remember was often accurate.

"Oui. She said that whenever she had a good vintage, the count's tax collectors came right away." In an aside to Joheved, Miriam whispered, "You wouldn't believe the curses Grandmama used when she talked about the count and his tax collectors."

Isaac was used to making decisions quickly when necessary. "I don't think we can take the risk. Let's at least try to remove as much of the free-run wine as possible tonight. We can leave the pressed wine in the cellar to avoid suspicion."

Salomon gave up all thoughts of celebration and turned his mind towards the problem at hand. "We must find all the merchants who sold me goods in return for wine. They can take their shares tonight, and we'll tally accounts when the fair closes."

"That will be a perfect job for me and the girls," Johanna said. She took Joheved and Miriam by the hand and pointed them into the crowd.

"First look for Nissim and Hiyya's agent, but if you recognize any of the others, send them over here too."

Sarah offered to take as many barrels as her small cellar would hold. Joseph made the same offer and went off in search of his servants. Joheved found Nissim almost immediately; he had been one of the first in line and had not moved far after his cup was filled. Once he heard enough to understand the gist of the problem, he rushed off to the fairground, promising that he would be right back with his cart and horses. Soon other buyers were located, and if anyone doubted the basis for Leah's fears, the merchants' hasty actions were all the confirmation they needed.

The night wore on. The revelers danced, sang, ate and drank heartily, while against this festive background, men stealthily filled carts with wine barrels and slipped away into the darkness. Salomon instructed Joheved to keep a careful record of how much wine was taken away and by whom.

A few streets away in the palace, Count Thibault and his advisors crowded around one end of a long table. Warmed by fires blazing in the great hearth nearby, the men sat discussing His Grace's upcoming nuptials. Much planning was involved—after all, the uniting of two prominent noble houses was of great political importance. Whom to invite, where to lodge them, what foods should be served, should he have hunts or a tourney for entertainment, or perhaps both? Soon their talk grew tedious, and during a lull in the proceedings, the merrymaking and music from Salomon's courtyard became noticeable.

"I'm glad to hear my fairgoers having a good time." Count Thibault's eyes took on a calculating look. "If they are happy, their business is profitable, which means that mine is as well."

"We can certainly use a successful fair this year, Your Grace," Guy, his chamberlain, said. "The wedding costs will make a large dent in your treasury." Thibault shot his chamberlain a dark look, and the man quickly replied, "I have been saving for the occasion for some time, and in any case, we can always tax the Jews if more is needed."

Girard, the seneschal, sat up and listened alertly, a frown on his face. "They certainly are loud down there. I hope I don't have to send my men over later to break up any fights."

Thibault rejected this idea with a wave of his hand. "As long as we hear music, I'm sure your intervention is unnecessary." He cupped his hand behind his ear to hear better. "It's quite loud to be coming from the fairgrounds. It sounds closer."

"Your Grace is correct about the closeness," Bernard, the cellarer, spoke in obsequious tones. "I believe the music is coming from the Jewish Quarter, where they are celebrating their winter festival."

"Well, if it's the Jews making noise, I probably don't have to worry about fighting." Girard relaxed back into his chair.

"And if the Jews are celebrating with that much enthusiasm," Guy rubbed his hands greedily, "then they are doing very well at the Cold Fair, and we can expect substantial tithes from them."

"Pardon me," Bernard interrupted politely. "One of the things they celebrate at this time of year is tasting the new wine. It has come to my attention that this year's vintage is expected to be one of the finest in years."

"If that's true, don't you worry that they will sell or hide the best of it before you can claim our share?" Guy asked.

Bernard stared at the chamberlain in disdain. "The Jews are His Grace's loyal subjects, who would undoubtedly be honored to provide wine for his table, particularly if it is very good wine and they are acknowledged as the vintners."

Girard was inclined to agree with the chamberlain and view the Jews as potential tax evaders. "I think it might be prudent for me to visit the Jewish winemaker first thing tomorrow morning and inventory his cellar."

"You shall do no such thing." The usually cool and civil cellarer was starting to show just a bit of pique. "If anybody is to go, it will be myself. And I am not going tomorrow!"

Count Thibault had heard enough. "None of my retainers is going to the Jewish Quarter tomorrow." He looked sternly at Girard and Guy. "The Jews take their Sabbath very seriously, and I will not have them or anyone else thinking that my men do not observe our Sunday rest with proper reverence.

"However," Thibault nodded in the cellarer's direction, "on Monday morning, Bernard will present himself at their winemaker's home to sample their new wine and decide how much to tithe for my use. I have no doubt that my Jews will cooperate with him fully."

As Count Thibault ordered, his punctilious cellarer arrived at Salomon's door late Monday morning. Joheved answered it, and was not surprised to find the smartly dressed nobleman and his retainers waiting there. Upstairs tidying the bedrooms, Marie had seen the knights riding up the street and had rushed to inform her mistress. The trap door to the cellar was open, and even with much of the free-run casks removed, the cellar looked well stocked. In fact, there was more than twice as much wine as the cellar had held last year.

Salomon was still at synagogue. He had announced earlier that his eldest daughter was perfectly capable of dealing with the count's cellarer, or whoever was sent in his place. Joheved had actually been in charge of the wine accounts for the last few years, ostensibly still learning the skill from her grandmother.

Rivka offered the visitors food and drink, but Bernard declined and asked to see the cellar. As the cellarer watched closely, Joheved identified the various casks and drew four small jugs of wine. Once back in the kitchen, the family observed him carefully as he tasted the wine.

Starting with the pressed wine, he chatted nonchalantly about the count's upcoming wedding and how a band of brigands had been discovered in the western forest, just waiting to attack the merchants returning to Paris from the Cold Fair. "The gallows at the city gates will soon be full," he announced.

Eventually he took a taste of Salomon's free-run wine, and his prattle stopped. Joheved had waited for this moment, and she was not disappointed. Like the other connoisseurs who had tasted Salomon's wine, Bernard could not hide his pleasure.

He saw them watching him and knew that they were equally aware of this wine's unique value. "His Grace will be pleased to serve such excellent wine at his wedding," the cellarer said. "I am not yet sure what his needs will require, so I must advise you not to sell over half your stock until he takes his tithe."

"Half the stock," Joheved protested with a gulp. "But at least half the barrels come from Montier-la-Celle's grapes, and we haven't given the abbot his share yet."

Bernard's bland expression didn't change, but inwardly he was furious. The abbey's produce was their own, not subject to Thibault's authority. Leave it to their wily abbot to have the Jews make and sell wine made from his grapes, thus greatly increasing its value and Montier-la-Celle's revenue. The cellarer had no choice but to modify his initial demand.

"I mean, of course, that your father should not dispose of more than half the wine coming from his own vineyard until you hear from me again." Bernard abruptly rose from the table and bid the family, "*Bonjour.*" He was already trying to figure out some way to obtain the abbey's wine; it was nearly as good as the Jewish vineyard's product.

Rivka couldn't wait to report the morning's events to Salomon when he returned from services. "Joheved was wonderful. While I was nearly mute with fright, she stood her ground against Count Thibault's cellarer and outwitted him too."

"But I was lucky," Joheved admitted, her face coloring. "I didn't realize the abbey's wine was exempt from their tithes. I only hoped to save a few barrels for the abbot's personal use."

"It doesn't matter how much Thibault wants." Filled with pride at his daughter's success, Salomon was philosophical about the loss. "Our creditors have been paid, we have enough for our own use, and I'm sure the Jewish community will not make our family bear more than our fair share of the wedding's cost."

He turned to Joheved and continued, "I want you to go with me to the fair this afternoon. We must settle our accounts now that the merchants are leaving, and we also need to buy a Hanukkah present for Meir."

"A present for Meir?"

"Isaac reminded me that it's customary for the bridegroom-elect and the father of a betrothed maiden to exchange gifts," Salomon explained. "A supply of parchment is waiting for me on Rue de la Petite Tannerie, so I should reciprocate. I thought you could help pick out something appropriate. It's for your fiancé."

"I'd love to go shopping with you, Papa." Everything with the wine had worked out so well, Joheved wanted to celebrate.

And in a way, Meir's family had given her a Hanukkah present as well. After the betrothal, Marona had sent over so much raw wool that Mama had been able to weave a new blanket out of the thread that Joheved and Miriam had spun from it. That reminded her—"May Miriam come too?"

So the three of them spent the afternoon at the Cold Fair. "Maybe we could find Meir some silk hose, like the new ones Papa has," Miriam suggested.

"What about a wine goblet?" Joheved remembered the fine ones that Isaac and Joseph had given her parents.

"That would make an excellent gift, but probably more appropriate for a wedding present," Salomon replied, his gaze sweeping over the merchandise as they walked along.

They continued past the booths and listened to the merchants' extravagant descriptions of their wares. "You would think they're giving things away at the fair's closing, their prices are such bargains," Salomon said, clearly not impressed.

Finally they passed a table with a few leather items left on it, including a beautifully worked belt. Joheved stopped to admire the intricate pattern.

The merchant immediately began his litany. "This beautiful belt was made in Spain, of the finest Cordovan leather. Look how fine the workmanship is." He picked up the belt and thrust it at Salomon. "It's my mistake that I have not sold this excellent piece already—it's too small for most men. After all, the men who can afford this kind of merchandise are too prosperous and plump to wear it. You can have it for a ridiculously low amount." And he named a figure that was actually reasonable.

"Meir is pretty skinny," Miriam said, trying the belt around her own tiny waist. "I bet it would fit him."

Once the merchant saw he had a potential customer, bargaining began in earnest, and the sale was quickly made. They would send the belt with some merchants going through Mayence after leaving the Cold Fair. Meir was not likely to expect a gift and shouldn't mind receiving it after Hanukkah was over.

nine

A week after Hanukkah ended, when Salomon asked Joheved to procure some fresh parchment for him, she was reluctant to go. Yet if Miriam went in her place, her sister and Catharina would surely gossip about her betrothal. So Joheved set off for Rue de la Petite Tannerie, determined to remain calm and unaffected no matter how much her friend teased her.

Catharina was helping a bald, brown-robed monk examine some parchment in the storage room, and her face lit up when she saw Joheved come in.

"Congratulations." She hurried over to give Joheved a hug. "I hear everything worked out between your father and Lord Samuel. My brother says we are to give you as much parchment as you want."

"Merci." Joheved returned the hug. At least Catharina hadn't teased her immediately. "Samuel's betrothal gift was very generous. For our part, my father only has to give him a cask of wine each year at Passover."

Before they could continue their conversation, the monk came over and, to their surprise, addressed Joheved. "Excuse me." His voice was gentle, yet he spoke with authority. "I couldn't help overhearing. You are the daughter of the Jewish winemaker?"

"Oui, I am." Joheved cast a questioning look at Catharina, who shrugged her shoulders in reply. But Joheved didn't want the strange monk to think that Papa was only a vintner. "My father is also a scholar. He needs parchment for the commentary he's writing on the Bible."

"I am Robert, prior of the Abbey of Montier-la-Celle." While his posture didn't change, he somehow gave the impression of bowing to them. "I owe your father a debt of gratitude for the excellent wine he produced from our grapes this year."

"Oh." Joheved relaxed at the monk's kind words. "Even Count Thibault's cellarer said the vintage is one of the best he's ever tasted. We are grateful to you as well, for sharing your grapes." She could see that Robert wasn't really bald; his hair was such a pale blond that his short tonsure only made it appear that way.

"Your father is writing a commentary on the Hebrew scriptures?" he asked, his pale brows furrowed in thought. "There are some passages that confound me, and perhaps he might spare a few moments to help me understand them better."

Joheved suspected that her father would rather not discuss Torah with the heretics who worshipped the Hanged One, but she merely suggested, "Perhaps you should ask him your questions when you come to get the abbey's wine." After all, Papa wouldn't want to antagonize anyone important at Montier-la-Celle.

"Give your father my regards and tell him I'll be visiting him soon," Robert said. Then he turned to Catharina and added, "Give your father my regards as well, and inform him that the abbey needs six more folios. Count Thibault has commissioned an illuminated psalter as a wedding present for his new bride." He left them with that delightful piece of news.

"It must be nice when somebody wants to marry you," Catharina said wistfully, thinking of Samuel's gift of parchment and Thibault's psalter. "But then look at you, you have new clothes on too. I'm glad things are going so well for you."

"You are a true friend to be happy in my good fortune." Joheved hugged her again and sighed. Now that Miriam was an apprentice midwife, the Jewish girls all wanted to be friends with her, but Catharina was still the only friend Joheved had.

"What's the matter?" Catharina could see the sadness in Joheved's face. "Is there something wrong with your fiancé?"

"No, no." Joheved made an effort to look more cheerful. "There's nothing the matter with Meir; that's his name, by the way. He's not handsome, but he's not ugly either, and he seems nice enough. He's a scholar, which is what Papa wanted, and his family is well off, which makes Mama happy. I just wish things could work out well for you too."

"I don't know about me." Catharina gathered up several sheaves of folded parchment and handed them to her friend. "But I bet my brother is thinking of getting married. He spends a lot of time with the daughter of one of the leather tanners on the next street. At least she'll be used to the stink."

"I'll pray for the Holy One to send you a good husband." Joheved took her parchment and walked home slowly, feeling guilty that her future looked so bright compared to Catharina's.

Her spirits brightened when Salomon announced that it was time to resume their nightly Talmud sessions. Since the holiday was still fresh in their minds, they would study the section in Tractate Shabbat that explained the laws of Hanukkah.

As always, the sages Shammai and Hillel were arguing over some point of law. This time the subject was exactly how one should light the Hanukkah lamp.

> For those who fervently pursue mitzvot, the School of Shammai says that on the first day of Hanukkah one kindles eight lights, and then continuously decreases the amount; but the School of Hillel says to kindle one light on the first day and continuously increase . . . Hillel's reason for a continual increase is that in sacred matters we elevate, not lower, the level of holiness.

Miriam and Joheved stared at their father in surprise. "That means Shammai starts with eight lights the first night, seven on the second night, and ends with just one light," Miriam said.

Salomon nodded. "That's right."

"But why light them backwards like that?" Joheved asked. Who would have imagined that other Jews did things so differently?

"Shammai believes this publicizes the true nature of the miracle, the single flask of oil that gradually diminished over eight days," he said.

"Everybody here does it like Hillel . . . I think," Miriam said.

"That's true; no one follows Shammai anymore," Salomon agreed.

Joheved continued reading.

> What is Hanukkah?

"Don't they know what Hanukkah is?" Miriam interrupted. "They've been discussing it for pages."

"Maybe they're asking how we know to celebrate Hanukkah," Joheved said. "It's not mentioned in Torah at all, not like our other holidays." She glowed with pride when her father said she was right.

Miriam continued reading, and there was the story of the miraculous small flask of oil that burned for eight days. When she finished, Salomon asked if there was anything in the Gemara about Hanukkah that puzzled them.

"Why did it take eight days to get new oil?" Miriam asked. "That seems like a long time."

"And why did the Sages make an eight-day festival?" Joheved frowned. "I mean, since the flask started with enough oil for one night, didn't the miracle really occur the next seven nights?"

"Those are both good questions." Salomon nodded in approval. "Miriam, some sages say the nearest pure oil was a four-day journey away. Others say that the Jews were impure due to contact with corpses, because of the fighting, and it took seven days for their purification. Then they needed one more day to press the olives into oil."

"Joheved, many scholars have asked your question," he said with a smile. "Some answer that the flask of oil remained full after the lamp was filled, so it was evident even on the first night that a miracle was occurring. Others suggest that they divided the oil into eight parts and only poured that small amount into the menorah, yet the lamp burned the entire night. Thus a miracle did happen each day."

They continued studying Tractate Shabbat for months, the Gemara's debates over the minutiae of observance becoming increasingly overwhelming. One night, after an arduous day working in the vineyard, Miriam refused to spend another moment reviewing Talmud with her sister.

"Joheved, I'm too tired to study. Let's just go to sleep." Miriam yawned and pulled the covers over her head.

"But we have to review every day or we'll forget." Joheved pulled the covers back. "And we've worked so hard to learn it."

"I know. But this Gemara is too hard. And it isn't as interesting as Berachot was."

"You don't want to study Talmud anymore because it's too difficult?" Joheved was stunned. If Miriam abandoned their nightly ritual, she'd never find out what was in all those other tractates. "But you mustn't give up; I can't do it alone."

"Joheved, I didn't say that I wanted to stop altogether, but we never play hide and seek anymore, or make the kittens chase strings, or do anything fun. Don't you want to do anything except talk about Talmud?"

"I like learning Talmud, and I thought you did too." A cold fear gripped Joheved. It would be like going back to stirabout for every meal after eating meat. "Maybe we could tell Papa we want to study Berachot again."

Miriam might have been kinder if she hadn't been so tired. "Don't you realize that no matter how much Gemara we learn, Papa will still wish he had sons instead of daughters?"

There was nothing Joheved could say to that. She put the pillow over her head and cried herself to sleep.

During their next session, Salomon was astute enough to see that his students' enthusiasm was flagging. He didn't fault them; it was his responsibility to make sure his lessons were challenging without being onerous.

"Joheved, did you know that Tractate Shabbat isn't usually studied until a student has been in yeshiva for several years?" he praised them. "And Miriam, some of the boys are almost twice your age. You two are doing an excellent job learning such advanced material. I'm very proud of you."

"Merci, Papa." They surreptitiously exchanged glances. Had he overheard their conversation last night?

Joheved looked back at him and quickly answered, "Tractate Shabbat isn't that hard, Papa; we can learn it."

"Even so, I intend to go back to Berachot after we finish this section on Hanukkah," Salomon said. "Be patient for now. There's only a few pages left about Hanukkah, and soon we will come to a part that you'll find particularly interesting."

It was Joheved's turn to read when they got to the discussion he meant.

> A woman may certainly kindle the Hanukkah light. Rav Yehoshua ben Levi said: Women are obligated in the mitzvah of Hanukkah for they were involved in that miracle.

Joheved's voice rose with excitement. This was the first time she'd read about women's ritual observance in the Talmud.

Now Miriam leaned forward eagerly. "Papa, how were women involved in the Hanukkah miracle?"

"The Greek oppression affected Jewish women uniquely, since every bride had to submit to the local Greek commander," he replied. "In addition, as you know, a woman was an instrument of their deliverance—the high priest's daughter who killed the Greek general."

Thus they continued all winter long, studying Talmud at night and pruning the vineyard during the day. Joheved tried to learn pruning techniques with the same determination she applied to learning Gemara, because she doubted that Grandmama would be able to instruct them next year. Last winter Leah had confidently directed her granddaughters; every cut came with an explanation of why it was best for this particular vine.

"Cane pruning requires the most skill, but spur pruning is quicker," she had told them. "Remember that shoots farthest from the stock bear the most, and that sunlight on the woody parts, especially the new canes, makes a more fruitful vine. Cut short, leaving only two or three buds, if the plant appears weak, aiming for quality over quantity. Cut long, three or four buds to a branch, when the plant seems vigorous and you want a more plentiful harvest."

Leah used to be indefatigable when it came to such knowledge, but now she volunteered little. She answered questions the girls put to her, but the fountain of her knowledge was a well they had to bucket water from, not a gushing stream. Joheved and Miriam asked any question they could think of, to try to learn everything Leah knew and also because her silence so distressed them.

"Grandmama, why do we have to cut the vines so close to the ground?" Joheved was tall enough now that it hurt to stoop over the low vines all afternoon.

Leah might appear frail, but she chopped off the branch in front of her as easily as slicing a piece of cheese. "Here in the north, dear, the closer the grapes are to the ground, provided they do not actually touch it, the better they will mature."

"How do we know when to finish the pruning?" Miriam asked.

"You can tell that the vines have completed their winter rest when they start to discharge sap from the pruning wounds. Be careful; these 'tears of the vine' are sticky." Leah held up the cut branch for them to inspect, but it was still dry. "Some say the sap has medicinal properties, and I try to take a little each year as a spring tonic."

This year when the sap rose, it was raining heavily, and no one would brave the muddy vineyard to harvest it. Leah never did get any sap that spring, because the rain continued for months. At first people were happy with the abundant rainfall. But too much wet weather and even those few crops that germinated would fail to grow properly.

If it rained into summer, rivers would become impassable and roads too muddy for merchant wagons to travel. Already one heard complaints in the synagogue that few were willing to endure such hardships to attend the spring fair in Provins. On the bright side, fewer anticipated guests had forced Count Thibault to scale back his wedding festivities, which meant lower taxes.

For Joheved and Miriam, the continual downpour meant far too many days indoors keeping Grandmama Leah company. To pass the time, they began to ask her about their father's childhood. To their disappointment, she told the same stories over and over again, mostly along the lines of what a prodigy he had been in school, instead of stories of his mischievous boyhood adventures. She also told them a particularly bizarre tale.

"For years after I married your grandfather, I was barren. One day, he acquired a valuable pearl that the bishop wanted for the cathedral. My pious husband—may his merit protect us—refused to allow such a jewel to be used for the heretics' idolatry, and he cast it into the Seine. Soon afterwards, there was a solar eclipse and he dreamed of an angel who told him that because of his sacrifice, he would be rewarded with a son who would become a great scholar," Leah said proudly. "Six months later, our little Salomon was born."

Joheved and Miriam didn't know what to make of such a story. Their grandmother did occasionally make up something rather than admit she didn't remember the answer to a question. At first it had been funny when she gave them different answers to the same query, but now her mental lapses were painful to hear.

When they asked Papa about his father's pearl and the angel dream, he shook his head and said, "She probably dreamed the thing herself. So now she thinks it's true." Yet Grandmama told them the strange story several times, and it never varied.

One especially rainy day, a terrible new tale emerged. When Miriam asked, "What was Papa like as a baby?" Grandmama Leah sat transfixed for what seemed an eternity. Then her face became distorted with pain and she began to cry.

"Please, Mon Dieu, make the rain stop. Are you sending another flood to kill us all? What sins have we committed that you sent this famine? Wasn't it enough that my poor husband died last year of starvation? Please don't take away my baby, my little Salomon. We would fast for penance, but we have been fasting for two years already. What more do you want of us?" Leah stared into space, tears streaming down her cheeks.

The girls listened in confused horror. What was Grandmama Leah talking about? Grandpapa Isaac didn't die before Papa was born, and he certainly didn't die of starvation. Papa had told them several times, when warning them about the sharp pruning knives, how his father had cut himself while trimming back the grapevines. The wound had festered, killing him before the month was over. Papa was only a boy then, but he was old enough to understand his father's death.

But their grandmother wasn't done with her tale of woe. "Finally, the rains stop, but it's too late for my poor baby. I have no more milk for you, my poor little Salomon, and I tried so hard to save you. Soon you'll be in the Garden of Eden with your father, brother and sister. How can I go on living without you?" Leah covered her face with her hands and sobbed.

Joheved had heard enough. Desperate to find Papa and bring him to Grandmama Leah, to prove to her that she was having some sort of terrible dream, Joheved raced down the circular stairway so fast that she was dizzy at the bottom. Salomon, who had been working on his Torah commentary, jumped up to meet her.

"Papa, Papa! You've got to come upstairs right away! Grandmama Leah—"

"What is it? What's happened to her?" He didn't wait for her answer, but bounded up the stairs to his mother's room.

"Grandmama Leah is having some sort of nightmare." Joheved caught up with him just as he entered Leah's room. "She kept telling us how you died as a baby, and that your father and her other children all died in a famine. It was awful!"

Salomon didn't know what disaster he'd find when he walked through the door, but he didn't expect to see his mother sitting calmly on her bed, Miriam holding her hand and asking how to make wine from fruit other than grapes. As Leah explained how she occasionally fermented blackberries along with grapes, especially in a year when such berries were plentiful, Miriam put a finger to her lips and shot them a pleading glance. Joheved, amazed at Leah's sudden transformation, held her tongue. Whoever would have thought that Grandmama's poor memory could be a blessing?

Despite his daughters' insistent questioning, Salomon could confirm nothing of his mother's traumatic story other than to say that his father,

Isaac, had been her second husband. As for siblings, his parents had often told him that they had nearly given up on having children until he was born.

Joheved wondered if Isaac haParnas could enlighten them. After all, he was nearly as old as Grandmama Leah. Joheved and Miriam waited until he came to watch as they inventoried the wine remaining after Passover. Then, in the privacy of the cellar, he was more than willing to describe the great famine of his youth.

"It was about forty years ago, when I was a student in Worms," Isaac began. "I remember that rain was still falling after Passover, and I was disappointed that what should have been an exciting journey was reduced to a fruitless effort to keep dry and prevent the wagons from getting stuck on the muddy roads. Then, a year later, my parents surprised me by arriving in Worms to celebrate Passover there instead of bringing me home."

He paused for a moment and his eyes focused on something far away. "You see, it was still raining in France and my father hoped to spend the summer traveling to a place where grain was plentiful, so he could buy wheat and bring it back to Troyes."

"So it was still raining in Troyes a year later," Joheved said as she exchanged a sober nod with her sister. "No wonder Grandmama got so upset with all the rain this spring."

"And that year, there was famine in France." Isaac sighed heavily. "Even though we had grain, it was impossible to return until the flooded rivers receded and the quagmires became passable roads again."

"So what did you do?" Joheved asked.

"We had to wait until summer. My father was determined that his seed wheat reach Troyes in time for autumn planting, so the Jews of Worms warned us to hire additional men-at-arms." Isaac's bushy brows narrowed in pain as he continued his tale. "Perhaps our well-guarded convoy deterred attack, for we met only beggars on the road, and I have never seen such pathetic creatures in my life. I pleaded with my father to help them, but he refused."

Miriam stared at him in horror. "You left them to starve?"

Isaac nodded. "We had no idea how bad things would be in Troyes, how long we might need to live off our provisions."

"And what happened when you got home?" Joheved wanted to get past the misery to the story's end.

"Everyone in Troyes was so relieved to see us, to see what wonderful cargo we carried," Isaac said. "But they had suffered too much grief to be happy. Even though they made my father the new Parnas, it was difficult for my parents to find a girl my age for me to wed. I ended up marrying a young widow, who, like your grandmother, lost her husband and children during the famine."

Joheved sighed sadly when she realized Isaac's tale was over. Poor Grandmama Leah, no wonder she'd never told them about her first family. She gazed up at the blue sky with new appreciation. She should be more thankful for her family's good fortune. Yet life was so uncertain; even during good times, people died unexpectedly. It had happened to her grandfather.

Now in services Joheved prayed with special fervor when she got to the part that went "We thank You for our lives which are in Your hand, for Your wondrous providence, and Your continuous goodness which You bestow upon us day by day." She never made a conscious decision to keep Isaac's tale a secret from her parents, but somehow there was never a good time to tell them. And once the rains stopped, everyone was far too busy.

Besides the vineyard, which required daily attention, both Leah and Rachel needed supervision. Rivka was sure the baby would toddle into the hearth or garbage pit the moment nobody was watching. The days when Rachel could spend hours sitting contentedly in Grandmama Leah's lap were but a pleasant memory.

By necessity, Salomon began keeping his youngest daughter with him while he taught. Much to her sisters' surprise, Rachel's behavior in the classroom was exemplary. She cruised from one bench to the next, smiling up at whoever was near. Sometimes she sat on the floor next to her sisters, playing with the small scraps of colored fabric left over from making last year's clothes or with the smooth, shiny pebbles that the boys collected near the river for her. Salomon discovered, to his delight, that she was satisfied to sit on his lap and watch as he dipped the long goose quill pen into the ink holder made of a cow's horn, and then wrote his letters or kuntres.

Salomon's time was increasingly spent writing. Besides expounding the deeper meaning of biblical texts to his students, he wrote down his explanations as well. Now anyone new could catch up with his other pupils. He continued to expand his Talmud notes, and he let Joheved and Miriam read his writings whenever they wanted, partly for them to proofread and partly to make up for his having less time to study with them.

He also wrote regularly to Meir in Mayence. Meir had begun their correspondence with a letter of thanks after he received his Hanukkah present. He filled the rest of the parchment with news of the yeshiva, and included regards to Joheved. Salomon had responded in kind and encouraged his daughter to add a few lines of her own. Meir's letters kept the old yeshiva world alive for him, and he was thankful for that tenuous connection.

That was until the most recent letter arrived. Meir wrote that Isaac haLevi had enacted an edict restricting how kosher cattle could be slaughtered. But the forbidden practice was precisely that used by French butchers, and Salomon was expected to retract his approval of it.

Joheved was usually eager to read Meir's letters after her father was done, but when she saw his clenched jaw and red face, she backed away. What had Meir said to cause such anger? She overcame her urge to run away and forced herself to wait for an explanation. It was not long in coming.

Salomon threw the letter down on the table and grabbed for parchment and ink. As he wrote, he put his wrath into speech as well. "Will our teacher please refrain from adding to the number of 'forbidden foods'? For it would be impossible to accept this; otherwise we in France would never be able to eat meat. We are unable to stop this practice—unless we are willing to pay for the entire cow, whether it is found fit to eat or not."

He took a deep breath to compose himself and continued writing. "If you wish to erect a 'fence around the law'—yours is the great court and you are worthy to enact restrictive measures. We prefer, however, that our teacher stand by the accepted law and not forbid doubtful cases."

Salomon saw that Joheved was watching him. "That one was a public letter for my teachers. This one is just for Meir." He took a fresh piece of parchment and began another letter.

"I, Salomon, your devoted, inform you that I have not retracted so far and do not intend to retract in the future. I do not find the words of my teachers fully convincing, their arguments were but superficial, and I shall reveal my view to you, my very discreet student. Were it not for the calamity that overwhelmed my family, I would teach them my position in person, even if they would not abide by it. For I cannot adopt a view that would cause the loss of money to Jews in a matter that is so obviously permitted."

He finished with a suggestion. "I urge you to relocate from Mayence to Worms. It is important to study with different masters, to learn the material each teacher knows. I myself studied almost ten years in Worms before moving to Mayence."

Now that Salomon had written down his fury, he seemed calmer. Joheved didn't understand why he was so angry and took the risk of asking, "Papa, what do the butchers in Troyes do that your old teachers don't like?"

He stroked his beard for a moment before replying, "None of the butchers in Troyes are Jewish. We slaughter our meat in cooperation with them, so that if the animal is found to be not kosher, the butcher can still sell it. But of course, Edomites do not want to buy meat that Jews have rejected, so the butchers make it look like the animal was slaughtered in the usual way. Isaac haLevi forbids this, even though he knows I permit it. He thinks I would not dare to contradict him, but I rely fully on my own judgment to advocate the more lenient view."

"Of course, Papa. Who would slaughter an animal if he couldn't eat or sell the meat?" It didn't seem right for the rabbis so far away to make eating meat difficult for Jews in Troyes. Then she thought of something else Papa had written.

"Papa, when you wrote to Meir about our family's calamity, did you mean Grandmama Leah, that she can't remember things anymore?"

Salomon nodded sadly. "I'm afraid that Potach has her firmly in his clutches." He sighed heavily and wiped away some tears. "My mother will never be able to run the vineyard without me."

He quickly added an incantation of protection against the demon. "I adjure you, Potach, Prince of Forgetfulness, that you remove from me a fool's heart, in the name of the holy names, Arimas, Arimimas, Anisisi'el and Petah'el." He looked down at the letters he had written and sighed again. "I doubt that I will ever study with my old teachers again. My life is in Troyes now."

ten

Spring 4831 (1071 C.E.)

Had the idea of starting his own yeshiva first come to him after writing that letter to Meir? Or had it been there earlier? Salomon knew only that enough merchants had approached him about teaching their sons that he'd agreed to open a modest yeshiva. He insisted on taking only those candidates just starting to study Talmud, like his current pupils.

The week after Passover, Salomon had four new students, beardless, bewildered youths just past their thirteenth birthdays. There was a vintner's son from Rheims, a pair of cousins from Provins, and a pudgy boy from Bar-sur-Aube with relatives in Troyes. The first three intended to lodge with Salomon, so Joheved and Miriam helped outfit the attic as quarters for them.

Marie and the girls swept the floors and covered them with fresh rushes. Then they brought up sweet hay for the boys' bedding, and a few benches as well. Getting things up to the top floor was difficult. The circular staircase inside the house extended only to the second floor; one reached the attic by means of a ladder in the courtyard below.

The larger household consumed so many eggs that Rivka bought some hens of their own, and Miriam found that she enjoyed hunting for eggs hidden in the courtyard grass. Joheved was still begging for a few more moments of sleep while Miriam was already outside, searching out the hens' secret nests. Benjamin ben Reuben, the new student from Rheims, was often there to help her.

Wavy hair was a common Jewish trait, but Benjamin's sandy hair was even curlier than Rachel's. Miriam liked to toy with the baby's curls by stretching one to its complete length and then letting it bounce back, and she felt a strange desire to similarly play with Benjamin's light brown ringlets.

"Merci, Benjamin," she thanked him as he handed her another egg. "You're a good egg hunter. You can find two eggs for every one of mine."

"I ought to be." He grinned back at her. "My mother keeps poultry too, and since I'm the youngest, collecting eggs is my job." Suddenly Benjamin's expression changed from cheerful to forlorn, and his grey-blue eyes filled with tears.

Miriam could see that he was fighting to control his sorrow. "Benjamin, what's the matter?"

He leaned against the apple tree and tried to shield his face with his arm. "I miss my family. I miss my mother."

Miriam watched helplessly as the tears rolled down the homesick boy's cheeks. "Do you want to go home?"

"I don't mean to complain," he said. "Your father is a wonderful teacher, and during the day, I'm usually fine. But it's different at night. I remember how far away my parents are, and I feel so alone. My roommates must think I'm a big baby."

The poor fellow, no wonder he was unhappy. Miriam tried to think of something comforting to say. "Did you know that my father left his mother, his only relative, at the same age as you, and traveled all the way to Worms? At least you're still in France; you don't have to learn a new language."

"Thanks for your encouragement." He smiled wanly at her and started searching for eggs again. "I'll try to keep it in mind."

"Benjamin, I'm sorry you're so unhappy." What could she do to make him less miserable? "Maybe if you save some tidbits at meals and share them with one of the cats, you could entice it to sleep with you in the attic. Then you won't feel alone at night."

"I suppose that might help," he said skeptically.

Miriam knew that Benjamin was several years older than she was, but he hadn't started growing yet and still looked more like a boy than a youth on the verge of manhood. It didn't occur to her that they shouldn't be alone together; to Miriam they were both still children.

She ran over to him, scattering the chickens. "I know, let's pretend that I'm your sister. Then it won't be like you're separated from all your family. What do you think?"

Benjamin's demeanor brightened immediately. He grabbed her hand and gave it a quick kiss, exactly as he had done with his parents hundreds of times. Miriam had kissed her share of palms, especially her grandmother's, but nobody had ever kissed hers before. In the nights that followed, she remembered the sensation of Benjamin's lips on her hand and marveled at the feeling.

After evaluating his new students' capabilities, Salomon decided to teach them Mishnah from Tractate Pesachim. After all, they had recently celebrated Passover, and its rituals should be fresh in their memories. Eager to study this Mishnah, yet unsure what the new pupils would think, Joheved and Miriam took up their spindles and settled unobtrusively in the back of the *salle*.

Salomon held up the leather-bound volume. "Every Mishnah has pages of Gemara, so you can be sure our Sages had many questions. Now I want you all to think about what questions they might have asked about our Mishnah." He paused to let this sink in. "Remember, if you don't understand something, it's likely that one of the rabbis shared your difficulty."

Salomon directed Ephraim to read. "We will begin with the last chapter, which I'm sure you'll have no trouble learning. To study Mishnah, you chant the words with a special melody, which makes it easier to remember. When we get to a certain part," he smiled mysteriously at the class, "you will find that you already know this tune, and you can all chant it for us."

When Ephraim began reading, Joheved listened carefully for the special section.

> They poured the second cup of wine and the son asks his father . . . Why is this night different?

He looked up triumphantly. "It's the 'Ma Nishtana,' the Four Questions! I'm the youngest son, so I have to ask them every Passover at our Seder." He shot his twin brother, older by moments, a resentful glance.

He started again, this time chanting the questions in the traditional singsong melody.

> Why is this night different from all other nights? On other nights we eat leavened or unleavened bread, but on this night, only unleavened? On other nights we eat all kinds of vegetables, but on this night maror (the bitter herb)? On other nights we eat meat roasted, boiled or cooked, but on this night only roasted?

He stumbled a bit on the question about roasted meat, since it wasn't in his family's Seder, but picked up his rhythm again with the next, more familiar, query.

> On other nights we dip our food once, on this night we dip two times?

By the time Ephraim had reached the last of the four questions, the other boys had joined him in chanting the well-known verses. The atmosphere in the *salle* was exultant. Except for Menachem, all the boys had recited them at one time or another, and a few, like Ephraim and Benjamin, had chanted them less than a month before. Even Joheved and Miriam had chanted them. Now many hands were raised with questions.

Hoping for just such a reaction, Salomon couldn't wait to start teaching. "Before any of you fall off your benches, I'll tell you that the full answer as to why we don't ask about roasted meat is in the Gemara."

Several of the students groaned with disappointment, sure that they would have to wait years for the explanation, but their teacher smiled and continued, "Suffice to say that after the Holy Temple in Jerusalem was destroyed, this question was replaced with one about why we recline at the Seder table."

In the sunny spring days that followed, Miriam and Joheved tried to be wherever their father was teaching, which often turned out to be the vineyard. There Salomon's pupils learned simple vineyard skills along with the last chapter of Tractate Pesachim. While the girls and Benjamin secured the branches to their supports, he instructed the others to remove all leaves from the old branches. Only new shoots were fertile, so leaves left on the old wood consumed needed sap and decreased the plant's vigor.

Once Salomon was confident of Benjamin's skills in the vineyard, he allowed the youth to work there without supervision. And it wasn't long before Miriam was trying to cajole her older sister into joining him there. Joheved suspected that Miriam was more interested in Benjamin's company than in improving her vineyard techniques, but she kept those thoughts to herself. She hadn't liked being teased about Meir and resolved not to turn the tables on her sister. At least not without extreme provocation.

But after spending hours with Benjamin and Miriam in the vineyard, Joheved wasn't sure about her sister's intentions. Mama had been so adamant that no potential suitor would be interested in such learned girls that Joheved never mentioned her studies in her letters to Meir, and she tried not to let Salomon's students catch her studying either.

Yet it was clear that her sister didn't care what Benjamin thought, because when he stumbled and improperly chanted some of Pesachim, Miriam jumped right in to correct him. To Joheved's amazement, he didn't appear offended at all, not even surprised, and they were soon reciting the week's lesson together in the vineyard. But Joheved couldn't bring herself to join them, though she knew the Mishnah perfectly.

It never occurred to Benjamin that Miriam wouldn't know the Mishnah. After all, she attended her father's classes nearly as often as the male students. Benjamin was the first in his family to attend yeshiva, so he hadn't been taught who could study Talmud and who couldn't. His father and his two brothers had started working when they reached their majority, but they were now sufficiently prosperous to delay his own entry into the workforce.

When Benjamin returned home for Shavuot in the middle of May, he proudly recited Mishnah Pesachim and explained how much of what they did during the Passover Seder originated in this very Mishnah. His parents were pleased to hear how wise and patient his teacher was, and how he studied in the *maître's* vineyard. For Benjamin to learn both Talmud and viticulture at the Troyes yeshiva was an unexpected bonus. When he innocently mentioned that he worked closely with Salomon's daughter in the vineyard, his parents decided to delay their search for his bride until he'd spent more time at his studies.

After the festival, Benjamin took solace in knowing that, with more students beginning their studies during the Hot Fair, he would no longer be the newest one. To celebrate, he decided to lead them on a beehive hunt when the vines flowered. The blossoms attracted thousands of bees from the surrounding countryside, and if a fellow were lucky, he could follow one of them back to its hive and plunder their supply of honey.

Soon the weather warmed, and morning found the vineyard shrouded in a soft haze. Salomon and his students were in the vineyard every day, tying up the branches and keeping the tendrils from entangling each other. There was a sense of urgency in their efforts; all work on the vines would halt when the buds flowered. During the delicate time of flowering and pollination, nobody was allowed in the vineyard.

When the first yellowish blossoms began to open at the base of the vine, the children's eagerness to search for beehives reached a fever pitch. Salomon wasn't optimistic about them finding a beehive, but as long as they stayed out of the vineyard, he had no objection. The days were long, and there was time enough for both lessons and games. He even agreed to let Joheved and Miriam join the hunt.

Salomon would put his extra time to good use by answering some legal questions that had arrived with the good traveling weather. Asking him to decide their difficult judicial issues was a sign that local communities recognized his scholarship. This question-and-answer process was called responsa, and the more renowned a rabbi became, the more time he spent on it.

The questions sent to Salomon were simple, and he spent more time writing a proper introduction than pondering the legal difficulties. He sighed as he quickly answered a query pertaining to Passover, probably sent after the fact by an inquirer hoping to have his decision upheld. "A Jew accustomed to receiving daily loaves of bread from a special (non-Jewish) client may not receive them during the week of Passover, but may receive them all after Passover for that missed week." Undoubtedly the more complex issues went to Worms or Mayence.

Salomon also spent hours conversing with Robert of Montier-la-Celle, both using their forced rest from vineyard duties to study scripture. Some of the students were surprised to find a monk calling on their teacher, but Joheved and Miriam were used to Robert's visits and didn't give the two men a second glance. They couldn't wait to start looking for beehives.

The first afternoon, the children alternated between enjoying the grape blossoms' perfume as they waited to sight a bee and running around helter-skelter chasing the bees they saw. Soon they became familiar enough with the location of the peasants' hives that they could quit following a bee as soon as it veered in that direction. After a few days, they were consistently ending up in the forest, but it was harder to follow a bee among the trees.

On Shabbat of the second week of flowering, they knew there wasn't much time left. The blossoms at the very end of the branches had opened, and soon pollination would be complete. They ran from the vineyard into the forest, through the trees, and then, once the bee was lost, back to the vineyard again, getting more discouraged as the afternoon wore on. Perhaps the beehive was farther into the woods than they could go on Shabbat.

When Benjamin and Miriam managed to follow a bee so closely that they were sure the hive couldn't be far away, only to lose sight of it among the fluttering branches, they sat down on the ground in dismay instead of running back to the vineyard to start over. That's when Miriam heard it, or rather, them.

"Listen," she whispered with an urgency that grabbed her companion's attention. "I hear buzzing."

They focused all their attention on their powers of hearing. "You're right," Benjamin whispered back. "I hear it too."

They silently made their way towards what was obviously going to be the hive. The humming was getting so loud that the number of bees involved must be enormous, but they couldn't see any.

Finally, when it seemed like they must be right on top of the hive, Benjamin looked up and pointed. Miriam gazed skyward, and there were more bees than she had ever seen, flying in and out of the top of a tall, dead tree. They stood and stared in awe.

They had actually found the hive.

By the time Joheved and the other students reached the dead tree, their enthusiasm had faded. They couldn't reach the honey without cutting down the tree, and that meant adults would have to be consulted. But when they returned to the yeshiva, Salomon didn't want to plan any work on this day of rest.

"We'll discuss it later, after Shabbat has ended, after we make Havdalah," he said.

In June the Sabbath ends late, and by the time three stars appeared in the sky, Rachel and Grandmama Leah had already gone to bed. Everyone involved in the frantic beehive hunt was nearing exhaustion as they gathered in Salomon's courtyard for Havdalah, the ceremony that marks the close of Shabbat. Even if she had been awake, Rachel was too little to hold the ritual braided candle, so the honor fell to Miriam, the next youngest daughter.

"Hold the candle high," Rivka urged her. "So you'll have a tall husband."

But Miriam kept it close to her, refusing to lift it above her own head. She kept her eyes on the candle's flame, which flared brightly with its three wicks, while Joheved surveyed the circle of students. Did anyone else find it significant that Benjamin was the shortest boy in the group?

Any woman who drank from the Havdalah cup would grow a beard, so Joheved passed the wine on for the boys to bless and taste. Rivka handed around the container of fragrant spices, a reminder of the Sabbath's sweetness to fortify their spirits as they reentered the regular workweek. Joheved recognized cinnamon and cloves, but there were more.

In the Talmud, the rabbis taught that wine and spices restored one's learning, so the scholars' Havdalah ceremony came to include the incantation against Potach, Demon Prince of Forgetfulness. Salomon made his students recite the incantation together with him, to protect them from forgetting their Torah learning during the coming week. Miriam said it out loud as well, but Joheved murmured it under her breath.

Finally, with many in the group stifling yawns, it was time to chant the final blessing. The candlelight cast strange shadows behind the circle of students, their faces distorted as the flame grew and danced about. There was a liminal moment of sadness as the candle was poised about the wine cup and then a soft communal sigh along with the hiss of the extinguishing flame. Everyone wished each other, "A good week, *shavua tov.*" The moon had risen, allowing Salomon to watch as the boys climbed up to the attic. Downstairs, Joheved and Miriam were waiting for him.

"Papa." Miriam had a worried look on her face. "What will happen to the poor bees when their tree is chopped down? Where will they go? How can they live if we take away their honey?"

"Don't worry, ma fille; the bees will be fine." He smiled down at her. Sarah was right; she would make a good midwife; she was even concerned about hurting insects. "Robert told me that the monks of Montier-la-Celle would send someone to move our bees into a new hive at the abbey. So we can't go for the honey until Monday; we have to wait until their sabbath is over."

"You and Robert planned all this before you even knew that we'd found the beehive." Joheved was more convinced than ever that her father was the wisest man in France.

As the three of them climbed the stairs, Salomon seemed to be thinking out loud. "It's interesting . . . I've read about honey so often in Torah, but I've never seen the inside of a beehive."

Once in bed, Miriam stayed awake only long enough for the implication of her father's words to reach her. "Joheved." She nudged her drowsy sister. "Maybe Papa will let us come too."

"That would be nice," Joheved mumbled, and she drifted off to sleep wondering how they could possibly arrange it.

As it turned out, Aunt Sarah made all the arrangements they needed by announcing that as long as everyone was spending an afternoon in the forest, she could use help gathering her special midwife's herbs. Now was the perfect time for Miriam to begin her education on the subject, and it wouldn't hurt for Joheved to become familiar with these things as well. They could even watch Rachel at the same time.

Monday morning at dawn, Miriam was collecting eggs and wondering why Benjamin hadn't joined her the last two days. Surely he wasn't ill. Suddenly the courtyard gate opened and he came in from the street, carrying several loaves of fresh bread.

"There you are, Benjamin." She ran over and closed the gate behind him. "It's thoughtful of you to get us fresh bread so early."

"It's more thoughtful than you think." He smiled at her slyly. "Can you keep a secret?"

Intrigued, Miriam nodded.

"I've been worried about somebody else getting our honey, so the last two nights, I slept in the forest, next to our tree."

"Benjamin, were you out of your mind? Don't you know how dangerous it is to be out in the forest alone at night?"

He looked at her in surprise. "But I was perfectly safe. There aren't any highwaymen so close to the town walls. And I wouldn't have gotten lost; there was a moon out."

"But what about demons, what about Agrat bat Machlat and her eighteen myriads? You know there's nothing they'd like better than to find you, all by yourself, in the forest, in the middle of the night." Miriam paused for emphasis after each danger. "I can't believe you'd be so reckless."

"I'm sorry, but I just had to be sure that our honey was all right." He stared at the ground, unwilling to face her. She sounded just like his mother did when she caught him doing something risky. "I thought you only have to worry about Agrat bat Machlat on Wednesday and Saturday nights. Besides, I had my tefillin with me, so I was protected." Not that all the tefillin and holy books in Salomon's house kept Lillit from finding him in the attic.

"That was clever of you to buy the bread, just in case somebody else saw you coming home at dawn," Miriam admitted. There was no point in scolding Benjamin now. They were going after the honey that day, so he wouldn't be spending any more nights in the forest.

The sun was high in the sky as Sarah and her three nieces accompanied Salomon and his students, Joseph and two strong servants, plus the beekeeper and a couple of novices from the abbey. When they reached the forest, the groups divided according to gender, the males swiftly heading for the bee tree, their eyes fixed skyward, while the females meandered slowly in no particular direction, their concentration focused on the ground.

Aunt Sarah directed most of her instruction at Miriam, pointing out the various herbs and explaining how each was used. "See these columbines' large downward-hanging violet flowers? An infusion of ragwort and columbine seeds helps speed the birth, so we'll come back in the fall to collect them."

They walked a bit farther and came to a small bush whose felt-like leaves were green on top and white underneath. "This plant has two names, artemisia and wormwood. Tea made from its leaves helps the anxious mother relax, while its seeds bring on a woman's menses when it's delayed."

Sarah talked on, explaining the properties of each herb as they came upon it. "Sage tea is good for a woman likely to miscarry, due to slipperiness of her womb, but it's best collected later in the season. Nettle juice and powdered bark of black alder help stop excessive bleeding. I mix mugwort with cowslip and pepper to help the mother sneeze her baby out."

"Sneeze her baby out?" Miriam asked in surprise.

"Oui," her aunt replied with a smile. "After a long labor, when the baby is close to being born, the mother may lack strength for the final effort. When she sneezes, though, she cannot help but push the child through the birth passage at the same time."

Miriam was fascinated with Aunt Sarah's lessons, but Joheved grew bored and directed her attention towards entertaining Rachel. Together they chased dragonflies and butterflies, stopping occasionally to help Sarah dig up a special root or pick some unusual leaves. In the distance, they could hear the sounds of men wielding axes.

Suddenly Joheved thought of something she'd never considered before. Sarah was Mama's older sister, which meant she ought to know about Mama's youth. They knew she'd grown up in Allemagne and that her parents were dead, but no matter how nicely she and Miriam asked, Rivka would not talk about her childhood. But now Mama wasn't here and Aunt Sarah was.

"Aunt Sarah." Joheved made her move. "What was it like when you and Mama were little? She won't tell us very much about it."

"I'm not surprised," her aunt said, picking some artemisia leaves and adding them to her basket. "Our mother—may her memory be for blessing—died in childbirth along with the next baby."

Miriam impulsively joined the questioning. "Is that why you became a midwife, Aunt Sarah?"

"You may be right." She was lost in thought for a moment, and then continued. "Of course, Judah, our papa—may his merit protect us—married again."

The girls waited silently for her to proceed. "His new wife was young and soon had babies of her own. She wasn't mean to Rivka, or anything like that, but she preferred her own children. She wasn't an educated woman either, not like your grandmama."

Sarah frowned in disapproval. "She filled your mother's head with tales of *mazikim,* evil spirits and demons, until Rivka was afraid to leave the house without our mother's protective amulet in her sleeve. Our father had to make a silver case so she could wear it around her neck instead."

"Mama still wears that amulet," Joheved said, helping her aunt strip the leaves off a mugwort bush. "Aunt Sarah, you go out at night all the time. Aren't you scared of demons?"

"Well, of course I want to avoid the *mazikim;* everyone does. But good, pious folk who say their bedtime Shema and don't brag about their good fortune shouldn't be bothered by demons. You two don't need to worry; your father is a talmid chacham."

They came to a grove of black alder trees and stopped to peel off the bark. "How did Mama end up marrying Papa?" Miriam asked.

"Being the oldest, I married while my father was still alive, so I got my share of his estate as my dowry." Sarah paused and a flicker of pain creased her forehead. "My first husband died without giving me any children, so I collected my *ketubah* payment and married his younger brother. I had just given birth to my son, Eleazar, when my second husband died too, and with that *ketubah* I had enough money to live on without getting married again. Which was just as well, since few men will marry a 'killer wife' who's already buried two husbands."

"So what happened to Mama after you got married?" Joheved wanted to hear about their mother's life, not Aunt Sarah's.

"Then our father died." Sarah sighed. "And that meant his estate was mortgaged to our stepmother's *ketubah.* Naturally she wanted to provide for her own children, rather than set aside money for Rivka's dowry."

"But Mama knew she'd marry eventually," Miriam said, thinking of Catharina, "instead of staying on as a servant."

Sarah picked up the alder bark that had fallen around the base of the tree. "Oui, and it fell to our brother, Isaac, to arrange her marriage. Salomon was also a student at the yeshiva in Mayence, and Leah didn't care about a big dowry; she wanted a daughter-in-law from a learned family. So it seemed a good match. Your mama met your papa only once before their wedding in Troyes."

Rachel began to lag behind and Joheved hoisted the toddler onto her hip. "So how did you come to live here, Aunt Sarah?" she asked. "Did you stay with Mama after her wedding or did you move to Troyes later?"

"I'm not proud of what happened next, but as long as I've told you this much . . ." Sarah paused a moment. "You may as well know that in-laws don't always get along. My brother and I stayed in Troyes for the celebratory wedding week, and what I saw of Leah's domineering ways convinced me that I should move to Troyes to help my lonely and frightened sister. I'm ashamed to say that I thought Leah would treat your mother badly."

Joheved had suspected there was some problem between Aunt Sarah and Grandmama Leah because their aunt didn't seem to visit anymore. She'd never dared to ask about it, but now at least she'd hear Aunt Sarah's side of the story.

"When I found out that Troyes' Jewish midwife had recently died, I made up my mind. My son, Eleazar, was grown, living with my brother Isaac in Mayence and studying at the yeshiva. So I bought a house here, in the same courtyard as Leah's. She was immediately suspicious."

Joheved and Miriam stared at each in amazement. Rachel was squirming to get down, and distracted, Joheved almost set her down in a stand of nettles. Who would have imagined her aunt and grandmother being jealous of Mama's affection?

"But there was no battle for Rivka's loyalty." Sarah shook her head wanly. "My sister was relieved, happy even, to be the dutiful daughter-in-law under Leah's overprotective wing, to let Leah run the household. Leah became the mother she never had."

They stopped to inventory the herbs they'd collected so far. "When Rivka had you, Joheved, and Miriam soon after, Leah became a doting grandmother," Sarah said. "And now I have to admit that Leah did an excellent job of teaching her granddaughters."

Sarah paused to let her nieces enjoy the memory of their grandmother in her better days. "But then Leah's illness started. She imagined that I was plotting behind her back, and she even accused me of putting a curse on Rivka, my own sister, so she wouldn't have any more children."

"It was too much for me." There was hurt and anger in her eyes. "I didn't want to cause any more grief than Rivka already had with Leah, so I tried to avoid her whenever Leah was home."

Joheved and Miriam stood in pained silence. Each struggled to find something suitable to say, but could think of nothing that might begin to address the years of estrangement between their mother and her sister. In desperation, Joheved said the first thing that came into her mind.

"Aunt Sarah, what's a wandering womb?"

The older woman turned to her in surprise. "Where did you hear about wandering wombs?"

"Somebody told me that girls who study too much will get it."

"Joheved." Aunt Sarah smiled and shook her head. "Girls don't get wandering wombs; only grown women do. And the proper term is hysteria," she continued, this time addressing Miriam as well, "which is caused by a wandering womb."

"What are the symptoms?" Miriam asked eagerly.

"It depends on where the womb wanders to. If it goes to her head, the woman suffers from headaches. When it presses against her lungs, she has trouble breathing, and if it lodges near her stomach or intestines, she experiences indigestion. But only the Notzrim get hysteria."

Observing her nieces' puzzled expressions, she explained, "Not all the Notzrim, of course, just women who don't marry, like nuns. Married women, Jewish or not, are not susceptible to hysteria."

Sarah had a good idea what the girls' next question was going to be, but before she could decide how to tell her innocent young nieces that it was regular sexual relations that prevented hysteria, the men's enthusiastic shouts interrupted their conversation. They picked up Rachel and the herbs they'd collected, and arrived in time to see the men carefully lowering the top of the honey tree, now severed from its trunk, to the ground with a contraption of ropes.

The hollow tree was almost completely filled with honeycombs. It took every container they had plus Salomon's empty wine barrels to hold it all. Benjamin immediately became a hero to his fellows, and his popularity grew when Salomon sold the excess honey at the Hot Fair and divided the proceeds among the students. His pupils couldn't believe their good fortune; here they were, at the largest fair in France, their purses full of spending money.

eleven

Summer 4831 (1071 C.E.)

Once the foreign merchants arrived in Troyes, Salomon's yeshiva gained more students. Shemiah ben Asher, an associate of Hiyya ibn Ezra, came all the way from Provence for this purpose. Shemiah was accompanied by two boys, the older one about the age for starting yeshiva, the younger perhaps attending school for the first time. Father and sons were very tanned, though not so swarthy as Hiyya, with dark, curling locks that cascaded out from under their hats. Shemiah had an unusual offer for Salomon.

"I would like my son Asher to begin his studies in Troyes immediately, and I also wish to secure little Eliezer's future education," Shemiah said. "In payment, I offer you a pair of Jewish slaves, Baruch and Anna. I intended to sell them in Andalusia, but since they converted to Judaism, I have no choice but to sell or trade them to a Jew."

"Slaves?" Salomon knew that some foreign Jews owned slaves, but they were a rarity in France.

"Few of us still trade in slaves," Shemiah said. "I have considered leaving the field, since it is getting more difficult to find pagans for sale." He paused and frowned slightly. "The Byzantines who worship the Hanged One are rapidly converting the Slavs to their misguided faith, and the French bishops will only allow pagan slaves to cross their lands."

Salomon's eyes narrowed with suspicion. "How do you get these slaves, and where do they come from?"

"The land of the Slavs, which is east of the Danube, is regularly invaded by barbarian armies who are only too happy to sell the vanquished occupants into servitude."

Hiyya leaned forward and addressed his host. "Surely you see, Salomon, how acquiring Jewish slaves would benefit you in your wine-making business. And with so many students, an extra maidservant will lessen the burden on your wife and daughters."

Salomon saw the hope in his wife's eyes. Taking care of his mother and the yeshiva students was a hardship for her. "I assume that Baruch and Anna are married?"

"Oui," Shemiah replied.

"Do they speak our language?" Rivka asked, encouraged that Salomon had asked about the slaves' status. "I need servants I can talk to."

"Baruch's French is very good, and Anna's is improving daily," Shemiah said. "Why don't you come meet them?"

He took them to the fairgrounds near St. Jean's square, where Baruch and Anna were waiting. "Rabbi Salomon ben Isaac, this is my servant, Baruch ben Abraham." Shemiah motioned to the woman. "And his wife, Anna."

The two couples exchanged glances, and Salomon hoped he didn't look too much like a shopper checking merchandise for defects. Baruch was trying to stand calmly, while Anna, a rabbit forced out of its hole into a predator's view, cowered at his side.

Rivka recognized the dread and panic in Anna's demeanor, and felt her heart swell with empathy. It had been so difficult when she'd first moved to Troyes, living with strangers and not knowing their language. She felt an urge to protect and shelter the frightened young woman. Rivka looked at Salomon, who was watching for her reaction, and gave him a nearly imperceptible nod.

Now that he had his wife's approval, Salomon examined the slaves more closely. The man was in his early twenties and the woman slightly younger. They were fair skinned and freckled, and the man had straight, reddish-brown hair. The woman seemed to possess red hair as well, but it was hidden under her cap. Both were unusually tall and looked strong and sturdy.

"Very well, I'll take them," Salomon said. "It will be a relief to have their help, especially during the wine harvest."

One morning in mid-August, Joheved was awakened by Leah's shrill voice, insisting that she needed to go on a walk. Joheved listened as Anna soothingly told her to be patient, to wait until her hair was done. Outside she could hear Baruch chopping wood in the courtyard. Oddly, it seemed as if the slaves had been with them for months instead of weeks. Baruch had easily learned his vineyard duties, and Anna needed no lessons in caring for Leah and Rachel.

And just in time, Joheved thought, recalling how difficult last summer had been. There were so many more wine buyers this summer, people who could show up at any time of day, and the accounts were more complicated too. A few customers paid cash, but most, like the baker and butcher, traded their wares for Salomon's wine. Thank heaven Anna was able to keep Leah occupied; otherwise Joheved would never have time to balance the household books properly. It was a shame that Grandmama was never able to remember who Baruch was.

In the next room, Leah complained again that she wanted to go out now, and again Anna calmed her, assuring her that Master Salomon was almost done with his prayers and then he'd be happy to walk with her. It was early Elul, the month preceding the Days of Awe, when Papa got up before dawn to add *selichot,* special penitential prayers and supplications, to his morning litany.

Joheved, sure she would have to lead Rosh Hashanah and Yom Kippur services for the women, wanted to pray *selichot* herself in preparation, but it was difficult waking up early.

But now she was awake with time enough for the longest prayer. When she heard her father join Grandmama Leah downstairs, Joheved stepped into the hall. Mama and the servants were below, preparing the morning meal. She tiptoed towards her parents' room, peeked in, and saw that Rachel was still asleep in her cradle. Another late sleeper like her.

Then she noticed that Papa had forgotten to put his tefillin away. Joheved stared at the worn black leather straps and boxes that made up the tefillin, one box for the hand and the other for the forehead, as it was written in Deuteronomy, following the Shema. "Bind them as a sign on your hand and let them be a symbol on your forehead." Before they were Papa's, they had belonged to Grandpapa Isaac. It didn't seem right for such holy objects to be left out on the bed, exposed and vulnerable. What if a mouse gnawed on the leather?

With every intention of returning the tefillin to their storage bag, Joheved silently entered her parents' room. She picked up the arm box first; its long straps were in disarray and she tried to gather them up quickly. She couldn't help but caress the lengths of black leather, supple from years of handling. Papa, and all Jewish men, wore tefillin when they said their morning prayers, as a sign of accepting the commandments. Tefillin were also powerful protection—Papa had hung them on the bed frame when Mama was in labor.

Joheved had almost finished folding up the straps when a shocking thought struck her. She accepted the commandments. Why shouldn't she pray with tefillin? Nobody would see her if she closed the door. She'd just try it once, to see what it was like.

Shaking with fear and excitement, she rolled up the sleeves of her chemise, unwrapped the tefillin's arm straps, and started putting them on. When she finished winding them around her hand, a sense of holiness enveloped her that obliterated any feeling of wrongdoing. The sacred leather, pressing tightly against her skin, gave her a constant awareness of the Holy One's presence. Before, it had been hard to shut out the world and concentrate on her prayers. Wearing tefillin, she had no difficulty devoting herself to her *selichot.*

When her morning blessings were done, she reluctantly removed the tefillin and carefully replaced them on the bed, just as she had found them. As much as she regretted leaving them exposed, she didn't dare put them away and have Papa wonder who had disturbed his things. Then, heart pounding, she slipped back to her room, leaving Rachel still asleep and nobody the wiser. The rest of the morning Joheved could feel where the tefillin straps had left their mark on her arm, and she was careful to keep her chemise sleeves lowered.

The next day, overcome with remorse, she fought the temptation to wear Papa's tefillin again. But she kept thinking how the tight tefillin straps made her feel as if the Holy One was holding her arm Himself, and she was unable to focus on her prayers. So the following morning, terrified but helpless to stop herself, she stole into Papa's bedroom and prayed with his tefillin. Again she felt the Holy One's strength fill her as she donned the ritual objects, and she knew she couldn't be committing a sin.

Except for Shabbat, when tefillin weren't worn because the holiday itself is the sign of devotion, Joheved began urging Miriam to wake her early. Then, as soon as Papa took Grandmama Leah on their walk, she quickly put on his tefillin and prayed.

It wasn't long before Mama, not Papa, discovered her, after coming upstairs to wake her sleepyhead daughters.

As Rivka watched in appalled silence, she couldn't help but observe the look of awe and concentration on Joheved's face. She shook her head, sighed heavily and waited for her daughter to finish, all the while trying to decide what she should say.

It was her inability to give Salomon sons that had made him teach the girls Talmud in the first place, Rivka thought bitterly. She had hoped that once the yeshiva was thriving he would concentrate on his male students and forget about educating his daughters; but no, he had encouraged the girls to listen to his lessons. Perhaps he had sanctioned them to lay tefillin too.

Rivka groaned inwardly. This could only lead to marital problems for her daughters. Salomon had made good on his promise to find Joheved a talmid husband and would likely find matches for the other girls among his students, but what would they think when their wives acted more like men than women? Rivka wrung her hands in frustration. How could she prevent her husband from raising the girls however he wished, particularly when they were willing accomplices?

The surprise and fear on Joheved's face when she turned and saw her mother convinced Rivka that Salomon knew nothing of his daughter's actions. Joheved had tried to think of what she would say when she was finally caught, as she knew she would be, but she was speechless. She quietly put the tefillin away while waiting for her mother's angry lecture, one she knew she deserved.

But Rivka couldn't bring herself to chastise her daughter. The girl had only been praying, after all. Besides, this was Salomon's problem. He had Joheved studying Talmud like a boy—how would he react when he found that she wanted to pray like one too? Rivka felt a surge of satisfaction at her husband's dilemma.

She addressed Joheved simply. "If your father allows you to pray with tefillin, then any objections I have are meaningless. You are a betrothed maiden, no longer a child, so I have no intention of running to your father with this tale of misbehavior. You must speak to him yourself, and not use his things again until he gives you permission."

Tears of remorse and shame filled Joheved's eyes; she had not expected to be treated with such respect. "I'll talk to Papa soon; I promise." Unable to face her mother, she slowly walked past her, eyes fixed on the floor. "I'm sorry, Mama. I should have asked him first."

But Joheved couldn't find the right time or the right way to ask Salomon about the tefillin, even though morning prayers no longer felt right without them.

Miriam was sympathetic, but not very encouraging. "It's too bad he's not still in Mayence," she said as they took turns braiding each other's hair. "Then you could write him, and not have to actually face him with your question."

Her sister's offhand comment was just what Joheved needed. "Miriam, I will write to him. I'll send him a query just like other people do when they have a difficult ritual question."

"A betrothed maiden (thus she is an adult) who studies Talmud (therefore she is learned) wishes to observe the commandment of tefillin. Is this permitted?" Joheved read the letter out loud for Miriam's approval. "There, what do you think?"

"Short and to the point, it sounds fine to me." Miriam gave Joheved a quick hug. "Good luck."

That evening Joheved paced the salon waiting for her father to come home. She wanted to give him the letter in private, and she hoped he would be in a pleasant mood after studying with other scholars. She tried to compose herself, to be ready to defend her position against any objections he might offer. But when she heard the door open, her heart began to pound.

Salomon, tired but satisfied after a long day in the yeshiva, slowly set down his manuscripts. He was taken aback when Joheved handed him the query; surely it hadn't arrived at this late hour. His daughter seemed unusually quiet. Normally she was full of questions if he returned while she was still awake. He began to tell her about his studies, but she stopped him and asked him to read the letter first.

Salomon read it twice, then surveyed his visibly nervous daughter and weighed how to respond. She couldn't know that, in Worms, the prayer leader in the women's section of the synagogue reputedly wore tefillin, or that Tractate Eruvin reported that King Saul's daughter, Michal, did so as well. In fact, a woman laying tefillin wasn't nearly as scandalous as a woman studying Talmud. But it was not something to be done lightly. Salomon decided this would be an opportunity for Joheved to learn how responsa answers were determined.

"This question is a bit more complicated than the ones I usually receive. My reputation must be growing," he teased her. "You can help me answer it by getting out Tractate Berachot. There's a section in the third chapter that should be useful."

Joheved's hands shook as she lifted the manuscript out of the storage chest. Papa must have figured out who wrote the query, yet he wasn't acting angry or even surprised. Did he really need to look up the answer? He knew Berachot by heart. Maybe he wanted her to see the answer herself, so she wouldn't be angry at him for refusing her permission. With great trepidation, she began to read from the spot he pointed to. It was in Hebrew, and she could see it was Mishnah.

> Women, slaves, and minors are exempt from reciting the Shema and from laying tefillin. But they are obligated in prayer and in the command to attach a mezuzah.

This didn't sound right. She and Miriam both said the Shema at night as protection against demons; every Jew did. "Papa, why are women exempt from these mitzvot?"

Salomon stroked his beard as he answered her. "In general, women and slaves are exempt from time-bound positive mitzvot, those that command us to do something at a certain time. And when you think about it, both the Shema and tefillin involve specific times. We say the Shema in the morning and at night. Tefillin are time bound because they are not worn at night or on Shabbat."

Joheved nodded and Salomon continued, "The reason women and slaves are exempt from them is because a slave's time belongs to his master and a woman's time belongs to her husband."

She could see the sentence that mentioned tefillin and nervously read on.

> Women are exempt from tefillin—this is obvious.

But Joheved didn't see anything obvious about it. "It is?"

"The Gemara wonders why the Mishnah even mentions tefillin, since we know it is time bound," he explained.

And indeed, the answer followed.

> Since tefillin is compared to mezuzah, you might think that women should be required to lay tefillin just as they are required to attach a mezuzah to their doors. The Mishnah informs us this is not so.

"Tefillin and mezuzah are both mentioned in the same section of Deuteronomy as the Shema, which is why they are discussed here together," Salomon said.

To Joheved none of this made sense. The Gemara's objection sounded logical to her, the Mishnah's rules arbitrary. And neither said whether women were permitted to wear tefillin or not. She was about to ask her father about this, when Salomon urged her to finish the passage.

> Since the commandment of mezuzah is compared to the commandment of Torah study, you might think that women should be exempt from mezuzah just as they are exempt from Torah study. The Mishnah tells us that women are obligated to attach the mezuzah.

"Women are exempt from Torah study because it says that fathers are obligated to teach their 'sons' Torah; daughters are not mentioned." Salomon stopped to think. "It also says those who study Torah prolong their days . . . but can this mean that only men need their life lengthened, not women?" He sat stroking his beard, a puzzled expression on his face. "A difficult question, and I don't have an answer."

Joheved's jaw dropped. She had never heard Papa admit he didn't understand something in the Talmud. She sensed that their lesson was over, but he hadn't answered her question. Or had he? The Gemara stated that women were exempt from saying the Shema and from Torah study, yet she and Miriam both recited the Shema and studied Torah. If these were permitted, why not tefillin?

She gathered up her courage and repeated these thoughts to her father. He stared at her silently, a small smile on his face, and then she realized that she had won. He had made no objection to her argument.

"You realize that once you take on this mitzvah, you are committed to it?" he asked with a sigh. At least she wouldn't be wearing tefillin in public, like the woman in Worms. Here in Troyes, they were worn only at home.

"Oui, Papa."

Salomon's voice became stern. "I cannot stress too strongly the importance of scrupulous cleanliness before you put on tefillin, especially when you're older. Do you understand?" Much of the opposition to women wearing *tefillin* stemmed from fear that they would not be sufficiently sanitary during niddah.

"Don't worry, Papa. I'll be careful to wash my hands first."

"But you are betrothed now." He paused and stroked his beard. "Perhaps we should write to Meir about this."

Joheved's heart sank. Did her time belong to Meir already? What if he didn't approve? And even if he did, it could take months before they'd find out.

"As long as you live in my house and not your husband's, my permission is all you need," he decided.

Joheved's belly relaxed and she gave a sigh of relief.

"And I suppose my permission is meaningless unless you have tefillin to pray with," Salomon continued to the logical conclusion. "Which means we must buy you some."

"Merci, Papa." Joheved hadn't thought that far. But Papa was right; she couldn't expect to borrow his every morning.

Even so, Joheved was surprised when Salomon presented her with her own set of tefillin the following Sunday, just before she went to bed. Miriam stroked the black leather and looked hopefully at her father, who responded that she was not yet old enough to take on the responsibility of tefillin. Yet as much as Joheved basked in her sister's admiration, her pride was tinged with trepidation at how Mama would react.

Walking downstairs the next morning, Joheved steeled herself to face her mother's wrath. But there were no clanging pots or words of recrimination; Rivka served breakfast and disner in a sullen silence. Overcome with guilt, Joheved had to say something to heal the breach. Rosh Hashanah was less than a week away.

Joheved finally found her mother alone, weeding the herb garden. "Mama," she said, stooping to help her. "I can't explain it, but tefillin makes me pray better. Please don't be angry."

Rivka shook her head sadly and sighed. Why did it upset her so much? "Joheved, just as the Holy One created roosters to crow and hens to lay eggs, so too it is with people. It's not natural for girls to study Talmud and pray with tefillin; it's not right."

"But Papa found me a husband more learned than I am," Joheved cried out. Wasn't that what Mama cared about?

"If your father wishes to indulge you and pretend he has a son, that is his affair. But Meir may prefer that his wife pursue more feminine pursuits." Rivka's voice softened and she said, "Joheved, dear, think about what I'm telling you. I don't want you to be unhappy when you're living with your husband."

Would Meir really object to her praying with tefillin? Joheved didn't want to know if her mother was right. She and Meir were married now, so her time belonged to him . . . except he didn't know about her tefillin. That was the answer; somehow she'd find a way to pray privately. Then he'd never know she wore tefillin.

Summer was drawing to a close, and just when vintners thought they'd managed to get through the season successfully, they were denied the fair weather they'd anticipated. The last week in August brought such a drop in temperature that Bernard the cellarer briefly considered delaying the grape picking. But cool, damp weather inevitably brought a grey woolly fungus, *pourriture grise,* which quickly ruined a vineyard full of grapes.

Many believed the ripening process was like pregnancy, that Le Bon Dieu decrees that a grape will be ripe one hundred days after flowering, just as a child will be born ten lunar months after conception. The weather affected only the flavor of the ripe grape, not the time to reach ripeness. Having originally set the harvest for the hundred-day mark, Bernard declared that it would be prudent not to change it.

Salomon held to a middle ground. "Just as most babies are born after ten months in the womb, with some early and some late, so most grapes ripen about one hundred days after flowering. But it seems to me that heat tends to speed the process while the cold delays it." He explained that cool weather had both a good and bad side for the winemaker. "The wine's flavor may suffer because the grapes can not reach optimum sweetness, but fermentation will be slower, and thus easier to control."

A few days later, when carts full of grapes began to arrive at Salomon's courtyard, Baruch declared to Anna, "If this is a slow fermentation, let the Holy One save us from a fast one."

For the next three weeks, except for prayers and meals, Salomon's household and students spent every waking hour on the vintage. First the grapes were piled into vats in the courtyard, the last job performed by non-Jews. Then Salomon's people took over. Wearing linen boots and their oldest chemises, they trod the grapes vigorously.

Then they waited for the stinging smell of fermentation to fill the courtyard. From then on they labored in shifts, both day and night. Morning and afternoon, Joheved, Miriam and Anna carefully climbed into one of the vats. Their combined weight was barely enough, even with a bit of bouncing, to break the thick raft of skins and grapes buoyed on the surface by the fizzling fermentation below.

Once into the warm half-wine, they used blunt wooden spades to turn the raft fragments upside down and tread them back in. Anna's years of hard living had given her a strength and stamina that now served her well, despite her pregnancy, and the girls agreed that they could not have worked an entire vat without her.

In the other vats, Baruch and the younger students did the same, all under the watchful gaze of Grandmama Leah. Leah no longer needed walks to soothe her agitation. She circled the courtyard like a hawk, intently observing the treaders, every so often dipping a finger in the vats and taking a taste. At night, the courtyard lit by torches, Salomon and the older students took their turn.

Joheved and Miriam had never spent so much time in the vats before, and never without their father's supervision. This stage of making wine had its risks. Once the deep wooden vat was full, too much carbon dioxide could form and suffocate the treaders. The danger was greatest in warm years when fermentation went quickly, but with the weather on the chilly side, Salomon didn't expect any such problems. He worried about the process halting before enough sugar had been changed into alcohol.

Everyone was relieved when the stormy first phase of the fermentation, *bouillage*, was over in time for the Days of Awe. Thereafter the fermentation would proceed calmly for another ten to twenty days, allowing time for the intense contemplation and prayer that the holiday period demanded. Joheved and Miriam successfully took turns leading the women for Rosh Hashanah and Yom Kippur, even though it took every bit of concentration they had to stay awake and follow the service.

Once the contents of the vats needed only a brief daily treading, the workers returned to their normal lives. One arduous task remained, that of removing the heavy stems, now free of grapes, from the vats and discarding them. Joheved listened carefully as Grandmama Leah and Salomon tasted the half-wine and consulted with each other about whether to leave all or part of the stalks in the vats, and for how long. In a good vintage they gave the wine more astringent tannins, greater flavor and bite. But in a cold, damp year they merely diluted it.

Baruch was working in one of the vats when Leah came over, took a taste, and suddenly prodded him with a large wooden rake. Before he could reply, Joheved rushed over to see what her grandmother wanted with him and to intercede if necessary. Leah poked Baruch again and demanded, "Young man, take this rake and pull it through the crushed grapes, from bottom to top. Then dump any stems that cling to it outside the vat."

Joheved stared at her in astonishment; Leah had never spoken to Baruch before. He raked out several large stalks and asked her, "Mistress, do you want me to take out all the stems?"

Leah took another taste and made a sour face. "Bah, this stuff has no flavor; the grapes were picked before they were properly ripe. You may as well take out all the stems before what little quality this wine has is lost altogether."

Baruch took a drink himself, not wanting to miss the subtlety Leah had discerned, but the liquid tasted sweet and syrupy. "How can anybody call this flavorless?" he whispered to Joheved.

Leah chuckled at his puzzled look. "When you've been making wine for as long as I have, young man, then maybe you'll know what I'm talking about."

Joheved had a taste too, and Leah looked at her expectantly. "It's sweet, but not as sweet as other years, I think," Joheved said hesitantly. Her grandmother's smile of approval emboldened her to continue. "It's definitely not as sweet as two years ago, when everyone said the vintage was superb."

Of course Leah didn't remember what the vintage was like that year, but she did know how sweet an excellent wine should taste at this stage in its formation. "Joheved is going to be a great winemaker some day, just like her grandmother," she announced.

Once the stalks were removed from the vats, their contents would sit undisturbed until the grape skins and other solid debris settled to the bottom. Then it was just a matter of running the wine into the casks and storing them in the cellar. When that final job was done, it would be time for the Cold Fair, with its return of merchants and students to Salomon's yeshiva.

But winter also brought the pox to Troyes, and Rachel was among those stricken. An endemic childhood disease, smallpox swept through a community about once a decade, sometimes so severely that a third of its children died. Worried about his youngest daughter, Salomon spent a week unable to study properly, even though Rivka assured him that Rachel wasn't nearly as ill as Joheved and Miriam had been during the previous epidemic. Indeed, this outbreak was milder than usual, with most of Troyes' children surviving it. Rachel recovered with no visible scars, and like others who survived the pox, she now enjoyed immunity for life.

twelve

Winter 4832 (1072 C.E.)

With the smallpox epidemic behind them, it seemed that the rest of winter would pass uneventfully. Then Anna's labor began. For two days she struggled, but the baby didn't come. Joheved wasn't sure how long labor was supposed to take, except that Mama had delivered Rachel in only one night. When another evening came and the women were still occupied with Anna, Joheved volunteered to divert her little sister's attention.

"Tell me the story of Rachel from the Bible."

Joheved groaned inwardly. "I told you that one last night."

"I like stories with Rachel in them." Her voice was a whine.

"What if I tell you one about a Rachel in the Talmud?"

"There's a Rachel in the Talmud? Tell me, tell me."

"All right, but let me put more charcoal on the brazier first," Joheved said. Then she began the story.

"Akiva was a poor shepherd who worked for one of the richest men of Jerusalem. His master's daughter, Rachel, saw Akiva's great potential and fell in love with him. She promised to be his wife if he would devote himself to Jewish learning."

Joheved wasn't sure this was the right tale for her self-centered little sister. It was more about Akiva than Rachel. "Now Akiva was over thirty years old and still didn't know the alphabet, but Rachel insisted that he could be a great scholar."

"Then what happened?" Rachel asked.

"Akiva went off to Babylon to study, and when Rachel's father found out she'd married one of his shepherds, he refused to support them."

"Were they very poor?"

"Oui, they were. Once there was so little food in the house that Rachel had to cut off her beautiful braids and sell them." Joheved tugged gently at one of her sister's braids.

"After twelve years at the yeshiva, Akiva returned to Jerusalem. He was approaching his house when he heard a neighbor berating Rachel, saying, 'How much longer will you live like a widow?' Rachel replied that she was so sure her husband was devoting himself to Torah that she would gladly wait another twelve years. So what do you think Akiva did when he heard that?"

Joheved wanted to hear that Akiva entered his home, embraced his long-suffering wife, and promised to study Torah in their own city from then on, but little Rachel knew the correct answer. "Akiva went back to his yeshiva."

"That's right. After another twelve years, he returned with thousands of disciples," Joheved said. "When Rachel saw Akiva surrounded by his students, she pushed through the crowd to greet him. They tried to turn her away, but Akiva embraced her and told them, 'All that I possess and from which you benefit, I acquired only because of her.' When Rachel's father heard that a great scholar had come to town, he went to Akiva and asked for help in making peace with his estranged daughter."

"Rachel's father didn't recognize his own son-in-law?"

Her little sister was getting excited in anticipation of the happy ending, and Joheved couldn't help smiling. "Rachel's father repented for making his daughter suffer all those years, and Akiva made his identity known. They were all reconciled, and Rachel's father gave Akiva half his wealth. And as a reward for his faithful wife, who had sold her hair for him years before, he bought her the finest hair ornaments in Jerusalem."

Joheved preferred the stories of Rabbi Meir and his learned wife, Beruria, but she knew Rachel wouldn't want to hear those. Soon her little sister's breathing was regular with sleep, and she could hear the men downstairs reciting Psalms to guard Anna from evil spirits. Maybe there would be good news in the morning.

Several hours later, Miriam tried not to wake her sisters when she came to bed, but Joheved stirred as soon as she felt Miriam sit down and awoke fully when she heard Miriam weeping.

"What's wrong?" It was quiet downstairs; maybe she'd slept through the birth cries. "Is everyone all right?"

Miriam turned and buried her face in Joheved's shoulder. "No, everyone's not all right; the baby died. It was horrible."

Joheved clutched her sister tightly. "What about Anna?"

"Anna is still alive." Miriam gulped down her tears. "She looks awful, but Aunt Sarah says it's normal after a hard birth."

"What happened? Why did the baby die?"

Miriam was only too willing to share the burden she carried. "He was strangled by the cord. Aunt Sarah had to unwrap it twice from around his neck." She choked back a sob.

"Poor Anna! She must feel terrible."

"But she doesn't; that's what's really awful." Miriam began to tremble. "Baruch wasn't the baby's father; it was one of the barbarians who captured her. Anna was glad the baby died."

"Mon Dieu," was all Joheved could say before she started crying too. The two sisters held each other in silent grief.

But Miriam wasn't finished. "It's so horrible what happened to her, but I can't stop thinking about it."

Joheved murmured something soothing, and Miriam continued. "When the raiders found her people, they killed everyone except the young women."

Joheved cringed inside and braced herself for the details that were sure to follow.

Miriam took a deep breath and began to whisper. "They took away the girls' clothes and locked them up naked in a hut. Every so often somebody opened the door and threw some food in for them, but it was never enough. Yet more often than they got food, one of the barbarians would open the door, leer at the poor naked girls, and take one of them away."

Miriam spoke so softly that Joheved could barely make out her words. "But he didn't take her far enough away. Anna and the others had to listen to the missing girl's screams and moans until she was dragged back in. Sometimes she never came back."

Miriam buried her head against Joheved's shoulder. "The girls who were virgins—it was worse for them. Anna had already married Baruch, so it didn't hurt her so much. Some of the men enjoyed it more when the girls screamed and cried, and they avoided her if she remained silent."

Miriam paused and Joheved could feel her sister's tears, wet against her chest. "One day the door opened and men entered who looked different from her captors, less coarse somehow. They pointed to her and a couple of others, and they took them away. Anna never saw the barbarians again."

"Was it Shemiah who bought her?" Joheved asked, her disgust rising. How could he deal with such evil people?

"*Non,* not yet," Miriam said, reassuring her. "Her new captors ran the slave market where Baruch saw her and got his master to buy her. They didn't know she was pregnant."

"So after all that, do you still want to be a midwife?"

There was a long silence, and Joheved thought that her sister had fallen asleep.

"I only know that I don't want to talk about it anymore," Miriam said. "Let's try and get some sleep before all the bells start ringing."

The next morning, Joheved dressed and prayed quietly so she wouldn't disturb her sleeping sister. Once downstairs, she learned that Baruch had been told nothing except that the baby had not survived the birth. If people interpreted this to mean that the boy had been born prematurely, which would have been the case if Baruch had fathered him, it was just as well.

Under Jewish Law, a stillborn is not entitled to the same bereavement rituals as a child who lives at least a month. Anna's son was buried without a funeral in an anonymous section of the cemetery reserved for stillborns, amputated limbs and worn-out holy books. Legally, Anna and Baruch were not mourners and thus would not interrupt their routines for the seven days of intense grief that a family death usually required. Anna told the women that this was fine with her; she wanted to forget the baby and everything having to do with it as soon as possible.

Once springtime arrived, Miriam was too busy in the vineyard to worry about being a midwife, especially after she began using Grandmama Leah as an excuse to visit Benjamin there. All went well until one warm afternoon when Leah decided to go for a walk less than an hour after returning home from shopping.

Rivka tried to discourage her, explaining that they had just come back from a walk, but that pacified her only briefly. Anna had just started to do the laundry, and when Leah persisted, she looked to Miriam with pleading eyes.

Miriam needed no urging, and they had almost reached the vineyard when Leah declared, "I need to rest."

Impatient to both see Benjamin and get off the hot and dusty road, Miriam had no choice but to stop until Leah regained her strength. They had walked only a little farther when Leah again complained that she was too tired to go on.

Miriam, trying to hide her annoyance, coaxed Leah to keep going. "It's only a little ways, Grandmama. We're almost there."

This worked a couple of times, but finally Leah protested, "I'm exhausted. I can't walk another cubit."

Miriam waited a bit before trying to get Leah going again, as she had done before, but Leah wouldn't budge. Now Miriam's irritation turned into fear. It wasn't good for Leah to stand so long in the hot sun, yet Miriam couldn't leave her grandmother alone to get help. The spring wheat had already been harvested in the surrounding fields, and the road was empty. Miriam tried to remain calm. Surely somebody would come looking for them if they missed services.

Just when she was about to start sobbing, Miriam heard a familiar voice call to them, "Are you two all right? You've been standing at this spot for quite a while."

Miriam spun around, sure she had imagined him, but there was Benjamin, trotting down the road towards them, a cloud of dust billowing behind him. She was so relieved to see him, it was all she could do not to collapse, crying, into his arms. Instead, she fought back her tears and explained their dilemma.

Benjamin looked at Grandmama Leah, patiently standing by the roadside, and announced, "Let's go home now; we need to get back for evening services." He motioned for them to accompany him.

Miriam followed his lead and could hardly believe it when Leah began walking along with them. Feeling both relieved and chagrined, she scolded herself for allowing her grandmother's behavior to upset her. But their pleasant stroll was short-lived; Leah soon stopped and proclaimed herself too weary to continue.

Miriam was about to suggest that Benjamin run home to get a cart, when Benjamin proposed that they each put an arm around Leah, thus supporting her enough that she could get home on her own two feet. In the past year he had grown several inches, and he was stronger now too, so that the two of them were easily able to walk with their arms pressed against each other behind Leah's back. It was strange. By all appearances they were chaperoned, yet Leah would remember nothing they said or did. Miriam felt a bittersweet sadness in their freedom.

"You know, Benjamin, Grandmama Leah used to be really smart when I was little." Miriam felt compelled to tell him that her grandmother hadn't always been like this. "She was my first teacher, and she ran the vineyard almost single-handedly, making such fine wine that the whole Jewish community admired her." She sniffed back tears and Benjamin squeezed her arm in sympathy.

"You're lucky to have had such a wonderful grandmother," he responded. "I'm the youngest child, and my grandparents all died before I was born."

They spent the rest of their walk sharing childhood memories, arriving home just in time for evening services. But even though Benjamin made a cane for Leah out of a large, woody vine shoot, Miriam was afraid to walk with her to the vineyard again. She kept Grandmama Leah's walks within the walls of the old city, never more than a few blocks from home.

Benjamin wasn't the only boy who'd grown. When they returned for the Hot Fair, several yeshiva students' fathers barely recognized their sons, many of whom were half a head taller than when they'd parted company at the end of the Cold Fair.

Salomon's family wasn't exempt from the growth process either. In the past year, Joheved seemed to have made the progression from girlhood to young womanhood, a development most apparent on a late Friday afternoon when Rivka and her two older daughters visited the bathhouse in readiness for the Sabbath.

It had been hot and sticky all week, so when Rivka prepared to go to the stews, Joheved and Miriam asked if they could join her. Rachel protested that she wanted to come too, but Rivka drew the line there. The baths were too deep; she'd have to wait until she was bigger.

The bathhouse was located on the Rû Cordé canal, near the edge of the Jewish Quarter. Rivka gave the attendant a small coin and received three towels in exchange. Encountering Johanna there was a pleasant surprise, and Rivka settled in for a leisurely soak.

Joheved and Miriam couldn't bear sitting in the hot water so long and amused themselves by perching at the edge of the large tub and gently splashing each other. It was only when they accidentally splashed the older women, causing Rivka to look up from her conversation and scold them, that the physical difference between her two daughters was evident.

Joheved's body was rounded, almost voluptuous, with full breasts and prominent nipples, her waist a definite indentation above abundant hips. Between her legs, the hair of her lower beard completely covered the skin beneath. In contrast, Miriam's shape was slim and childlike. Her breasts were mere buds, and her lower beard was skimpy, little more than down. They were only a few years apart in age, but it was evident that Joheved had completely crossed the threshold that Miriam was just approaching.

Johanna observed the naked girls as well. "My goodness. Joheved looks so grown up now. Have you set her wedding date?"

"Non, not yet." Rivka was embarrassed to admit that she'd been caught unaware by her daughter's maturity. "We wanted to wait until she started her flowers, so there'd be no doubt about her ability to bear children." A woman's menses were commonly called her "flowers," because, just as a tree without flowers will not bear fruit, so too women without their "flowers" were not fruitful.

"Non, of course not." Johanna glanced at Joheved and then, not wanting the girl to catch them scrutinizing her, quickly turned back to her friend. "From the looks of her, she's sure to flower soon. I wouldn't wait too long if I were you, not with all those yeshiva students at your house."

After bidding Johanna a "Good Sabbath," Rivka observed her daughters closely. Both belted their Shabbat bliauts loosely, and the difference in their figures disappeared under the billowing, wine-colored wool. No wonder she hadn't noticed.

Johanna's admonition was still in Rivka's mind when she and Salomon went to bed that night. "Salomon," she whispered. "Joheved and Miriam came with me to the bathhouse this afternoon, and I don't think we should wait much longer to set Joheved's wedding date. She's not a little girl anymore."

"But I thought you told me she hadn't flowered yet."

"Non, she hasn't yet," Rivka acknowledged. "But she definitely looks like a woman now. It can't be much longer."

Salomon had to accept his wife's expertise in this matter. "Very well, I will write to Samuel and suggest that our children marry next fall, after the harvest. It will give Meir a year to finish his studies in Worms." That would work well, he thought. More merchants had approached him about sending their sons to the yeshiva, and he would need someone to assist the new, younger students while he continued teaching the older ones.

Meir returned to the Rhineland after spending a bittersweet Rosh Hashanah and Yom Kippur with his family. His parents had informed him that his wedding date was set, that next year he'd be moving to Troyes to help his father-in-law with the yeshiva there. As happy as he was with the news, he couldn't help viewing his teachers and fellow students with a sense of impending loss. He was even sorry to leave the family he lodged with.

Two years ago, when Salomon convinced Meir to move to Worms, Sarah had arranged for him to board with her son, Eleazar. Ever since the patriarch Abraham entertained the Holy One's messengers, Jews have considered it a mitzvah to offer hospitality to strangers. It was particularly meritorious to host a yeshiva student, and thus assist him in fulfilling the commandment to study Torah.

Not that Meir spent much time with Eleazar's family. All yeshiva students attended synagogue, both morning and evening, where a talmid chacham expounded a portion of the Talmud. After this, his learned colleagues, Meir now included among them, asked questions, pointed out difficulties, and argued about the legal principles involved. During the afternoon, when the older men were occupied with business affairs, Meir and the other youths remained in the synagogue and continued their studies.

Many of the students developed a favorite among the Talmudic sages. Some favored the wise and gentle Hillel, who never lost his temper, no matter what the provocation. He once advised a pagan, upon hearing that the man would convert to Judaism if Hillel taught him the whole Torah while standing on one foot,

> What is hateful to you, do not do to your fellow man. This is the whole Torah, all else is commentary, now go and study.

Others preferred the heroic Rabbi Akiva, the poor shepherd who became one of the greatest scholars in the Talmud. When the Romans forbade the study of Torah, Akiva continued to teach his students until he was caught and executed. A few, like Meir, gave special regard to their namesake among the Sages.

The Talmudic Rabbi Meir was so learned that the Mishnah alone contained over three hundred laws that bear his name. His wife, Beruria, one of the few women mentioned in the Talmud, was a sage's daughter and a brilliant scholar. Meir ben Samuel liked the fact that he too was marrying a scholar's daughter, but he wasn't sure he wanted one quite as brilliant as Beruria.

Now that his wedding date was set, Meir's friends encouraged him to join them in visiting the local brothel. After all, merchants and older students, who spent months separated from their wives, required a sexual outlet. Meir didn't disparage those who needed women in addition to their wives, but he didn't want his first experience to be with a harlot.

So they let him be. A popular student, Meir was never shy about asking questions that others, less assured, might think were stupid. He was confident that if he had difficulty with a passage, he would have plenty of company. He remembered how Salomon had befriended him when he was homesick and tried to be especially helpful to the youngest students.

One of these was a loner from Paris. Intelligent as he was pious, Judah ben Natan avoided the foolishness typical of boys his age. Was he stuck up or just shy? It was difficult to know since he discouraged attempts to discuss any subject other than Torah. He admired both Meir's refusal to frequent brothels and Meir's determination to learn as much as possible during this final year.

One warm afternoon, when most students were off swimming, Meir sat alone in one of the smaller rooms off the main sanctuary. It was a perfect place to emulate his future father-in-law and work on his note taking. He was trying to recall exactly how the Rosh Yeshiva had explained a particular passage, when he was distracted by someone's presence.

Judah ben Natan had entered, and when he saw that Meir had paused in his work, asked what he was doing. New students were always curious about his note taking, and Meir tried to explain himself quickly, before he lost the thread of his teacher's words. Yet Judah continued to stand next to Meir, silently watching him.

"Is there anything else I can help you with?" Meir didn't like being observed while he wrote.

"Actually, oui." Judah's gloomy tone of voice jerked Meir out of his studies, and he turned around to look at the youth.

Like a typical student, Judah was thin and pasty, but his face was fair, with large brown eyes framed by long black lashes. Meir's own beard had started to fill out, but Judah's face was as soft and hairless as a girl's. His dark hair was cropped unfashionably short, possibly to avoid that very misconception. The youth cleared his throat, and then asked Meir his age.

"I'm almost eighteen," Meir answered curtly. He was about to ask Judah why he wanted to know, when the boy asked him why he wasn't wed yet.

Jewish men tended to marry young, but there were those who didn't complete *nisuin* until they were eighteen. The Talmudic maxim was that a man should be wed no later than age twenty. And Meir wasn't unmarried; he had been betrothed for some time.

"I'm not sure why our parents have delayed *nisuin* for so long," Meir replied, "but I suspect it was to give my father-in-law time to accumulate my wife's dowry. He's a vintner and a rabbi, not a wealthy merchant."

"Oh," said Judah. "You're marrying a scholar's daughter. Does that make you happy?"

"*Mais oui.*" Meir wasn't sure what Judah wanted to know. "Her father heads the yeshiva in Troyes, so I'll be able to continue my studies and eventually teach there."

"I'd be happy too, if I could stay in a yeshiva and study Torah my whole life." Judah sighed. "But are you happy about getting married? I'm not betrothed to anyone, and I was wondering what it's like."

"I can't wait for the wedding," Meir said, trying to sound more confident than he felt. He wasn't about to tell this unknown boy that he was also anxious, maybe even a bit scared. "It's the first commandment to marry and procreate. That's why the Holy One created us in two sexes, men and women."

"Oui, I know." Judah proceeded to quote from the Mishnah, chapter Yevamot.

> A man may not refrain from fulfilling the commandment, "Be fruitful and multiply" unless he already has children. Shammai ruled that he must have two sons; Hillel ruled, a son and a daughter, for it is written "Male and female he created them."

His voice held a hint of impatience, as if explaining something simple to a dull child.

Meir felt compelled to defend marriage as more than a vehicle for procreation, and show this youngster that he was not without knowledge himself. "And in the Gemara on that Mishnah,

> Rav Tanhum said: When a man is without a wife, he lives without joy, without blessing, and also without Torah."

Judah quickly rose to the challenge. "In Tractate Kiddushin, it says:

> A man should first study Torah and then take a wife. But if he cannot live without a woman, he may take a wife and then study Torah."

Judah obviously had a poor opinion of the man who cannot live without a woman.

Meir quoted the next line, hoping that Judah also had an affinity for his Talmudic namesake.

> Rav Judah said: The ruling is that a man must first take a wife and then study Torah.

But Judah responded with the following line,

> Rav Yohanan said: With a millstone around his neck, is he expected to study Torah?

He smiled at Meir, apparently pleased that the discussion in Kiddushin concluded with disapproval of marriage for scholars.

Maybe Judah hadn't studied Tractate Sotah. Meir quoted from that text.

> The Sages taught: A husband and a wife, if they are worthy, the Divine Presence abides with them and they are blessed.

But Judah knew this section as well and his grin widened.

> If they are not worthy, then the Divine Presence departs from them.

Meir saw that this contest could only end in a draw. For every rabbi who praised marriage and considered his wife a blessing, another saw her as a source of misery. Yet everyone knew that a man must marry; it was the Creator's command. Meir went back to their first tractate, Yevamot, for what he hoped would be the final word on the subject.

> Rav Eliezer taught: He who does not procreate is as if he spills blood, for in Genesis, "Whoever spills a man's blood," is followed at once by "Be fruitful and multiply." Rav Akiva said: A man who refuses to procreate diminishes God's image, for "In the image of God He made man," is followed by "Be fruitful and multiply." Ben Azzai said: He both spills blood and diminishes God's image.

Meir's tone made it clear their discussion was at an end. Judah's smile disappeared, and he completed the quote that Meir had started.

> Rav Eliezer said to Ben Azzai: Such words sound good when they come from those who practice them. You preach well but do not practice well. Ben Azzai replied: But what shall I do, my soul yearns for Torah? The world can increase through others.

He looked at Meir with his usual serious expression and said, "Actually, my favorite sage is Ben Azzai, not Rabbi Judah." Then he apologized for taking Meir away from his studies and retreated out the door.

What a strange fellow. Meir shook his head in puzzlement. Why would anyone choose Ben Azzai for special admiration?

Simeon Ben Azzai was famous for his diligence and piety, and it was written in Tractate Berachot that anyone who saw Ben Azzai in a dream might expect to become pious. A disciple of Rabbi Akiva, he had married Akiva's daughter. But he became estranged from his wife and died while still a young man, never having fathered any children.

Meir considered Ben Azzai's life a warning against such extreme piety, and he felt sorry for Judah. He tried to return to his studies, but his thoughts remained on the topic of marriage. He decided that he would do everything he could to ensure that the Divine Presence abided between him and his wife. He also thought that, as sorry as he felt for Judah ben Natan, he felt more sorry for the poor woman who ended up married to him.

thirteen

Fall 4832 (1072 C.E.)

In Troyes, Salomon was also trying to catch up on his writing. With the vintage finished, Salomon finally had time to add to his kuntres the new insights he had gleaned during the Hot Fair. His students were gone for the Days of Awe and would not be back until the Cold Fair. Rivka, in the early stages of pregnancy, had barely enough energy to supervise the servants. She went to bed as soon as they finished souper.

His daughters were also occupied elsewhere. Sarah had approached him about teaching the older girls to ride, reminding him that Joheved was about to marry a man whose family owned a manor nearby and Miriam would soon be a midwife. Salomon required no more convincing and Rivka added her blessing. Women on horseback were assumed to be nobility; knights would feel obliged to protect them, and no peasant would dare molest them.

At first the girls rode their hired ponies slowly around the streets of the Jewish district, but eventually Aunt Sarah allowed them to ride wherever they liked within the city walls. Joheved marveled at how different everything looked from a mounted position. Even the tallest man was shorter than they were, and they could easily see through open windows into people's houses.

They learned to trot by accident. Rivka let them feed the horses any apples too bruised to use, and the mares, eager to reach the courtyard, began trotting as soon as they approached the street leading to Salomon's house. Their pace quickened as they neared the courtyard gate, and though frightened at first, the girls came to enjoy the brief burst of speed.

The days had shortened perceptibly when Sarah took them into the forest to look for the medicinal plants best picked in the autumn. On the off chance that they might find some, the midwife described alkanet to her two helpers. This particular type of borage made an excellent healing salve, but Sarah had never found any growing around Troyes. Still, she hoped to come across the elusive herb some day.

Joheved loved riding through the fall foliage. Every autumn she'd admired the trees changing color in the distance, but to be enveloped by it all was glorious. It was impossible to remain focused on the ground, looking for plants with dull grey leaves, when each tree seemed more colorful than its neighbor, all of them vying for her attention. Meir had his own horse. If he enjoyed riding through the beautiful autumn forest, maybe they could go together next fall?

Aunt Sarah's sharp voice brought her out of her reverie. "Joheved, please try to make yourself useful."

Miriam saw her sister blush in response and wondered what she'd been daydreaming about. "If you can't stop and pick some wormwood with me, at least try to keep your horse from trampling it," she added her own reprimand.

Joheved looked down and saw the familiar shrubs with silvery, almost white foliage. She made an embarrassed apology, quickly dismounted, and began to fill her hemp bag with the aromatic leaves. She was careful not to bruise them, so the medicine concentrating in the leaves all summer would not be diminished. Miriam was also filling her bag with grey foliage, but the bush she was working on had more feathery leaves, darker than those in Joheved's collection. Joheved hadn't been paying attention when Aunt Sarah explained the difference between the two kinds of wormwood, but at least she knew what they looked like and could find them again if she had to.

When they had finished collecting the herbs Sarah needed, the girls begged their aunt to let them ride in the beautiful forest by themselves. Perhaps they'd find the elusive alkanet. They promised to be back in time for disner. Sarah reluctantly agreed, also making them promise to always leave and reenter Troyes by the same gate, so that the guards would become familiar with their routine. After a few weeks, they grew adept at recognizing when the sun was almost at its zenith, thus arriving home before their father, who rarely left the synagogue until the bells finished chiming the noon hour.

Their one close call came when they were distracted by a hunting party from the palace. The men and women on horseback, noisily enjoying themselves, were easily visible through the trees. Joheved and Miriam watched in fascination as, again and again, they sent their hawks and falcons aloft in search of prey. The birds were wonderfully graceful and swift, and it was amazing how faithfully they returned to their owners. It was only when servants began spreading robes on the ground and taking out baskets of food that the girls realized how late it was.

Sure the bells would begin chiming sext any moment, they urged their mounts through the trees. When they reached the road, Miriam's horse sensed her rider's haste and broke into a run. Joheved felt herself flying as well and closed her eyes, holding on for dear life. After a few moments of terror, Joheved forced herself to peek to make sure she was at least going in the right direction. Her sister was in the lead, her horse still cantering, the city walls growing closer.

Once they passed the gate, both mares slowed to a trot, and as the girls tried to calm their rapid breathing, the bells began to toll. The final chime rang as they closed the courtyard gate behind them, and they just had time to wash their flushed and shiny faces when their father arrived.

The next day Joheved noticed blood stains on her chemise, which Rivka happily interpreted as her oldest daughter's first flowers. But there was no bleeding the next day, nor the next, and a short exam by Aunt Sarah revealed that Joheved had merely torn her hymen, probably the result of her vigorous ride the previous day. It was disappointing, but Sarah reminded Rivka that Joheved's wedding night should be easier as a result. Still, Rivka didn't give up hope until two months passed with no further bleeding.

By then she had a more serious problem to worry about. Outside in the courtyard one windy day, Leah had noticed some apples still hanging on the tree. Anna, digging onions in the garden, saw the old woman swinging her cane among the apple tree's branches and ran over to stop her. But she was too late. Leah lunged at one of the remaining apples, lost her balance, and crashed to the ground. When Anna tried to help her up, Leah groaned with such pain that the doctor was sent for.

It took only a few prods here and there, with resulting yelps from his patient, before the physician announced his diagnosis.

"Her left hip is most likely broken, although it may only be a bad bruise. If the latter, and Le Bon Dieu wills it, she might be up and about after some bed rest." He didn't need to describe the consequences for the former.

The doctor wrote out instructions for a painkiller, and Joheved ran off to the apothecary's. Leah's moans only grew louder as Salomon and Baruch gently carried her upstairs to bed. When Joheved returned, Aunt Sarah was preparing one of her own remedies for pain. They gave Leah both medicines, and to everyone's relief, she quieted down and slept.

Now Joheved led all the women's services at synagogue, but she was too distraught to notice that the other girls looked at her with awe instead of disdain. Rachel continued to sit downstairs with Salomon, even though most small children, and certainly all girls, joined their mothers in the women's gallery. She sat patiently on his lap during the study session after services as well, and Salomon became convinced that she could understand both Hebrew and Aramaic, so keenly did she appear to follow the scholarly discussions.

When the Cold Fair ended and the merchant scholars went home, Salomon was left with just his students and daughters to teach again. Leah remained bedridden, although her pain had diminished considerably. But what little intellect she had previously possessed now deserted her altogether, and she neither spoke nor seemed to understand when others did. She allowed Anna to feed, bathe and swaddle her like a baby. Her only reaction to her surroundings came if somebody inadvertently jostled her sore hip.

For her part, Joheved found her grandmother's degeneration so distressing that she avoided her room as much as possible. Filled with shame each time she passed Leah's door, Joheved threw herself into doing chores that Rivka, as her pregnancy advanced, was increasingly unable to perform. Nobody complained about her neglecting Leah, but Joheved still felt she was stealing time to study. Not that she stopped studying Talmud; she just felt guilty doing it.

The household's mood brightened when Rivka easily gave birth to a fourth daughter in early spring, her labor so rapid that Miriam learned little from it. This time Salomon had a full cadre of students praying with him, and when Joheved woke the next morning, she had a baby sister. Two weeks later, when Papa was called to bless the Torah in honor of his youngest daughter's naming, she learned that her new sister was called Leah.

Spring brought a present for Joheved. She had written Meir about learning to ride, and he had asked his parents to loan her his horse until he returned to Troyes in the fall. Always the youngest child at his family's Seder, Meir was thrilled when Sarah's son suggested that he spend Passover with them in Worms. Now he'd be an honored adult guest instead.

Exercising Meir's horse was a pleasant chore, except that rides with Miriam kept ending up at the vineyard when Benjamin was working there. Joheved didn't like being an accomplice to these clandestine rendezvous, but she wouldn't tattle on Miriam, who at least worked on the vines while visiting her friend. But her sister only became more persistent about sneaking off to see Benjamin as the season progressed.

"I can't explain it," Miriam told her, "but it's frustrating to spend all this time in public with Benjamin, at meals or in the salon during Papa's lessons, yet we never have any time together without Papa's supervision."

Joheved nodded, even though she didn't understand. What difference did it make whether Papa was there or not?

"Maybe we could take Rachel on a walk along the Seine tomorrow afternoon?" Miriam asked, her expression not quite as innocent as she hoped. "Then once we're outside the city walls, I'll meet Benjamin and the two of us can go to the vineyard together."

Joheved's jaw dropped, and it took her a moment to respond. "Miriam, have you lost your mind? You know that nobody is allowed in the vineyard now—the grape blossoms are beginning to flower." How could her sister be so reckless?

"We aren't going inside the vineyard," Miriam said, her hands fidgeting with her skirts, "just near enough along the road to smell the flowers."

Joheved's concern heightened. Both girls had been repeatedly warned not to disturb the vineyard during the delicate pollination process. But Miriam obviously didn't care, and when Joheved tried to look her in the eye, Miriam blushed and avoided her gaze.

That's when Joheved remembered hearing that the blossoms' perfume was reputed to be an aphrodisiac. "Miriam, don't go there alone with him, not now," she pleaded, but to no avail.

"Joheved, we'll be on a public road in broad daylight. Don't you remember last summer when we found the honey? We all smelled the grape blossoms then and nothing terrible happened."

Miriam too had heard tales of the grape flowers' effect on men and women, and it was exciting to imagine her and Benjamin enjoying the fragrance together. She had no idea how they might be affected, but that was part of the attraction.

Joheved realized that her sister might go off with Benjamin even if she refused to be an accomplice to their scheme. "All right, we can go on a walk along the river tomorrow, but promise me you'll be home well before sunset. And please be careful."

Miriam gave her older sister a grateful hug. She didn't know how she was going to wait until the next day. For her part, Joheved couldn't imagine any man being so compelling, but at least Miriam had promised to tell her everything that happened.

The following afternoon, all went as planned. As the bells began to chime vespers, Miriam saw Benjamin waiting for her just outside the Preize Gate, the one closest to the vineyard. At first they walked the familiar road in silence. Miriam could sense that Benjamin was nervous, but was too shy to ask what was bothering him. She tried to think of a subject they could discuss and remembered the Gemara they had been learning.

"Benjamin, could you help me remember what we studied today from Tractate Pesachim? You know, the disagreement between Hillel and Shammai about which blessing is said first at the Seder, the one for the wine or the one for the holiday."

He easily recalled the beginning of the Gemara. The class had been studying this tractate ever since the students returned from celebrating Passover with their families.

> Shammai says: First one recites the blessing of the day and afterwards recites the blessing over the wine, because the day causes the wine to come.

He smiled at Miriam and said, "Now, it's your turn."

She had no difficulty taking up where he had left off.

> But Hillel says: First one recites over the wine and afterwards over the day because the wine causes the blessing to be said.

"And the law accords with Hillel," Benjamin finished for her. "I know. So what does Shammai mean when he says that the day causes the wine to come?" He was sure she knew the answer.

"The festival begins at sunset, before the wine is served." She paused for a moment. Did she actually smell something pleasant or was she imagining it?

When Benjamin first noticed the faint sweet scent on the breeze, he missed a few of Miriam's words. He forced himself to calm down and listen to what she was saying. "Thus, because the holiday arrives before the wine, its blessing should come first." There was another reason, but he couldn't seem to remember it.

Miriam no longer cared about Hillel and Shammai. As soon as she became aware of the vineyard's lovely fragrance, she began to happily reflect on why Benjamin had wanted to get her under its influence. "Oh, I can smell the grape flowers." She tried not to sound too excited. "We probably shouldn't get much closer."

Benjamin stopped. The perfume was already powerful enough; they didn't need to go farther. "Miriam, I . . . "

He began to speak, but when she turned around to look at him, he couldn't think of anything to say. Had it only been a year ago that they had ignored this wonderful smell and followed bees instead? Somehow in that time, he had left childhood behind. He stood staring at her, inhaling the wonderful fragrance that surrounded them. Were her eyes blue, green or grey, or some of each?

Miriam tried to continue their discussion, but the look in Benjamin's eyes flustered her. To avoid his compelling gaze and concentrate on the beautiful scent, Miriam closed her eyes.

Benjamin, interpreting her actions as an invitation, leaned forward to kiss her. She momentarily gloried in his embrace, but then she noticed the rough beginnings of his beard against her skin and came to her senses.

What on earth was she doing, allowing herself to be kissed in the middle of a public road, where anyone could see them? What could have possessed her to act so shamelessly? She spun out of his grasp and began to vent her outrage.

"You must be in league with demons! You've cast a spell on me. I can't believe I followed you up here and let you kiss me in front of the world. We aren't married, or even betrothed."

Benjamin was stunned by her sudden wrath, but he had to say something to overcome her distrust. "But, Miriam, I do want to marry you, more than anything. I've wanted to marry you for over a year. I've even talked to my parents about it."

"Try to understand," he pleaded with her. "You're the daughter of a talmid chacham with his own yeshiva, your older sister already has a great match arranged for her, and your parents probably hope to do even better for you. I know they can find you a greater scholar than I am, and a richer one too. My only hope is to make you want me."

His confession washed away Miriam's anger. He wanted to marry her! And he worried that he wasn't good enough. She threw her arms around him and kissed him, not caring who saw them.

This time he broke their embrace. "Miriam, if you want, I'll ask my father to speak to yours just as soon as I get home for Shavuot." Despite her apparent pleasure in his company, Benjamin still wasn't sure that she wanted to marry him.

She took his hands in hers. "Please make your parents hurry. Our *erusin* must be complete before the merchants return for the Hot Fair, before somebody else approaches Papa about me."

"I'll have them come back with me immediately after the festival," he assured her. "Your father wouldn't make another arrangement without your knowing, would he?"

Miriam shook her head. "I don't think so. He made Joheved consent to her betrothal, in front of witnesses. And speaking of witnesses," she quickly looked up and down the road, "if we don't want any to our behavior today, we'd better get home."

"We're safe enough." He was so happy, he couldn't help but laugh. "Everybody knows that they should stay away from a vineyard while it's flowering. And by the way, weren't you saying something about Hillel and wine?"

After souper, when the sisters had gone to bed, Joheved insisted on finding out exactly what had transpired outside the vineyard. Miriam shyly told her that she had never smelled anything as wonderful as the grape flowers and that Benjamin was bringing his parents back to Troyes as soon as Shavuot was over to arrange their betrothal.

More relieved than disappointed when Miriam became reticent about sharing the romantic details, Joheved gave her younger sister a happy embrace. "It's about time."

Miriam wanted to lie back and reflect on her wonderful afternoon, but she couldn't let Joheved have the last word. "You should take Meir to smell the blossoms next year," she said with a yawn.

"When the time comes, I'll try to remember." Joheved didn't want to spoil Miriam's happiness by arguing. But by this time next year, she'd be married, hopefully pregnant even, and therefore not likely to be interested in smelling any aphrodisiac flowers.

The days passed, and eventually Salomon looked up from his studies and Rivka from her new baby, and they became aware of the mutual satisfaction emanating from Miriam and Benjamin. There didn't seem to be much else to do except ask Benjamin to invite his parents to return with him when Shavuot was over, to which he shyly answered that he had already planned to do so.

Under the guiding hand of Isaac haParnas, negotiations went smoothly. Benjamin's parents easily agreed that their son would live in Troyes and help manage Salomon's vineyard so Miriam could remain there as the community's midwife. Salomon hosted his daughter's *erusin* feast just as the Hot Fair began, disappointing several merchants who had hoped to negotiate on behalf of their own sons that summer. It was a good thing that Rivka still had a substantial supply of honey down in the cellar, because the quantity of honey cake she was obliged to serve in honor of the happy couple was so great that she needed to utilize the baker's large ovens for two days.

A happy couple they were. Sitting next to Benjamin at their betrothal banquet, Miriam reveled in her good fortune. Love matches were rare, and she squeezed Benjamin's hand under the table as she reflected on the difference between her *erusin* and Joheved's. Now that Papa had made good on his promise to find them both learned husbands, Mama was beaming.

And with her raven curls, big green eyes and perfect oval face, there was no doubt that when the time came, Rachel would have her choice of Papa's finest students.

"What a lovely child, *tres belle,*" murmured the guests as they admired her, "may the Holy One protect her." Automatically they invoked Divine protection to guard her against the Evil Eye.

Enough people mentioned Rachel's beauty to her parents that they were forced to devise an appropriate response. "I suppose she's *belle assez,* beautiful enough," Mama or Papa would reply whenever their young daughter was complimented, as if they had never considered the subject before.

Oui, Rachel was certainly beautiful, Miriam thought with pride, as she watched her little sister dancing with the older women. Then the musicians began to play a dance for pairs, and Joheved beckoned her to join them. When Benjamin applauded as the two sisters performed the dance's intricate steps, Miriam began to feel sorry for Joheved. Her older sister hadn't seen Meir in nearly a year, and when he did stop by on his twice-yearly return to Allemagne, he spent most of his time with Papa.

"Oh, Joheved." Miriam gave her an extra hug as they twirled each other, "I hope you and Meir will be as happy as me and Benjamin when you're married."

"Happy?" Joheved gave a snort of disbelief. "Marriage is to have children, not for happiness."

Miriam was in too good a mood to be intimidated. "Well, then, I hope you and Meir have lots of children and a happy marriage."

Joheved gave a quick glance to Leah's upstairs window. "It's too bad Grandmama can't enjoy these good times with us," she said. But even that thought dampened Miriam's joy for only a moment.

Leah's sad condition was the only taint on that otherwise happy summer. Her situation was stable; she did not regain her former health, but neither did she get worse. She seemed to appreciate her family's company, that is to say, she smiled at whoever sat and talked to her, and held fast to their hands. Rivka warned the invalid's visitors to be sure her limbs were kept well inside the bed, so demons couldn't grab them.

Hopeful that Leah might remain this way indefinitely, Joheved and her family turned their attention to her nuptial preparations. At the Hot Fair, they bought material for wedding clothes and bed linens, plus a chest and cabinet to house the new couple's possessions. Aunt Sarah had graciously offered one of her bedrooms to the newlyweds, and Rivka decided to outfit it with new wall hangings as well.

The fair was in its second month when Grandmama Leah began to fail. She had difficulty breathing and was often so drowsy that they could barely wake her for meals. The doctor came regularly and bled her, but to no avail. Salomon and his students spent hours praying and reciting Psalms on her behalf, but her condition continued to deteriorate.

One morning a worried Anna confessed that she had not been able to give Leah breakfast. The old woman had clenched her teeth tightly together and refused to swallow any food. At midday, Rivka attempted to feed Leah herself, with the same unhappy result. In late afternoon, Miriam had success getting her grandmother to drink some well-diluted wine, but no one could persuade her to eat the evening meal.

The next day, Rivka directed Maria to prepare a chicken stew with garlic for disner, and to set aside a portion of the rich broth for Leah. But despite encouragement by both granddaughters, even this delicacy failed to tempt her, and Rivka tearfully brought the untouched dish downstairs later. Salomon's household, which had so recently been joyfully anticipating the future, now viewed it with dread.

Joheved sadly packed away her new fabrics. Clutching the amulet she always wore, Rivka lit candles near Leah's bed and removed the chicken-feather pillow, hoping to lure away any demons who would prolong her death agony. The family avoided wearing new clothes, knowing that they would have to rend them at news of her demise. Bowls of water were set out as traps for demons, to be dumped outside immediately after the death was discovered, and Rivka sternly warned the household never to drink from them.

Thus it was that Miriam, awake early and gathering eggs in the courtyard, learned of Leah's passing when she saw Anna tearfully pouring a dish of water into the dirt outside the kitchen door. One by one the other members of her household appeared, each emptying a container of water outside. Joheved went all the way to the courtyard gate and spilled hers in the street, just in time to meet a neighbor on her way to the bakery.

Instantly recognizing the significance of these events, the woman crossed to the other side of the street. The dead woman's ghost was surely nearby, and perhaps the Angel of Death was still in the vicinity as well. But Joheved knew the neighbor would inform the community of Leah's passing. Now somebody would be sure to prepare food for the mourners before midday, and people could arrange their affairs to free them for an afternoon funeral.

One of the most rigid rules of Judaism is that a funeral must take place at the earliest possible moment after death. If Leah had died on the first day of a festival, non-Jews would have carried out her burial. But her early morning demise left plenty of time to attend to all the funeral minutia and still have her body under the earth before nightfall.

While Baruch and Benjamin were at the riverbank, cutting fresh rushes for the floors where the mourners would sit during the next week, the women of Salomon's family focused their attention on *tahara,* ritually preparing Grandma Leah's body for burial. Joheved dreaded the next few hours, but she had to do it. *Tahara* was one of the most important mitzvot a woman could fulfill, an act of unselfish kindness whose recipient could not possibly return any favors. It was performed for the sake of the mitzvah, knowing that one day it would be done for her.

Joheved steeled herself as she helped Miriam, Mama and Aunt Sarah lift Grandmama Leah's corpse onto a wide board. But it wasn't as bad as she feared. Mama encouraged them to recall Leah in her prime as they washed and salted the body, and even Aunt Sarah found good things to say about her. During the occasional silences, Joheved could hear Papa praying outside the door, performing his watchman's duty. The body had not been left alone since the moment of death and would be accompanied constantly until burial.

Mama made sure that the corpse was wrapped in a new linen shroud; Leah had been a proud woman, and they wouldn't want her shamed by appearing in the Garden of Eden poorly dressed. Joheved shivered as she remembered tales of ghosts who refused to leave their former homes because their shrouds were too shabby to be seen in.

She knew that some of Salomon's students were trying to find an appropriate coffin, while others were in the cemetery, digging the grave. Mama had given strict instructions to prevent them from choosing a plot next to any of Leah's old adversaries, lest the two ghosts return and make their displeasure known.

By midday, when Johanna had laid out a small repast in the kitchen for the family, Leah's covered body had been placed in the coffin and all was ready for the procession to the cemetery. Before they left, Mama marked the side of the board on which the corpse had lain; heaven forbid it be turned over and incite the deceased's ire, resulting in an untimely death for another in the household.

Benjamin and several of Salomon's bravest students carried the coffin down the stairs and out of the house, followed by the immediate family and then the rest of the mourning congregation. As they walked beside Salomon, Joheved and Miriam recited the antidemonic ninety-first Psalm to prevent the spirits awaiting the corpse from seizing a living victim instead.

The heart of the funeral service was "The Justification of the Judgment," a short prayer that affirmed the rightness of the Creator's disposition of humanity. Here, and as part of every service prayed during the seven days of mourning, the congregation would proclaim verses from Deuteronomy:

> He is our Rock, His work is perfect; for all His ways are judgment; a God of truth and without iniquity, just and right is He.

The Hot Fair had not yet ended, so there was no lack of pious and learned men to repeat the ninety-first Psalm seven times as Grandmama Leah's coffin was lowered into her grave.

> He will cover you with His pinions, you will find refuge under His wings, His fidelity is an encircling shield. You need not fear the terror by night or the arrow that flies by day, the plague that stalks in the darkness or the scourge that ravages at noon.

They continued reciting as the body was buried, until the grave was full of earth, but Joheved could barely hear them; she was crying too hard.

Then Papa and Mama, followed by the congregation, reached down to tear up and smell a portion of grass and dirt, which they then threw over their shoulders while reciting the verses from Psalms,

> They shall flourish as the grass of the field, . . . Remember that we are dust.

Now Leah's soul had permission to leave her grave, and the prayer also prevented her ghost from following the mourners home. A double line of people formed for her family to walk between, and the entire company escorted them to Salomon's house.

Upon entering the courtyard, Joheved found that washing utensils and water had been prepared for them. Everyone bathed their hands, and some, including Mama and Papa, their eyes and face as well. On the dining table, the traditional mourners' meal of boiled eggs and lentil stew was laid out. Even the breads were round, to remind the mourners that bereavement is like a wheel, ever recurring. But even though she'd barely eaten anything since yesterday, Joheved had no appetite.

For the next seven days, her family would sit on the ground, abstain from meat and strong wine, and not leave the house except on the Sabbath. Daily prayers, each including the Justification of the Judgment, would be recited at home, as the community joined the mourners to share their anguish and console them.

Although Salomon was the legal mourner and tradition demanded these strict rituals for his benefit, Rivka, Joheved and Miriam felt greater grief than he did. The woman who died was a stranger, not the mother he remembered from childhood. As far as Salomon was concerned, he had lost his mother long ago.

Rivka had mixed feelings. She loved Leah as the mother she never had, yet she couldn't help but feel relief when Leah died. The old woman had lain in a bed of pain for six months and hadn't been able to function in dignity for several years. In addition, the burden of Leah's care had become increasingly onerous with the new baby's arrival. Rivka felt sad about Leah's demise, but she knew that it was time.

Throughout the week of bereavement, Salomon was amazed at the number of people who came to mourn with him and eulogize his mother. Merchant after merchant told stories of how she had befriended them, providing advice as well as room and board.

"When I was only nineteen, at my first Hot Fair, my purse was stolen," a thirtyish man with a Flemish accent said. "Leah—may her merit protect us—boarded me for free and loaned me money until I could repay her at the next year's fair."

"My father is too old to travel now." This man's accent proclaimed him a Lombard. "But he still tells the story of how he became ill one summer and Mistress Leah—may her memory be for blessing—nursed him back to health and saw to it that other merchants sold his merchandise for him while he was disabled."

Even Isaac haParnas had praise for her. "Whenever I came across a young merchant, newly arrived in Troyes, disoriented and alone, I knew I could send him to stay with Leah and he'd soon be feeling at home."

Salomon's family listened with wonder as Leah was revealed to rival the biblical Abraham and Sarah for gracious hospitality. Joheved and Miriam had their own fond memories of Leah that they were glad to share with those who came to console their family. More than their own mother, who seemed rather like an older sister, their grandmother had raised them. She'd provided their food, clothing and shelter, and she made sure they acquired the skills necessary to run a Jewish household and make Jewish wine.

"She was the one who taught us how to read scripture," Joheved said, recalling how they used to sit in front of the hearth and recite the text together. "And she taught us all the prayers too."

"When we were little, she helped Mama bathe us and get us dressed," Miriam added, a tear rolling down her cheek. "She loved to braid ribbons into our hair."

"She tucked us in bed and kissed us goodnight . . ." Now Joheved was crying too.

"And she gave us hugs each morning when we came down to breakfast," Miriam finished for her. With Leah gone, it was easy to forget the recent past and remember the good times.

For Salomon, a new picture of his mother emerged as seen through his daughters' loving eyes, and he realized that his only chance of receiving such a fond eulogy lay in being a devoted father to Rachel and little Leah. He would have to make sure that they grew up with equally warm and affectionate memories of him.

fourteen

Fall 4833 (1073 C.E.)

As *shiva,* those first seven days of intense mourning after the funeral, drew to a close, Rivka sadly suggested that perhaps they should write to Meir. With Salomon in mourning, the wedding must surely be canceled.

"*Oy,* I forgot about Meir completely." Salomon shook his head. "He's probably already on his way here by now."

"What are you going to do with him?" Rivka asked. "Send him back to Worms or to his parents' house?"

"My mother's death doesn't change my need to have Meir help with the younger students." Salomon paused and stroked his beard. "He may as well stay in Troyes. The wedding is only postponed, not canceled. He and Joheved can wait a few months."

Joheved almost cried with relief at Papa's announcement. Now she wouldn't be wed to a stranger. She and Meir would see each other every day, share meals, get a chance to know each other. Joheved would never admit, even to herself, how much she envied Miriam's love match.

At first Joheved kept a sharp eye out for any young strangers at synagogue. She wasn't sure she'd recognize her fiancé when he arrived; she hadn't seen him for almost a year, and during their brief times together she'd been careful not to stare at him. After a week went by without Meir's appearance, Joheved grew less vigilant, and three weeks later, she gave the men's section only a cursory glance as she climbed the synagogue stairs.

Thus she didn't give a second thought to the young man who stood hesitantly at the cellar entrance one afternoon. She was fully occupied with a wine buyer who could not decide which cask's contents to purchase. Papa and the others were in the vineyard, stringing up netting to keep the ripening grapes safe from hungry birds, and Joheved would much rather have been outdoors listening to her father's lessons than down in the cellar drawing unending wine samples for this merchant who was drinking more wine than he'd likely end up buying.

Her impatience grew. The only reason they even had such a choice of wine to sell this late in the season was because Salomon no longer needed it for her wedding. So when she noticed the second man coming into the cellar, she sighed in resignation. Another customer—she'd never get out to the vineyard now.

She forced herself to politely greet the stranger. Tall and brown haired with a full beard, he had a lanky frame that proclaimed his youth. He seemed ill at ease, probably a new junior partner, one who undertook the risky journeys to distant markets while the senior partner provided the capital and stayed safely at home. His dark green côte was of excellent quality, somewhat dusty from travel, and rather handsome with his deep yellow chemise and hose. At least it seemed likely he could afford their prices.

She was drawing him a cup of wine when Rivka called to her from the kitchen. "Joheved, are you still in the cellar?"

"Oui, Mama. I have two buyers down here with me. Do you need me for anything?"

"Nothing that can't wait," the voice from upstairs replied. "Don't let me keep you from the customers."

Meir's suspicions were confirmed. The young woman handing him a cup of wine was his betrothed, but she had no idea who he was! And after all he'd endured to get here to marry her.

It had never been difficult to find companions traveling home for holidays, but any merchant going to the Troyes Hot Fair had left long ago. Meir had waited in Worms for weeks. He'd nearly despaired of finding anyone going west, when word came of a party of knights attending the fair. They were likely to be poor company, but he would get to Troyes in safety. The journey had been as irritating as he had anticipated, and this morning, when he knew he could make Troyes' gates before dark if he rode hard, Meir gladly bid his comrades *adieu.*

Meir's annoyance evaporated as he surreptitiously watched Joheved. The wine was very good, and after downing the contents of his mug, he decided to conceal his identity a while longer. In Worms, Meir always drank his wine well diluted, so he was unprepared for the effect of a full cup of strong wine on his empty stomach. His mood began to lighten considerably as he continued observing his fiancée.

She had certainly grown up to be an attractive woman. Her skin looked soft and creamy next to her dark hair, braids that ended well below her waist. He briefly wondered what all that hair would look like, loose and flowing against a pillow, and then chided himself for harboring such unseemly thoughts.

Her bliaut was a deep rose color, and her pale blue chemise was embroidered with flowers in shades of blue, pink and burgundy. Meir couldn't help but notice that the figure under her bliaut was definitely not that of a young girl, and when she lifted her skirts to climb upstairs to bring them more bread, he openly savored her exposed ankles and calves, instead of modestly looking away as he normally would have done. Why shouldn't he admire her? In less than a month they'd be sharing a bed.

Upstairs in the kitchen, as she tried to relax and slow her racing heartbeat, Joheved was also having a silent conversation with herself. For shame, she scolded herself, getting flustered just because a handsome stranger couldn't keep his eyes off her. *Don't encourage him; you're a betrothed woman! Don't waste the fresh bread on him; give him some from yesterday.*

Joheved knew she should listen to her conscience, even as she knew she was going to ignore it. She resolutely cut the source of her consternation a large piece of the freshest bread and brought it downstairs to him. As he ate, she silently refilled the young man's cup from a different cask, feeling flattered yet annoyed that he was staring at her so brazenly. Did he think his fine looks and clothes gave him such license? She felt her face growing warm and was mortified that he might notice her blushing. This was definitely going to be a trying afternoon.

The older merchant finally made up his mind, so she tried to ignore the impertinent young one's interest in her and concentrate on negotiating a price. But both tasks proved difficult. Implying that there must be something wrong with the wine because it hadn't sold earlier, the first merchant made a ridiculously low offer.

Joheved expected bargaining, but this was outrageous. Her eyes narrowed in anger, and Meir, emboldened by his second cup of wine, entered the fray by loudly remarking that this fine vintage was certainly worth more than such a paltry amount. Perhaps the good mistress should deal with him first. The older man, furious at his competitor's interference, turned to Meir and ordered him outside to discuss the matter.

Meir gallantly agreed, and after suggesting that Joheved might bring down some more of her excellent bread, followed him into the courtyard. Joheved returned to the kitchen, sure that there was something familiar about the young merchant's voice. But she couldn't seem to place it.

"What do you mean by meddling in my business?" The older man kept his voice low but the anger was unmistakable. "If you keep quiet we may both profit well."

"Shalom aleichem, Master . . . ?" Meir said.

"Simon haLevi." The merchant rudely ignored Meir's greeting.

"Meir ben Samuel, at your service." He bowed deeply. "Now Master haLevi, perhaps you aren't aware that the vintner in question here is the town's rabbi, their Rosh Yeshiva. What are a few *deniers* to you when the Day of Judgment is nigh and the Holy One is about to weigh your deeds?" Meir held out his hands as if balancing something invisible. "Which do you want written by your name in the Book of Life, that you generously supported a Torah scholar or that you deprived one of sustenance?"

Simon's face blanched. He reached over and clasped Meir's shoulders. "You are absolutely right, my friend, and I thank you." This young man's warning may have just saved his life.

He turned and walked back down into the cellar, thanking his lucky stars that there was still time for such a good deed to be inscribed onto his heavenly ledger.

Joheved was waiting for them with some cheese as well as bread, and Meir forced himself not to wolf down his share, no matter how hungry he was. Before she could say anything, Simon surprised her by agreeing to match whatever price the previous customer had paid. Joheved looked back and forth at the two men, who now seemed on the most amicable of terms. What on earth had transpired between them?

As they marked the casks his carter would collect later, Simon made friendly conversation. "Mistress, I must admit it is unusual to have so much wine still available this late in the season. You must have had a fruitful harvest last year."

"I'm afraid not." Her faced clouded and she fought back tears. "My father had saved this wine for my wedding, but a few weeks ago his mother died. So we are in mourning and there will be no wedding."

No wedding! Meir sat down hard; it was as though he had just been punched in the gut. He listened in shock as Simon offered Joheved condolences on the loss of her grandmother. By this time, Meir's head was swimming so badly that he was unable to stand and wave good-bye when Simon took his leave.

"Farewell, and shalom aleichem, Meir ben Samuel," the older man saluted him. "I will offer a toast for your good fortune in the coming year whenever I drink this wine."

"Shalom aleichem, indeed, Meir ben Samuel." Joheved's voice was slow and controlled as she approached him.

Meir couldn't tell if she was hiding anger or amusement. He didn't dare look at her.

Joheved was more astonished than anything else. She had been looking for him in vain for weeks, and now he appeared out of nowhere in her own cellar, just in time to hear from her own mouth that their wedding was off. Any annoyance she felt at being misled vanished when she saw how forlorn he looked, lying on the bench, arms crossed over his belly, face to the wall.

"Are you all right?" Had he really gotten so upset when he'd heard that they weren't getting married? How flattering.

"Am I all right?" He turned to face her. "I haven't had anything to eat since dawn, my stomach feels like a horse just kicked it, and my bride, who doesn't even recognize me, just informed me that our wedding is canceled. And you ask me if I'm all right?" He tried to sit up, but his head hurt too much. With a grimace of pain, he reached out to support himself.

"Don't move." She helped him lie back down on the bench. "I'll get you some food."

Meir closed his eyes and berated himself for staring at her legs when he should have been noticing the tear at the neck of her chemise. How could he have missed that obvious sign of recent bereavement? And now what was going to happen to him?

His pessimistic thoughts were interrupted by the sensation of being watched, and he turned to see an orange-striped cat staring at him, less than an arm's length away. To his surprise, the cat walked over to him and pushed its head under his hand. His horse liked its ears scratched, so he proceeded to do the same for the cat. He was rewarded with a loud purr and was soon so engrossed in petting the cat that he almost forgot his miserable situation.

Joheved heard Meir's stomach growl as she came down the stairs with a large bowl of stew and two loaves of bread, and she tried not to smile. She was sure he hadn't had such a nice beard the last time she'd seen him. No wonder she hadn't recognized him. She let out a sigh of relief. Thank heaven this attractive man had turned out to be not such a stranger after all.

Meir finished his stew so quickly that Joheved insisted on bringing him a second helping. Ashamed at how he'd openly scrutinized her legs on the stairs earlier, he made a point of looking at her face as she returned to the kitchen. She smiled down at him in return.

He ate more slowly this time, while Joheved enlightened him about what her family had suffered recently. When he heard Joheved say that Salomon intended for him to live in Troyes despite their postponed nuptials, Meir was feeling almost happy. His bride-to-be had proved herself to be kind and forgiving of his less than admirable behavior. And she had very nice-looking legs. Feeling a rush of generosity, he left the last of his stew for the cat.

In the weeks that followed, Meir decided that, in spite of remaining unwed, life in Troyes was good. He enjoyed giving his young students their first taste of Talmud, watching their eyes light up with understanding and their faces shine with the pride that comes from mastering difficult material.

The grape harvest and winemaking went by in a blur, and then Rosh Hashanah was upon them. Meir's family came to Troyes to worship, and he listened proudly as his female relatives praised Joheved's skill in leading the complicated Yom Kippur service. Salomon and his father didn't set a new wedding date, but Meir hoped he would not have to wait a full year of mourning.

Next came Sukkot, Festival of Booths, commemorating the temporary shelters the Israelites lived in as they wandered in the desert after leaving Egypt. The yeshiva students took great pleasure in building a *sukkah* in their *maître*'s courtyard. For seven days they would eat, study, and, if the weather was decent, sleep in the rickety structure, thus fulfilling the commandment to "dwell in the *sukkah*."

Besides dwelling in the *sukkah,* Jews celebrated Sukkot with special blessings made while holding four varieties of plants, as it said in Leviticus: "Take the fruit of goodly trees, branches of palms, boughs of thick trees and willows of the brook, and you shall rejoice before your God seven days." The fruit traditionally used for Sukkot was the *etrog,* or citron, considered "goodly" because it was both fragrant and flavorful. Thanks to the generosity of Hiyya ibn Ezra, who brought them all the way from Cairo, Salomon's family was assured one of the beautiful fruits.

Joheved and Miriam couldn't believe their good fortune at having their very own *etrog.* Even their pious grandmother had never been able to obtain one. For the whole week, it sat in its special dish, bright and yellow like a miniature sun. Any time they wanted, they could pick it up and inhale its sweet, citrusy perfume. Everyone who came to their house couldn't help but stop and smell the *etrog* when they saw it.

Boys had a great time during the week of Sukkot. They held competitions, played ball games, and, when no adults were watching, gambled with nuts or dice. Meir was constantly being asked to lend out his horse. It was difficult to refuse, even though he knew the boys intended to race her. It was Sukkot—the Season of Simcha (Joy).

It wasn't all fun and games for the girls. While the resident students were gone, Rivka had Joheved, Miriam and Anna replace the attic's dirty straw. Sweeping up the old stalks and dumping them into the courtyard was easy. But the next part, carrying clean straw up a rickety ladder into the attic, was both awkward and a bit scary.

They were busy with carrying and spreading the stuff on the attic floor when Meir, having interrupted his studies to use the privy, stopped at the well to wash his hands. At this particular moment, Joheved was starting up the ladder with a load of straw while Miriam was waiting at the top to take it from her. Remembering what a prude her sister had been when she wanted to be alone with Benjamin, Miriam was struck with a mischievous idea. Joheved had indignantly told her how Meir had enjoyed watching her on the cellar stairs, and she couldn't resist this opportunity to tease them.

After assuring herself that Anna was occupied at the rear of the attic, Miriam called out, "Meir, can you give us a hand and hold the ladder steady for Joheved?"

Meir couldn't refuse—not that he wanted to—and Miriam chortled with glee at the furious look on her sister's blushing face as Meir took hold of the ladder. Her initial notion was to tempt Meir with a view of Joheved's legs as she climbed higher, but Miriam soon concocted a more devilish idea. She waited until Joheved's hips were level with Meir's shoulders, then gave the ladder an abrupt shake. When she peeked over the ledge, what she saw surpassed her wildest expectations.

Miriam had imagined her sister stopped with Meir's upper body pressed against her legs as he steadied the ladder. But instead, Joheved lost her balance entirely. Miriam watched open-mouthed as Joheved, falling backwards off the ladder, managed to knock Meir down as he attempted to catch her. They landed in a pile of debris from the attic.

For a moment they were too dazed to move, then Meir gently rolled Joheved off him and helped her up. "You're not hurt, are you?" he asked, trying to brush the stems off his clothes.

Joheved shook her head. She ought to ask how he was, but she was too flustered to speak. Physically unharmed, she had never felt more embarrassed in her life. She glanced around the courtyard and thanked heaven that nobody was outside to see her and Meir lying in the straw together. Up in the attic, Miriam howled with laughter as she watched the couple awkwardly trying to remove the stalks from each other's hair and clothes.

As much as she wanted to contain her mirth, Miriam was still giggling when Meir, insisting that Joheved rest a bit while he carried the straw upstairs, reached the attic and dropped his load at her feet. His inquisitive look made Miriam giggle even more, until it occurred to her that he might tell her father what had happened. Her smile froze and then disappeared as she returned his gaze. But he only winked at her, then climbed down to get more straw.

That night, it took great willpower on Miriam's part not to laugh as she helped Joheved remove the final pieces of straw from her hair. And it took even more willpower on Joheved's part not to accuse her sister of orchestrating the incident that neither one dared to acknowledge. But discomfited as she felt, Joheved had to admit that falling on top of Meir had not been a completely unpleasant experience.

Early the next morning, Salomon made his way to the courtyard *sukkah* and began prodding the bundles of cloaks and blankets containing Meir and the students to wake them for morning prayers. Meir was still trying to recapture the pleasant feeling of Joheved's body on top of his, when his reverie was suddenly interrupted by a woman's screams coming from the house.

Salomon had already closed half the distance between the *sukkah* and his house by the time Meir threw off his bedding and took off after him. Meir reached the open door, hesitated about whether to go in or not, and nearly collided with Joheved's Aunt Sarah as she bolted past him and on up the stairs. Now there were more female voices wailing above. Behind him, the small band of frightened students congregated in the pale dawn, some of them shivering in their light chemises. He motioned them near the hearth and tried to compose himself enough to lead them in Psalms.

Just then Salomon stumbled down the stairs, tears streaming down his cheeks, and Meir hurried to support his teacher. Salomon buried his head in the young man's shoulder and wept loudly. "My baby, my poor little girl. She was perfectly fine when Rivka put her to bed; we never even heard a peep from her during the night, and now she's dead."

Meir's response was automatic. "Baruch ata Adonai . . . *Dayan Emet* (Blessed are You . . . the True Judge)." Since Talmudic times this was the prayer Jews said when first informed of a death.

As the significance of Meir's words reached him, Salomon's wild weeping ceased, and he looked down at his clothing for a place to tear. He was wearing a new outfit for the festival, one originally made for Joheved's wedding. Meir could see him hesitate and knew Salomon didn't want to ruin his fine holiday *côte.* But his chemise had already been rent at his mother's death. As Meir and the other students watched in trepidation, Salomon grabbed the beautiful embroidery and tore the neckline open nearly to his waist.

For Joheved and Miriam, the next few days seemed almost a repetition of Grandmama Leah's death. Yet some things were different. Their grandmother had been the rabbi's mother, thus deserving of honor for his sake, but she was also a respected elder of the community in her own right, their vintner and women's prayer leader. Nearly every Jew in Troyes had attended her funeral and visited their house during the week of mourning.

But baby Leah's demise went almost unacknowledged. Babies died regularly in their first year, and usually another child came along soon enough to console the parents. Besides, it was still Sukkot, and it was forbidden to mourn or lament during the joyous festival. Only Salomon's students and a few of the men who studied with him regularly attended the funeral.

The family members' need for consolation was the opposite of when Grandmama Leah had died. Joheved and Miriam, who had deeply mourned their grandmother's loss, felt little grief for the baby sister they had barely known. Rachel was almost relieved at the disappearance of this competitor for her parents' attention, although she was old enough to know that she shouldn't show it.

Rivka, who had discovered baby Leah dead in her cradle, had recovered from her initial hysterics only to become terrified that this second death, so soon after Grandmama Leah's, portended an imminent third visit from the Angel of Death. Sure that some lapse during her mother-in-law's bereavement had brought this misfortune upon them, she clung tightly to her amulet and turned her efforts towards ensuring that all mourning rituals were carried out punctiliously.

When Rivka was a child, her stepmother insisted that she cut her nails starting with the first finger, explaining that starting with the third finger caused the death of one's children, with the fifth, poverty, and with the second, a bad reputation. Rivka was always careful to cut her thumbnail first, even if a different one needed paring, but maybe Salomon hadn't been so meticulous. When she got up the nerve to ask him, he assured her that he invariably trimmed his nails in the same order: left hand, 4,2,5,3,1; right hand, 1,3,5,2,4. Scholars were taught to never pare any two nails in sequence because it caused forgetfulness.

Still Rivka fretted about the next death, and only when Joheved reminded her that Anna's baby had been the first recent death in their household, thus making little Leah the third, did Rivka become resigned to her fate. She had lost babies before, and this one was only a girl.

Strangely, while Salomon had been the least bereft by his mother's passing, he now suffered the most. Once he got over the initial disappointment at not producing a son, little Leah had been a joy to him. Rachel was starting to prefer the company of her sisters, and just as he was looking forward to cuddling another toddler on his lap as he studied, she was suddenly taken from him.

It had to be his fault. Baby Leah couldn't have committed any sins during her short lifetime. Was there some sin he'd forgotten to atone for at Yom Kippur, some person he had wounded yet neglected to ask for forgiveness, a vow unfulfilled? He searched his memory in vain for such a lapse, yet he knew it must exist. How many mourning fathers came to his Bet Din, begging the court to release them from a careless oath before another child died? At least those men knew what they'd done wrong.

Sitting on the rushes that covered the floor of his house, he surveyed his three remaining daughters and felt a stab of regret that he would never know the little girl or young woman that baby Leah might have been. The infant had died sometime during the night, yet he'd gotten up and gone outside without even noticing anything was amiss. A sudden terror seized him—what if another of his daughters were to die in her sleep tonight?

Emotions in turmoil, he surveyed the small group who had come to his house of mourning so he'd have nine men to pray with. Meir prayed with the family every day, but the other students had been encouraged to enjoy their Sukkot holiday. Today Hiyya ibn Ezra and Shemiah ben Asher, in addition to a couple of other foreign merchants and a few local men, sat in silence until services began. Because of the holiday, it was inappropriate for them to offer words of consolation.

When they reached the place when one would usually say the Justification of the Judgment, Salomon paused, and Joheved sensed the distinguished visitors' uneasiness. This bereavement prayer was never recited on Shabbat or during a festival, yet at the appointed time, Salomon stood up and said it alone. None of the men challenged him, but they didn't join him either.

Once the service was over, she could tell that the men stayed only long enough to be polite. Hiyya and Shemiah motioned to Meir to walk with them, and she followed at a distance.

"I don't understand why Salomon is so distressed that he laments even during the festival." The Egyptian looked more puzzled than angry. "After all, he only lost a baby girl, and he already has three daughters. Now if the infant had been male . . ."

"Perhaps this daughter wasn't destined to be fruitful and build something great for him in this world," Shemiah suggested.

Meir shook his head. He didn't want to criticize Salomon, but he couldn't explain such a blatant disregard for accepted mourning practice. Meir no sooner closed the gate behind the men than Joheved and Miriam approached him. They too were upset with Salomon's breach.

"What was there to grieve over?" Miriam asked, lifting her hands towards the heavens. "Baby Leah died peacefully in her sleep and is surely in the Garden of Eden now."

Meir had had no answer for Miriam's question. None of them dared ask Salomon directly, and he never offered an explanation.

fifteen

Winter 4834 (1074 C.E.)

Gloom enveloped Salomon all winter. Pupils returning after the fall holidays noticed that their *maître* no longer began study sessions with a joke or funny story. Despite a successful wine harvest, the new vintage celebration at Hanukkah was subdued, and Salomon left the festivities early, pleading a headache.

That night he dreamed that he was back in Mayence, attending synagogue with his mother. Dressed in her new violet silk bliaut, she looked younger, like when he first left home to study with her brother, Simon haZaken. The expression on her face was fearsome, and she proceeded to denounce him to the scholars.

"Look how he ignores me, how little he mourns for me," she screamed, "and after all I sacrificed for him. Well, I gave him something to mourn about. If he wouldn't grieve for one Leah, he can grieve for another!"

Then Uncle Simon stood up and pointed a finger at him. "Have you forgotten everything we've taught you?"

Salomon woke up in a sweat, his heart pounding. How could he have forgotten the Talmudic discussion that began, "Why do a man's children die when they are young?" The answer was a sword in his breast. "Because he did not weep and mourn over a kosher person."

Only fear of demons kept him from rushing to the cemetery immediately, and when the roosters began crowing at dawn's first light, he was dressed and ready to visit his mother's grave.

"Please forgive me, Mama!" He threw himself down on the few tufts of grass that had grown since the funeral and cried out, "Have mercy on me and your granddaughters; pardon my iniquity, please, I beg you." But he could not bring himself to weep.

All that day, he was so visibly disturbed that Rachel, the only one not intimidated, finally asked him, "Papa, why are you so upset?" She inquired with the self-centeredness of childhood, "Did I do something wrong?"

Salomon, ashamed that his emotions were so obvious, assured Rachel that she had done nothing to anger him.

She was not deterred. "Then who did make you mad?"

"Well, it's not something anyone did." He had no intention of revealing his nightmare, so he stroked his beard and finally thought of something else he could tell her.

"You remember Robert, the monk from Montier-la-Celle, who comes to visit me and ask questions from time to time?"

"The one who gives us grapes to make wine from?"

"Oui, and for one of the Notzrim, he's not so bad." Robert's naive interest in Torah had forced Salomon to formulate plain, simple explanations to deceptively deep questions. The process had honed Salomon's intellect in a way that was different from teaching Talmud, and he'd come to relish their meetings.

"He is leaving Montier-la-Celle to found an abbey at Collan."

Joheved couldn't restrain herself. "But what about the wine, Papa?" Without the abbey's grapes, their household income would drop considerably.

"Don't worry; the abbot at Montier-la-Celle has no intention of changing our current business agreement." He was quiet for a moment, then sighed. "I will probably never see Robert again, and we had an argument the last time he was here. He asked me about the creation of man, and I should have been able to answer him without getting angry."

The students around the table came to attention. Creation was taught only to the most advanced pupils.

"You see," he told them, "Robert brought up the subject of 'original sin' and wanted to know what we Jews believed." The confusion on Rachel's face told Salomon that he needed to back up.

"Original sin is what the *minim* believe is the nature of man. They say anyone not baptized, even babies, cannot enter the Garden of Eden in the World to Come and must spend eternity in the flames of Gehenna." His voice, which had begun with mild derision, rose into fury. "How can they possibly think the Creator would condemn innocent babes to such torment?"

Whether it was this horrible concept or her father's angry voice, tears formed in Rachel's eyes. Salomon fought to contain his outrage and decided that somebody else should speak until he calmed down.

He turned to Meir and asked, "In the last chapter of Tractate Berachot, what does Rav Huna say about the creation of man?"

Joheved knew the quote and felt relieved that she had not been forced to display her Talmud learning in front of Meir. He was sitting next to her, and she felt him tense in response. Lately she'd noticed that Benjamin and Miriam's adjacent hands often vanished together beneath the table, and she suspected that Meir had launched a campaign to similarly take hold of her hand.

He had begun by keeping his nearer hand on his lap, and each day he moved it closer to her, apparently waiting for her to bring hers down as well. Today, with a decision that had her pulse racing, Joheved was slowly moving her hand towards the table's edge when Papa suddenly spoke to him.

Meir snatched his hand back and rested it on the table. "Pardon me, Master Salomon, could you repeat your question?"

Salomon did so, and Meir responded with alacrity.

> Rav Huna asks: What is the meaning of the verse in Genesis, "And God formed man," the word "formed" being spelled with two *yods?*

Of course Meir knew the reason why "formed" was spelled with two "*yods*" instead of its usual one, and he immediately provided it.

> The Holy One, Blessed be He, created man with two *yetzers,* two inclinations, one good and one evil, the *yetzer tov* and the *yetzer hara.*

Salomon had Miriam bring them the Bible. "See," he showed the words to Rachel, "the Hebrew word for 'to form' is *yotzar* and for 'inclination' is *yetzer.* It's a pun, a play on words." The Hebrew was written without vowels, so the two words looked exactly the same.

"This teaches that we are not condemned at birth, because man can choose between his good and evil urges," he concluded, this time keeping his voice steady.

"But why did God create the yetzer hara? " Rachel asked, her eyes wide. "Why not just the yetzer tov?"

The others at the table knew that the term, yetzer hara, had come to be associated, not with evil in general, but with the sexual urge in particular. They were curious how Salomon was going to edify his little girl about the yetzer hara.

While waiting for Salomon's reply, Meir sensed an almost imperceptible movement at his thigh, and with a quick intake of breath, he saw that Joheved's hand had vanished from the table. His heart beating wildly, he reached down and captured her hand with his own. She flinched slightly in response, but didn't pull away. His spirit was suddenly soaring, and he hoped his surge of happiness wasn't obvious. But everyone except Joheved, whose concentration was focused on how strong and warm Meir's hand felt on hers, was too interested in Salomon's imminent answer.

> "Because if it were not for the *yetzer hara,* a man would not build a house, take a wife, beget children or engage in commerce,"

the scholar explained, quoting Ecclesiastes. Rachel saw the abashed looks on the students' faces and sensed that there was more to this discussion than she was being told. But whenever she brought up the yetzer hara, and how come none of the students would talk to her about it, all Joheved or Miriam would say was that she'd have to wait until she was older, much older, before they'd explain it to her.

Every day for the next two months, ignoring both rain and snow, Salomon went to the cemetery and begged his mother's forgiveness for not crying over her death. If it hadn't been unlucky to visit the same grave twice the same day, he would have gone more often. When February came and went without his mood improving, his family began to wonder if his good humor would return in time for the raucous holiday of Purim in late March.

Last year Anna had been too busy ministering to Grandmama Leah to take much notice of Purim. But when she saw how eagerly everyone anticipated the holiday, she approached Joheved and Miriam for an explanation.

"Purim celebrates how Queen Esther and her cousin, Mordecai, saved the Persian Jews from Prime Minister Haman's evil plan to exterminate them," Joheved explained succinctly. "His scheme was thwarted when Esther convinced the king to nullify the decree."

"That's enough history," Miriam interrupted. "At Purim Jews read the Megillah (book of Esther) in synagogue, send gifts of food to friends and relatives, and give charity to the poor. But best of all, we feast, eat and drink to our heart's content, and then some." She continued with a grin,

> The Talmudic sage, Rava, said that on Purim a man must drink wine until he can't tell the difference between "blessed is Mordecai" and "cursed is Haman."

With their love of food and wine, French Jews excelled in Purim revelry. After a day of fasting before the holiday, there was one banquet in the evening, followed by another the next day after services. Because Queen Esther's position as a new wife enabled her to influence the king, betrothed and newlywed couples celebrated Purim with special enthusiasm.

No one was sure how the decision was made, but it became common knowledge that Salomon, with two betrothed daughters, would host this year's midday Purim celebration in his courtyard. After all, where better to observe a holiday that required excess drinking than at a winemaker's? Salomon accepted the *fait accompli* reluctantly. But he only needed to provide the place and the wine; the community would supply the rest.

Recruiting the requisite *jongleurs* and musicians would be easy this year. Two years after presenting her husband with their first son, Eudes, Countess Adelaide had recently given birth to another boy, Philippe, and the entertainers hired for his christening were still wintering in the palace.

As the month of March approached its close, the Jewish community filled with nervous anticipation. For days the weather had been drizzling and overcast. Rain on Purim would be a disaster, and if the day before was wet, the courtyard would be too muddy for dancing. But damp weather did not hamper the children.

They ran through the streets, eager to deliver Purim gifts and take others in exchange. Rachel was beside herself with glee as she waited for Rivka to decide which sweets she and Anna would deliver to whom. Someone seemed to be continually knocking at the door, and the dining table was piled high with dishes. Joheved and Miriam helped sort the gifts, trying to keep track of what they received and sent out again. Heaven forbid they should accidentally give an item back to the family who had originally sent it. But with all the coming and going, mix-ups were inevitable and a source of great amusement in the community.

With great relief Joheved had stopped delivering Purim presents once she was betrothed. She could still see the looks of pity on the faces of the prosperous women who had condescendingly taken her small offerings and replaced them with much larger ones containing more staples than luxuries. Mama made Miriam stay home this year too, but even so, Miriam had no intention of missing the Purim frivolity. She and Benjamin concocted a scheme that was sure to fluster both Meir and Joheved. First, they moved Meir's bedding next to Benjamin's, directly above the girls' bedroom. Then they waited impatiently until evening.

"Who moved my things?" Meir carefully checked his possessions, sure that some Purim trick was being played on him.

Benjamin allowed himself a slight smile. "Miriam and I did. She told me that Joheved would rather you slept over here now."

"What's the difference between this spot and where I used to sleep, which was very comfortable, by the way? Why should Joheved want me to sleep next to you?"

"If you can't figure it out, I'll show you."

"I'm not interested in games; just tell me." Meir was in no mood to talk. Though Joheved continued to hold hands with him at meals, she seemed unable to carry on a conversation with him. As soon as he tried to speak to her, she blushed and stammered and found an excuse to flee. Everyone said she was intelligent and articulate; why wouldn't she talk to him?

"There's no need to act so touchy." Benjamin grabbed some pieces of straw and arranged them in a layout of Salomon's house. "Here's the chimney; it goes up through our teacher's mother's old bedroom and out the middle of the attic. To the right is his room, and here on the left is where Joheved and Miriam sleep."

"How do you know where everyone's bedrooms are?" Meir asked. Had Benjamin been in Miriam's room?

"When Miriam's grandmother died, I helped carry the coffin downstairs." He waited as Meir surveyed the diagram, then the attic, and then the diagram again.

Meir's face reddened as understanding dawned on him. "Mon Dieu, you've got us lying right on top of them!"

"An appropriate arrangement, don't you agree?" Benjamin replied with a grin.

"Won't it, uh, bother us at night?" Meir asked. How could he sleep knowing that Joheved's naked body lay just a few cubits below his?"

"You mean Lillit's visits?" Benjamin lowered his voice to a whisper. "I'm used to them now."

Meir didn't want to ever "get used to" the night demon molesting him. Even when Lillit came to him in Joheved's guise, he still felt as if he were being unfaithful.

In the room below, Miriam was setting up her side of the prank. "Joheved, why don't you want to speak to Meir? You don't even say '*bonjour*' to him in the morning."

"It's not that I don't want to talk to him; it's just that somehow I get shy and flustered whenever I try." She couldn't talk to Meir without looking at him, but as soon as her eyes met his, she became tongue tied. "I can't explain it."

"Shy and flustered! You, who can speak at least four languages, who leads services and negotiates with wine merchants all the time, who outwitted Count Thibault's cellarer. I don't believe it. I tell you what. You just start slowly," Miriam said slyly. "Tomorrow morning, when you first see him, wish him '*bonjour*' and ask him if he slept well."

The next morning, after Meir's sputtering response to her question sent Miriam and Benjamin into gales of laughter, Joheved pulled her sister aside and demanded to hear the joke. In between giggles, Miriam told her what they'd done.

Joheved slammed her hand against the wall. "That's your idea of a Purim prank? How could you disgrace me like that?" She was going to die of humiliation the next time she saw Meir. "Meir's going to believe I deliberately set him up for embarrassment this morning. I can't imagine what he thinks of me for enticing him to move his bedding above mine and then asking him how he slept!"

"I'm sorry, Joheved, we didn't mean to hurt anybody. It was only a joke for Purim." Joheved looked exactly like a feminine version of their father when he lost his temper, and Miriam realized that she had gone too far. "Do you want me and Benjamin to apologize and have Meir put his bedding back where it was?"

"I don't want either of you telling him anything," Joheved hissed. "You've said enough already. I'll talk to him myself."

But she had no opportunity that day or the next. Meir was taking his meals at his cousins' house, where his parents were staying, and he spent the rest of his time with the students. Joheved found that she missed holding his hand at the table, and she worried how displeased he might be with her. Tomorrow was Purim; maybe all the wine she'd drink would help her find a way to speak with him.

The day before Purim the gift exchanges were finally finished. The congregation observed the Fast of Esther under grey skies, but when the day ended and they prepared to exchange fasting for feasting, the weather cleared. Before Meir left to attend the evening banquet with his parents, he presented Joheved with the present he had carefully saved until last. It was a miniature pair of men's boots, sculpted completely out of sugar.

Asher had told Meir about a Provençal Purim custom, the special confection a bridegroom gave his intended. Made of sugar, it represented a common item belonging to his gender, and Meir had hired a baker to make one of the simpler designs.

Relieved that he wasn't upset with her, Joheved managed to whisper "Merci." But she could never eat anything so beautiful, so she placed the sugar shoes on a shelf in the pantry before joining everyone at the dining table. It was covered with nearly every dish and bowl her family owned, each one filled with such savory fare that she didn't know what to eat first.

The evening Purim feast finished, a sated community gathered in the synagogue, goblets in hand. Casks of wine had been set up in the rear to enable those goblets to be replenished as often as necessary. Before the service started, a tray was passed around, and each man gave a small donation. This was a symbolic offering; the community leaders had already collected for widows, orphans and others in distress. As the tray progressed through the room, the sounds of adults trying to hush restless children increased.

Finally the blessings were said, and the congregation's most recent bridegroom opened the Megillah scroll and began to chant. In the women's gallery, Joheved translated his words into French. Everyone listened quietly, at least until the villain's name, Haman, was read, at which time pandemonium broke out. The congregation stamped their feet, clapped their hands and made as much a clamor as possible to drown out the hateful word. With Haman mentioned more than fifty times in the scroll of Esther, the reading was continually interrupted by shouts, screams and every other noise a person could make.

Those who wished to fulfill their religious obligation and actually hear every word, crowded close around the reader. Room was made for Salomon near the stand holding the scroll, and he motioned for Meir to squeeze in next to him. Rachel perched on her father's shoulders with a saucepan in one hand and a spoon in the other, and Meir couldn't imagine how Salomon could tolerate such a din so close to his ears.

This was the first time Meir had been near enough to see the Megillah read, and when he turned his attention to the words written before him, he was astonished. The scribe, in order to make up for the absence of the name of God in the book of Esther, had written its constituent letters larger whenever they occurred close together, so that those reading might see the Holy Name emerge, as it were, out of the text.

It seemed as though the cacophonous recitation would never end, but finally Haman's name was chanted for the last time, as he was hung on the very gallows he had built for the Jews. Families reunited downstairs, exhausted children slung over their parents' shoulders and friends bid each other, "*Bon soir.*" Most went home to get some sleep before the merrymaking started again in the morning. But many of the men, including most of the yeshiva students, adjourned to the Parnas's house for a night of gambling.

The next morning, Salomon's household was up early as Rivka and Sarah prepared for a busy day. Soon women would be arriving with dishes of every kind of delicacy. Poultry was preferred above all else at Purim, so there was sure to be a large selection of chicken and goose. Meir's family provided a lamb, usually in short supply this early in the season. Roasting on a spit, it took up the entire hearth in Sarah's kitchen.

The baker's helper had delivered so many loaves of bread that he needed a cart to carry them all, and he would return later with savory pies containing pigeon and quail. Finally he would bring the sweet cakes and pastries, more varieties than can be imagined, giving him a short respite before another batch of bread was needed for the evening meal.

Rivka wanted both Joheved and Miriam to stay home and help, but they argued that at least one of them should be at services to translate for the women. Not that many women would be there, most of them being just as busy in their kitchens as Rivka was. Still, she sent Miriam with Rachel and Salomon.

He had planned to dress in his regular festival attire, but his daughters insisted that he wear something unusual, especially since he was hosting the feast. Not in a jolly Purim mood, he finally agreed to wear mismatched hose, one leg red and the other yellow, to give his children pleasure. Then they joined the other Purim revelers in the street, boisterously making their way to the synagogue.

Last year Miriam had been one of the pot-banging children downstairs on Purim morning, so she was disappointed to see that her mother was right; the women's section was nearly deserted. Miriam recognized the few elderly ladies sitting down, but not the four young women looking over the railing. Maybe they were visiting Troyes for the holiday.

"Shalom aleichem, ladies." Miriam felt proud of herself for offering hospitality to strangers, but to her dismay, the women ignored her. Perhaps they couldn't hear her over the din.

She came closer, but they avoided her. Determined to be heard, she maneuvered herself directly in front of the nearest ones, only to discover that it was Menachem and Ephraim in women's clothes. She let out a shriek of astonishment and then quickly dissolved in giggles.

They each had a veil, fancy headpiece and matching girdle. Neither had a beard yet, so except that their bodies lacked the distinctive feminine shape, the disguise was quite good. One would have sworn they were young women, just past puberty.

"What are you doing up here?" Miriam scanned the older women for signs of ire, but they smiled back benignly.

"How do you like our masquerade?" Menachem gave her a wink. "We must look pretty good if we fooled you for so long."

"You won't tell anyone, will you?" Ephraim asked, looking around nervously.

"I suppose not," she replied. The women here probably wouldn't recognize them, and even if they did, the boys weren't likely to get in trouble on Purim. "But why come up here? It's more fun downstairs."

"It was all his idea." Ephraim pointed to what looked like another young woman, heavily veiled. "Everyone was treating us like women, so he suggested we come up here and have a look. I told him it was nothing special, that we used to spend lots of time up here with Mama, but he still wanted to see it."

"Who is 'him,' and how many of them are you?" Miriam looked suspiciously at the old ladies in the back.

"Just the four of us." The "woman" lowered her veil and Asher's scraggly bearded face grinned back at her, looking ludicrous in the feminine head covering.

Asher motioned for his veiled companion to come over, and his/her familiar gait filled Miriam with apprehension. She could barely bring herself to watch as the last veil came down to reveal her fiancé standing in front of her. At least he had the decency to look embarrassed.

"You are two of the ugliest women I have ever seen," she teased them in return. "You'll need large dowries to attract a decent-looking husband."

"For your information, we are both engaged already," Benjamin retorted truthfully, but in falsetto. "And my betrothed is so fair that the sun pales in comparison."

Miriam blushed at his compliment, but before she could say anything clever in return, the noise level began rising below. "The Megillah reading is starting. I have to go translate for the real ladies," she said. "You fellows stay out of trouble."

The four students amused themselves for the duration of services by watching to see which men winced the most when Haman's name was read. They told Miriam later that while it was more fun to be in the middle of the crowd below, the view from the women's gallery was better.

sixteen

Spring 4834 (1074 C.E.)

As Miriam walked home with her four new "girl friends," they could hear the music playing blocks away. Inside the courtyard, musicians with lutes, violins, and cymbals played so loudly that normal conversation was impossible. Many of the guests were sitting at long tables set up in a large square, while others danced in the empty area formed in its center. Concentric circles, each of men or women, danced in opposite directions from each other, slowing and speeding up as the tunes varied.

Youngsters preferred to watch the jugglers and jesters. Miriam was heading towards a man who seemed to have no difficulty producing coins from people's ears, when she passed Joheved and Meir speaking seriously under the apple tree. Meir was wearing his fur-lined cloak inside out, and with the hood drawn tight around his head, he looked like a large hairy animal. Miriam got near enough to overhear the word "bedding" and quickly turned back towards the dancers.

"Meir," Joheved began, her face growing warm. He turned to face her and she had to force herself to keep speaking. "I'm sorry for what I said the other morning. I mean I apologize if I embarrassed you; I didn't realize . . ." Why was it so difficult to talk to him? Even several cups of wine weren't helping.

"You have nothing to apologize for. Benjamin told me all about their Purim joke."

"You weren't angry? I was so mad at Miriam that I wanted to break something." She smiled ruefully and added, "And I nearly did break my hand."

"I was angry at first, but when I saw how upset you were, I knew that you had to be a victim as well."

Maybe the wine was affecting her, because she then asked him, "So did you return your bedding to its old spot?"

He moved closer to her. "I left it exactly where Benjamin put it. I didn't want the students to think we'd had an argument."

"I'm glad it's still there." The wine was definitely affecting her. "It comforts me to know you're up there."

Comfortable was not how Meir would describe his feelings about their sleeping arrangement, but at least she didn't object. "I like knowing you're down there too."

"Meir, what are you thinking when you look at me like that?"

She was looking at him so earnestly, those big blue eyes staring up at him. "I was admiring your eyes," he answered. "They're exactly the same color as the sky today."

"Really? I'm not even sure what color my eyes are."

"You've never seen yourself in a mirror?"

"Not that I can remember. My family doesn't own one."

They had been gazing into each other's eyes too long. Meir was slowly leaning towards her and she realized that he was going to kiss her, no matter how many people were watching.

Joheved had just closed her eyes and tilted her face up when Miriam called out from the crowd, "Joheved, come and dance with me. They're playing our favorite tune." The spell was broken, and with mingled relief and regret, she ran to her sister's side.

Meir watched the dancers for a while. A gentle melody provided the backdrop for pairs to turn and sway in intricate patterns, all the while gracefully swirling their skirts. The sky deepened, and the clouds parted to reveal the full moon rising.

He was about to head for the dining tables when the music grew lively again. Recognizing the tune, a young man jumped up and challenged him. Immediately another pair joined them, then another, the crowd cheering as the men performed an athletic dance involving jumps, spins and fancy footwork. Two by two, each pair kept up the frantic pace until one of them dropped in exhaustion and his partner was declared the winner. Joheved applauded proudly at how well Meir danced.

Once it was dark and the torches lit, the merrymakers separated into two groups, one of each gender. Outside, the men recited various Purim parodies that imitated famous Talmudic passages, their themes usually the praise of wine and those who drink it to excess. The women, who found these mystifying rather than clever, gathered indoors at Sarah's, where a female *jongleur* was singing.

Joheved was curious how much she'd understand of the men's humor, so she joined them, standing close by Meir and her father. Somebody was chanting, in the Talmudic style, a ditty enumerating the diverse foods that must be eaten on Purim.

> Rabbi Mordecai said: Twenty-four dishes were told to Moses on Mount Sinai, all of which a man must prepare for Purim. Tortes, pastries, ragout, pouches, venison, buck flesh, geese, chickens, pigeons, swans, ducks, pheasants, partridges, moor hens, stuffed fowl, quails. But it is taught that we must also prepare pancakes, preserves and jellies.

But men didn't have to prepare all those Purim dishes, Joheved thought to herself; the women did. Then she was distracted by screams of laughter from across the courtyard and realized she was the only female left among the men. She made her way to her aunt's house and squeezed in next to her sister. The *jongleur* was strumming a lyre and singing a riddle song. Adding to her audience's glee, many of the riddles were double entendres, with both an innocuous and a sexual solution.

"Here's a special riddle for the new brides and betrothed maidens among us." The *jongleur* grinned salaciously at the group.

I heard of something rising in a corner
Swelling and standing up, lifting its cover
The proud-hearted bride grabbed at that boneless
Wonder with her hands, the master's daughter
Covered that swelling thing with a swirl of cloth.

Amid peals of laughter, one of the women cried out the answer, "bread dough." Joheved giggled nervously, but Miriam, too innocent to understand the phallic innuendo, asked what was so funny. A blushing Joheved found herself unable to say the thing out loud, but an older matron leaned over and whispered it in Miriam's ear.

"Speaking of dough, here's another verse for our newly and about-to-be marrieds," the singer announced. "But first let me slake my thirst." Immediately one of the many vessels of wine making its way around the room was handed up to her.

Both swayed and shook. The young man hurried,
Was sometimes useful, served well, but always tired
Sooner than she, weary of the work.
Under her girdle began to grow
A hero's reward that good men often love.

Again the room was raucous with merriment, until it was finally quiet enough for someone to gasp out the explanation: "A churn, they are making butter."

This time Miriam had an idea what the other meaning was, but Joheved felt obliged to inform her that the couple could also be making a baby. Strumming a chord on her lyre, the musician announced that the next riddle was for the learned among them.

A man sat at wine with his two wives
And his two sons and his two daughters,
Beloved sisters and their two sons, noble, first-born.
The father of each noble one was with them as well,
Uncle and nephew. Altogether there were five
Men and women sitting together.

The room was silent as the women, heads dizzy with wine, tried to count on their fingers and otherwise solve the mystery. Hopeful faces turned towards Miriam and Joheved, expecting them to uphold the town's honor and provide the answer. Joheved was deep in thought, but Miriam was too drunk to figure out any more than that the man was married to sisters. She looked around the *salle,* and there was Benjamin. Mon Dieu, how long had he been there?

Suddenly it felt as if all the wine she'd consumed had gone straight to her bladder, and she hurried out to the privy. Luckily Joheved was less intoxicated and was able to provide the riddle's key: the five were Lot, his two daughters, and their sons, Moab and Ammon. Murmurs of praise for her knowledge of scripture filled the room. Nobody noticed that Benjamin had infiltrated their group, or that he left as soon as Miriam did.

Outside, the moon's brilliance illuminated several women waiting near the privy. Miriam impatiently went upstairs to use her own chamber pot, only to find Rachel asleep in bed and Salomon snoring there as well. Miriam smiled at the familial scene. He must have been telling her a story when they both nodded off.

Benjamin was waiting for her below. Fearful of waking her father, Miriam had hurried her business and been inattentive in tidying up. An admiring Benjamin couldn't help but notice that her skirt was stuck in her girdle, exposing her calves and thighs. He pointed out her carelessness, and as she struggled to straighten her bliaut, he offered his assistance and guided her under the stairs where they weren't likely to be disturbed.

Sometime later, Meir began to tire of the men's scholarly humor, and he wondered what the women were finding so hilarious. It seemed as if he hadn't seen Joheved for hours. None too steady on his feet, he made his way to Sarah's house and listened.

Splendidly it hangs by a man's thigh
Under the cloak of its master. In its front is a hole.
It is stiff and hard, and has a good place.
When its master lifts his garment over his knee,
He intends to greet that familiar hole
With the head of his hanging thing
Which has so often filled it with even length before.

The room rang with mirth. Meir's chuckles turned to shock when he noticed not only Joheved, but his mother and his sister also enjoying themselves within. Repulsed at the vulgarity displayed by women he expected to be modest and pious, he turned away before hearing the answer of "key and lock." But he couldn't stop thinking about the riddle's apparent answer, and his loins responded with an uncomfortable pressure.

Such an onslaught by his yetzer hara had become increasingly frequent, and his usual remedy was to douse his face with cold well water until the condition dissipated. But his trip to the well was interrupted when he noticed Salomon's open front door. The noises within drew him to investigate, and what he discovered there staggered him further.

At first he thought it was two women having a *tête-a-tête,* but as he watched, he could see they were embracing, their hands busy under each other's clothes. He shook his muddled head, trying to make sense out of what he was witnessing, when a shaft of moonlight played on the pair long enough for him to identify them. One of the women was his fiancée's sister, and the other was no woman at all, but Benjamin in feminine dress.

Meir backed away, intending to find Salomon, but once outside, he remembered seeing the man carrying his sleepy daughter upstairs, not to return. By now the moon was low in the sky, and most of the guests had gone home. The ache beneath his chemise continued to throb, and his frustration mounted as he recalled the lasciviousness he had witnessed.

Then he noticed Joheved at one of the far tables, trying to collect the dirty dishes. This was perfect—he would help her bring things into the kitchen and make sure she saw what her supposedly innocent sister was doing. His plan worked, except that Joheved didn't seem to be as upset as he was.

Thanking him for bringing the matter to her attention, she shooed him outside and told him she'd deal with her errant sibling herself. Minutes later she appeared in the doorway, supporting a pasty-looking Miriam, and the two of them walked quickly over to a nearby wall, where Joheved offered comfort as her sister's stomach rejected its contents. Then she helped the sick girl upstairs to bed. But this was complicated by Salomon's presence, and she needed Meir's help to move him to his own bedroom. When that was accomplished, Joheved was nearly exhausted, but she felt an irrational determination to continue cleaning up.

Meir waited until they were out of earshot and vented his displeasure. "What are you doing? Let your servants do the job tomorrow."

Why was he so mad about her trying to tidy up? "You mean today, not tomorrow," she said as a rooster crowed nearby. "I do believe it's nearly dawn."

His anger increased when she ignored his question, and he brought up the true source of his indignation. "I can't believe the depravity I witnessed tonight. You laugh your head off at the most bawdy entertainment, your sister embraces her lover with impunity in your own house and your father lies upstairs in a drunken stupor, oblivious to everything." Meir had consumed so much wine that any shred of discretion was gone.

Intoxication loosened Joheved's tongue as well. "How dare you accuse me and my family of immorality! And on Purim yet, when we're supposed to drink and celebrate! Besides, your mother and sister were laughing just as hard as I was."

She continued to berate him. After all, he had practically called Miriam a harlot. "And you have the self-righteousness to complain about immorality on Purim. The entire holiday encourages excess. Why do you think the rabbis in Tractate Megillah complain so much about licentiousness at Purim if it didn't happen to them all the time?"

"And I suppose you've studied Tractate Megillah?" Meir's voice dripped sarcasm.

"I certainly have! And Tractates Berachot, Shabbat and Pesachim too." Joheved immediately covered her mouth in horror.

Meir stared at her in stunned silence, trying to process the indictment he had heard from her own mouth. He couldn't resist challenging her learning with his own from Tractate Sotah (the suspected adulteress). "Since you're such a talmid chacham," his tone was icy, "I'm sure you'll understand when I say that I agree when Rav Eliezer says that teaching a woman Torah is teaching her lechery. I suppose your sister studies with you, and we can see where it's gotten her."

"Adultery!" Her eyes were blazing and she would have screamed except for fear of waking everyone up. "I have never even looked at another man. As for my sister, the man she was kissing was consecrated to her in *erusin,* and I won't have you accusing her of adultery either." She turned and stalked away, terrified that he intended to put an end to her studies.

But before she'd turned away completely, Meir had seen the tears well up in her eyes. Overcome with remorse, he condemned himself for his drunken rage, for letting his yetzer hara ruin six months of exemplary conduct in his attempt for the Divine Presence to abide with them. So what if she knew Talmud? What did he expect with her growing up in her father's yeshiva? Wasn't a learned wife what he wanted, to make sure his sons became scholars? He took off his mantle and replaced it right side out. He'd been enough of an animal tonight.

The next morning, Joheved slept through services. She didn't want to face Meir, and she suspected, correctly, that there wouldn't be many other women in synagogue either. She woke in time for the midday meal, and as she prepared to put on tefillin, she wondered if he would forbid her that as well.

Meir had gotten up early, hoping to apologize to Joheved on their way to services. Once it became obvious that she wasn't coming, he accompanied Salomon, who was in a surprisingly good mood. Under the influence of much wine, Salomon had experienced a catharsis. After depositing a drowsy Rachel in her bed, he had sat down next to her, observing her innocent beauty as she slept. Drink loosened his inhibitions and he began to sob, first for his poor baby Leah, taken from him so young, and eventually, for his mother too. The next thing he knew, it was morning and he was lying in bed next to Rivka, feeling as if a great weight he'd been carrying had been lifted.

At services, Salomon prayed with joyful thanks, while Meir prayed for forgiveness for desecrating the Creator's festival with ugly words. He also prayed that the Merciful One would open Joheved's heart and allow her to forgive him as well. Maybe he'd be lucky and find that she had consumed so much wine the previous night that she'd forgotten their argument altogether.

When Joheved finally came down to eat, her first thought was to sit as far away from Meir as possible. But even the students who'd slept through services were on time for disner, so the only place available was her customary one next to him. Not wanting to publicize their quarrel by squeezing in next to Miriam, Joheved took her usual seat, but she kept her hands resolutely on the tabletop.

"Master Salomon taught an amusing text this morning about Rabbah and Rav Zeira," Meir said cheerfully, teasing the students who had overslept. "Since so many of you missed it, maybe we can convince him to repeat it now." More important, he wanted Joheved to know that he thought she should hear the Talmud lesson too.

Salomon was happy to comply. "Naturally I taught from Tractate Megillah. I suspect Meir is referring to this passage,

> 'Rabbah and Rav Zeira once made a Purim feast together. They got very drunk, and Rabbah went and cut Rav Zeira's throat. In the morning, Rabbah prayed and brought Rav Zeira back to life. The next year, Rabbah invited Rav Zeira to another Purim feast. But Rabbi Zeira said: No, thank you. A miracle may not happen every time.'"

Those around the table broke into laughter, as much for the funny story as for the knowledge that Master Salomon had recovered his good humor. Benjamin couldn't resist adding, "It's a miracle Rav Zeira could even remember what happened if he was that drunk."

The only one not smiling was Joheved, and the sadness on her face was enough to convince Meir that their argument was neither forgotten nor forgiven. She avoided him the rest of the day, and he grew determined to speak with her.

After souper, he discreetly lingered in the courtyard until she finished in the privy. The orange-striped cat seemed to know Meir needed support and twined companionably around his legs.

"Joheved, please wait." He stepped in front of her and nearly tripped over the cat. "I have to talk with you."

"Didn't you say enough last night?" She nearly bit her tongue in shame at her harsh words. She had hoped he wanted to apologize, but maybe he intended to break their engagement and was being polite by telling her first.

"I want you to know how terribly sorry I am for what I said last night." He corrected himself, "I mean this morning. It was the wine talking. I've been thinking about it all day, and I swear to you that—"

"Stop. Don't make any oaths." Joheved covered his mouth with her hand, but before he could fully appreciate the feel of her skin against his lips, she pulled away as though burned.

"Let me rephrase that," he said carefully. Taking oaths was a serious matter that Jews avoided whenever possible. Children died young as the result of their parents' broken vows. "When we're married, Le Bon Dieu willing, I will hire as many servants as you need so you have time to study." His eyes pleaded with her. "Now that I have repented, will you forgive me?"

"I forgive you, Meir," she replied, her heart bursting with happiness. "And I, in turn, will try not to get upset over anything you say on Purim."

The relief of her forgiveness felt so good that he decided to open his heart to her. "I must also confess that when I got mad at your sister and Benjamin, part of my anger was because it was them embracing so openly, not you and me." There, he had said it. He nervously waited for her response.

"*Moi aussi,*" she said softly and went back indoors, leaving him standing there in elation.

He tried to recapture the fleeting feel of her fingers on his lips, while imagining the two of them in a passionate kiss. The response of his body jolted him back to reality, and he headed to the well. The cat, realizing that there was no food in Meir's direction, turned and followed Joheved into the kitchen.

Between holding Joheved's hand at meals and picturing her sleeping body below him at night, Meir found cold water on his face increasingly ineffective. Springtime filled him with pent-up energy, and he took to swimming in the Seine, where the amused fishermen regarded him as a crazy penitent bathing in the chilly river for some kind of Lenten sacrifice.

Joheved was also growing restless. At night, she knew it was only a few planks of wood that separated her from Meir, and she wondered if he was thinking of her too. Sometimes she could almost pretend that he was lying next to her snoring, not Miriam. It was only four months until the anniversary of Grandmama Leah's death. When was Papa going to set a new wedding date?

At the end of April, Meir went home for Passover and spent more time thinking about Joheved than enjoying the Seder with his family. To make matters worse, it had been unseasonably warm all week and he was having trouble sleeping. He awoke Friday before dawn, keenly missing the pleasure he usually felt as he imagined Joheved waking up below, and decided to return to Troyes.

When Meir entered Salomon's courtyard, he didn't know which was warmer, the weather or the smile Joheved gave him when she saw him. At home on such a day, Meir would have been barefoot and wearing only his chemise, but Salomon's family took disner fully dressed. Sweltering in his wool *côte,* Meir bent over to roll down his hose. At least his legs, hidden beneath the table, wouldn't be quite so hot. But he hadn't anticipated how eager Joheved would be to hold hands. Instead of demurely waiting for him to reach for her hand, she took the initiative, and Meir nearly choked when he felt her fingers on his bare thigh. Immediately he grasped her hand and pulled it away, but it was too late. He was excruciatingly aroused.

The only thing Meir could think of to divert his yetzer hara was intense Torah study, but when he asked Salomon to help him with Song of Songs, the biblical text traditionally read on Shabbat during Passover, the scholar declared that it was too hot. He wanted to take his Sabbath nap first. Perhaps Meir could find a study partner at the synagogue. But the place was empty, forcing Meir to study alone.

Salomon taught his students that the Song of Songs should be read as allegory, a duet of longing between God and Israel. Meir knew this, but the literal meaning of the words assailed him.

> Let him kiss me with the kisses of his mouth, for his love is better than wine.

Meir savored the line and forced himself to recall that Salomon taught that this really meant that Israel longed for God to teach her Torah, "mouth to mouth," as at Sinai. When he read,

> I am faint with love, his left hand is under my head and his right hand embraces me,

it became difficult to remember that this referred to Israel in the desert, enveloped in God's cloud.

The room was sweltering like a desert, and after what had transpired at midday, Meir could only think about real kissing and real embracing. Exasperated, he tried to control his yetzer hara by going back to the text once more. The third chapter began with,

> By night upon my bed, I sought him whom I love,

and through a fog he recalled something about Israel wandering in the wilderness before reaching the Promised Land. The fourth chapter contained a litany of verses describing the bride's beauty: her eyes, hair, teeth, lips, mouth, neck and finally,

> Breasts like two fawns, twins of a gazelle, which feed among the lilies . . . all of you is fair.

Salomon had taught that this referred to the Two Tablets of the Covenant, which nourish Israel, but Meir found himself visualizing a real woman. Finally, it was too much to read,

> My bride, you have ravished my heart with one look from your eyes.

Meir gave up and closed the book.

His damp hair clung to his skin; sweat trickled down his face and through his beard. He mopped his brow with his sleeve and decided that this would be a perfect time to take a swim. He set off down the street, but somehow his feet led him, not to the Seine, but to Salomon's courtyard gate.

Inside Salomon's wine cellar, attempting to avoid the heat, Joheved was also reading Song of Songs. Salomon, Rachel and the servants were taking naps, while Rivka and Miriam had gone to Johanna's to relax now that the ordeal of preparing for the leaven-free eight days of Passover had ended. They had urged Joheved to join them, but she had begged off.

Even as a child, she'd hated going to other women's houses during the festival week. She'd never been taught chess or any of the nut games the other girls liked to play, and they made fun of her when she lost. She couldn't remember ever enjoying Passover; it was so much work to clean everything, and then Papa came home for such a short amount of time that it was mostly a disruption.

Joheved knew things were different now, but the old feelings still surfaced this time of year. Miriam was an apprentice midwife now and friendly with all the young women, but Joheved felt comfortable with women only if she was leading them in prayer. Their talk of husbands, children, clothes and where to find the freshest meat was not the least bit interesting.

Joheved sighed and focused her attention on the text. Some time ago she had heard Papa discussing Song of Songs with the monk, Robert. The prior declared it an allegory about love between God and the Church, while Papa countered that the song told of God's relationship with Israel through time. After Robert left, Papa had muttered angrily about the *minim* appropriating the holy song for their heresy, when it was obviously a message of consolation to the Jews.

Now Joheved was determined to study the song herself, to see if she could find the historical verses Papa said were there. It wasn't difficult. There in the first chapter was

> I have compared you to a mare in Pharaoh's chariots,

an obvious reference to Egypt, and in the second chapter, she found

> He brought me to the banquet house and his banner over me was love . . . his fruit was sweet to my lips,

which was about God's giving Israel the Torah. Solving this riddle was far more entertaining than visiting with a bunch of gossipy women, Joheved thought, and eagerly began chapter three. She had finished chapter six, where

> You are beautiful, my love, comely as Jerusalem

meant building the Holy Temple, and was deep into chapter seven when Meir discovered her reading by the light of the clerestory windows. Dressed only in her chemise, her silhouette was clearly outlined beneath it.

Meir's body responded like lightning coursing through him and a gasp escaped his lips. Joheved looked up, smiled in recognition, and any hope he had of leaving undetected vanished.

"Meir, what perfect timing." She jumped up and showed him the book. "Papa told me that the verses in Song of Songs teach the history of Israel. Here, let me show you."

Excited to share her knowledge, Joheved was oblivious to the effect her nearness and thin clothing were having upon Meir. "See all the verses that mention wine or vineyards. Papa says that a vineyard often means study hall in the Gemara, so that these lines symbolize the progress from Mishnah to Talmud:

> Come my beloved . . . let us see if the vine has budded, if its blossoms have opened.

Meir automatically continued with the line that followed,

> If the pomegranates are in flower, there I will give you my love.

Joheved remembered how smelling grape blossoms had affected Miriam, and was suddenly very aware of the words she and Meir had just recited, as well as his proximity.

In the weeks that followed, whenever Joheved thought about that sultry afternoon in the cellar, which was often, she could never recollect exactly how it had happened. One moment she and Meir were quoting Song of Songs, and the next, he was kissing her with the hunger of a starving man presented with a banquet. And she was responding just as ardently.

He fervently kissed her lips, cheeks and ears; he kissed her neck and inhaled the fragrance of her hair. When she turned so he could kiss her lips again, he sank onto a bench and pulled her into his lap. Time seemed suspended, and Joheved had no idea how long they were lost in each other's arms. She also had no idea that her father, standing at the top of the cellar stairs, had discovered them and was trying to restrain his outrage.

seventeen

Salomon had awakened, hot and thirsty. He was about to descend into the cellar for a cool cup of wine when he heard the unmistakable sounds below, and a glance was all he needed to identify the lovers. At first, his anger blazed at how Meir had taken advantage of his hospitality and at how enthusiastically his daughter had abandoned her modesty. But by force of habit, Salomon's intellect began to temper his emotions.

He could see the passion that enveloped the couple, rendering them oblivious to his presence, and contrasted it with his own awkward wedding night. He suddenly realized that the Creator had just given him an opportunity to ensure himself grandsons.

The sound of a polite cough shattered the lovers' private world, and disoriented, they looked up into what Salomon hoped was a face of furious disapproval. They sprang apart immediately, and he angrily demanded an explanation for their disgraceful behavior.

"Rabbenu," Meir used the honorific title, intending to say whatever was necessary to protect Joheved's reputation. "I apologize for subjecting you to this display. It was entirely my fault. Joheved did nothing to entice me." He seemed to be groveling, but Salomon noticed that Meir hadn't actually said he was sorry for his actions, only for exposing his teacher to them.

Joheved was humiliated beyond belief by her father catching her in such a compromising position. Her yetzer hara, coupled with years of resentment and adolescent rebellion, fanned her anger. She stepped forward and challenged her father.

"Don't you blame Meir, Papa; it's not his fault." Her voice rose. "This wouldn't have happened if you'd arranged for us to be married already!"

Now Salomon had no need to feign indignation. How dare his daughter address him in such an insolent tone? In a voice of barely controlled fury, he began lecturing Joheved about showing proper respect for parents, reminding her that, according to scripture, a rebellious youth forfeits his life.

"Well, what do you expect?" she retorted. "You were never here to teach me appropriate behavior."

Salomon's eyes blazed as he shushed her. "Keep your voice down; people are trying to sleep upstairs." He had better end this confrontation before his daughter said anything more she'd regret. "Joheved, go to your room and think about the fifth commandment and repentance until you come to your senses."

Then he turned to Meir, who was nearly frozen with shock, and said, "Come with me, Meir. Let's take a walk."

They mutely trod the city streets. Most people were either indoors or at the river, and while Meir felt relieved that they weren't likely to meet anyone he knew, he waited in dread for Salomon's chastisement.

"If it weren't Shabbat, we'd be on our way to Ramerupt," his future father-in-law finally broke the silence.

Now Meir was even more worried; surely Salomon didn't intend to inform his parents of the afternoon's debacle. He summoned the courage to face Salomon again. "I apologize for being unable to control my yetzer hara; I beg you to forgive me." He ought to have promised that it would never happen again, but he didn't dare make such a vow.

Suddenly Salomon started to chuckle. "The yetzer hara certainly took control of you and Joheved today. Are you sure you want to marry my daughter now that you've experienced her temper?"

There was nothing Meir wanted more than to marry the woman who had kissed him with such fervor, but he said merely, "I do."

Salomon sighed at the young man's glum tone. Then, to Meir's amazement, Salomon told him that in a way, Joheved was right. "We do need to set a wedding date, and the sooner the better."

Meir's heart soared as his future father-in-law teasingly scolded him about their poor timing. "Instead of marrying quickly next week, you two must now wait a month until Lag b'Omer."

Since Talmudic times, when a plague among Rabbi Akiva's students lasted thirty-three days from Passover until Lag b'Omer, those days have been ones of semimourning when no weddings are held. "As soon as Shabbat is over," Salomon said, "we will ride to Ramerupt and confirm the wedding date with your parents."

They walked again in silence, Meir basking in his sudden good fortune, until Salomon interrupted his musing. "Meir, I have never told anyone what I am about to share with you."

"When Rivka and I were married," he began somberly, "I had no father or older brother to advise me about 'using the bed.' To my shame, I thought that what I'd learned from Talmud was all I needed to know." Salomon paused a moment. "I assume you've studied Arayot?"

Meir nodded. Last summer, a chacham reputed to be happily married had taught him and another student the various Talmud texts having to do with sexual matters.

"Well, then, let me remind you of the discussion in Tractate Ketubot about the pain women bear when they lose their virginity."

"I remember it," Meir replied. "There's a debate over whether a rapist should pay for the pain he inflicts on his virgin victim since she would otherwise suffer the same pain when she married. The Sages decide that the rapist must still pay damages for pain because,

> There is no comparison between engaging in relations on a dunghill and engaging in relations in a bridal chamber."

"That's right," Salomon said. "Then they wonder if a seducer should also pay damages for pain, and they ask their wives to describe what a woman feels at that time.

> Rava said: The daughter of Rav Hisda told me that it is like the prick of a blood letter's lancet. Rav Pappa said: The daughter of Abba Sura told me it is like a dry crust in the gums.

"So the rabbis conclude that a woman feels almost no pain in consensual relations, and like a fool, I asked no questions." Salomon's voice grew so quiet that Meir had to strain to hear. "When the time came, I found my wife's passage so tightly blocked that it took all my strength to break through. Rivka never cried out, and I only realized later how much I must have hurt her."

"Even now, I doubt she has much pleasure in the holy deed." He shook his head sadly. "I didn't realize that only when a woman feels desire will it be as Rava and Rav Pappa described."

"I see," Meir said. And also when she and her husband have a relationship where they can discuss such an intimate subject.

Salomon proceeded to explain his plan. "I will pretend to be angry, while you arrange to see Joheved alone. Remember what it says in Proverbs: 'Stolen waters are sweet and bread eaten in secret is pleasant.' If you increase her desire for you, she will find pleasure in your bed, emit her seed first, and conceive fine sons."

Meir nodded in dazed agreement, recalling that the Sages taught that the quality of a child's traits reflected the quality of the marital act that conceived him.

Salomon turned to face Meir and asked, "Can you do this and still control your yetzer hara?"

"I believe so. After all, it'll only be for a few weeks," Meir replied with apparent confidence. He hoped he could.

While Salomon and Meir were plotting, Miriam had come home early, hoping to study Song of Songs with Joheved. But she found the house silent, all the bedroom doors closed. Sure that everyone was enjoying the traditional Sabbath nap, she tiptoed up the stairs and quietly entered the room she shared with her sisters.

Joheved, who had been lying face down on the bed, snapped to a sitting position. She had obviously been crying.

"Mon Dieu, Joheved. What's wrong?" It couldn't be a death or injury; somebody would have gotten her and Rivka earlier.

Reluctantly, and with great embarrassment, Joheved related her story. Miriam didn't know what to say. She couldn't imagine which was more unlikely, Joheved speaking so rudely to their father or him catching her and Meir kissing.

"It's not fair," Joheved said between sobs. "You and Benjamin steal kisses all the time and never get caught, but the first time it happens to me, Papa has to walk in on us."

"Do you think Papa is more angry about you and Meir kissing, or your talking back to him?" Miriam longed to know how they had come to be embracing in the cellar, but that would have to wait.

"I don't know. And what difference does it make anyway?"

"The difference is that you'd better come up with an appropriate apology before Papa gets home."

They were still trying to compose one when they heard voices below. Joheved began pacing the room. "I can't face them yet. Please, Miriam, tell Mama that I'm not well, that I'm not coming down to eat." She was shaking with fright.

But it was too late. Salomon stuck his head in the door, and in a voice that brooked no excuses, said he expected them both to join the family for the final Shabbat meal. At the table, he and Meir discussed the historical allegory of the Song of Songs, and Miriam added a few comments of her own. Joheved said nothing—her gaze fixed firmly downward, her face blazing with shame, both hands clearly visible on the tablecloth. Papa obviously intended her discipline to wait until the festive day had ended.

After Havdalah, when Salomon announced that he and Meir were riding to Ramerupt that very night, Rivka expressed her alarm. "Can't it wait until tomorrow? You know how dangerous it is to go out tonight?" Saturday night was particularly perilous because the evil spirits released from Gehenna for the Sabbath were angry at being forced back to their eternal punishment.

"Don't worry, Rivka; we'll be safe. The moon is nearly full and we'll stay out of the shadows." He reassured her even though he knew from Tractate Pesachim that Wednesday and Saturday were the very nights the demon Agrat went abroad with eighteen myriads of destroying angels. "Besides, a ride in the cool evening air is just what I need after such a warm day."

They would also be protected because they were on their way to perform the mitzvah of arranging a wedding, but Salomon wasn't ready to make that announcement yet. He had Joheved walk them to the gate, where he sternly told her that he'd hear what she had to say when he returned. As soon as they left, she ran upstairs, threw herself on the bed and burst into fresh tears.

Was he sending Meir away? She couldn't imagine a single good reason for them to see Meir's parents in the middle of the night. Miriam couldn't think why the two of them needed to go to Ramerupt either, but she forced Joheved back to the task at hand.

When Joheved finally felt that she had the proper penitent words fixed in her memory, she went outside to wait. The full moon lit up the courtyard, reminding her of last month's Purim celebration. How ironic that

Miriam, who had shared her fiancé's embraces with impunity, had been too drunk to remember them the next day. Right now, Joheved would have given anything to have her own memory erased in the morning.

Suddenly she heard men's voices. Unable to stand the suspense, she threw herself at her father as soon as he opened the gate. "Oh, Papa, I'm so sorry I said all those terrible things to you." Her carefully composed apology had disappeared from her mind. "I'm so ashamed of myself. I didn't mean to show you disrespect." She babbled on with words of contrition and remorse.

"Very well, ma fille, I forgive you." Salomon gave her a hug. "And I hope you will forgive me for delaying your marriage when I tell you that I have arranged with Meir's parents for a Lag b'Omer wedding. His mother has sent some fabric for your wedding dress." He thrust a bolt of material at her.

Joheved looked back and forth several times between her father's smile, Meir's beaming face, and the blue silk in her hands, then she almost knocked Salomon down hugging him in return. Salomon extricated himself from her arms and warned the couple to control their yetzers until the wedding. "I expect no repetition of today's incident," he said, giving Meir a wink.

In the weeks that followed, Meir managed to steal ever more kisses and caresses from Joheved. At first she was reluctant, and he had to carefully choose a time when Salomon was away. But soon she was taking the initiative, even using Miriam to make sure the coast was clear. Meir knew that Salomon was trying not to discover them, but they still had to stay clear of Rivka.

Finally it was Meir's last night in the attic. Tomorrow several students would ride with him to his parents' home, and from then on, as a precaution against demons, neither he nor Joheved would be left alone until the wedding. Tonight would be their boldest meeting yet; they had arranged that he would stay downstairs studying until the household was asleep; then Joheved would sneak down when the bells began to chime matins.

Joheved met him wearing only her chemise, and he reached out to caress her through the thin fabric. Her two yetzers warred within her: the good one telling her to stop him, that they should wait until their wedding night, and her yetzer hara, its attention focused on Meir fondling her breasts. She could feel her nipples harden between his fingers, and her hips began to rotate every so subtly against his.

Meir couldn't imagine how he would be able to end this glorious encounter, but he needn't have worried. Salomon had been sleeping fitfully, expecting such an assignation. When the sounds below grew loud enough to make him think things had gone far enough, he began to cough heavily and make more noise than usual using the chamber pot. Sure enough, it was only a short time later that he heard his daughter sprinting back up the stairs.

The next night, Salomon and Samuel began the task of instructing their respective children in proper marital behavior. Arayot were traditionally taught to two students, so Salomon decided to teach Joheved and Miriam together. He brought out Tractate Shabbat and showed them a spot nearly at its end. Joheved read the text aloud.

> Rav Hisda said to his daughters: You should be modest before your husband. You should not eat herbs at night.

This was amazing—the Talmud never addressed women.

"But I eat herbs in front of Benjamin all the time," Miriam objected.

"He means the herbs that give your breath an unpleasant odor," Salomon explained.

Miriam continued eagerly.

> You should not eat dates at night, and you should not drink beer at night. And you should not relieve yourselves where your husbands relieve themselves.

She couldn't help but giggle at this advice.

Salomon remained serious. "Dates and beer can cause flatulence," he said, "and if you and your husband both relieve yourself in the same place, he may see some traces that remain and be offended."

Now both sisters were fighting back nervous laughter, and Joheved forced herself to recall that this was holy text. She'd better say something. "But Papa, eating herbs and dates and drinking beer . . . that's only a problem at night . . . when they go to bed with their husbands?" She felt herself blush as he agreed.

"Joheved," he pointed out the text to her, "the next passage is rather important for a new bride. Why don't you read it?"

> Your husband will hold a pearl in one hand and a *kora* in one hand.

Joheved stumbled over the Aramaic word *kora.* She had no idea what it meant, but she continued to read. The previous verses had been easy to understand; perhaps the next one would clarify things.

> You should give him the pearl, but the *kora* you should not give until you both are tormented, and only then should you give it to him.

Though she understood what every word except *kora* meant, the text was incomprehensible. She looked at Miriam, who shrugged her shoulders helplessly.

Salomon knew this passage referred to a delicate subject, and he had thought carefully about how he would explain it before finally deciding that frankness was best. "Rav Hisda is using very tactful language to instruct his daughters about the role they will have in marital relations. When he says 'pearl' he means breast, and when he says '*kora,*' which is best translated as 'forge,' he means the womb."

Salomon might as well be discussing any unremarkable Talmud passage.

"You are no longer children, so I will not use euphemisms." He cleared his throat and said very quickly, "When your husband caresses you to arouse the desire for relations, and he holds your breasts with one hand and your womb with the other, give him your breasts first to increase his passion, but do not allow him the place of intercourse too soon, until his passion increases and he is in pain with desire."

Both girls' faces were flaming, but their father ignored their embarrassment and calmly asked if they had any questions. Miriam was speechless, but Joheved, equally disconcerted, felt she had to query him at least once to show she'd grasped the material.

She forced herself to speak seriously. "Papa, why does Rav Hisda call the womb a forge?" A pearl did make a suitable symbol for the breast.

"I'm not sure," he replied. He had never taught this text to any of his yeshiva students; they were too young. And he had only studied it once himself, just before he married Rivka. "Perhaps it is because, just as a forge refines precious metals, the womb refines the man's seed into a child."

That made sense, Joheved thought. She had the feeling there was more to the text, that she should be asking other questions. But she needed time to think about it, time she didn't have.

That same evening in Ramerupt, Samuel was presenting a manuscript to his son. Meir opened the slim volume, titled "Tractate Kallah (Bride)," and looked at his father with surprise. He had never heard of such a tractate.

Samuel smiled at his son's bewilderment. "Tractate Kallah is not actually part of the Talmud; it's additional material. Before my *nisuin,* my father gave me this book to copy. I gave it to your brother before his wedding, and now it's your turn. I'm sure you will find its lessons well worth learning."

Meir took the mysterious volume up to his room and began reading. After the first few pages, he was blushing furiously. The author, with the intent of extolling erotic pleasure within marriage, had provided detailed and salacious descriptions of sexual techniques. No wonder this wasn't part of the Talmud. Yet the book started out innocently.

> He should give her pleasure and embrace her and kiss her and sanctify himself with sexual intercourse. He should not use foul language and should not see in her anything contemptible, but rather arouse her with caresses and with all manner of embracing in order to fulfill his desire and hers.

The author continued by explaining the various kinds of caresses and embracing, and in what order to use them most efficaciously. And should the reader be affronted that any of these were unnatural, a quote from Talmud (Tractate Nedarim) followed.

> The Sages say: Anything that a man wants to do with his wife, he may do, like meat that comes from a kosher butcher. If he wants it salted, he may; roasted, he may; boiled, he may; braised, he may.

Even nonprocreative practices were permitted, if performed "once in a while, not as a habitual practice." But it was forbidden to force his wife in the holy deed; this was sure to produce wicked and sinful children. And if a man wanted male children, he should perform the holy deed twice in a row.

The new husband was advised to eat spicy foods to increase the flow of semen. Salty fish, strong wine, lentils, cheese, eggs and roasted garlic were also recommended. There was a section on love potions, the least complicated of which involved cutting one's fingernails, toenails and pubic hair, burning them to a powder, and steeping this in water for nine days before serving the drink to one's beloved.

The manuscript continued in this eclectic fashion, combining folksy advice with licentious commentary. There was even a blessing, the Birkat Betulim, for the new husband to say after seeing his bride's blood of virginity. Meir had never heard of such a benediction, and he kept reciting it until he had it memorized.

> *Baruch ata Adonai* . . . Who put an almond tree in the Garden of Eden, roses in the valley; let no stranger control the sealed fountain. Therefore her lover's holy seed she keeps pure and does not break the law. *Baruch ata Adonai,* Who chooses Abraham and his seed to make Israel holy.

What a strange blessing. Was he supposed to say it right after they used the bed for the first time or should he wait until the next morning when it was light? Tractate Kallah didn't say.

Meir was pondering this question when one of his father's menservants knocked on the door. Samuel was taking no chances with demons. Not only would his young grandson share Meir's bed, but a servant would sleep on the floor as well. The next night Meir's room was more crowded. Meshullam's family arrived, and now another nephew shared his bed.

The day before the wedding, the house was overflowing with relatives, so when Meshullam suggested they ride together along the Aube River, which bordered the manor, Meir was eager for respite. At first they rode together in silence.

Eventually Meshullam cleared his throat and said, "Meir, I assume Papa showed you his copy of 'Tractate Kallah.' Do you have any questions?"

"Well," Meir hesitated. He'd been trying not to think too much about Tractate Kallah. It was difficult enough to sleep already. "How do I make sure that she emits seed first? . . . I mean, how do I make sure I don't emit mine first?" So far he hadn't been very successful at controlling his yetzer hara when Joheved was around.

Meshullam stopped to let his horse munch on a clump of grass. "Concentrate on remembering the Birkat Betulim."

"You mean I'm supposed to recite it that night? But how can I see any blood in the dark?"

"You wait until morning to say it, but just thinking about it should slow you down," Meshullam replied, giving his horse a soft kick to get her going again. "Now, remember, your bride's passage is closed, and it will probably cause her some pain when you first open her. Some say it is best to enter quickly with a strong thrust, but I think gentleness is important, even if it is more difficult for you to control yourself."

Meir, recalling Salomon's sad tale, grimaced at the idea of causing Joheved pain.

"Don't worry," Meshullam's voice was reassuring. "If you have aroused her desire sufficiently, it will only be a momentary discomfort for her."

"One last piece of advice, Meir." They were approaching the manor gate. "I know we're taught not to waste seed, but if you get too aroused reading Tractate Kallah, you may need to. You'll want to get a good's night sleep tonight."

Meir knew his brother meant well, but his yetzer hara had never forced him to deliberately waste seed before, and he wasn't about to start now, the night before his wedding. Besides, thus far his prenuptial anxieties had been more than enough to counter the stimulating effects of Tractate Kallah.

eighteen

Ramerupt
Late Spring 4834 (1074 C.E.)

The next morning, it seemed as though every member of Meir's extended family came in to offer advice and good wishes while he dressed. It was just as well that the bride and groom fasted on their wedding day; he couldn't have eaten breakfast anyway. Marona had just finished sewing closed the sleeves of his fine new linen chemise when they heard the clattering of horses and clanging of weapons in the courtyard.

Meir ran to the open front door, where the household had assembled to watch Benjamin, Asher and several yeshiva students in mock combat with Meshullam and Meir's cousins. He raced to get a sword and join the fray, but his mother barred his way.

"Meir, are you crazy?" she said. "After all the work I put into your new silk côte, you want to go out there and ruin it?"

He reluctantly replaced the weapon and waited for the ruckus to die down. It was traditional for the groom to be escorted to his wedding, "just as a king is attended by his guards." The encounter was so likely to result in damage that Jewish law held: "If a man or horse is injured when a fellow rides to greet the bridegroom, and he pleads that he did nothing wrong, but rode normally, he is not believed, and must provide evidence."

Meir threw on his mantle and adjusted his ornamented hat. This was it. He mounted his horse, waved good-bye to the servants, and with great fanfare, the wedding party set off, accompanied by a wagon of musicians to provide entertainment as they made their way to Troyes.

When they crossed the Seine and reached Bishop's Gate, much of the Jewish community was there to meet them. Though it was broad daylight, many of the men held torches. The boisterous crowd escorted Meir to the synagogue, where morning services were in progress. Then, having done their duty for the bridegroom, the torchbearers and musicians left for Salomon's house.

Joheved had spent a restless night. She had been so eager for this morning to arrive, each day looking longingly at her beautiful blue silk bliaut. But yesterday, after returning from her first trip to the mikvah, reality sunk in. Tomorrow, Meir would be her husband and master. She had seen him angry once, and though he had quickly apologized, maybe he wasn't always so contrite. And would he really approve of her studies?

Then of course, there was another worry—their wedding night. Mama had said nothing except that when it was time, Aunt Sarah, the midwife, would tell her all she needed to know. Mama had offered the excuse of being busy with the wedding banquet, but Joheved had seen the anxiety in her mother's eyes. What was it that Mama wouldn't talk about?

She knew brides were expected to bleed, but how bad would it hurt? She tried to recall how much she longed to be with Meir when they were apart, how much she enjoyed his kisses.

But what if she wasn't ready and he forced her? And what about Rav Hisda's words—not offering the forge until they were both tormented? Tormented? Was she supposed to suffer before they coupled? Why hadn't she asked Papa about this? She prayed that Meir wouldn't cause her too much pain.

Each new worry chased another through her mind, until she forced herself to concentrate on the prayer she'd recited earlier, before her immersion:

"Mon Dieu, may it be Your will that Your presence dwell between my husband and me. May his thoughts always be about me, and about no other, as it is written, 'Therefore shall a man leave his father and his mother and cleave to his wife.' May we be worthy to see with our own eyes children from our children who are committed to Torah and to good deeds. May You hear my prayer with mercy and great compassion. Amen."

She whispered it again and again, until she fell asleep.

Too soon it was morning, and she had overslept. Everyone had already eaten when Mama entered her room, carrying the chemise for her wedding bliaut. Mama and Anna had spent hours embroidering its neck, sleeves and hem with blue flowers to match the silken côte. Behind their mother trailed Miriam and Rachel, eager to help their sister dress for her finest hour.

While Rivka and Miriam sewed up her sleeves, Rachel brushed Joheved's hair. Her wedding day was the last time her hair would be fully visible in public. Until the ceremony was over, she would be veiled, but afterwards everyone would see her long, unbraided hair. Just as a new mother's hair was loosened during childbirth, it was best to have nothing constricted upon the nuptial bed. Certainly not the bride's hair.

The three sisters took turns admiring themselves in the shiny new wall mirror that Meir had sent as a wedding present. Joheved stared at the stranger who looked back at her so intently. How grown up she looked, dressed in her wedding finery. She took a step closer and examined her face. Meir was right; she definitely had blue eyes. But her nose was so big, and where did all those freckles come from? She glanced at Miriam and then back at the mirror. She really did look like her younger sister. Miriam's nose was a little smaller and her face was thinner, but otherwise, they had the same visage.

Joheved turned slightly, trying to see her profile. Nobody would call her a beauty, but at least she wasn't homely. Look at her—such serious expression. She stuck out her tongue, struck a few poses, and then laughed aloud at her silliness. Well, she certainly looked more attractive when she smiled. At least she had nice, straight teeth.

Miriam was reluctant to spend much time staring at herself. Compared to Joheved she was too thin, and all those days in the vineyard with Benjamin had tanned her as brown as a peasant. But she couldn't resist making faces back at Joheved, and when Rachel joined in, the three of them nearly collapsed in giggles. After that, it was impossible to coax Rachel away from the mirror. She stared at her reflection as if transfixed, and only when they heard the musicians approaching was the mirror forgotten.

Her heart beating furiously, Joheved climbed on the white mare and gave one last glance homeward, her gaze focusing on the window of the bedroom she would no longer share with her sisters. When she reached the synagogue entrance, Meir came forward to receive her, and surprisingly, she felt neither eager nor frightened. It was as if she were somehow outside herself, watching.

He took her hand, and as they stood together, the congregation threw wheat and shouted, "Be fruitful and multiply!" Then Mama escorted her up the stairs, while Meir hurried to his seat at the front of the synagogue.

Services continued as usual, except that the penitential prayers were omitted.

Once in the balcony, the women surged forward to weave flowers into Joheved's hair and help her into her jewelry. Most of it was Leah's, but two items were new, gifts from Meir. Those close enough to see their detail oohed and ahhed as Marona fastened Joheved's new girdle and placed the matching headpiece over her veil. Both were fashioned of shining silver, woven into a wide braid and decorated with delicate silver birds. The eye of each bird was either a pearl or a sapphire, the stone of Issachar, of understanding and of Torah. Just before it was time for the ceremony, Aunt Sarah anointed her with perfume.

Escorted by Rivka and Marona, Joheved walked outdoors to the raised platform in the center of the synagogue courtyard. Under the safety of her veil, she stared at Meir with impunity, but his expression was inscrutable. His côte was made of the same blue silk as hers, and she could hear people saying that they made a handsome couple.

When she reached his side, he lifted her veil and threw it over his own head as well, forming the wedding canopy. Two young students called as witnesses were told to observe carefully as Meir wedded Joheved by reciting the ancient formula, "Behold, you are consecrated unto me by this ring, according to the Law of Moses and Israel."

As he slipped the ring onto her right forefinger, Joheved could feel his hand shaking. How was it possible for her to be so calm? She put her hand over his to reassure him and barely heard the *ketubah* and marriage settlements being read to the witnesses. The crowd was so large that not everyone fit into the courtyard, so they moved into the street for the *chazan* to chant the seven wedding benedictions.

"Soon may there be heard in the cities of Judah, in the streets of Jerusalem, the voice of gladness and joy, the voice of bridegroom and bride, the grooms jubilant from their canopies and the youths from their feasts of song. Baruch ata Adonai, who makes the bridegroom to rejoice with the bride."

As the *chazan* finished this last blessing, Meir took up a cup of wine, drank deeply and gave it to Joheved. His eyes never left hers as she lifted the cup to her lips. When she was done, Meir turned and threw the goblet at the synagogue's outer wall. The cup shattered, and several maidens raced to pick up the shards, possession of which assured them a good marriage.

Immediately the musicians broke into song, and the company, shouting with joy, rushed at the newly wedded couple and carried them to Salomon's house. No sooner did they enter the gate than Benjamin and Asher, swinging a loudly squawking hen and rooster over their heads, forced them up the stairs and into Leah's, now their, bedroom.

Suddenly, they were alone. Their mad dash had gotten Meir to the bridal chamber before any demons, confused by the noise, could prevent him from enjoying his newly won nuptial happiness.

Joheved sat on the bed, decked with blooming honeysuckle, and looked around at everything except her husband. She knew this was her grandmother's old room, but it seemed different now, bright and cheerful. Mama had fastened rose-colored hangings on the walls, and there was new linen on the bed. On an unfamiliar chest, which Joheved supposed must contain Meir's effects, was a tray holding bread, wine, half a roasted chicken, two cooked eggs and some fruit preserves. There was also a small dish of salt.

Still feeling unnaturally calm, she tore off some of the bread and dipped it into the salt, then handed a piece to Meir and joined him in the blessing. They ate in silence, listening to the sounds of people celebrating outside. Mixed with the sweet scent of honeysuckle, Joheved could make out the fennel strewn among the fresh rushes and ferns. More protection from demons.

A sudden thought filled her with panic. Was she expected to use the bed with Meir now? Nobody had told her and, though she'd been to weddings before, it hadn't occurred to her to ask. One thing was certain; somebody had left food for them, and she was hungry. Still, it was all she could do to keep her hand from shaking as she dipped her bread in the preserves and took a bite.

Joheved felt Meir watching her; she looked up and their eyes met.

Those beautiful blue eyes, he thought, the same color as the silk they both were wearing. That was enough waiting for Meir. They were married now, and he should be kissing her, not sitting there staring at her. He pulled her down on the bed, fastened his lips on hers and reveled in her ardent response.

She pressed her body against his, and her perfume, which had first enticed him when they stood together under her veil, smelled stronger now.

His hands sought out her curves, but other than reaching directly under her chemise from below, which seemed too brazen, there was no way to caress her bare skin. They were both sewn into their clothes.

Meir broke their embrace. They eyed each other hungrily, and Joheved reached for him again. "We can't," he told her between kisses. "We have to wait until we can get out of these clothes." He sat up and attempted to replace the flowers his fingers had dislodged.

"We'd better eat our food then," she said, offering him one of the eggs. Relief coursed through her. Meir hadn't tried to force her, and his kisses were just as sweet as she remembered.

They finished the small meal and did their best to smooth their rumpled clothes. Joheved wanted to enjoy their privacy a while longer, but Meir pulled her towards the door.

"Come, my bride, the sooner we get down there, the sooner we can leave."

Rachel, who had stationed herself at the bottom of the stairs for this purpose, ran outside to announce the honored couple's imminent appearance. Rivka had made Joheved's bliaut so frugally that there was enough fabric left over to make one for Rachel as well, and the girl was beside herself with joy. The blue silk set off the contrast between her dark curls and fair skin, and now she was the one to wear red ribbons.

The musicians burst into a fanfare as the newlyweds entered the courtyard, and dancers ran to grab their hands and pull them into the quickly forming circles. Before she knew it, Joheved was going one way and Meir was moving in the opposite direction. She danced with Mama, with Miriam and finally with her new female in-laws before the musicians struck up the tune for a mixed-couple dance and she could be back in Meir's arms.

When the dance ended, the musicians signaled for everyone to sit while they serenaded the bride and groom. Secular songs, particularly love songs, were officially discouraged in Jewish households, yet everyone knew them. The *jongleur* began with one that was often sung as a lullaby, and was rewarded with wet cheeks on many of the older women. Meir's mother was seated next to him, and he could hear her sniffling as she reminded Samuel that she used to sing that very song to their son when he was small.

Rejoice, O Bridegroom, in the wife of your youth
Let your heart be merry now and when you shall grow old
Sons to your sons shall you see, your old age's crown
Your days spent in good, your years in pleasantness.

Joheved and Meir remained seated at the head table under the apple tree while relatives and guests chatted with them. The only taint on the happy occasion came when a guest began arguing with Benjamin and Asher. In a voice so loud that the musicians' efforts to drown him out were unsuccessful, he accused the two students of stealing his chickens. A hen and rooster were missing from his coop, and he demanded their immediate return. Of course this was impossible; the wedding party had eaten them.

Salomon rolled his eyes and stood up, intending to get some coins to pay for the purloined poultry. He knew of the responsa that stated "Young men with the bridegroom should not steal from anyone, neither chickens nor anything else," and he was fairly certain that his pupils were not ignorant of this rule either. Still it was rude for the aggrieved man to interrupt the wedding banquet. If he had complained in private, Salomon would have promptly reimbursed him.

Then Meshullam stepped in and insisted on dealing with the indignant guest himself. Having made off with his share of birds at other weddings, he knew that the students would be terribly shamed if their *maître* ended up paying for their prank.

The afternoon wore on, with more singing, dancing, and of course, more eating and drinking. It was almost like Purim, except that Meir and Joheved would be the first, rather than the last, to leave. Meir began to wonder how soon they could make their exit, how he would know when the time was right.

Samuel must have noticed his son's increasing impatience, because, just before sunset, he stood up and motioned the musicians for quiet. He raised his cup and toasted the newlyweds, "For a happy life!"

The guests understood the signal and began to yell out their good wishes as well. Meir and Joheved rose to thank everyone, and wheat was soon flying at them from all directions. There seemed no escape but to run for the house, with the chants of "Be fruitful and multiply" in their ears. Hannah and Aunt Sarah, having been delegated the task of helping the couple out of their finery, followed discreetly.

In his new bedroom, Hannah carefully undid the stitches on her brother's chemise. She suspected that he had already received advice from the male members of their family, and she wanted to give him the female point of view.

"I don't want to worry you, Meir, but please remember that what feels good for you might be painful for your new bride, especially the first time."

She finished one sleeve and moved to the other side. "There's no way of knowing in advance," she said. "I'm just telling you not to be shocked or feel like you've done something wrong if Joheved bleeds a lot or cries."

Meir knew his sister was trying to be helpful, but right now, he didn't want to think about how much this might hurt Joheved. "I promise I'll be as gentle and considerate as possible," he said, and when Hannah removed the last thread, he directed her out the door. Moving quickly to the chest that held his belongings, he pulled out Tractate Kallah.

In Joheved's room, Sarah was telling her niece exactly what she could expect to happen between her and her new husband, but her explanation was far more clinical than Rav Hisda's words to his daughters. "You should encourage Meir in what gives you pleasure, Joheved," she told her, "because it is through your mutual satisfaction that you will merit worthy children."

"But, Aunt Sarah, how do I give my husband pleasure?" Joheved asked. It seemed selfish to ignore his needs.

Sarah smiled and said, "Don't worry about his pleasure. Young men like Meir have strong yetzers, and it will be a challenge for him to control his desire while stimulating yours. You mustn't be disappointed if he can't do it at first."

Joheved had more questions, but that was all Aunt Sarah would say. They removed her new outfit, and soon Joheved stood dressed only in an old chemise. Aunt Sarah anointed her with more perfume and walked with her into the hall. Joheved took a deep breath, then opened the bedroom door and stepped inside.

Meir was standing by the window, trying to read in the fading light, when he heard the door open. He too was wearing just a chemise, and Joheved felt a surprising sense of relief that he hadn't undressed and gotten into bed already. He immediately closed the shutters, but she could still see quite well. That there was some light remaining in the room disconcerted her; she had expected that it would be dark when they first cohabited.

Joheved hung her new clothes on the pegs next to his. She hadn't had time to turn around when she felt Meir's arms encircle her waist and his lips kissing her neck. Chills went down her back and she shivered. It was a pleasant sensation, but she wanted her lips and arms in a position to reach him. She squirmed around to face him, and was suddenly aware that only two very thin pieces of cloth separated their otherwise naked bodies. It was both exciting and scary.

Meir looked down at Joheved and tried to read her expression. He wanted to ask her what her aunt, the midwife, had told her, but he was afraid that she would want to know what his sister had said in return. He gently ran his fingers through her hair and tried to think of something to say that wouldn't make him sound foolish.

She startled him by speaking first. "What are you thinking?"

"I can't believe how lovely you look; your hair is so beautiful." Meir somehow made an inspired reply, and asked in return, "What are you thinking?"

Her face colored with that question and she averted her gaze. Before she was forced to give a response that would only embarrass her further, he said quickly, "I also think that we have better uses for our mouths than asking questions."

His hands were still in her hair, so he tilted her face up and bent over to kiss her. Her perfume was intoxicating, and he reveled in the feeling of her lips on his. His right hand, which had been moving over the linen that covered her back and shoulders, slowly made its way to her breast. He marveled at its soft fullness, and gently rubbed his thumb across the nipple, which hardened under his touch. He heard Joheved's quick intake of breath, but she didn't flinch.

Joheved's anxiety over the lack of darkness was forgotten in the agreeable sensation Meir's lips were giving her. His caresses were so sensuous that she understood why the cats purred with pleasure when she petted them. When he began fondling her breast, she remembered Rav Hisda's advice and was reassured that things were as they should be.

But as soon as he touched her nipple, the reaction this caused was extraordinary. It was as if she had been burned, but with pleasure rather than pain, and it radiated out from her breast, down her belly to that place between her legs. She felt an intense yearning unlike anything she had ever known, something like an itch that cried out to be scratched and a need to use the privy.

When Meir brought his left hand around to cup her other breast and tease that nipple as well, she thought she would swoon with the intensity of her desire. Her arm went up behind his neck to grasp his shoulder, and she kissed him harder, as if this would somehow keep her on her feet. Her weakness only increased with his tender ministrations, finally forcing her to slip out of his embrace and sit on the bed.

Meir, sensing that the opportunity was ripe, lay down next to her, pulled the covers over his body and eagerly removed his chemise. As it fluttered to the floor, he beckoned Joheved to join him, hoping that he looked more encouraging than lustful.

Fear and desire warred within her. The sun had set, but dusk still lit the room. Colors had faded into grays, but she could easily make out details. Joheved took a deep breath and gathered her courage. She mustn't keep her husband waiting, but she couldn't bring herself to undress in front of him.

"Close your eyes," she instructed him, and Meir obligingly flipped over to face the opposite direction. She pulled her chemise over her head and hurriedly got into bed, drawing the linens all the way up to her neck.

He turned towards her and searched her face for an indication on how to proceed. She looked worried, but hopeful. He took her in his arms, intending to hold her until they got used to the feeling of their bare flesh pressing against each other. But the softness of her skin, her breasts pushing against his chest, and the warmth of her belly and thighs so close to his loins were almost more than he could bear. He fought to control his yetzer hara, which was urging him to take her right then and there.

Joheved was enthralled with the sensation of his naked body pressed so tightly to hers. She had tensed when she first felt his unclothed skin, but when he made no attempt to do more than hold her, she allowed herself to relax. He must have noticed her stiffness easing, because he started kissing her again. When he bent down to kiss the hollow of her throat, the combination of his lips and beard on her exposed skin was so exquisite she thought she wouldn't be able to bear it if he stopped.

His lips on her neck felt her heartbeat quicken, and her breath was coming faster as well. The perfume she wore combined with her own sweet fragrance to permeate his senses. He reached for her breasts and was rewarded with a soft moan as his fingers made small circles around her nipples.

Joheved couldn't believe the passion coursing through her. The aching between her legs returned with more intensity than before, and, without the slightest volition on her part, her hips began to rotate and push against his. His answering heat and hardness caused her great consternation, yet she could not hold herself still.

But further delights were in store. When Meir lowered his lips from her neck to her breasts and shifted his caresses to her lower body, she squirmed sensuously in response. She didn't understand how his fingers and lips could have such delicious effects on her, only that she yearned for more. He took one of her nipples in his mouth and, almost simultaneously, began to stroke the skin of her inner thighs. She gasped and tensed a moment, and then separated her legs, desperate for him to do something to quench the fire that was now burning between them.

His hand sought that aching place, and his fingers gently explored every fold and crevice. Joheved whimpered with pleasure. She had never imagined that such delights existed. Every time he tongued her nipple, a jolt of heat seemed to shoot directly down to where his hand was creating an inferno in her womb.

Meir didn't know how much longer he could curb his lust; his bride was writhing under his stimulation, but he wasn't sure how he'd know when she was truly ready. Her warm dampness was on his fingers, and he could feel a fresh surge of wetness whenever he sucked on her nipple, but he restrained himself.

By this time Joheved was beside herself with passion, with a suffering that she somehow knew only her husband could cure. Each additional caress caused her ardor to flare, and she understood why Rav Hisda called that burning place a forge.

And she realized that it was time to end the torment engulfing her by giving herself to her husband. "Please, Meir." She pulled him closer. "I can't endure any more."

He was throbbing with eagerness as he shifted his hips above hers and gently spread her open to receive him, but he forced himself to push carefully into her body that was moving so voluptuously beneath him. Again he controlled his yetzer, which was demanding that he draw back, thrust hard and bury himself in her. He slowed when he felt the impediment in front of him, but Joheved, impatient desire banishing any fear, wrapped her legs around him and insistently pulled him towards her, past the momentary blockage, until he had penetrated fully.

The incredible pleasure of feeling her warm passage envelop him was nearly overwhelming. If he moved even slightly, it would be over, so he held himself still and thought about the Berchat Betulim. He dimly heard Joheved asking if he was all right, and himself answering that he was fine, was she all right? When she responded in the affirmative, he felt calm enough to begin moving again.

He withdrew some and then reentered, each time with increasing strength. For Joheved, the torment she had felt before paled in comparison to what she was experiencing now. Each time he drew back, her legs urged him back in, and each time he reached her depths, she groaned blissfully. He knew he shouldn't move so vigorously; he ought to slow down and make it last longer, but when he tried to rest, Joheved forced him back into motion.

Was it an almond tree or a walnut in the Garden of Eden? Lilies or roses in the valley? Meir tried to concentrate on the Berchat Betulim.

Joheved was panting now, and, curious what her passion looked like, he opened his eyes a sliver. The sight of her breasts below immediately reversed the effect of his calming exercise, and he found himself thinking instead about how good it felt, wondering how soon they could do it a second time. Again, he approached the brink and compelled his passion to cool.

Let no stranger control her sealed fountain. Let her keep her lover's holy seed pure and not break the law. No wait, that wasn't how the blessing went.

Suddenly the intensity of her cries increased, and Meir felt her passage contract and throb around him, caressing his entire length. It was the most marvelous thing he had ever felt. He tried desperately to compose his thoughts again, but a burning ecstasy surged from deep within him. He plunged in to the hilt, and drove into her again, and again, with a frenzy he didn't know he was capable of.

Joheved was sure she was going to die of rapture. Her body was seized with paroxysms of the most incredible pleasure, and, at the same time,

Meir felt a searing fire coursing in his loins. His deeper cries mingled with hers as he spilled his seed into her womb and then collapsed on top of her.

For a time they remained joined, too exhausted to move, until Meir, concerned about crushing her, slowly disengaged himself.

Joheved wanted to tell Meir how wonderful she felt, how happy he had made her, but she had no energy to speak. She lay beside him in blissful satisfaction, silently thanking the Creator for giving them the mitzvah to be fruitful and multiply.

Meir was drowsy himself, and, having decided that he would wait until morning to say the Berchat Betulim, had almost dozed off when he remembered that Tractate Kallah had cautioned the new husband to speak sweetly to his bride afterwards, so that she would know he cared for her and not just for the act.

"Cherie," he whispered, but her only reply was a soft snore. Joheved was fast asleep.

"*Bonne nuit,* Cherie." He snuggled up next to her spoon-fashion, and, savoring the feel of her naked backside against his chest and thighs, he slept as well.

nineteen

Troyes
Summer 4834 (1074 C.E.)

In early June Joheved persuaded her new husband to visit the flowering vineyard. Meir agreed that the blooms smelled very nice, but he didn't need any aphrodisiacs other than his wife's unclothed body in bed with him. He thought himself the most blessed of men; by day he prayed, studied Torah and helped with the vines, while at night he fervently tried to fulfill the Creator's commandment to procreate, with a partner whose yetzer hara seemed every bit as strong as his own.

Times were sweet for Joheved as well. She enjoyed showing Meir how to care for the vineyard, and at night she studied Talmud with Miriam until he returned from the synagogue. No one had ever intimated to her that getting married could be so wonderful, and she suspected that it had not been so for Mama or Aunt Sarah.

Joheved's contentment that summer would have been complete but for an incident at the Hot Fair. Now that Joheved was a married woman, she needed to have her own medicine box, stocked with all the remedies her family might require. Aunt Sarah offered to help her two nieces shop for them.

There were several merchants who sold herbs and potions, but Aunt Sarah preferred to deal with an old man named Ben Yochai. His origin was unknown, as was his first name. Some said that he came from lands east of the Saracens, while others said he lived south of the Mediterranean Sea. He was reputed to be a sorcerer as well as a merchant and scholar, with knowledge of esoteric and mystical texts.

The three women arrived at his stall to find the oldest man Joheved had ever seen, as well as the most oddly dressed. Most men wore bright colors, but the robe that covered Ben Yochai from shoulder to ankle appeared to be pure black. It was only when she got closer that she could see it was actually a deep, midnight blue. Instead of the flat, round hats that men usually wore, Ben Yochai's was tall and conical, the same dark blue as his côte.

"If it weren't for his hat," Miriam whispered to her sister, "he'd be shorter than I am."

Sharp, intelligent eyes squinted out at them from beneath bushy, white eyebrows. "Shalom aleichem," Ben Yochai said, his voice surprisingly young. "I may be a stranger to you, but at synagogue Rav Salomon pointed you out to me as his daughters."

He turned to Joheved. "I congratulate you on your recent nuptials." He spoke with a strange accent, similar to Hiyya ibn Ezra's. "When the time comes, I can provide you with an excellent selection of birth amulets."

"That's very well, Ben Yochai, but what Joheved needs now is more mundane," Sarah said. For her nieces' benefit, she described the uses of each herb she wanted. "We'll take some cowslip flowers—its tea is excellent for headaches and insomnia—ginger to treat colds, horehound for coughs, and of course, comfrey, both root and leaf. Joheved, are you listening?"

Joheved, who had been reviewing a Talmud lesson in her mind, quickly looked up and Aunt Sarah continued, "Moistened comfrey root, when applied around a broken limb, sets it like plaster, and its leaves make an excellent poultice for all sorts of wounds."

Ben Yochai produced the herbs that Joheved's kit lacked and then took Aunt Sarah and Miriam aside to describe some contraceptives. Bored, Joheved wandered over to the nearby square, where two acrobats were balancing on a tightrope. She might as well wait there for Miriam and enjoy the entertainment. But before the show was over, Miriam joined her, complaining that Aunt Sarah had dismissed her when the subject turned to love potions. Suddenly Miriam gasped with dismay.

Joheved followed her sister's gaze and was shocked to see Catharina, the parchment maker's daughter, leaning boldly against a wall. Her hair was uncovered and her neckline was cut so low that the swelling of her breasts was exposed. There could be no doubt; their old friend had become a common woman, a prostitute.

Their first impulse was to pretend they hadn't noticed her. After all, they had hardly seen her since Baruch and Anna came to live with them.

The reputation of the alleys between the two Rues de la Tannerie was as unsavory as their odor, and Salomon had been quick to make procuring parchment his manservant's assignment. Yet they couldn't leave without finding out how she had come to this lamentable state.

They started off towards their friend, but when they were about halfway there, perhaps aware that she was being stalked, Catharina saw them. Her initial happy expression abruptly changed to one of shame. Joheved worried that she might try to avoid them by slipping into one of the alleys branching out from St. Jean's square, but she dejectedly walked forward to intercept them.

"Miriam, it's good to see you. I trust your family is well," she said quickly, forestalling the questions they were sure to have for her. She turned to Joheved, "I heard you finally married the sheep rancher's son. Does wedded life agree with you?"

Even her concern for Catharina's fate couldn't hide the joy Joheved felt when she thought about being married. But when her face lit up, Catharina's eyes filled with tears.

Eventually Catharina stopped crying long enough to tell her story. "Two years ago my father died," she said, waving her hands to ward off her friends' proffered sympathy, "and my brother took over the business. At first things seemed the same. I helped my brother make the parchment and my sister-in-law take care of the house. I told myself it didn't matter if I never married. I had food to eat and a roof over my head."

"But last year my brother brought his wife's younger brother into the shop. The brute immediately had eyes for me, and I foolishly imagined that he might marry me."

She laughed derisively, not a happy sound. "But he intended no such thing. Why should he marry me when another woman would bring a dowry with her? But that didn't keep him away from me. Oh no. Whenever we were alone he was after me, making lewd remarks, his hands groping my body. I never had a moment's peace. When I finally complained to my brother, he got angry and said it must be my fault for encouraging the fellow."

Catharina's face hardened in anger. "Well, that was all the villain needed to hear. He increased his disagreeable advances, and I began sleeping in the workroom, near where we kept the knives. One night, I awoke to his unwelcome presence. I tried to grab a knife, but he caught hold of my hand and nearly crushed it. He said that if I tried to call my brother, he'd tell them that I was a tease and a slut, that I'd invited him to my bed only to reject him. I was trapped; no one would believe the truth." A sob escaped her, but she stifled it quickly.

Her voice became louder. "He didn't care about hurting me, and probably thought it was amusing to watch me hobble around the next day and tell my brother that I had tripped going down the stairs. Still, I hoped that once he'd ruined me, he'd leave me alone. That's how little I knew of men. He was back the next night, and the next. The following Sunday, I told my brother I was sick and waited for them to leave for church. Then I took my things and found a merchant going to the Mai Fair de Provins."

Catharina paused and surveyed her audience. So far they had listened quietly, their expressions sympathetic. But how would they feel after hearing what she was about to recount? "It was simple to pay the merchant to take me with him with the same commodity my brother-in-law wanted, the same commodity all men want. Many in Provins were willing to pay too, and I did so well that I decided to come back and try my luck at the Hot Fair."

Joheved and Miriam stared at each other in dismay. Catharina sounded almost proud of herself.

"Catharina, just because your brother-in-law forced you doesn't mean you have to keep doing this." Joheved was filled with pity. Her friend would never know how wonderful it could be with a husband who was considerate and gentle.

"People are always looking for good servants," Miriam said. "You could save your wages and get married like our Marie did."

"I'm sure you're trying to be kind," Catharina said obdurately. "But in one season of Champagne fairs, I can earn more money than your maidservant does in years." Catharina's defiant expression softened and she sighed. "Well, it's been nice seeing you again. I wish you both very happy futures."

She turned and disappeared into the crowd, leaving Joheved and Miriam to walk dejectedly back to the herb dealer.

It was autumn when Joheved and Meir encountered the first thorn in their marital bed of roses. The Days of Awe were over, and the new vintage was sealed in casks and undergoing its final fermentation in the cellar. Salomon was working on his kuntres for Tractate Rosh Hashanah, which he planned to teach when his students returned, when the thought came to him that he needn't give up teaching Talmud to his daughters just because one of them was married. Meir could join them.

When Joheved saw her husband walk in and sit down next to her and Miriam, her stomach tightened into a knot. Yet as desperately as she wanted to escape, Joheved couldn't get up and leave Meir to study alone with Miriam and Papa.

Salomon had no idea anything was troubling Joheved. He began with a section at the end of the third chapter that dealt with the commandment of *shofar* blowing. The shofar, or ram's horn, was sounded each day during the month before Rosh Hashanah, and several times on the holy day itself. The Sages were debating whether one who heard the shofar, but without the intent of fulfilling the mitzvah, had indeed fulfilled the commandment.

Salomon motioned to Joheved to start with the Mishnah. She fought down her panic, swallowed hard, and began to read.

> One whose house was next to a synagogue and he heard the shofar, if he applied his mind to it, he has fulfilled his obligation, but if not, he has not fulfilled it. Even if this one heard it, and that one heard it.

But she asked no questions and offered no explanation of what she had read. It was Miriam who asked about the last line, and Salomon explained, "This teaches that only the men's intent mattered, not the quality of the sound they heard. 'This one' heard the shofar with intent to perform the mitzvah, and 'that one' heard exactly the same shofar without intent."

Miriam continued with the Gemara.

> Rava maintains that the commandments do not require intent.

Joheved was usually first to interrogate him, so Salomon tried to direct his questions towards her. "Can one in fact perform a mitzvah by accident? What if one is studying Torah and happens to recite the section containing the Shema at the commanded time? What if a man hears the shofar on Rosh Hashanah, but thinks it is a donkey braying?"

Even if she'd wanted to speak, Joheved couldn't. Her mind was too frozen to think of any response, let alone an intelligent one, and she could only defer to Meir or Miriam. Miriam began to speak less, to encourage her sister to say more, and soon even Meir could tell something was wrong.

Joheved was focused on how much longer she'd have to endure this ordeal, when Meir, sure that his presence had somehow spoiled their studies, stood up and addressed Salomon. "Please excuse me, but you three might be able to study better without me."

Hoping that they would call him back, Meir slowly walked to the door. He hadn't said it, but inside her head Joheved could hear him clearly—I know when I'm not wanted. She felt miserable for rejecting him, but she still couldn't study Talmud with him.

Meir had no time to feel sorry for himself. Rachel was sitting on a bench near the hearth, head bent over a book, and she called out when she saw him, "Meir, can you help me? I'm not sure what these words mean." Rachel was struggling with Leviticus, the book of Torah traditionally taught to beginning students.

Meir couldn't help but grin at her call for aid. When she smiled sweetly and looked up at him with those innocent big green eyes, he could almost imagine what it would be like teaching Torah to his own children, assuming Joheved ever gave him any. Still he was pleased that somebody wanted him around, so Meir sat down and looked at the page Rachel was having difficulty with.

She was in chapter Kedoshim, the Holiness Code.

> You shall not hate your kinsfolk in your heart . . . You shall not avenge, neither shall you bear a grudge. Love your fellow as yourself.

Rachel chanted the text and looked up at Meir. "What's the difference between 'avenge' and 'bear a grudge'?"

Meir was delighted to explain it. "Here's an example. Suppose that Reuben says to Simon, 'Lend me your sickle,' and Simon replies, 'No.'" Meir made his voice change to imitate the two imaginary men, high pitched and whiny for Reuben, low and gruff for Simon.

"Then the next day, Simon says to Reuben, 'Lend me your hatchet,' and Reuben says, 'I'm not going to lend it to you, just as you refused to lend me your sickle.'" This time Meir acted out the two men's argument. "That's avenging."

Rachel giggled in response and he continued his little drama.

"And if Simon says to Reuben, 'Lend me your hatchet,' and Reuben replies, 'No,' but on the next day Reuben says, 'Lend me your sickle,' and Simon answers, 'Here it is—I am not like you who would not lend to me . . .' "

Rachel clapped her hands in glee as Meir dramatized the second scenario. "This is bearing a grudge; Simon bears hatred in his heart even though he does not avenge himself."

He listened patiently as she read more and helped her as necessary. It brought back fond memories of tutoring Eleazar's children during his final year in Worms. Sarah's grandchildren were his cousins now, and he had been remiss in not writing to them. He found a quill and parchment, and when Rivka put Rachel to bed, he had something else to keep him busy while Joheved studied Talmud without him.

Later that night, after they'd gone to bed, Joheved did her best to make up for neglecting Meir earlier, and the next morning, he seemed his usual sanguine self. But after Joheved finished her prayers in the room the two sisters used to share, Miriam couldn't wait to bombard her with questions.

"Joheved, what's the matter with you? Why on earth didn't you say anything in the salon when Meir was there?"

Joheved had been asking herself the same questions. "I'm not sure why, but I felt too nervous to speak."

"But that's silly. You talk to Meir all the time now. Why should talking about Talmud be different?" Miriam thought for a moment while she folded the straps of her tefillin and put them back in their bag. "Try to remember last night, and what exactly you were afraid might happen if you spoke up in front of him."

Joheved put her tefillin bag away in the chest next to her sister's. Despite her marriage, she continued their custom of saying the morning prayers together. Like studying Talmud, it was something she worried her husband wouldn't like a woman doing. She realized that was part of the answer.

"After everything Mama's said, I can't believe that Meir really approves of my learning Talmud." Joheved could see that Miriam was about to protest, but insisted on finishing her thought. "And even if he does think it's all right, I still worry what he'll think of me after I do speak. If I say something stupid, he'll think poorly of me, and if I say something clever, he might get upset that I make him look bad in comparison."

How her sister had changed, Miriam thought, that this man's opinion meant so much to her now. "Are you sure you haven't misjudged Meir? Why don't you ask him how he feels?"

"I'll think about it." Joheved felt a sense of relief that she'd figured out why studying Talmud with Meir bothered her, but that didn't mean she was ready to face his possible disapproval. Maybe she should explain to him how she felt; maybe they could try to study together again.

But that night, Meir announced that he intended to spend the evening reviewing Tractate Sanhedrin, the text Salomon had taught during the Hot Fair. "After all, I missed most of the scholar's night sessions this summer."

Joheved was stung by his rejection and by the implication that he regretted spending those nights with her instead of staying up late studying Talmud. Maybe he didn't want to study with women and was glad of an excuse to leave. Maybe he didn't mind them studying without him.

But Meir did mind. Several strange things about his wife came together to unsettle him further. Why would a normal woman want to study Talmud and wear tefillin? He knew she did because he had glimpsed her at prayer once when Rachel left the door ajar. Also, she didn't have flowers like other women did.

And what about her yetzer hara? Weren't women supposed to be modest and demure? Perhaps her unwomanly pursuits explained why she wasn't getting pregnant; after all, it wasn't for lack of trying. What Meir didn't know, and neither did Joheved, was that she was enceinte, and had been for many weeks.

That Friday night, Salomon's family was looking forward to an evening of singing Sabbath table songs together. Next week the Cold Fair would begin, and this was the family's last Shabbat dinner without a houseful of students and guests.

So everyone was taken aback when Joheved yawned and apologized, "I hate to miss all the singing, but I'm too tired to stay up a moment longer."

Sarah listened to this announcement and rose to accompany her niece to the privy. "Joheved, are you feeling all right?" she asked shrewdly. "Having any stomach aches?"

"I'm feeling quite well," Joheved replied. "I just can't seem to stay awake." She finished in the privy, and this made her remember another thing. "And I need to pee all the time. I even have to go in the middle of the night. It's so annoying."

"Tell me, do you think your breasts are larger? Do they feel tender?" It was too dark for Joheved to see her aunt's smile.

"I suppose they might be bigger, but they've been growing for several years now." It was also too dark for Sarah to see Joheved blush. Her breasts and nipples were sore, but she'd thought that was due to Meir's frequent handling.

Sarah walked upstairs with her. "When you wore your new girdle at Rosh Hashanah was it tighter than at your wedding?"

Joheved was beginning to get an inkling of where Aunt Sarah's questions were leading. "Oui, I had to buckle it differently to make it larger." She pulled out the jeweled accessory. "I thought marriage was agreeing with me, like Mistress Johanna."

"I'm sure marriage does agree with you, Joheved, which is why I'm asking you all these questions. Let's see how your wedding girdle fits now." Sarah watched with satisfaction as Joheved attached the ends at their widest setting.

"Good heavens, how could I get so fat in just six months?" Joheved looked in awe at the evidence of her increased girth and then up at her aunt's grinning visage. The evidence was undeniable, but she still had to ask, "Am I going to have a baby?"

Sarah embraced her. "It certainly looks like it. Now *bonne nuit* dear, pleasant dreams."

Joheved was too excited to sleep; she kept thinking about how happy Meir and her parents would be with the news. She could hear everyone still singing below, so she went back down to join them. Then she stood uncomfortably at her seat, unable to overcome her shyness at bringing up such a delicate subject.

Aunt Sarah broke the ice for her. "Meir, Joheved has something she wants to tell you."

She tried to pretend that she was addressing him alone. "I think you should know that . . . if Le Bon Dieu wills it . . . next summer you will be a father."

It took a little while for the message to sink in, but as her family shouted their delight, Meir jumped up and kissed her, right in front of everyone. Anna was particularly pleased; she too was pregnant and their children would be playmates. Rivka silently wiped away tears with her sleeve.

But happiest of all was Salomon, who couldn't help remembering that it was almost a year ago that he had lost his precious little Leah. He silently thanked his Creator and, though it was probably more than forty days since conception, prayed for a grandson.

Alone in their bedroom that night, Meir felt chagrined at his earlier doubts. He needed to confess and have his wife forgive him. Surely the explanation for her odd behavior was that her father, lacking sons, had treated her like one. But when Meir revealed his previous fears, Joheved's reaction surprised him. He had expected her to be hurt or angry.

But she admitted that she harbored the same concerns herself, "Ever since my grandmama told me that too many masculine interests could give girls a wandering womb."

Meir had never heard of a "wandering womb," but he wanted to reassure her. He placed his hands around her waist and whispered, "Joheved, I have no doubt that your womb is exactly where it's supposed to be."

Meir was gazing at her with that familiar look in his eyes, and Joheved could feel the answering warmth within her. It amazed her how her yetzer hara responded to just the expression on his face. But she was pregnant! Should they still be having relations? Would it hurt the baby?

When Joheved didn't respond to his initial caresses, Meir had a good idea what was worrying her. His studies had assuaged his own concerns; both the Talmudic Sages and the author of Tractate Kallah advocated marital intimacy during pregnancy.

"You needn't worry about the child," he whispered as he nuzzled her neck, an approach he knew she enjoyed. "In Tractate Yevamot, Rav Shmuel recommends the holy deed during pregnancy."

"And none of the other Sages contradict him?" Joheved admitted that she had never studied Yevamot, one of several tractates that dealt with the status of women.

"No, his opinion stands." He stroked her belly, very much aware of the new life growing within, and had a flash of insight. "You also needn't worry about knowing more Talmud than I do."

"You know me too well, Meir." How had he ascertained her anxieties so accurately?

He moved his hand up to caress her breasts. "And I intend to 'know' you much better," he said softly in Hebrew.

twenty

Winter 4835 (1074–75 C.E.)

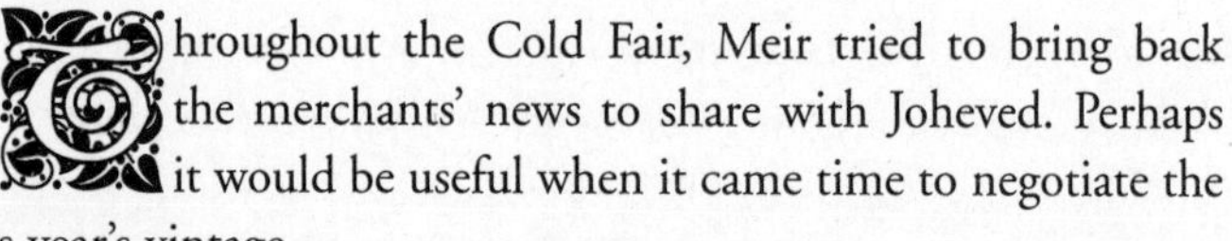

Throughout the Cold Fair, Meir tried to bring back the merchants' news to share with Joheved. Perhaps it would be useful when it came time to negotiate the price of this year's vintage.

"Last night I heard that it's dangerous to travel near Paris without a goodly number of men-at-arms," he told her one morning. "King Philippe seems helpless to control the petty nobles of his fief. The counts of Beaumont have even pillaged estates belonging to the Abbey of St. Denis."

"Hmmm." Joheved reached for her hairbrush. "If attending the St. Denis fairs is dangerous, perhaps more business will come to our Champagne fairs," she replied.

Meir's expression became grim. "But it's not just the local barons who have sunk to banditry. They say that Pope Gregory is threatening to excommunicate King Philippe himself for robbing pilgrims and Italian merchants."

"But Meir, if the king makes it so difficult to bring goods to Paris, then anyone who succeeds will make a handsome profit," Joheved said. Maybe she should hire guards for their wine's trip down the Seine. "Isaac haParnas says that what really angers the pope is Philippe's refusal to give up the king's authority to appoint bishops in his lands."

"Of course he refuses!" Meir was a lord's son; naturally he supported the king. "How can Philippe depend on the fealty of a bishop selected by the pope?"

Joheved smiled at her husband's defense of the nobility. "Some monarch Philippe is," she countered. "First he lets William the Bastard unite Normandy and Angleterre, then he allows his vassals to behave like brigands. If that's not bad enough, he and the queen have been childless for over five years."

Meir's voice became somber. "I know. If he dies without an heir, those same vassals will fight like mad to claim his throne."

"Le Bon Dieu be thanked that we live under Count Thibault," Joheved said, tucking her braids under her veil. "He's a decent ruler, with three healthy sons, who keeps his roads secure and his nobles under control."

They both said "amen" to that.

More than bringing Joheved the merchant's politics, Meir wanted to share their Talmud discussions with her. The yeshiva students gossiped that Miriam knew as much Talmud as Benjamin did, and that Joheved surpassed her sister. How was it possible that he had married a chacham, yet they never studied together? He racked his brain until he found an argument so compelling that Joheved would have to conquer whatever aversion she had to learning Talmud with him.

"After all," he told her, "what could be a better influence on our unborn child than words of Torah spoken by his parents?"

"I suppose you're right," Joheved said slowly, her throat tightening. She couldn't help but agree with Meir's premise, even though it obligated her to study with him.

"You don't sound convinced. What's so terrible about studying with me anyway? Do you think I'm such a bad teacher?"

"No, of course not." She was quick to reassure him. "I've seen you with the boys and I think you're an excellent teacher."

She could see he was waiting for her to answer his earlier question. She took a deep breath and explained in a rush, "I'm sorry, Meir, but I find it hard to believe that any man beside Papa would approve of my learning Talmud."

Meir lifted up her chin and forced her to look at him. "I know it didn't sound like it at Purim, but I can honestly say that I don't object to your studying Talmud."

"But if I say something clever, you might get angry because it makes me look smarter than you."

"Joheved, I'm sure I'll feel proud when you say something clever, not angry."

"And if I say something stupid?"

"No sincere question about Torah is stupid."

Despite Meir's reassurance, Joheved was so reticent that it took several sessions before he saw that he didn't need to teach her the texts; she'd already memorized them. Even then she merely listened to his explanations and repeated them back. It was only when they reached chapter four of Tractate Rosh Hashanah, which dealt with women blowing the shofar, that she threw off her timidity and questioned him like a real study partner.

The debate started with the Mishnah and continued with the Gemara.

> We do not prevent children from blowing the shofar . . . But we do prevent women.

Joheved reacted immediately. "What? How does the Mishnah's statement about children imply a prohibition on women?" If women weren't allowed to blow the shofar, maybe they weren't allowed to wear tefillin either.

"Both women and boys are exempt from the shofar obligation," Meir began slowly, not sure how much she already knew.

"Of course." She tried not to sound impatient. "Boys are exempt because children are not obligated to perform any mitzvot, and women are exempt because shofar is a positive time-bound commandment, performed on the day of Rosh Hashanah."

"Well, boys will eventually be obligated when they're grown." Meir tried to remember exactly how Salomon had explained it. "And because they must be trained, we allow them to practice."

"As for women (he suspected she was about to ask this), the sage in the Gemara apparently holds that if a woman blows the shofar when she's not obligated to do so, she violates the prohibition against adding anything to the commandments."

Joheved's eyes narrowed in anger, and Meir quickly pointed to the next line.

> But it was taught: We do not prevent either women or children from blowing the shofar on the holy day.

Her expression softened. Now the discussion would attempt to resolve the obvious contradiction. But would the final decision keep women from performing the mitzvah or not? She had to know.

> Abaye said: There is no difficulty. The Mishnah prohibiting women is the view of Rav Yehuda, and the other teaching is that of Rav Yose and Rav Shimon.

Joheved jumped in with a question before Meir could say anything. "But how does Abaye know the first sage is Rav Yehuda and the others are Rav Yose and Rav Shimon?" She looked up at him eagerly and her eyes were shining.

Meir felt his own excitement growing. He smiled and told her the text would answer her question.

> It is taught, regarding Temple sacrifices: The sons of Israel lay hands over their sacrifices, but the daughters of Israel do not. These are the words of Rav Yehuda. Rav Yose and Rav Shimon say: Women may lay hands if they so desire.

"Since Rav Yose and Rav Shimon's opinion permitting women, and Rav Yehuda's opinion restraining them, are known from the teaching about sacrifices, Abaye presumes that they hold the same opinions about the mitzvah of shofar," Meir explained.

"Very well, I see that." Joheved started pacing the room. "Papa taught us that the prohibition against adding anything to the mitzvot only applies to things like putting five paragraphs of Torah in tefillin instead of four." Her voice began to rise. "I don't see why it should prevent anyone from voluntarily doing a mitzvah from which they are exempt."

"That's not what Rav Yehuda says." Meir could see his wife's anger growing and he quickly added, "Not that I agree with him."

Joheved sat down, and they started in on the next paragraph. For the next hour, their words fairly flew around the room.

Why does Rav Yehuda believe that? The Gemara may explain this situation, but what happens in another one? Are you sure that's what Abaye means? Perhaps he means this? We must remember to ask Papa about this case. Rava's explanation doesn't make sense—he must mean something else. But that can't be right; it contradicts the Mishnah. What do *you* think? What do you think?

Meir hadn't felt such excitement studying Talmud since he'd moved to Troyes. No wonder women weren't allowed in the yeshiva.

Suddenly Joheved was silent for a moment. "But what is the law, Meir? The Sages haven't said anything else about women, just more about shofar blowing in general."

"There is no decision to prevent women from performing mitzvot. Rav Yose and Rav Shimon, Rav Yehuda—they maintain their respective opinions." Meir gave her a small smile. "You know very well whose rule we follow here. I've seen you perform time-bound commandments myself."

Joheved didn't know how to respond. Had Meir discovered that she prayed with tefillin? What else could he be referring to? "What do you mean?" she asked tentatively, her eyes wide.

She looked like a startled doe Meir had suddenly encountered while riding in the forest. Well, let her hide her tefillin if that's what she wanted. "Joheved, everyone in your family eats in the *sukkah* during Sukkot; the women are not restrained. So you all fulfill the mitzvah of dwelling in a *sukkah.*"

"And I suppose Rava would say that my mother also performs the mitzvah of *sukkah,* even if she has no intention of doing so." Relieved that her secret had not been exposed, Joheved laughed at the absurdity of this conclusion, while Meir noted proudly that she still remembered the text they had studied months earlier.

Meir continued to share Talmud with Joheved, but they weren't the only ones attempting to influence their unborn child for the better. Anna now attended services the three days a week when scripture was read publicly. This particular Shabbat, they had come to the part where Joseph was reunited with his brothers after years of separation, hiding his identity from them until he'd ascertained that they had repented of their sins against him.

Many of the men in the congregation used this time to chat amongst themselves. After all, they had been studying this portion of the Torah all week. There was also much coming and going; people greeting friends, those with weak bladders leaving to relieve themselves, latecomers just arriving. With the Cold Fair in full swing, there were foreign merchants to be speculated about as well.

The reader had just begun to chant the section from Prophets that followed the Torah reading, when a large, red-haired stranger entered. He was so tall that he had to duck to get through the door, and he seemed poorly dressed for the holy day. The man peered around anxiously, as if not sure what his welcome would be.

The hubbub, which had increased with his entrance, was suddenly split by a shriek from the women's gallery. The reader halted in midword, and the congregation's attention was riveted as Anna pushed her way through the women and raced down the stairs.

"Nicolae, Nicolae," she called out, while the stranger watched in astonishment as this hugely pregnant woman bore down on him. Despite the men's presence, she tore off her veil so he could see her clearly. "Nicolae, don't you know me? It's Anna! Anna, Mihail's daughter."

Their audience watched in awe as his face lit in recognition. This real-life drama was even better than Joseph's story in the Torah. Tears running down both their faces, the man picked her up and swung her around as if she were a child, oblivious to the public display they had created. Only when Salomon and Baruch approached them did Anna notice the sea of curious faces turned in their direction. She quickly replaced her veil, and, all eyes upon them, the foursome exited into the courtyard.

Anna was too overwrought to speak, so Baruch introduced them. Nicolae was Anna's uncle, her mother's youngest brother. If his appearance wasn't amazing enough, the tall man proceeded to correct Baruch, and, using passable Hebrew, tell Salomon that his name was no longer Nicolae, but "Samson," an appropriate moniker considering his size and strength. He too was a convert.

Like any other Jew arriving in a new town, he had presented himself at the local synagogue. But a convert like Samson was at a disadvantage. His poor Hebrew plus his lack of familiarity with the holy texts made it difficult to prove that he was truly a Jew. Samson's outlandish appearance only emphasized his foreignness, but he was prepared for suspicion.

He pulled a well-worn sheet of parchment from his sleeve and handed it to Salomon. It was a "letter to the communities," written by none other than Salomon's old *maître*, Isaac haLevi of Mayence. First, in case he was unknown to the reader, Isaac haLevi filled the letter with examples of his Talmudic knowledge, written in erudite Hebrew, so that his testimony could be relied upon without doubt. Then he requested the reader to "receive Samson ben Abraham graciously, and treat him the same excellent way you are accustomed to treat every traveler."

Salomon couldn't wait to invite Samson to disner and hear about his travels. And what tales they were! The yeshiva students listened eagerly as Samson described how he spent several years in the Carpathian mountains fighting barbarians, becoming expert with many types of weapons, before he was finally captured and sold into slavery. He laughingly told them how his conversion to Judaism had come about because of a Romanian priest.

"The fellow told me that unless I became a Christian, excuse me, one of the Notzrim, I would be castrated and sold to the Moors as a harem guard." Samson didn't understand the Jews' touchiness about the word, "Christian," and sometimes he forgot to use an acceptable substitute. "But if I accepted the Church, he would save me, since Jews weren't allowed to own Notzrim slaves."

"Well, I certainly wanted to keep my balls," he continued, "but I wasn't about to worship a man who was hanging dead on a cross. What kind of god is that?" Samson shook his head in disgust. "At first my master was furious when I asked him about becoming a Jew," he said with a smile. "But I told him it was either Judaism or the Church for me, that I had no intention of ending up a eunuch."

Samson explained how he continued to travel as a man-at-arms for his Jewish master, from their base in Mayence to Russia for furs or to Byzantium for silks and spices. Once, when they were attacked by bandits, his earlier training stood him in good stead and enabled him to save his master's life. The merchant had freed Samson in gratitude, and since then, the former slave made his living as a guard with various merchant caravans.

This year, having heard that roads to Paris were particularly dangerous, he hoped that he might be of service to those wishing to export goods, particularly wine, to that city. Hearing this, Meir and Joheved nodded to each other in silent assent. Several wine buyers at the Cold Fair would be very eager to meet Samson.

Salomon invited Samson to stay in the attic with the students, who were thrilled with the opportunity to hear some of his more exciting stories out of the women's hearing. Several of the older ones, including Benjamin, encouraged him to give them some lessons in self-defense, the better to protect themselves in future days of traveling.

By the end of the Cold Fair, Samson had contracts with several wine dealers to transport their casks, including much of Salomon's wine, to Paris. He was barely gone a week when a series of snowstorms swept through Troyes, forcing everyone indoors. Joheved fretted that they wouldn't be able to finish the pruning in time, but there was nothing she could do about the weather.

It was two weeks before a clear day dawned. The students took deep breaths as they climbed down from the attic; air outdoors smelled so fresh and crisp compared to the stuffy, smoky atmosphere inside Salomon's salon. When Benjamin saw Baruch assembling the pruning knives, he suggested to Salomon that, with nobody able to work on the vines recently, perhaps the man could use some assistance.

Then Salomon couldn't help but observe the remaining students' envy as they watched the pair put on their cloaks and gloves. He was torn. He really shouldn't allow the class to take an afternoon off from Talmud study, yet they wouldn't learn much if their hearts were yearning to be outdoors. Besides, Benjamin was right. They were weeks behind on pruning the vineyard.

It wasn't only because of bad weather. During the previous fortnight, Joheved had started bleeding, and Sarah had confined her niece to bed in hopes that the pregnancy might be saved. Privately, Sarah confided in Miriam that she didn't have much faith in the bed rest cure. While it might be useful in late pregnancy, there was little a midwife could do with bleeding this early. The outcome was in the Merciful One's hands.

So far, all was well. Joheved spent most of her day in bed, spinning wool, helping Rachel with her studies, or going over each day's Talmud lesson with Miriam. Salomon sorely missed her in the vineyard. Leah had taught her granddaughter well; Joheved knew exactly where and how much to trim each vine. But Joheved was bedridden and likely to remain so for some time.

Salomon finally gave in to the reality that sometimes his livelihood must take precedence. When he announced that he too would be going to work in the vineyard, and that any student who wished to labor with him was welcome, the entire student body swiftly made for their warm clothes. Even Rachel demanded to go out, which prompted Rivka to insist that Miriam accompany the group in order to watch her little sister.

Rivka took advantage of the break in bad weather to go shopping with the new maidservant, Claire, leaving Anna and Joheved to work their way through a pile of clothes that needed mending. Periodically they sipped from cups of hot liquid, sage tea for Joheved to prevent a miscarriage, and elder leaf tea for Anna as a precaution against curses. The charcoal brazier provided warmth, but it also served another purpose. Sarah burned some foul-smelling herbs on it, hoping to discourage either fetus from leaving its present lodging too soon, and Joheved tried to tolerate the stink for her baby's sake.

All morning Joheved had been feeling uncomfortable with what she hoped was indigestion, but now the ache in her belly was too strong to ignore. The previous day she had been in pain too, but then the cramps had gone away, allowing her a few hours of sleep. It was Anna, looking up from her sewing in time to see Joheved grimace, who decided to go next door for Aunt Sarah.

"Mon Dieu, please don't let me lose the baby," Joheved prayed, at the same time fearing that it was already too late. She could hear Aunt Sarah on the stairs, asking Anna if the bleeding had increased and when was the last time they changed the cloths in Joheved's *sinar.*

Every married Jewish woman owned a *sinar,* a special article of clothing worn when she was niddah. Shaped like an apron, it served the dual purpose of holding absorbent rags in place to catch the menstrual flow and letting her husband know that she was forbidden to him while she wore it. Joheved disliked wearing a *sinar* so continually; the material rubbed annoyingly against the inside of her thighs, chafing her skin.

"Let's pull these covers off and get a look at you." Aunt Sarah's voice was cheerful, yet professional. "I need to know how much blood you've lost."

With the stained sheets exposed, Joheved could see that her *sinar* cloths were insufficient, and she started to cry. She waited anxiously while Anna brought some fresh rags and Sarah examined the bloody ones. Then, seized with another cramp, she doubled over in pain, and when it passed, they needed to change the cloths again.

Sarah turned and said sadly, "I'm sorry, Joheved, but your womb is starting to empty. There is nothing I can do to prevent it. I'll be right back with the birthing stool."

Joheved lay back in bed, tears streaming down her cheeks. Two more spasms came and went before Sarah reappeared. Then she and Anna helped Joheved support herself over the birthing stool's opening. The pain intensified now, and when it abated, Joheved felt a cup in her hand.

"Drink this," Aunt Sarah told her. "It's wine with ragwort and columbine seeds, to quickly empty your womb."

Joheved downed the strange-tasting wine, and before Rivka and Claire returned from their errands, the process was complete. Aunt Sarah helped her into bed in her old bedroom while Anna hurried to replace the bloody linens with clean ones.

Rivka arrived home to find her sister stirring soup in the kitchen, not an auspicious sign. "I'm sorry," Sarah said, "but Joheved has miscarried." Rivka crumpled into her sister's arms as Sarah said softly, "Don't worry. Joheved is uninjured, and this shouldn't affect her future pregnancies."

Rivka straightened up, took a deep breath and hurried upstairs. Anna, still making Meir and Joheved's bed, pointed her mistress down the hall. Rivka cautiously opened the door, and when she saw that Joheved was awake, rushed to her side. As she consoled her weeping child, now taller than she was, Rivka couldn't help but remember how she used to hold Joheved in her lap, years ago, to comfort her when she cried.

Outside the city walls, those in Salomon's vineyard were oblivious to the misfortune in his house. The sun shone brightly, the snow-covered fields contrasted dazzlingly with the blue sky, and everyone was full of energy after weeks of forced inactivity. Once Salomon explained that the vines needed to be cut as close as possible to the soil, the boys enthusiastically began hacking off the taller shoots.

They were a jolly group. Careful to avoid Salomon's notice, one student made a snowball and pelted another, only to return immediately to his pruning in apparent innocence. The victim then felt that he had no choice but to hurl one back at his suspected attacker, who most likely was not the guilty party. And so the cycle continued until Rachel, aiming to hit Miriam, slipped in the snow just as she threw the snowball. Her missile flew straight up into the air and landed on Salomon, who was concentrating on an exacting cut nearby.

Splat! The students stood in chastened silence as Salomon dropped his knife and began to curse vigorously. In no uncertain terms, he reminded them all how dangerously sharp the pruning knives were, how the slightest misstep could result in a lost finger or gouged eye. He continued by questioning their maturity, their conscientiousness and their intelligence in general. His voice echoed like thunder across the frozen landscape. Most of the students had never seen their teacher lose his temper before, and it was a sobering sight.

Rachel was trying not to cry, and the sight of her quivering chin had an immediate calming effect on her father. The boys looked uncertainly from one to another, none of them wanting to indict the frightened little girl, and then Menachem and Ephraim almost simultaneously stepped forward to each admit his culpability. If only one of them had spoken, the subterfuge might have succeeded, but Salomon knew he had been pelted just once and quickly recognized whom the twins were protecting.

"Rachel, do you know how my father died?" He kneeled down next to her and spoke soothingly, but loud enough for the boys to hear, "He cut himself with a pruning knife, and it never healed. I was not much older than you when it happened."

"Papa, I'm sorry. I don't want you to be hurt. I didn't mean to hit you. I was aiming at Miriam." Rachel immediately realized that she shouldn't have said this, but the image of her father, orphaned when he was her age, had clouded her judgment.

"But surely you didn't want Miriam to cut herself either," he asked, and she nodded silently in reply. Salomon had no intention of chastising her in public and returned his attention to his students, who stared at the snowy ground in guilty silence. "Now let's get back to work. Darkness comes early this time of year."

"Belle Assez, why don't you work over here by me and Miriam?" Benjamin called her by the nickname all the yeshiva students used for her since the wedding.

"My name is Rachel, and I'm not about to get close enough for Miriam to put snow down my chemise." There was no use complaining when the students called her "Belle Assez." It only amused them and made them use the vexing name even more.

"All right, Belle Assez, have it your way," he said, breaking into a laugh when she stuck her tongue out at him.

The sun was low on the horizon when they gathered their tools and headed for the road to town. Peasants who'd been plowing nearby joined them, and one man let Rachel ride his horse. The students tumbled noisily into the house, but the somber look on Sarah's face silenced them even as she put her finger to her lips.

Rivka was still upstairs with Joheved, leaving Sarah to explain the sad circumstances. Meir's face fell and he bounded up the stairs to see his wife, while Salomon restrained himself from doing the same. Let the couple have some time to mourn their loss in private.

He turned to his sister-in-law and asked, "Sarah, you're the expert in such matters. Is there any reason to think that Joheved might not have another child in the near future?"

"Not as far as I can tell," she replied. "Your daughter appears perfectly healthy."

"And were you able to determine the baby's gender?"

"Yes," the answer came, "it was a girl."

When Rivka saw Meir at the door, she prudently remembered something in the kitchen that needed her attention. By now, Joheved had cried all the tears that were within her, so it was she who consoled her tearful husband the best she could. It was frustrating not being able to hold him, or even touch him, but a miscarriage caused impurity just as the blood of childbirth and menstruation did. Because her child had been female, Joheved would be niddah for fourteen days.

She tried to reassure him with Sarah's confident prognosis, but she kept yawning. The day's exertion had exhausted her, and Aunt Sarah had given her a sleeping draught. So Meir sat silently beside her, and when her breath was soft and regular with sleep, he went gloomily downstairs to be comforted by the others.

twenty-one

Spring 4835 (1075 C.E.)

During the weeks that followed, Joheved found consolation from the women in the congregation. No one had snubbed her for some time now; after all, she was the Rosh Yeshiva's daughter. There were no more looks of pity either; she and Miriam dressed as well as anyone. She wouldn't have called these women her friends, but when she returned to lead them in prayer, they overwhelmed her with their sympathy and encouragement. Nearly every mother among them had suffered miscarriages, and after listening to their stories, Joheved's vague sense of guilt began to lessen.

One old woman, who admitted to ten pregnancies resulting in four grown children, said it was like shelling peas. "In every pod or two, amongst all the nice solid, plump peas, is a tiny, shriveled pea. Only the Creator knows why these are big and healthy, while that one is not."

"And just because you've lost this first one," Johanna reassured her, "doesn't mean you won't have any more."

The mothers in the group glanced at the few childless ones and quickly looked away. "Don't worry, Joheved," they told her. "You're still young."

Joheved tried to remember those words as she was continually confronted with Anna's new baby boy, born just before Passover. Salomon had just given the slaves their freedom, and because their son would be named during the festival week, Baruch and Anna decided to call the boy Pesach, the Hebrew word for Passover.

Whenever Joheved began to fill with envy, she reminded herself how good her life was compared with Anna's many sorrows. If fate decreed that one of them suffer a miscarriage, better it should be herself rather than poor Anna. Yet she couldn't help but wonder what Anna had done right, and she had done wrong, during their respective pregnancies.

Far more disconsolate was Meir, who, believing that any show of grief on his part would only further distress his wife, kept his own anguish inside. When Salomon tried to offer support by sharing that his own firstborn had been stillborn, Meir felt the need to apologize for failing him.

"I don't see how I can possibly conceive sons." Meir shook his head sadly. "No matter how determined I am that Joheved should emit seed first, I cannot restrain myself. As soon as I feel her emitting her seed, mine comes as well."

"At least yours doesn't come first," Salomon said, sure he'd never felt Rivka emit seed at all. "Remember what it says in the last chapter of Berachot: When a man and woman emit seed simultaneously, then the child may be of either gender."

But no matter how much he wanted to, Salomon wasn't able to provide Meir with the comfort that Joheved received from the many women who had miscarried before her.

When Joheved began using the mikvah, Meir accompanied her and joined the men who spent their evenings at the synagogue. Some, like himself, were waiting for their wives to immerse in the ritual bath below, but others came for the masculine company. They discussed, and occasionally argued, business, politics and Torah. The mood was cheerful; after all, more than a few of them were on their way to an amorous reunion with their wives. These men were glad to find Meir among their number and made sure that their wives encountered him before they went home.

Meir tried to greet the women, who were often more flustered than he was, with as pleasant a demeanor as he could manage. It embarrassed him to be admired in this fashion, but he understood their motive. What a woman saw before cohabitation made an impression on her, one transmitted to any resulting offspring. If she saw a dog after immersing in the mikvah, her child might have a dog's ugly face. If she saw a donkey, the child would be simpleminded. Meeting a talmid chacham was a good sign, for then her child would delight in learning Torah.

Meir was relieved when the Hot Fair arrived and men began introducing their wives to the other scholars at the synagogue, but he was disappointed that Joheved wasn't pregnant again. One night, while waiting for his wife to ready herself for bed, he decided to consult Tractate Kallah. There was a section on resuming relations after childbirth, but he hadn't paid much attention to it. He was so engrossed in the book that it was only when Joheved began to hang up her clothes that he realized she had entered the room. He abruptly turned to face her, trying to hide the manuscript behind him.

"What are you reading?" Joheved had thought he was studying one of her father's kuntres, but his guilty behavior belied that.

"Oh, nothing that I can't finish later." Meir didn't want to lie to her by naming a scholarly text. So he moved to embrace her, hoping to forestall her curiosity.

"Let me see." She tried to get around him, but he put his arms around her waist and drew her to him.

"I doubt that you'd find it interesting. Why don't we go to bed now, and you can read it tomorrow if you like." He tried one last gambit to avoid what he suspected was inevitable.

"Meir, if you just let me see it, then we can go to bed."

Realizing it was hopeless, he stood aside and watched helplessly as his wife began to read.

The first thing she saw was a commentary on Psalm 128:

> "Your wife shall be like a fruitful vine in your house, your sons, like olive saplings around your table."

What Tractate Kallah said was:

> "Your wife should adorn herself like a fruitful vine, so that your yetzer will be inflamed like a fire and you will shoot semen like an arrow. You should delay your climax until your wife has her climax first, and then she will conceive sons."

"Mon Dieu! " she exclaimed, cheeks flaming, as she read further. "Where did you get this . . ." Joheved restrained herself from saying "this obscenity" as she snapped the pages shut.

"My father gave it to me just before our wedding. It's called Tractate Kallah."

"This is part of the Talmud?" Her disapproval softened with the idea that this was holy text. After all, Song of Songs was bold stuff.

Meir couldn't help but appreciate their identical reactions. "That's exactly what I said when I first saw it. But it's not Talmud; my father says it's additional material."

Joheved began to leaf through the book again. "So this is where you learned how to do all those things. I assumed that some common woman in Worms must have taught you."

Meir put his arms around her and whispered in her ear, "I have never bedded any woman but you, and I hope that I will be blessed to bed only you my whole life."

Her husband's close presence and sweet words, in addition to what she was reading, began to affect her. "Would you show me your favorite part?"

Meir could hear the desire in her voice. He took the book out of her hands, but instead of leafing through it, he blew out the lamp and kissed her. When she began to protest, he said, "You told me to 'show' you my favorite part, not read it to you."

Despite his ardent efforts, Meir found himself back at the synagogue later that month, again waiting for Joheved to exit the mikvah. The Hot Fair was well under way, with men attending from nearly every land inhabited by Jews, and Meir heard disturbing news from the east. Pope Gregory had intensified his efforts to free the Church from the authority of King Henry of Germany, much to the consternation of the German bishops, most of whom had been appointed by the king or his father. It was bad enough that Gregory insisted on celibacy for all clergy, not just monks; but the bishops were the king's vassals. They depended on Henry and his knights for protection.

The merchants passing through Allemagne heard rumors of increasing tension. Henry appointed new church councilors and Gregory demanded their dismissal. Men whispered that Gregory would excommunicate Henry if he did not obey, and others said the king was preparing his army for an attack on Rome, intending to put a new pope in Peter's Chair. A war between king and pope would have tremendous implications for those doing business in Allemagne and Italy, and much deliberation was spent on how to best profit from it.

Salomon was untouched by these political discussions. Scholars who had studied in Mayence had brought him news that his old teacher, Isaac haLevi, had died, and that Rivka's brother, Isaac ben Judah, was the new Rosh Yeshiva there. But relations between the brothers-in-law were cool. The Germans had never forgiven Salomon for exerting his own authority over how French beef was slaughtered, and when he'd opened his own yeshiva, it only exacerbated the breach.

But neither scholars' rivalry nor political intrigue could dampen the happy anticipation of the Jewish community's biggest social event of the Hot Fair, the feast Isaac haParnas was giving in celebration of his grandsons' betrothal. The yeshiva students looked forward to congratulating Menachem and Ephraim with such good cheer as only a group of youths presented with unlimited food and drink could provide.

Salomon and Meir weren't in a celebratory mood and spent most of the banquet discussing Talmud with their more serious colleagues while Miriam coaxed Joheved into partnering her in the women's dances. Rachel started out watching her sisters, but it was difficult to see them with so many adults in the way. When she tried to find her mother, she saw only strangers, and her calls for Mama were drowned out by the musicians.

She rushed through the crowd, desperate to find a familiar face, when suddenly a thin, skeletal hand reached out and grabbed her. Terrified, she looked up to see that she was the prisoner of a little old man in dark robes. She fought to get away but he held her fast.

"You are Rav Salomon's little girl." His accent was so strange that she could barely understand him, but his kind voice calmed her. "Are you lost? Shall I take you to him?"

She nodded and started to cry. The old man sounded nice, but Rachel knew about witches and warlocks, how they kidnapped innocent children. And if anyone fit her idea of what a warlock looked like, it was this gaunt white-haired man whose skin was as dry and scaly as a lizard's. But she obediently followed him.

"Salomon, I believe this valuable commodity belongs to you."

Rachel looked up to see her father, standing next to Meir, and several men she recognized as having dined with them on occasion. "Papa!" she cried out and ran to his outstretched arms.

He kept his hand on her shoulder as she took a tight hold on his tunic. "Rachel, you should thank my friend Ben Yochai for bringing you to me," Salomon said as the old scholar held out his bony hand.

But she couldn't bring herself to kiss that reptilian palm, and squeezed closer to her father, as if hoping to hide in his bliaut, as she had often done when she was little. Ben Yochai, either out of pity or because the ritual of hand kissing was not important to him, moved his hand up to stroke her curly hair.

"What a delightful child; may the Holy One protect her." Ben Yochai smiled his toothless grin. "She will be a treasure for you in your old age, Salomon." He smiled wider as Joheved ran up and scolded Rachel for slipping out of her sight. "Scholarly sons are well and good, but when you're old and frail, you'll appreciate your daughters and granddaughters."

"And you, Ben Yochai, have so many children, grandchildren and great-grandchildren that you can't even keep track of them anymore," Hiyya ibn Ezra teased his elderly colleague. "Your presence here is fortuitous, my friend. I'm trying to persuade Salomon that it is time for him to study the mysteries of the Torah. You are an authority in these matters, don't you agree?"

Before Ben Yochai could reply, Salomon interrupted. "I have no interest in such perilous subjects; I leave them to you in the hot climates. Between my commentaries on scripture and my Talmud kuntres, I have more than enough to study for a lifetime."

Joheved changed her mind about returning to the dancing and listened closely to their debate. Papa discouraged his yeshiva students from investigating

> What came before (creation), what came after (death), what was above (heaven and angels), or what was below (the domain of demons).

He said that the Torah's secret knowledge was so dangerous to explore that Talmudic sages who'd attempted it had either died or become insane in the process. Joheved never expected to meet a master of the esoteric wisdom, but apparently Ben Yochai was one.

"I have no doubt that Salomon has the necessary background, but if he has no interest, he would make a poor student," Ben Yochai replied. "To fully grasp the material, a pupil must study for years, from a mentor who only takes one disciple at a time. Even then it is a waste of effort if he lacks the proper *kavanah.*"

Was it really possible, Joheved wondered as the men talked, to use the hidden names of God to summon demons and make them do one's bidding, to make potions that could heal or kill, to foretell the future? What would it be like to wield such power? Certainly Ben Yochai was not an imposing man, except that he had lived to an exceptional age.

Salomon turned to admonish Hiyya. "I don't believe the Creator intended us to know His secrets. If others wish to engage in this risky venture, I will not encourage them." Then his expression softened. "In any case, I am only thirty-five years old, and it is forbidden to study these things until one is forty. Perhaps when I am older, I will feel the urge to delve into them."

As August and the Hot Fair drew to a close, Joheved, to her surprise, was asked by her father-in-law to attend the livestock sales with him and his daughter, Hannah. Since it was unclear which of his children's sons would eventually inherit his manor, Samuel wanted all their parents to become more knowledgeable about sheep. As long as he was in Troyes, Joheved might as well begin her husbandry education.

"This summer we must purchase at least one new ram for our flock," he told her. "You see, during last fall's mating season, the old lead ram killed a younger one in a battle for dominance, but he was mortally wounded in return."

As they walked around the holding pens, Samuel pointed out each ram's desirable characteristics to the young women. One sturdy fellow impressed them all, but they could not agree on a second. Samuel waited patiently until they came to the conclusion to buy this one animal only and see how the lambs he fathered did in the spring. They could always purchase another ram later.

Hannah, in the early months of pregnancy, found the odors emanating from the livestock area overpowering. "Joheved, I would be grateful if you could finish shopping for me," she said. "After all these animals, I'm afraid the spice merchants' scents will be too much for me."

"I'd be glad to." Joheved gave her sister-in-law directions home (it wouldn't do for Hannah to end up near Rue de la Petite Tannerie) and set off for the spice sellers' stalls.

Hannah slowly walked from the bustling streets surrounding the fairgrounds to the Rû Cordé bridge. All the alleys with their daub and wattle houses looked the same to her, and it took longer than she expected to find Salomon's courtyard. Relieved, she stood at the gate waiting for her nausea to pass.

The warm weather had persuaded Meir to take his small group of students outdoors to work on the week's Torah portion, and their high-pitched chanting was pleasantly soothing. Eventually the singsong came to a stop, and Meir heard a sound behind him.

He turned to see his sister slumped against the wall. "Hannah, what are you doing here alone? Are you all right?"

She nodded her head, and he continued, "Are you too warm? Shall I get you some wine from the cellar?"

"Merci, non," she said. "But perhaps we could walk along the river where it's cooler. The fresh air there would be nice too."

He directed the boys to continue with their study partners and led Hannah towards Bishop's Gate. There, far from the tanneries and fairgrounds, they strolled along the tow path that bordered the Seine.

Between the exercise and clean air, Hannah began to feel better. "Thank you for leaving your students to accompany me," she said. "The first months of pregnancy are always difficult for me, and I probably should have stayed at home."

Meir winced. Here his sister was expecting her third child, and he didn't have any. Maybe she could help him figure out what he was doing wrong. But it was a delicate subject.

She interrupted his thoughts to tease him. "Why is my usually talkative little brother so quiet? What deep and scholarly subject is he contemplating?"

There would be no peace until he told her something, so he took a deep breath and prepared to confide in her. "Hannah, I need your advice."

"I don't believe it. My brother, the talmid chacham, doesn't know everything?" She raised her eyebrows in mock astonishment.

"Would you please be serious? This is important."

"I'm sorry, Meir, I'll listen until you've said your piece." His troubled tone of voice, rather than his words, convinced her of his sincerity.

"Joheved and I have been married almost eighteen months and we still don't have any children." Surprisingly, it was difficult to speak without crying. "We must be doing something wrong, but I don't know what it is."

Hannah patted his arm in sympathy. "I think it's too early to worry about being barren," she said. "Besides, you've had one pregnancy already."

"But she lost the baby six months ago, and we've been trying so hard since then." He was ashamed to admit he still suspected his wife was lacking in feminine attributes.

"Meir, I lost the pregnancy after my daughter's birth, and it was more than a year after that before we conceived this one. I doubt that you use the bed any less than Simcha and I do."

"You miscarried? You didn't tell me." It was sobering to think that they had this kind of loss in common.

"It was just after we heard that Joheved was expecting, and I didn't want to spoil your happiness."

He sighed in remembrance of those carefree times. "I know I should be patient, but it's so frustrating. Joheved's flowers aren't regular—sometimes they're a month apart, sometimes more. Just when it's been so long since she last immersed that I'm sure she must be pregnant, then I find out she's niddah again."

"I know it's difficult, getting your hopes up and then being disappointed, but these things take time." She smiled up at him. "After all, there's almost ten years difference between Meshullam and me. Look how many years Mama and Papa have been married, and still they've only had the three of us."

Meir began to blush. Of course his parents used the bed—all married couples did. But the thought of his father doing with his mother the same things he did with Joheved was disconcerting. Despite Samuel's gift of Tractate Kallah, Meir hadn't considered that his father might also have benefited from its wisdom.

"Surely you don't think that they only had marital relations three times?" Hannah couldn't help but laugh at her younger brother's consternation.

"All right, I'll try to be more patient." His sister often teased him about spending so much time with his books that he was oblivious to the real world, and now he had given her new evidence of his naiveté. "Let's change the subject. How are you feeling?"

"I'm feeling better, merci. And I have a question for you." Now her voice became serious. "How can you stand to live in such a crowded and noisy city when our own manor is so close by? How can you sleep at night or think during the day with so many bells ringing all the time? Don't you miss the sound of birds singing? And the tanneries' stink that permeates the town during hot weather is nearly unbearable."

"That was more than one question, but I can answer them all by saying that studying Talmud is my life—and that means living in a big city." Meir didn't want to hurt his sister's feeling by saying that, after spending years in Mayence, Worms and Troyes, he preferred the cosmopolitan hustle and bustle to rural torpor.

"I'll gladly put up with the summer stench in order to talk Torah with the learned merchants who come to the Hot Fair," he added. It also meant a great deal to Joheved to learn what she could from the yeshiva, and her happiness was becoming more important to him every day. "Besides, I don't live a completely urban life. I work in Salomon's vineyard and I might even become a vintner some day."

"You a vintner?" Hannah shook her head in disbelief. "I'd love to see that."

They discussed the possibility of growing grapes in Ramerupt and spent the rest of their walk speaking of inconsequential matters. Neither wanted to broach the difficult subject of who would be the one to inherit the family estate. If Meshullam's sickly son didn't live to adulthood, then by law the manor should go to Meir. But what if he preferred life in the yeshiva?

twenty-two

Early Spring 4836 (1076 C.E.)

The clattering of horses' hooves followed by loud, urgent men's voices jolted Miriam awake. Rays of light appeared from below, and as Papa hurried downstairs, she heard Mama complain, "Just when I was hoping to get some sleep after those night-long Purim parties . . ."

Miriam peered out the window. With the moon just past full, the scene below was clearly visible. Aunt Sarah's manservant was speaking with men at the courtyard gate, men whose horses and swords proclaimed their nobility. Now Sarah herself came out, and the relief the knights displayed proved that they had come to the midwife's home for the usual reason. Miriam couldn't contain her curiosity, and when she saw Papa join them, she threw on her clothes and raced outside.

As she listened to the men's story, her apprehension grew.

Countess Adelaide was in labor and unable to find another midwife at this hour. The knights knew nothing of their lady's condition save that she had been laboring for nearly two days.

"Miriam, will you help me pack my midwife kit?" Sarah asked. They walked back together, and she whispered to Salomon, "I don't like this. What could have made the regular midwife disappear?"

"Must you take Miriam with you?"

"Oui. It may be that the first midwife failed because more than one attendant is necessary."

At Count Thibault's palace, Miriam held tightly to Aunt Sarah's hand as they passed through rooms so large that, as hard as she tried, she could see only the small circle of illumination cast by their escorts' torches. They ascended a staircase wide enough for Miriam, Aunt Sarah and their guide to walk abreast, before arriving at a door that opened immediately when they reached it. Miriam saw that the floor was not wood, but laid with different colored tiles, and the walls were covered with embroidered hangings.

Even more impressive was the bed, carved with animal shapes. Miriam stopped to stare at them and Aunt Sarah hissed at her, "Never mind the fancy decorations. On the bed lies a pregnant woman struggling in long travail, no different from any other."

The countess looked ghastly, her eyes sunken and her pallid skin tinged with grey. Sarah asked the calmest-looking woman what had happened and learned that Her Grace's water had broken two nights ago and the usual midwife was called.

"The midwife tied agrimony to Her Grace's thigh and rubbed her body with the ashes of burnt donkey hoof, but the baby did not come," the lady-in-waiting said. "We massaged Her Grace's belly for hours, to no avail. Finally the midwife said she had to get some special herbs for a difficult birth, but that was well before Matins—"

Suddenly, Countess Adelaide was seized with a contraction. Her face contorted and she moaned in agony. "Let me die. By the bones of Saint Margaret, let me die." She clutched at Sarah's hands, which were intently probing her belly. "Or help me to die. I know you have the means."

Miriam didn't know which was worse, that the Countess sought death or that she thought Aunt Sarah could provide it. Did she know a Jewish midwife was attending her, reputedly wise in the ways of poisons? Adelaide didn't seem capable of knowing anything besides the pain that was making her mewl like an injured cat.

Sarah stood up and confidently addressed the nearest maidservant, "Get me some pure olive oil, and make sure the vessel that holds it is large enough for my entire hand to fit in."

Then she turned to Miriam. "The child is laying sideways. Until his head or feet are pointing towards the womb's opening, he cannot be born. So when the oil arrives, you will stick your hand into the vessel, and then, quickly before the oil drips off, reach into Her Grace's womb and feel for the child's hip or shoulder."

"What?" Miriam's eyes opened wide in astonishment. "Me, stick my hand up into the countess? Won't that hurt her terribly?" She didn't dare mention how repugnant she found the procedure. "Isn't there another way?"

"Non, Miriam, there isn't another way. My hand is too big." Sarah gave her niece an encouraging smile. "You must turn the baby from within while I turn him from the outside."

Sarah poured out a cup of wine for her patient and crumpled some leaves into it. "Ragwort and wormwood," she informed Miriam. "The first to give the mother fortitude, the second to relieve her pain."

A large clay pot was offered to Miriam, and she plunged her hand into the warm oil. Then, praying for fortitude for herself, she gingerly inserted her dripping fingers into Adelaide's birth canal. Telling herself that it wasn't much different from cleaning a chicken, Miriam slowly slid her way forward. But the opening wasn't big enough for her whole hand, and she said so.

"Can you get a finger in?" Sarah inquired, and when Miriam nodded, she said, "Try to insert two fingers so you can massage the opening larger."

Eyes tightly closed, Miriam worked the aperture wider as gently as she could. When a contraction came, the countess thrashed and flailed, causing Miriam to think that her arm would surely break. But Aunt Sarah was encouraged that Adelaide still had strength enough to react so vigorously.

Miriam finally managed to gain access to the womb, and there was the baby, wedged tightly on its side. But it was difficult to tell one part from another. Wishing she'd spent more time bathing baby Pesach, she decided that she'd found this babe's shoulder, mainly by its proximity to his head. But all this maneuvering was taking its toll on the countess, just when she needed to be as strong as possible.

Sarah gave new instructions to the ladies-in-waiting. "Any rubies Her Grace owns, bring them in immediately, along with two cups of strong wine and some ground pepper." Then she threw some sweet-smelling herbs on the brazier, to attract the child so reluctant to be born.

Aunt Sarah's directions to Miriam were simple. "In between contractions, we will try to rotate the baby into a proper position, each pushing as hard as we can."

When Miriam whispered her concern about injuring the child, Sarah quietly insisted that she push with all her might. "The baby must be born soon, no matter what his condition."

The hours passed. Somehow Miriam found the strength to keep pushing, though she longed with all her heart to be home in her own bed. Count Thibault agreed to sacrifice one of his wife's small rubies, now ground up in wine for her to drink. In addition, the countess gripped two larger stones, one in each hand. Sarah crushed a strange root into the other wine cup, but this potion she set aside.

Dawn was lightening the room, and Miriam distracted herself from her cramping fingers by trying to figure out what scenes the colorful wall hangings depicted. Some were obviously from the Bible: Creation, the Flood with Noah, and so on down to King David. Others showed great battles. She had progressed from admiring the wall hangings to examining the ceiling, painted with signs of the zodiac, when the baby suddenly made a larger turn than before and Sarah yelled for Miriam to withdraw her hand.

Now things happened quickly. Too exhausted to move, Adelaide was carried to the birth stool and supported there by her ladies. When the next contraction came, Sarah blew the ground pepper up her patient's nose, generating a large sneeze accompanied by a glimpse of the baby's feet.

Sarah took hold of them and waited. One more sneeze, a firm pull, and the entire body was out.

"A boy! It's a boy!"

One last dose of the expensive spice brought forth the head and afterbirth. At first the infant cried feebly, but his cries grew stronger as he was cleaned up and swaddled. Sarah hastily removed the agrimony, lest it draw the womb itself out afterwards.

Miriam was physically drained, but emotionally elated. They had saved both Countess Adelaide and her baby boy! The new mother settled back into bed, her ladies trying to pretty her up for her husband's expected visit. Only Miriam noticed that Aunt Sarah emptied the untouched second cup of wine into a chamber pot.

Miriam heard roosters crowing as she and Sarah were escorted home. Somebody had given Aunt Sarah a purse full of coins, but she would not open it until she was secure at home. One thing kept Miriam awake. What had been in the untasted cup?

"Powdered iris root, very hot and dry." Aunt Sarah showed her where she stored the dangerous herb. "When a woman is feeble and the child cannot come out, it is better that the child be killed than the mother also die. The Merciful One be blessed that we did not need it tonight."

Miriam kept her eyes open long enough to don her tefillin and say her morning prayers. When Joheved entered their old bedroom, ready to put on her own tefillin, Miriam was sound asleep. She, and everyone else in the household, would have to wait to hear a firsthand account of the night's events.

Miriam was chopping vegetables in the kitchen a week later when one of the countess's ladies-in-waiting knocked on the door. She jumped up and eagerly asked how mother and child were doing.

The lady replied that both were healthy, the boy suckling well from his wet nurse. "Her Grace is especially appreciative of the part you played in the birth of her youngest son." She held out a small wooden box. "And she wanted to reward you."

The box was intricately carved, and Miriam hoped it contained some valuable spice, perhaps pepper for use in future midwife duties. By now Rivka, Joheved and Rachel had gathered around the smiling stranger, who encouraged Miriam to show everyone the box's contents.

The room filled with awed exclamations. The box contained a small red jewel, and Miriam knew it had to be a ruby. She looked in awe at the countess's lady, who explained that this was a twin of the one Her Grace had swallowed, one of a pair of earrings. Her Grace still had two ears, so she'd decided to send this lonely stone to the brave young midwife's helper.

Miriam couldn't take her eyes off the ruby. "Please thank Her Grace for me. One day my future patients may benefit by holding it."

"Oh no, my child," came the reply. "Her Grace thanks you. What is a ruby worth compared to her life and that of her son?"

"A woman of valor who can find? Her worth is far above rubies." Joheved quoted the final Proverb, its meaning clearly demonstrated.

They urged the noblewoman to share some bread and wine with them, but she declined. If she tarried here too long, Her Grace might think she'd been waylaid and the jewel stolen. Rivka took upon herself the obligation of seeing their guest to the gate; it would be impolite for the lady to find her own way out. They were still admiring the ruby when Rivka came back.

"Miriam, Joheved! Take my keys to the jewelry box and put that stone away before Claire comes downstairs." Rivka trusted Marie's replacement, but that didn't mean she wanted valuables flaunted in front of the girl.

Rivka's position as mistress of the house entitled her to custody of the keys, which she wore pinned to her bodice like a brooch. She even had a decorated pin to hold them on Shabbat, so she would be legally considered to be wearing jewelry, which was permitted, rather than carrying keys, which was not.

She was the one who locked the doors at night and unlocked them again at dawn. She kept a key to every chest and cupboard in the house, excepting Meir's. If Anna or Claire needed pepper or cloves from the spice cabinet, she opened it for them, and it was she who unlocked the jewelry box before Shabbat or a festival, to take out what she and her daughters would wear on the holiday.

Rivka handed a key to Miriam, and the three sisters climbed down to the cellar. The jewelry box should have been hidden behind a wine cask, but Joheved couldn't feel it there.

"Are you sure you put it back behind this cask, Miriam?" Her sister had been the last one to bed on Purim.

"I thought it was this one," she replied sheepishly. She had consumed a large quantity of wine.

"Well, it has to be in here somewhere; you did put the box behind one of the wine casks, didn't you?" Joheved snorted with impatience. Now they'd have to search behind all the casks.

They started from where Miriam thought she had put the box. Rachel was too little to reach behind the casks, but she could look underneath them. "I see it," Rachel squealed suddenly. "But I can't reach it. It's fallen behind this barrel."

It took Joheved's entire arm's length to reach the object. But it was a leather-bound volume, not the missing jewel box. "It's in Hebrew and it's mostly numbers," Joheved announced after reading silently for a while. "I think it's Grandmama Leah's old ledger, but there's more here than just accounts. Some of the pages are about things that happened to her, like a diary."

"Are there dates in it? Can you tell when it was written?" Miriam squeezed around to get a better look.

"I can't tell exactly, but I think the first date is 4700-something. Goodness, that's before Papa was born." Joheved thumbed through a few pages. "We certainly get a higher price now than she did back then."

Rachel didn't try to hide her impatience. "Never mind what wine cost then, read some of the diary part."

"All right, here's a couple of pages near the beginning." Joheved began to read aloud, "The townspeople are trying to ruin me with their taxes, and I shall have to go to the Bet Din (Jewish court) over the matter. They insist that my vineyard and grapes be taxed separately. They dare say that vineyards are the same as capital of a loan, while the harvest is equivalent to interest."

Joheved paused to turn the page. "They don't understand that a vineyard cannot be compared to capital, nor even to merchandise. A vineyard requires not only a heavy yearly investment in both money and effort, but also a great deal of expensive labor to harvest the grapes. And even after all this, I am rarely sure of a profit. Every year the lords come and carry away their portion. Sometimes the crop is lost completely and I receive no return whatever for all my invested money and labor."

Leah's complaints continued: "If the court upholds the townspeople and allows them to take away my painfully small profit and to even tax the land itself, I would be left with nothing. Heaven forbid! Such an injustice is a practice typical of Edom, not the Jewish way. The Jews should equitably allocate all taxes based on the person's ability to pay, in accordance with the principle: Love thy neighbor as thyself."

Miriam sighed. "What a shame that Grandmama Leah's profession gave her so much trouble."

"But imagine, she was ready to take her protest all the way to the Bet Din," Joheved said, nodding in approval.

"What about now?" Rachel asked. "Do we still have to pay taxes like that?"

"Non, Rachel," Joheved assured her. "As long as I can remember we've only paid tithes on the value of the wine itself, never on the vineyard or the grapes."

"Maybe Grandmama Leah did challenge her taxes at the Bet Din," Miriam said. "And that's why we don't pay so much now."

"Find something else to read," insisted Rachel, "something about Papa when he was little or when he got married."

But there was no mention of Papa, or of Mama, at all. In between the pages of numbers, there were sporadic complaints that bad weather or disease had nearly ruined the crop, but there were also many years when she wrote nothing except the accounting. Occasionally Leah objected to the harlots in the marketplace, which made it difficult for respectable women to do business there. Much to her granddaughters' disappointment, it appeared that Leah wrote only about winemaking.

"Wait, listen to this final entry," Joheved said suddenly. "It's dated 4825; that's three years before Papa came home."

Leah had written: "I have had some distressing symptoms that I have not told anyone. New instructions do not penetrate; I hear them, but I can't retain them. A thick fog begins to descend after a few sentences. I make the appropriate responses, but I am aware that I am not understanding. It is driving me mad."

Joheved fought back tears. "Even when I make a notation to trigger my memory, I have no idea to what the notes are referring. Instructions on how to get to someone's house or a new recipe—these are old skills at which I excelled and now I cannot believe how this curtain always comes down.

"I am reluctant to try anything new for fear I will come off as an idiot, and people will notice. There are parts of the city I know nothing about and I do not go there. I do not go out at night anymore. Everyone is always talking to me and giving me instructions, but I cannot seem to assimilate new procedures or ideas. My thinking process frightens me—my mind is spent."

Joheved stood stone silent. That was the last thing Leah had written. How terrible for Leah to know that her intellect was failing, how painful to suffer such a thing in secret. Leah had always been so proud of her learning; the shame and fear of losing it must have been unbearable, not to mention the humiliation of people thinking she was crazy.

Tears were running down Miriam's cheeks. "Why didn't she tell us?" she asked helplessly. "We would have helped her. Poor Grandmama, so afraid and so alone."

Even Rachel, who barely remembered her grandmother, was sad. When they finally found the jewelry box, they no longer had quite the same enthusiasm for the valuable ruby. The stone's beauty was tarnished by Grandmama Leah's revelation. Miriam put the jewel away with their other valuables and carefully replaced the box behind the proper wine barrel.

Joheved put the old ledger back behind its cask too. She suspected that Leah herself had been the last one to read it, and had never intended for anyone else to do so. The sisters couldn't bring themselves to speak of what they'd found. Their grandmother had agonized so long over her secret, and now they had exposed it. It seemed best to leave well enough alone.

Leah's secret receded in importance as Passover approached. Rachel grew increasingly excited because this year she would finally join her sisters in making matzah, the unleavened bread that Jews are commanded to eat during the festival. For the eight days of Passover, it was forbidden to eat, or even possess, bread, cake or any kind of pastry. Consequently, the Jews of Troyes had to make enough matzah to last the entire community a week.

For Joheved and Miriam, making matzah was the most, if not the only, pleasurable part of the festival preparations, and they volunteered to help at the bakery nearly every day. Rivka spent a few afternoons there as well, for both the camaraderie of her peers and to participate in the holy work.

Rachel, and all the town's children, wanted to help too, for part of their fun in baking matzah came from watching the adults working in such great haste. To eliminate any contamination by leaven, the women moved as quickly as they could. Those who mixed the flour with water, those who poured the dough and those who kneaded it, those who cut it into cakes and those who smoothed it, those who shoved the cakes into the oven, not to mention those who carried the dough from one worker to the next—they all raced through their tasks at lightning speed, taking care to insure that the dough never stood for a moment.

One special task was delegated to the children, that of using the little cog wheels to perforate the dough and prevent it from rising in the oven. The children tried to make perfect pointed lines across the round cakes, and, for them, it was more game than work. Even for the adults, it was equally merry and pious labor. The women sang as they whisked the dough from one station to the next, songs as lively as their pace.

Salomon accompanied Rachel on her first day of matzah baking. The most learned Jew in Troyes, it was his responsibility to supervise the workers and admonish them to remain diligent. But no one, not even Salomon, stood around and watched. Speed was unnecessary when it came to removing the baked unleavened cakes from the oven, and from this warm vantage point, he could make sure the dough was not delayed before it reached the oven.

Rachel was so excited that she found it impossible to concentrate on making quick straight lines with her little cog wheel. People hurrying about, circles of dough practically flying from one hand to the next, these were far more fascinating to watch. It seemed as though collisions would be unavoidable, yet the workers always managed to move out of each other's way in time. Then Rachel would let out her breath and return to her task, inevitably too late. But this learning period was expected; in time she would master making the perfect lines.

Joheved and Miriam were experienced dough rollers, and, sitting next to each other at the large table, they rapidly yet calmly smoothed their balls of dough into flat circles. When it came time to bake the very last batch, the baker's wife took out decorative molds for the workers to make fancy-shaped matzah for their own seders. Joheved used a bird-shaped form, and Miriam chose one shaped like a flower. Salomon made sure nobody took longer making the special matzah than the regular ones. Finally, the matzah was sorted and stored in tall stacks. As the festival week progressed, each family would come and take what they needed.

Meir's family baked their matzah in the manor's large oven, along with extra for other Jewish families in the vicinity. But they were distracted this Passover. Hannah had been bleeding off and on for the last month, painless bleeding, sometimes heavy and sometimes scant. But the babe remained inside her womb.

Passover in Ramerupt passed uneventfully, and one week later, Meir was sleeping fitfully. Joheved was niddah again after a long interval, and he had been unable to hide his disappointment. This only heightened her sense of failure, and when he tried to comfort her, he succeeded only in making her feel worse. She finally asked him to stop talking and just let her go to sleep.

Meir had no idea how much Joheved hated being niddah, and wearing the uncomfortable *sinar* with its associated mess was but a minor part of it. Niddah meant more than not being able to use the bed with her husband. To avoid even the temptation to sin, she and Meir never touched each other. For almost two weeks, they slept with separate linens, sat on separate benches, ate from separate bowls, and handed items to each other indirectly either by placing them somewhere for the other to pick up or by using another person as a go-between.

After the miscarriage, when she first began her flowers, Joheved was proud of her niddah status. It proved she was a normal woman after all.

During meals she sat with Rivka and Miriam and shared their dishes. She carefully avoided giving Meir anything from her own hand and vigilantly made sure that he never ate from anything she'd sampled. It was like a game.

But a year later, niddah was more like a punishment. The abrupt changing of seats from her husband's bench to her sisters' was a shameful announcement that yet another barren month had gone by, and she now understood why Rivka preferred to sit with the women all the time rather than endure the monthly humiliation of moving her place. Joheved found it easier to not share her bowl with anyone during niddah, lest it inadvertently end up in front of Meir, even if it did make her feel like a leper.

Yet when she and Meir walked back home after she'd immersed, it was wonderful. The sheets were freshly washed, they drank wine from the same cup and fed each other dessert. Their hands found every excuse for touching each other—her veil was crooked, his côte needed straightening. The orange-striped cat, who slept between them during niddah, would vanish for the night and reappear at the foot of their bed the next morning.

Was their renewed passion worth the price? Joheved didn't know, and it didn't matter. The law was the law. One thing she did know. Nothing lessened the pain of acknowledging that another month's attempts at pregnancy had failed.

For Meir, besides the halt to marital relations, what he missed most during niddah was the casual intimacy of marriage. When Joheved sat with the women at meals, it was difficult to even talk with her. At night, he wished he could just snuggle up to his wife's warm body and hold her. Despite the incident in the cellar, Meir felt confident he could control his yetzer during niddah. Forbidden was forbidden—he would no more approach Joheved while she was niddah than he would eat bacon at a tavern.

But he had no intention of testing his resolve and pulled his own covers tighter around him. He was still half awake when he heard the whinny of horses and the voice of his father's servant below. He sat up and listened carefully. This was no dream. In a moment, Meir was dressed and out the door.

Outside, he saw Aunt Sarah frantically trying to mount his horse. The servant's distress had communicated itself to the animal, increasing its agitation. Meir ran over and took hold of the bridle, his familiar presence calming the nervous filly.

"Your sister is in labor and I've come for the midwife," the servant whispered. His anxiety made the simple words imply the worst. "Your horse can easily find her way to Ramerupt in the dark."

Meir tried to control his increasing fear. "What's the matter?" His father had sent the servant to Troyes on his own horse, the fastest in their stable. What was the emergency that couldn't wait for dawn?

"This is no time for talk," Sarah called to Meir. "You can be useful by closing the gate behind us."

When they were gone, he slowly walked back to the house. He was trembling, but not with cold. Childbirth was the domain of women, and he knew little of the process except that it was so dangerous that Jacob's beloved Rachel, one of the four Jewish matriarchs, had died from it. And that ratio hadn't changed much since then.

Sleep was impossible, so he spent the hours until dawn reciting Psalms. But he kept interrupting his prayers to see if it was getting light. Suddenly a rooster crowed. It was still dark outside, but Meir knew his waiting was nearly over. Heart pounding, he cleared his mind and focused on the eighty-sixth Psalm:

> My God, deliver Your servant who trusts in You.
> Have mercy on me, O Adonai, for I call to You all the day;
> Give ear, O Adonai, to my prayer; heed my plea for mercy.
> In my time of trouble I call You, for You will answer me.

When the sky finally began to lighten, Meir was astride Sarah's horse and ready to ride for Ramerupt. He rode past sleepy peasants, who watched with surprise as the young horseman raced across their lands. But he barely noticed them. His concentration was focused on guiding the mare over any obstacles that might hinder them.

The sun had risen completely when he galloped through the manor's gates. A servant ran out to meet him, but Meir ignored him and bolted through the nearest door, which led into the kitchen. Maidservants preparing breakfast scattered as he rushed for the stairs, and he slowed only when he reached the landing and heard the unmistakable sound of an infant's cry.

Meir's heart swelled with relief. Sarah had arrived in time, the baby was born, everything was all right. The need to see his sister overcame all else, and without thinking, he opened her bedroom door and strode in. And stopped, horrified, in his tracks.

As a child Meir had watched the villeins slaughter sheep, but he had never seen so much blood indoors—the bedding, the attending women's clothes, even the floor. The scene in front of him seared into his mind: his mother holding the small wailing bundle, tears streaming down her face, the serving women staring at him with dread, Aunt Sarah grimly sewing up the large hole in his sister's belly. He suddenly felt nauseous, and the room began to swirl around him.

The last thing he heard before he fainted was a woman screaming, "Get him out of here!"

twenty-three

Ramerupt
Spring 4836 (1076 C.E.)

Meir awoke to the sound of Joheved's voice. "Meir, please wake up. You need to get up now."

Relief coursed through him; he'd just had a horrible nightmare, but it was over. He slowly opened his eyes and saw Joheved bending over him, her face etched with sympathy and concern. Then he looked beyond her and saw that he was in his boyhood bed at his parents' house.

"Non, Merciful God, Non! " Meir sat up, grabbed the neckline of his chemise and ripped it open to his waist. Then he rolled over and pounded the bed in anguish.

Joheved watched helplessly as her husband bewailed his loss. His back was towards her, and she wanted to reach out and stroke his shaking shoulders. But she was niddah. They couldn't touch each other until she immersed.

Tears running down her cheeks, she gazed at him and sighed. She hated to think about it, yet Joheved knew that if she died in childbirth, Meir would take a new wife. But now his only sister was gone, and with her an irretrievable piece of his past.

"I'm so sorry." She didn't know what else to say.

Her voice reminded Meir that he wasn't alone. Gulping down his sobs, he sat up and faced her squarely. "Tell me what happened. How did my sister die?"

Joheved was taken aback by his direct question, but she had listened carefully as Aunt Sarah explained the circumstances to Miriam. "I'm terribly sorry, but the placenta was in between the baby and the birth passage," she explained. "Aunt Sarah said there was nothing anyone could have done for her. At least they saved the baby, which, by the way, is a boy."

"When I heard the baby crying, I just had to see for myself that Hannah was all right," he muttered bitterly. "It never occurred to me that she wouldn't be." He had barely spoken the last phrase when he began to weep.

Joheved repeated, "I'm sorry," several times and wondered how long Meir intended to sequester himself in his old bedroom. She didn't want to leave him alone, but she was needed to help prepare Hannah's body for burial.

Just then the door opened to admit his parents, both wearing ripped bliauts. His father's barely controlled grief was too much for Meir, and when he broke into tears again, his mother took him in her arms and they wept together. Joheved felt like an intruder observing what should be her in-laws' private sorrow, but she couldn't get up and leave without forcing them aside.

Finally Samuel cleared his throat and suggested that Meir come downstairs where Salomon and his students had congregated. Of course, Meir realized, they were gathering for the funeral. Was everyone waiting for him? Had he been unconscious so long that his sister's body had already been ritually prepared?

Marona answered his unspoken question by asking Joheved, "Are you ready, dear? We have everything we need for *tahara* upstairs."

Joheved gave Meir what she hoped was an affectionate look and then walked with her mother-in-law to the room where Miriam and Aunt Sarah were waiting with the corpse. She told herself not to be so nervous. After all, she had performed this mitzvah for Grandmama Leah, whom she had loved deeply, while Meir's sister was practically a stranger. Her thoughts were interrupted when she saw that Marona had hesitated outside the door. The woman was trembling and Joheved instinctively took her arm to offer support, berating herself for being insensitive to the mourner's needs.

They each took a deep breath and walked in. Hannah's bed had been dismantled and in its place was a narrow table on which her body lay, covered by a sheet. Aunt Sarah was instructing Miriam in the procedures needed for *tahara* when a woman died in childbirth, assistance the midwife was expected to provide. She lapsed into respectful silence when she saw Marona, and the four women quietly took their places around the table.

Marona, the only legal mourner among them, positioned herself at her daughter's head to wash her face and hair. Sarah would prepare the torso, thus preventing anyone except herself from viewing Hannah's disfigurement. There was a subtle odor in the air, and Joheved recognized it as the smell of death. She had only experienced it twice, with Grandmama and baby Leah, but the fetid odor was unmistakable.

At Grandmama Leah's *tahara,* they had talked among themselves as they performed the mitzvah. But Jewish law prohibited anyone from addressing a mourner first, and here, the deceased's mother was entitled to contemplate her sorrow uninterrupted, if that was her choice. They worked in silence, changing the body's position as necessary, maintaining its modesty under the sheet.

Suddenly Marona's eyes brimmed over and a few tears slipped down her face. "I haven't washed or brushed Hannah's hair since she was a little girl." Her voice quivered as she spoke.

Her listeners made sympathetic comments and she continued, "Once Meir was married, and Hannah had survived two births, I thought my days of burying children were over. You see, while I was still nursing Hannah, I lost two children to smallpox in a month. It was the most pain I've ever borne, until now."

"You have much company," Aunt Sarah said gently. "It's a rare mother who sees each baby grow to honor her in her old age."

"True." Marona sighed. "Smallpox made mourners of every woman I knew, and we comforted each other. And others were worse off—I had some children survive, plus the likelihood of having more in the future. Now I am like Naomi—there are no more children in my womb."

Joheved could not restrain herself. "Please don't say that; it will tempt Satan. Naomi said it to Ruth when all her sons were dead. You have two sons still living; may the Merciful One protect them."

"May the Merciful One certainly protect them," Marona said hastily, clearly horrified at endangering her sons.

They were nearly done now. Hannah's body was shrouded and all that remained to do was to cover her head with a white hood, the front of which resembled a veil. This honor was reserved for her mother, and with trembling hands, Marona gently smoothed the delicate fabric over her daughter's face and hair.

Then she sighed and began to weep anew. "She looks just like a bride."

Sarah, who had helped prepare too many young matrons for burial, was ready for this reaction. She took the sobbing mother in her arms and held her, offering the consolation that Hannah had lived to womanhood, had known the joys of a husband's and children's love. Then she sent Joheved and Miriam out to find whoever was going to watch the body next.

Meshullam arrived two days into the week of mourning for his sister, and by then the family had settled into a routine. Each day, shortly after breakfast, Salomon and his students arrived to pray the morning service with the mourners. This was followed by Torah study, the midday meal, more study and the afternoon service, after which the contingent from Troyes returned home.

Salomon taught only from the sorrowful sacred texts—the books of Job, Lamentations, and Jeremiah, and the two tractates of Talmud dealing with mourning or the destruction of the Temple—while the bereaved men in Meir's family sat silently on the floor. Joheved longed to sit by her husband's side and console him, but no matter how comfortable she might feel listening to scholarly discussions at home, she thought it would be inappropriate for her to sit here with the men.

Besides, Marona had no other woman to console her, and she seemed content to pass the time showing her daughter-in-law around the estate that Joheved had only glimpsed on her ride over. Unlike houses in the crowded Jewish district of Troyes, which were protected by the castle and city walls, the manor sat isolated, surrounded only by fields. And compared to the house of Isaac haParnas, one of the finest in Troyes, this place was enormous. Besides the imposing main house, there were several other buildings as well.

What were all those rooms and buildings for? What did people do here all day? What was it like, this place where her husband had grown up? Joheved couldn't hide how impressive she found it.

"It was either my husband's grandfather or great-grandfather—may his merit protect us—who was the first lord here." Even grief couldn't conceal Marona's pride. "The Count of Ramerupt needed money—don't they always—which Samuel's ancestor loaned him, and the count repaid him by deeding him this land."

They walked past a large chicken coop built against the far wall, and Marona patted the grey stone with satisfaction. "Samuel told me that at first it was one big structure, half hall and half barn, but over the years, they built the kitchen and bakehouse, the dovecote, the sheepfold, the stable and storage barns."

Joheved admired each building, so different from home. The bakehouse oven was as large as the matzah bakery's, and the enormous kitchen had its own granary built against one side. The round, thatched dovecote held at least a hundred doves, while the wooden sheepfold, also thatched, was big enough to accommodate all the estate's sheep at night. In the stone stable, she saw horses and oxen, as well as carts and farm tools.

While Joheved knew that other people didn't reside in large cities, she had never given much thought to what rural life was like. She felt provincial and ignorant, and suddenly understood her father's driving need to question the foreign merchants about their lands and customs, to learn how everything worked or was made. As Marona pointed out detail after detail, Joheved grew ashamed that she knew so little about her husband's home.

"And Samuel is still making improvements," Marona said, ushering Joheved into a building that seemed newer than the others. "When Meir was little, we built this dairy, to make cheese from the ewe's extra milk."

Marona earnestly explained how the milkmaids used the churns, settling pans, strainers and cheese presses. Joheved was intrigued with the little blocks with inverted Hebrew letters carved into them, and one of the milkmaids showed her that when they were pushed into the hardening curd, the resulting cheese was clearly labeled so that Jewish customers could tell it was kosher.

When they came to the large cellar under the main house, Joheved was surprised at all the wine barrels stored there. She recognized Salomon's, but these were by no means the majority. She knocked on a few and, finding them empty, asked when they had last been used.

"Before your betrothal, we used to buy grapes and make our own wine here, though it was never as good as your family makes," Marona said. Then, unable to remain content with such a short reply, she elaborated, "In Provence, where I grew up, most Jews owned land, and my family had olive orchards and vineyards. They told me that Samuel's father specifically looked for his bride in Provence, to find one who was familiar with a landed estate.

"I wish I had been raised like you, Joheved, to know all about growing grapes as well as how to make wine from them." She sighed with nostalgia.

"We all had to help with the vintage, of course, but my father wouldn't let me or my sisters work in the fields."

Joheved remembered the girls in Troyes who used to snub her for working in the vineyard, but she said nothing.

"I must admit that nowadays, harvesting the wheat is so time consuming that it's a relief not to be bothered with a vineyard too," Marona continued. "Yet I loved the way the grapevines looked back home, all green and tied up on their stakes, and they smelled so nice in the spring. I've never quite given up the idea of having our own vineyard here, which was, of course, one of the things that was so attractive about having my son marry you."

Joheved thanked Marona for the compliment and tried to listen attentively as her mother-in-law babbled on. At least she'd been able to offer the woman some diversion from her grief.

Unfortunately, she was less successful at consoling Meir. Questioning him about the day's studies brought brief monotone responses, not at all like the enthusiastic Talmud lessons they had previously shared. She told him about exploring the manor and tried to draw him out by asking about his favorite childhood memories. But they all seemed to involve Hannah, which, instead of offering the comfort of pleasant recollections, only deepened his dark mood.

Even sleep brought him no peace. Joheved would wake in the dark to hear him tossing and turning. Sometimes he cried out and she was afraid of the demon, the night *mare,* that invaded his dreams. How she longed to pull him close to her and hold him tight until he relaxed back into sleep.

Each night Meir had a similar dream. Someone or something was chasing him, but he dared not look back to see his pursuer's face or how many of them there were. When he could almost hear their breathing behind him, he reached a flight of stairs and raced up them, only to find himself stopped by a closed door. Just as an arm or claw reached out to grab him, he forced the door open, only to find himself in Hannah's bedroom, her bloodied body on the bed. The pursuers laughed raucously and Meir would wake up in terror.

Meir briefly considered telling Joheved or Marona about his bad dreams. When he had woken up crying as a child, his mother would have Samuel,

Meshullam and herself bless him the next morning, turning his bad dream to good. But he wasn't a child anymore; he couldn't bring himself to ask for three people to bless him because a night *mare* disturbed his sleep.

Yet reciting the antidemonic Psalm 91 didn't help. He couldn't wait to return to Troyes, where he wouldn't have to pass by that dreadful door every day. Once he was back at Salomon's with his mind engaged by the yeshiva's routine, surely then he would rid himself of the horrors that stalked him.

But Meir's troubles were only beginning. The night *mares* followed him back to his marital bed, and the night before his wife was due to immerse in the mikvah, they took on a new, more frightening, aspect. This time, instead of opening the door to behold his dead sister, it was Joheved's corpse on the stained bedding. It was her open belly he saw, and her lifeless eyes stared at him accusingly.

"Non!" Meir jerked awake with a cry that woke Salomon's entire household. Heart pounding, his body drenched with sweat, it took Meir a few moments to get his bearings, to realize that his wife was very much alive and sitting right next to him.

"It's all right," Joheved said soothingly. "You've had a bad dream, that's all. But we're home now; there's nothing to worry about here."

She wanted to find a cloth to dry his clammy skin, but he clutched her tightly. Miriam was trying to comfort a frightened Rachel in the next room and the murmur of her parents' voices carried from down the hall. Light glimmered from beneath the door—downstairs someone had lit a lamp.

"Meir, let go of me; I haven't immersed yet." Joheved struggled to get away, and he slowly loosened his grasp. "Let me get Papa and Mama to bless you over your bad dream, so they don't think we've been murdered in our beds."

Meir tried to speak in a firm, calm voice. "I'm sure they can hear us talking in here; they'll know we're all right." He'd been so terrified that he'd actually touched his wife while she was still niddah, not to mention waking up a house full of people. Even the orange-striped cat seemed offended; it had jumped off the bed immediately and was balefully staring at Meir from the floor.

As for Joheved getting up to make her parents bless him, he was embarrassed enough as it was. "Just stay here with me, and I'll be fine."

"Very well," she said. It was certainly more pleasant in their warm bed than walking about in the cold night air, even if they did have to sleep with separate linens.

Joheved soon fell asleep, but even the sound of his wife's breathing next to him couldn't dispel Meir's lingering anxiety. He kept thinking about the second Mishnah in Tractate Shabbat, the one that stated:

> For three transgressions women die in childbirth; for neglecting niddah, the dough offering of Challah, and lighting the Sabbath lamp.

Surely Joheved would never fail to observe any of the women's mitzvot—she was so eager to perform mitzvot that she even performed the ones women were exempt from. But he couldn't believe that Hannah had been guilty of such things either, and still she had died.

The next night, Meir accompanied Joheved to synagogue and waited with the other men for their wives to use the mikvah. This time he couldn't bring himself to join in their high-spirited mood. How could these men laugh and joke when any one of them might be signing his wife's death warrant tonight by impregnating her? How could they be so callous?

Immediately he rebuked himself. The Holy One commanded man to be fruitful and multiply. Life and death were in His hands.

Meir walked his wife home in silence. Despite his best intentions, once he was alone with Joheved, his yetzer refused to cooperate. He kissed her and tried to enjoy the sensation of her lips moving against his, but the vision of her dead body lying on the bloody bed appeared before him. He stroked her backside and belly, trying to concentrate on how soft her skin felt under his hands, but again the horrible image assailed him. It was all he could do not to pull his hands away, so strong was the feeling that if he did so, he would find them covered with blood. He struggled to discover something that would excite his desire enough to banish his nightmarish memories, but he failed.

Joheved sensed there was something wrong almost immediately. There was no pleasure, no passion, in Meir's kisses. Yet he kissed her so hard that it almost hurt her lips. The hands that wandered over her flesh were not those of an experienced lover, confident of arousing his wife's desire, but somehow conveyed desperation, and finally, hopelessness.

He was kissing her neck almost frantically when she pulled away to ask, "What's the matter? Have I done anything to upset you?"

"What do you mean? There's nothing the matter," he lied. "It's just taking me a bit longer than usual. Try to be patient."

Joheved submitted to more vigorous caresses, her own desire now as diminished as her husband's. How could she end this without humiliating him?

"Meir, please stop for a moment," she whispered. "I know you're tired, that you didn't sleep very well last night. Let's just go to bed now and get a good night's sleep. I'm sure you'll be your old self again once you're rested." Maybe he'd be fine in the morning after they'd spent the night snuggled together.

But he wasn't.

So they decided he must still be despondent over Hannah's death and agreed to wait until *sheloshim,* the thirty-day period of less intense mourning, was over. This time, walking home from the mikvah, Meir felt more anxious than on his wedding night. Nervous as a bridegroom, he thought ruefully, but with none of a groom's eager lust. Joheved was worried too, though she tried to hide it under a mask of forced cheerfulness. Their artificial gaiety only made things worse, and again they were disappointed and frustrated.

It was during the Hot Fair, three months later, while Salomon was teaching at the synagogue, that he noticed something that disturbed him so greatly that he dismissed the merchants in order to walk home alone with his son-in-law.

"Tell me, Meir, did my eyes deceive me?" Salomon tried to keep the apprehension out of his voice. "Did I see Joheved leave the mikvah earlier, while you remained here?"

Meir knew he could no longer hide his incapacity. "Oui, Rabbenu Salomon, you did."

The misery in his son-in-law's response almost broke Salomon's heart. "And so?" He waited for the confession that was sure to follow.

Meir took a deep breath. "Rabbenu, I am no longer capable of marital relations. A demon has bound me," he answered, using the Hebrew euphemism for "impotent." "I have been this way since my sister died." There, he had said "impotence" without crying.

Salomon couldn't hide his shock. Impotent! How could this young man, whose yetzer was so strong that he could barely keep the fellow off his daughter before the wedding, be impotent? A sudden memory of Meir screaming in the night answered his question. Rivka had begged him to go with her right then and bless their son-in-law, and when he demurred, she'd insisted that he get two other scholars to bless Meir in the morning. But he had done nothing, and here was the result.

It must have been a powerful demon to bind Meir. Well, Torah scholars were not without power themselves. Salomon immediately resolved to bring a Torah scroll into his home and hold daily services in his salon. Instead of waiting until the month before Rosh Hashanah to rise at midnight for penitential prayers, he would begin reciting them forthwith. His piety would drive this demon out from under his roof.

"Don't worry, *mon fils.*" He put his arm around the young man. "I'm sure your yetzer hara is too strong to be bound for long. But even so, I believe I am developing a craving for lentils cooked in garlic."

When Salomon announced his sudden food preference and insisted that Meir share the dishes with him, Joheved knew their secret was out, and this gave her the courage to consult Aunt Sarah. For if Meir remained in his current state, she'd never get pregnant.

But Sarah only shook her head. To free Meir from the demon's binding was beyond her skill. "You must go see Ben Yochai, the herb and potion merchant," she said. "Do you know who I mean?"

"Oui, Aunt Sarah. I've seen you buy herbs from him, and he has shared meals with us on occasion." Joheved remembered the wizened old scholar well. If anyone knew how to expel this demon that bound her husband, it was Ben Yochai.

Joheved waited for an afternoon when everyone was going to the vineyard and then feigned a digestive problem that necessitated her remaining at home with easy access to the privy. As soon as the house was empty, she set off for the fairgrounds. To her dismay, quite a few customers were gathered at Ben Yochai's stall, apparently more interested in discussing politics than potions. She made herself inconspicuous and resigned herself to wait.

"Ben Yochai, you know everything that happens in the south. Is it true that King Henry tried to assassinate the pope, and when that failed, he deposed him from office?" one man asked.

"I heard that while the misguided ones in Rome were celebrating the birth of their false messiah, men at arms seized the pope and offered him a choice between abdication and death," another man announced. He sounded excited.

"Bah, he was freed the next morning, no worse for the experience, and his captors fled back to Allemagne," said a man with a deep voice. It seemed that Ben Yochai wasn't going to get a word in edgewise.

"But that's old news. That attack took place over six months ago. Does anyone know what's happened since?"

The deep-voiced man answered, "Let me see; I think it was just before Purim that Henry deposed Gregory officially, who in turn excommunicated not only the king but all the bishops who signed the decree."

"But Gregory is only bishop of Rome. Doesn't Henry have the authority to appoint and remove his own bishops, just as Count Thibault does for the bishops of Troyes and Provins?" This speaker sounded like a local man.

"That's certainly what Henry thinks."

The discussion continued as the men weighed the arguments for and against war, and if so, where and when. None of them seemed to have the slightest interest in buying anything from Ben Yochai, or in getting his opinion. Joheved was seething with impatience.

Just when it seemed that she'd have to leave and return another day, who should arrive to consult Ben Yochai but Johanna? In a voice of authority, she announced that she had business with the herb dealer, private business. As the men backed off to let her through, Joheved shrank into the shadows.

But Johanna must have met with Ben Yochai earlier, because she left immediately after collecting a small packet, after which, he motioned Joheved to enter his stall. Then Ben Yochai closed the shutters, took a kettle off the brazier, and poured them each a steaming drink. The voices of the men outside gradually drifted away, undoubtedly to a nearby tavern.

Ben Yochai sipped his beverage in silence. He knew very well who his client was and what ailed her, since her father had spoken to him only yesterday. But he waited patiently for Joheved to speak first, to hear how she would describe the problem. Right now she was eyeing her cup with skepticism.

"It's an herbal infusion from the East called 'tea,'" he said. "A pleasant change from wine or ale, more stimulating."

As far as Joheved was concerned, only sick people drank hot water steeped with herbs. But never mind the drink; enough time had been wasted this afternoon already. "I need your help, Ben Yochai. My husband has lost his virility; a demon has bound him."

Excellent, Ben Yochai thought. The girl was straightforward and spoke to the point. The cure he had in mind needed fortitude, not timidity. "Tell me when this all started, and how," he urged her. "It will help me identify the demon we are dealing with."

She explained about Hannah's death and Meir's night *mares,* while he nodded thoughtfully, stroked his beard and asked a few questions. This was a difficult business, and there was more to it than she knew. But he had heard enough.

"Joheved, you know that demons hate human beings, but they hate Torah scholars most of all. They will do whatever they can to harry us, with their worst efforts aimed at preventing our procreation." Ben Yochai spoke quietly, as if not to be overheard, but his tone was urgent.

"You are Rav Salomon's daughter and your husband is one of his disciples. Surely the demons would consider it a great victory if they could prevent the birth of your sons. But have no fear; we will thwart them."

Joheved almost wept with relief at his confident tone. He rummaged through one of his chests and took out a silver mirror and a small knife. He handed them to her and told her to carve Meir's name into the finish. He watched as she did so, all the while explaining exactly what she had to do.

"Take this mirror, and when you see a pair of dogs copulating, hold the mirror up to capture the image of their coupling. Then, three days before the new moon, put the mirror under your husband's bed and recite the fifth verse of chapter eight of Song of Songs three times in Aramaic. Then, starting three weeks later, give him a drop of this liquid in wine every night for seven days." Suddenly there was a small vial in his hand.

"It may take a while, but when your husband's yetzer is first released, that doesn't mean the demon is banished, only that you have temporarily overcome it. You must encourage your husband's yetzer to grow strong, and while I realize you've been taught to be modest, you must avoid cohabiting in darkness. Demons have their greatest power in the dark; light weakens them."

The warning in Ben Yochai's voice sent a shiver of fear through Joheved. What had she gotten herself into?

"One last thing, Joheved. It would be best not to share our plans with anyone, particularly not your husband. The demon will be most vulnerable when surprised." He opened a ceramic jar and handed her a large green leaf. "Put this betony under your husband's pillow; it will keep the *mares* away. It will also serve as a convenient excuse for your visit here."

The betony leaf proved effective, but during the next several weeks, Joheved wished that her true assignment was as easily accomplished as ridding Meir of bad dreams. Even if she were free to wander the alleys of Troyes all day, it seemed unlikely that she would encounter any mating dogs. But she refused to give in to despair, and kept the mirror tied up in her sleeve should any opportunity present itself. As it turned out, it was Miriam who offered a way out of her predicament, albeit quite inadvertently.

twenty-four

Troyes
Summer 4836 (1076 C.E.)

With less than a week left until the new moon of Elul, Joheved returned discouraged from another fruitless foray. She had wandered around for hours but on this hot, August afternoon, the few dogs she saw were sound asleep. So she was astonished to find Miriam in the courtyard, furiously chopping wood.

"Miriam, what are you doing? Can't you find somebody to help you in this heat? Where are all the students?"

"I don't need any help," Miriam said through clenched teeth. "I want to chop wood, if you don't mind." She whacked the ax a few more times. "In honor of Asher's impending nuptials, his friends have gone to Ramerupt to observe the rams sporting with the ewes, after which they intend to return and sport with the local harlots."

Joheved suspected that Miriam was imagining Asher or Benjamin in the log's place. "And I suppose Benjamin went with them?"

"With great enthusiasm, I'm sure." Miriam's log split in two with a loud crack. "Rest assured that your faithful husband stayed home."

Joheved wouldn't have minded if Meir had gone to watch the rams and ewes if it produced the results the other young men anticipated. But no—in hopes that his piousness would oust the demon, Meir joined Salomon in midnight penitential prayers, fasted Monday and Thursday and ate meat only on the Sabbath.

Joheved sighed and tried to calm her sister. "Miriam, I know you're upset, but what else can men do when they don't have wives? If they didn't relieve their urges with common women, they might not be able to restrain themselves with decent ones."

"Just because everyone condones it doesn't mean I have to like it," Miriam shot back.

"Well, maybe Asher and Benjamin are hoping to learn about women from them." Joheved was certain most men did not have access to anything like Tractate Kallah. "Wouldn't you prefer that your husband practice on a common woman, so he can come to your bed with experience?"

"No, I wouldn't. I want him to practice on me!" Miriam turned around and went back to chopping wood.

Joheved didn't like her own argument either, but if men wanted to visit harlots, what could women do about it? It was their nature, and maybe it did protect their wives and daughters. It did seem excessive to go watch the rutting sheep first.

The sheep! Good heavens—she'd been an idiot! She'd wasted weeks trying to find mating dogs in Troyes when the rams were pastured with the ewes in Ramerupt. And a rutting ram would be even more powerful than a lowly dog. She couldn't go today; the students would be there. But tomorrow, or the next day . . .

Four days before the new moon, Joheved got up early and caught up with her father as he left the privy. Finding him alone was almost as difficult as finding mating dogs. "Papa, I need your help. I want you to invent an errand that requires me to take a horse and be gone for several hours."

Salomon could see his daughter's desperation. "Let me think," he said slowly, and stood there stroking his beard. "Ah, I will say that Robert seeks my advice about his new vineyard in Molesme. His duties prevent him from coming to Troyes, and I, of course, cannot spare the time now to call on him. In my stead, I will delegate my well-qualified eldest daughter."

To Salomon's gratification, his old friend Robert had found the location at Collan unsuitable and set up a new monastery at Molesme, which was only as far south of Troyes as Ramerupt was north of it. Robert was abbot now, with responsibilities that left little time for visits, but the two men had managed to renew their relationship through correspondence.

"What do you think, Joheved?"

"Merci, Papa. That should cover my absence very well." She gave him a hug. "Just as long as Robert doesn't decide to show up suddenly while I'm gone."

The next day Salomon acted so disappointed at not being able to help Robert that Miriam took the bait and suggested that Joheved go.

Benjamin, trying to escape from his fiancée's bad graces, enthusiastically supported her idea.

Meir, who had begun to harbor suspicions about his wife's recent absences, wasn't happy about her embarking on another one. After overhearing Miriam complain that Joheved kept disappearing and leaving the kitchen chores to her, he'd followed her one day. She must have sensed his presence though, because instead of secretly meeting anyone, she'd led him on a wild goose chase through the alleys of Troyes. Still, he kept his misgivings to himself and ended up loaning her his mare.

Riding Meir's horse, who knew the way home, saved Joheved the trouble of inquiring for directions to Ramerupt. Once in the estate's vicinity, she found the right pasture almost immediately. She moved into position behind a mass of shrubbery and took the mirror in her hand.

However, an unexpected difficulty soon presented itself. As Joheved observed the coupling sheep and tried to make sure she captured a good likeness in the small mirror, she began to feel an uncomfortably familiar heat between her legs. It was impossible to watch a ram mount his ewe without yearning to experience the same act herself with Meir.

But if Joheved thought it was disturbing to watch the mating sheep, horseback riding in her aroused condition was torture. The jostling she received while trotting was intolerable, but walking back would take forever. She finally decided there was nothing to do but gallop back as fast as she could; at least that would get her off the horse the quickest.

When she finally reached her family's courtyard, she was aflame with unrequited desire. And if that wasn't bad enough, Meir was outside with his students, waiting for her. He rushed forward to help her dismount, and she prayed that he wouldn't sense her frustrated passion.

Seeing the well reminded Joheved of how Meir said he used to quell his desire for her before they were married. Without a word to anyone, she pulled up a bucket of cold water, carried it into the privy, lifted up her skirts and dumped the bucket's contents over her exposed flesh. The cold water raised goosebumps, but heaven be blessed, it also had the salutary effect she hoped for.

Joheved exited the privy with water dripping down her legs, then nonchalantly replaced the bucket and went inside to change her chemise. She realized that Meir was following her, but she couldn't talk to him now.

"Could you please wait a moment while I change?" Alone in their room, Joheved quickly slipped the mirror under Meir's side of the bed and chanted the incantation from Song of Songs as she changed clothes.

> Under the apple tree I roused you; it was there your mother conceived you, there she who bore you, conceived you.

Thank heaven she didn't have to chant the verse backwards. She repeated the words twice more and then opened the door to face her husband.

"What took you so long?" He advanced on her, his mouth a snarl of fury.

Joheved chose her words carefully; she didn't want to lie. "It takes a long time to ride to Molesme and back, especially if you've never been there before." She avoided Meir's angry gaze.

"Look at me when you talk to me!" He grabbed her arm and roughly pulled her around. "What have you been doing that, as soon as you see me, you have to go wash yourself?"

"The ride back was dusty and hot—is it so terrible that I wanted to wash away the dirt from the road?" Joheved suddenly realized that Meir was jealous, that he had almost accused her of being unfaithful. How dare he distrust her after all she was doing to try to fix things between them!

"It was you who told me how effective cold well water is to cool you off when you're hot and frustrated, which is what I feel every night when you get into bed and turn your back on me."

She might as well have hit him. The blood rushed to Meir's face; then he released her and slumped down on the bed.

"Meir, I'm sorry. It hasn't been that bad, really." How could she have used such hurtful words, especially so close to Rosh Hashanah, the Day of Judgment? She knelt in front of him and begged him, "Please forgive me."

"You're the one who should forgive me," he replied sadly. "I've been so caught up in my own misery that I haven't given much thought to yours." He looked into her eyes and sighed. "Well, if all this fasting and praying doesn't dispel the demon by Yom Kippur, I'll write you a divorce. You deserve a husband who can . . . ," he hesitated while he tried to think of a delicate way to say it, "give you children."

The words "divorce" and "children" were more effective at chilling Joheved's insides than well water. "Non, I won't accept a divorce, and

Rabbenu Gershom decreed that no man can divorce his wife without her consent."

She stood up and faced him. "Which I will never give you, never! I don't want another man's children. I want yours." The thought of somebody else touching her intimate places made her feel ill.

She sank back down to the floor and burst into tears. But in her heart of hearts she knew that no matter how good a vintner she was, how much Talmud she learned, it would be bitter compensation for not having children. The shame would be a thousand times worse than being poor. Every time she saw another woman holding a child she'd be filled with bile, her affection for Meir eventually replaced by resentment. She clutched his legs convulsively. Ben Yochai's magic had to work; it had to!

Meir looked down at the woman he loved weeping in his lap and stroked her hair. Imagining Joheved pregnant with another man's child was almost more than he could bear. Curse this wretched demon that bound him and wouldn't let him go. He sighed heavily. Maybe cursing the evil spirit was useless, but he was helpless to do anything else.

Now that he understood Joheved's frustration, Meir felt even more reluctant to share his wife's bed. That night he quickly volunteered when Rachel asked for a bedtime story, even though it only delayed the inevitable. But when Rachel asked for a Rosh Hashanah story, Meir's mind went blank. Purim, Hanukkah, Passover—these were holidays with stories, not Rosh Hashanah.

"I'm sorry, Rachel, I don't think there are any Rosh Hashanah stories in scripture," he said. Just what he needed, another female he couldn't satisfy.

"Are there any in the Talmud?"

There was something in the third chapter of Tractate Berachot. "I do know one from the Talmud, but it's a ghost story. I don't want to frighten you."

"A ghost story!" Rachel's face lit up. "Tell me, tell me. I'm not a baby any more—I won't be scared."

"All right. But be sure to tell your parents about any nightmares, so they can find three people to bless you," he warned her. Something he had neglected to do, with disastrous results.

He made sure the bedroom shutters were latched and began speaking.

> Once there was a pious man, who gave his last *dinar* to charity on the eve of Rosh Hashanah. His wife got angry, so he went and sat in the cemetery. There he heard the ghosts of two girls who had recently died, talking to each other.
>
> One said: Today is Rosh Hashanah. Let's go hear the Holy One decree what misfortune will happen in the world this new year. Her friend replied: I cannot come with you, since I am buried in reed matting. You go, and tell me what you hear.

"You see," Meir explained, "her family was too poor to afford a proper linen shroud, and she was ashamed to be seen before the other ghosts."

> When the first ghost returned, she reported: I heard that anything planted at the time of the first rain will be destroyed by hail. So the pious man waited to plant until the second rain, and when everyone else's crops were destroyed, his were not.
>
> The next year, he went to the cemetery on Rosh Hashanah night again and heard the same two ghosts talking. This time the well-dressed one reported: I heard that anything planted at the time of the second rain will be blasted by a dry wind. So the man planted at the first rain, and when everyone else planted later, at the second rain, their crops were blasted and his were not.

"Your papa teaches us that the crops planted early have grown so tall and stiff by the time the second rain comes that hail breaks them, while the small flexible shoots are spared. However these young tender plants are most affected by the dry wind, not the older, tougher ones. Do you understand?"

"Oui, Meir," she replied.

> Then the man's wife grew suspicious and asked him: Why is it that last year everyone's crops were destroyed by hail and ours were not, and now everyone's crops were blasted by wind and ours were not? So he told her the story. But a few days later, she quarreled with the mother of one of the dead girls and said to her: Shame on you for not burying your daughter in a proper shroud.

Sensing that the denouement was coming, Rachel looked up at Meir expectantly.

> The next year, he went again to the cemetery and heard the two ghosts talking. But this time, when one suggested that they learn what misfortune would happen in the world that year, her friend refused, saying: We cannot, for the living have heard our words.

"Thank you, Meir." Rachel yawned and rubbed her eyes. "That was a good story. But what happened to the pious man after that? Surely he wasn't still poor after the two good harvests."

He shrugged his shoulders. "I don't know; that's all the Talmud says about him. But I suspect that even after his good fortune he never became rich, because whatever money he acquired, he gave to charity."

There was only a week left before Rosh Hashanah when Joheved added the first drop of Ben Yochai's potion to Meir's evening drink. But she wasn't able to complete the dose because, a few days before the festival, her husband took ill. All morning he was feverish, and after throwing up disner, took to his bed. He spent the rest of the day curled up under the covers, clutching his belly in pain.

By evening, Meir was nearly delirious with fever and unable to keep down any nourishment at all. Joheved, terrified that something had gone wrong with the magic elixir, spent the night by his bedside, trying in turn to spoon some soup into him and to get the chamber pot under him. She had no success at all with the former and only moderate success with the latter.

When it was light enough for her to see how terribly Meir had soiled himself during the night, Joheved realized that she would have to cast modesty aside and give her husband a thorough washing. Intending to get a bucket of warm water and some rags, she stopped when she saw the pitcher and basin outside the door.

Joheved silently gave thanks for her mother's prudence. Sickrooms tended to attract demons, and one as foul as Meir's even more so. When she washed her hands before crossing his threshold, any demons would be trapped in the water. The supplies Joheved needed were also waiting for her, as well as some clean bed linens (another silent thank-you to Mama).

After returning to the bedroom, she tried not to breathe in the stink as she rolled her barely conscious husband onto his stomach. This was the first time she had seen a man naked, and she kept expecting someone to walk in and scold her for her brazenness. It was impossible to clean him without looking at him, but she found that if she concentrated on a small area, it became merely skin, not much different from her own.

But when it came time to turn him over and bathe his private parts, she nearly panicked. Maybe she should get Baruch or Papa to do it? But that was ridiculous; she'd be running to them continually. She was Meir's wife; they were one flesh, she told herself decisively. She could and should do this. Joheved put her arms under him, swallowed hard, and pushed him over.

Strange how that member, which had always felt so large and hard inside her, now appeared so humble and vulnerable. She picked up a wet cloth, wrung it out, and gingerly began to wipe clean the surrounding area. He twitched slightly when she accidentally brushed the fleshy thing, and she pulled her hand away.

Don't be such a silly goose; do it now and get it over with. He'll get cold if you leave him uncovered much longer.

Joheved gathered her courage and took hold of him, marveling at how this thing had once given her so much pleasure. She cleaned between all the folds, as well as around the sac below. She washed the dark curls of his lower beard and carefully patted him dry. Then she called downstairs and, while Baruch held the helpless man in his arms, she changed the bed linens.

But her work soon had to be repeated, and by the time the roosters crowed the next morning, she was washing her husband's private parts with no more embarrassment than she felt washing his face after he vomited. Her concern had changed from what was coming out of him to what was not going into him. Even by the spoonful, he could scarcely tolerate wine or ale. All Joheved could do was give him a wet cloth to suck.

Unfortunately there was little help available from the rest of the household. Anna was ailing, and several of the students had taken ill as well. More people in Troyes were coming down sick every day, and merchants were trying to wrap up their business so they could leave immediately after the holy days. Benjamin had already left for Rheims, after desperately seeking and finally receiving, Miriam's forgiveness.

Joheved spent another sleepless night at Meir's side, and by morning she was so exhausted she didn't realize it was Erev Rosh Hashanah until Miriam volunteered to lead the women's evening service in her stead. After breakfast she struggled up the stairs and resumed her post next to the bed.

Her head began to droop, and had just come to rest against the bed frame, when the door opened and there was Meir's mother.

Resplendent in her holiday finery, Marona took a long look at the room's occupants. Her daughter-in-law hadn't combed her hair or changed clothes in days, and her son, with his pallor and hollow eyes, looked ghastly. She approached the bed, felt his forehead and sighed deeply.

Before Joheved knew what was happening, her mother-in-law was leading her to her old bedroom and tucking her into bed. "You get some rest now, dear, and don't worry about Meir." Marona's voice was soothing. "I'll take care of him for the time being. We don't want you getting sick too."

Then Marona went downstairs, where her anxious husband was deep in conversation with Salomon. "It's not good." She shook her head despondently. "You need to ride home and bring back as much wool swaddling as you can carry."

After repeating the instructions to her bewildered spouse, she whispered fiercely to him, "I intend to stay here until our son is well. The Angel of Death has taken too many of our children already. I will not let him have this one!"

Joheved slept that night and the entire next day. When she felt Rachel climbing into bed with her, it took her a moment to realize that it was her sister's bedtime. She had missed Rosh Hashanah services entirely. She jumped out of bed in a panic—what had happened to Meir?

"*Shana tova* (Happy New Year), Joheved." Rachel knew what worried her older sister; she was worried herself. "I don't think Meir is any worse than he was this morning. His mother has been tending him all day."

"*Shana tova* to you too," Joheved said, giving Rachel a quick hug. "Now it's my turn for '*shmira.*'" She used the Hebrew word that meant both to watch and to guard.

When Joheved entered the sickroom, Marona was spooning some clear liquid into Meir. There were fragrant herbs burning in a charcoal brazier, and rather than linens, the laundry basket was half-full of used wool swaddling. Joheved eyed it with trepidation. How many times had it been emptied while she slept?

"*Shana tova;* I hope you slept well." Marona tried to sound cheerful and confident. "You're just in time. Now I can show you what to do before I go to bed."

She lifted the covers to expose her son's lower body, and Joheved couldn't help but smile at Marona's resourcefulness. Meir was swaddled as if he were an infant.

"I had your mother prepare some chicken soup, well seasoned with salt and garlic. But Meir gets only the broth, and very little of that at one time." Marona demonstrated how she slowly allowed a few drops of broth into Meir's mouth. Sure enough, after he swallowed, nothing came back up.

"The doctor came today, but I chased him away." She continued to drip soup into her son. "He only wanted to bleed Meir, and I think we need to get more fluid into him."

Salomon had called in the doctor, who had taken one look at Meir and concluded that the fellow would probably die before Yom Kippur anyway. Thus he was not too upset to be dismissed by the patient's mother; he didn't need another failure on his record.

From that night on, Joheved and Marona fell into a routine. Marona spent the daytime with Meir, while Joheved shared his nights, each feeding him broth, bathing him and changing his swaddling. At first Joheved found it difficult to feed him slowly enough, but either because she became more adept, or because Meir was getting better, she was eventually able to give him an entire bowlful without him vomiting. Yet as soon as the broth went in above, it seemed to come out below. Much of the time Meir was delirious. Only in early morning did his fever drop enough to give him some lucid moments, but this was sufficient to encourage Joheved greatly.

On Yom Kippur, Joheved spent the day at services rather than sleeping. Sure that her plot to expel the demon was exacerbating Meir's illness, she needed to pray for forgiveness. By Sukkot, two weeks after Meir had first taken ill, the worst seemed over, and thus this traditionally joyful festival was particularly so for Salomon's household. Yet Meir's painful diarrhea continued, and Marona would only allow him to eat bread soaked in broth.

The day after Simchat Torah, he woke early and seemed unusually alert. He looked around and sniffed the scented air as if smelling it for the first time. "Mm—that smells nice. What it is?" Before Joheved could answer, he continued, his hands exploring the swaddling, "And what in heaven's name have I got on?"

Joheved did her best to explain his circumstances, but he insisted, "Is this really necessary?"

"If you can ask for the chamber pot in time, then probably not," she replied, hopeful that this might be the case. "But you'd best speak to your mother."

"My mother? Is she here too?" And when Joheved nodded, he said, "I thought I was dreaming about my mother."

"You've been very ill. Your mother and I have been taking care of you for weeks."

"How long have I been sick? What day is it?" When Joheved told him, Meir fell back into the cushion in shock. "I can't believe it. I missed Rosh Hashanah, Yom Kippur and Sukkot too."

"Are you at all hungry?" she asked eagerly. "One of Papa's merchant friends heard about your ailment and offered a bag of some special grain from the East. He says people there eat it with every meal, like we eat bread, only it's easier to digest. It's called 'rice,' and Mama cooked some for you."

He agreed to try it, and Joheved hurried down to the kitchen, where a small amount of the strange beige seeds had been cooking in chicken broth all night. She had wanted to be the one to introduce this new food to Meir, to give Marona the good news that here was something he could eat without discomfort.

Meir's brow furrowed as he stared at the bowl of rice; the stuff looked like maggots. He was more thirsty than hungry, but Joheved was looking at him so hopefully that he took a spoonful to please her. After chewing it carefully, Meir had to admit that the rice didn't taste bad. It didn't have any particular flavor at all, besides that of the broth. He took another spoonful, then another, and then downed the bowl completely.

He felt as if he could have eaten more, except that any food he ate was soon followed by cramps, and he didn't want to make them worse by eating too much at one time. Eventually his sore insides did protest, but the merchant was right—the rice soup was definitely less painful to eat than soup with bread.

twenty-five

Fall 4837 (1076 C.E.)

A week later, Meir was able to eat rice soup and drink ale with almost no discomfort. Best of all, he could control his bowels well enough to dispense with the swaddling. Sitting up tired him, and standing was out of the question, but he was able to spend a few hours each morning helping his students with their lessons.

Friday morning, Meir woke so early that the lamp was still lit. He could see Joheved half-dozing nearby, one of Salomon's kuntres in her lap, and his heart swelled as he observed her sleeping form. Then his stomach rumbled with hunger and her head jerked up. Another growl, and she hurried downstairs.

He could smell his breakfast before she opened the door. Despite Joheved's concern that he was eating too fast, he quickly downed the entire bowlful. When the only response from his belly was more hungry rumbles, he begged her to refill the bowl and to put some meat and vegetables in it this time.

Meir ate his second helping slowly, savoring each bite. He couldn't remember when he had eaten anything so delicious. He mopped the bowl with his last piece of bread and sighed with contentment. He was still hungry, but he decided to be sure this meal agreed with him before attempting thirds.

Joheved leaned over to remove the empty dish, and as she did so, her chemise's neckline gaped open. Between the lamp and approaching dawn, there was sufficient illumination to afford Meir a splendid view of her exposed breasts and belly. An explosion of desire flooded his loins, and he groaned with the intensity of his need.

"What's the matter?" Certain that he was in pain, Joheved was furious with herself for allowing him to eat so much, so fast.

It was all Meir could do to keep his hands down; he was so eager to reach up and caress that bare flesh. He looked up into his wife's eyes, so full of apprehension, and replied hoarsely, "I'm starving, but not for food."

Joheved recognized her husband's lust and couldn't believe her eyes. But her doubts disappeared when Meir took her in his arms and pulled her onto the bed beside him. His kisses rained down on her and Joheved reveled in every one. She tore off her chemise to give his hands free access to her body. His excitement was contagious, and she let him know she wanted him too.

"Oh no!" Meir moaned when he found himself too weak to assume the customary position above his wife.

Joheved wasn't going to let anything stop them. "Don't worry. I have strength enough for both of us. Just lean back and close your eyes." Then she climbed up and straddled him.

Meir felt her damp warmth envelope him and he almost cried out with pleasure. The most exquisite feelings emanated from his loins as she slowly moved up and down. It had been so long, so very long. It was then that he began to remember his fears, and desperate to avoid the demonic visions, he opened his eyes . . .

The scene in front of him was overwhelming. Joheved's naked body, displayed before him in all its glory, was sensuously moving over his. Control was impossible under such circumstances, and with a sudden convulsion of release that was almost more pain than pleasure, it was over. Meir sank back into the cushions, dazed from the intensity of his experience, disappointed that it had ended so fast. He couldn't possibly have satisfied Joheved.

But when he looked over at her, stretched out next to him, she returned his concerned gaze with one of love and happiness. He stroked her hair and assured her, "It will be better next time, Cherie, I promise."

She hadn't experienced the physical release that he had, but Joheved felt more than satisfied. A wave of affection rushed through her and she reached over to kiss him. Baruch ata Adonai . . . who heals the sick.

Surprisingly, Meir didn't feel tired. He felt refreshed, as if he had just awakened from a long nap. He leisurely returned her kisses, enjoying the memory of what he had just experienced. This time, rather than a sudden assault, his yetzer hara sneaked up on him. Under its influence, he took hold of the bed linens that concealed his wife's body and slowly drew them back.

By now the room was bright with early morning sunlight, and Joheved's cheeks flamed as he stared at her naked flesh, his eyes widening to take in every curve. Remembering what Ben Yochai had said, she fought the urge to pull the covers up again. Soon Meir could no longer confine his pleasure to his eyes, and he reached out to caress the beauty displayed before him.

"Are you sure we should be doing this so soon?" Joheved's emotions warred between the excitement his attentions were beginning to elicit and anxiety that he'd become ill again if he tried to push his body beyond its limits.

As if to answer her question, he took her hand and placed it between his thighs, where she would have no doubts as to his need and capability. He chuckled when she promptly pulled her hand away, enjoying her embarrassment as well as the passion her brief touch ignited.

"Your yetzer hara has become brazen in its freedom," she teasingly scolded him. Now he was caressing her more intimate places, compelling her rising passion to match his, and any reservations Joheved had were soon overwhelmed by the intense pleasure his touch gave her.

This time he felt more in control as she mounted him, and he whispered, "Try to make me take longer this time, Cherie." As much as he wanted to feast his eyes on her, he knew he had to resist that temptation unless the demon threatened him.

Joheved discovered, once she paid attention, that she could tell when Meir was reaching his peak. And if she ceased moving at that point, his ardor cooled sufficiently that they could continue a while longer. But eventually her own yetzer refused to let her stop until she reached the climax she'd been so long denied. And Meir found that, like before, it was impossible to control himself when he felt Joheved's contractions convulsing around him.

Joheved fell back onto the bed and Meir snuggled up to her. Then, as he drifted off to sleep, he conjured up the memory of his wife's naked body, not lifeless and bloodied, but beautiful, alive with passion and coupled with his.

When Marona peeked in Meir's room later that morning, she was unprepared for the scene that greeted her. Her son and daughter-in-law lay sleeping together, her head on his chest and his arms intimately entwined around her. Marona keenly observed the crumpled chemises on the floor, the empty dishes piled carelessly nearby, and came to the conclusion that her son was well on his way to recovery. She quietly backed away and closed the door.

As she stood in the hall, relief flooded through her and she began to sob, the anxiety of those terrible weeks dissolving in her tears. Rivka saw her weeping and rushed upstairs, fearing the worst. But when Marona showed her a glimpse inside, Rivka embraced her counterpart and shared her cries of happiness.

"You must tell me your son's favorite dishes, so we can have them for Shabbat dinner." Rivka picked up the pitcher and basin. "I guess I can put these away."

The most mouth-watering smells were in the air when Meir woke up again. Joheved was sleeping next to him, and he reached out to caress her bare shoulders and back. A stirring in his loins convinced him that he hadn't been dreaming; his virility had finally returned.

"Ahem." A voice coughed discreetly and his hand immediately came to a stop. He quickly sat up and then sank down again in a wave of dizziness.

"If you sit up slowly, I'm sure it will be easier," his mother said, smiling down at him.

"*Bonjour,* Mama." Meir did as she said, his face crimson. This time his head remained clear.

Marona nonchalantly handed him his chemise, then arranged the cushions so he could sit up straight and asked, "Are you hungry?"

"I'm famished." Meir had no idea how much time had passed since his last meal. "I'm so hungry I could eat a cow."

"Well, you're in luck. I believe that Rivka has stewed beef and onions especially for you." Marona laid Joheved's chemise on the bed and stood up. "I'll get you some."

Joheved, unable to sleep through their conversation, opened her eyes just in time to see Marona leaving. She quickly got up and dressed before her husband's appreciative eyes. "I hear Papa downstairs," she said, giving Meir a quick kiss. "Everyone must be back from services already. I have to go and help Mama get ready for the Sabbath."

He grabbed her hand. "Stay and have disner with me."

"I'd like to." She really wished she could. "But your mother is leaving for Ramerupt after Shabbat, and I think she'd like to spend some time with you now that you're feeling better. Don't worry, Meir; I'll be back tonight." She blew him a kiss and made her way down the stairs, humming a merry tune.

That afternoon, Joheved volunteered to make the *challah,* the braided loaves traditionally eaten on Shabbat and festivals, and as she kneaded, she hummed the riddle song about the bride and her rising dough. When the loaves were ready for the baker's oven, she pinched off a tiny piece and tossed it in the fire, to observe the law that required part of each challah be separated and given to the priests. Since the temple's destruction, however, women fulfilled this mitzvah by burning the piece of dough instead.

"Baruch ata Adonai . . . Who commanded us to separate challah from the dough." Joheved made the appropriate blessing.

She wrapped up the six loaves, two for each Shabbat meal, and set off for the bakery, a happy skip in her step. She would bring them home later, along with the other loaves their household would consume over the Sabbath. On impulse she decided to visit the bathhouse while the bread was baking.

Joheved returned home from the bakery to find a row of capons roasting in the hearth—they looked nearly done. She laid down the breads and looked around for something to do, but the table was already set and everything seemed in readiness. Had she stayed at the baths too long? At least the men weren't back from synagogue yet.

"I'm sorry if I'm late, Mama." She suddenly felt guilty for luxuriating in a hot tub while her family was working. "I stopped in at the 'stews' and lost track of the time."

Miriam began to protest, but Rivka cut her off. "What a good idea. I'm sure a nice, warm bath was just what you needed."

Just then Marona entered the kitchen. "If souper is ready, is it all right if Meir eats his now? He woke up from his nap early and is quite hungry."

"I'll take his tray up to him," Joheved immediately volunteered. "That way you and Samuel can have a nice Shabbat supper together down here." She hoped it wasn't too obvious that she wanted to be alone with Meir.

"As a matter of fact, my son made the same request himself," Marona said as she and Rivka exchanged knowing looks.

"I'll fix up enough for both of you, so your poor husband doesn't have to eat by himself." Rivka smiled in anticipation of her daughter's happiness. "Le Bon Dieu willing, maybe Meir will be well enough to join us down here next Shabbat."

To say that Meir was happy to see his wife carrying in his meal would be an understatement. Since his last student had gone downstairs, it had been difficult to think about anything besides that morning's events, and he'd barely managed to prepare the next day's Talmud lesson. In the past, he would have firmly controlled any erotic thoughts that attempted to interfere with his studies, but tonight he needed reassurance that his yetzer was still unbound. Besides, it wasn't as if this was a prelude to sin; it was Shabbat and his wife would be the recipient of his desire.

He tried to wait patiently while she put down the dishes, some of which were giving off plumes of delicious-smelling steam. His two appetites warred within him, but when Joheved bent down to kiss him hello, his yetzer hara took over, and he turned her gentle buss into a passionate embrace.

"I brought your food up right away because your mother said you were hungry," she teased him.

He pulled her down on the bed and kissed her again, enjoying her full cooperation. "I am hungry . . ."

". . . but not for food." Joheved, extricating herself from his arms, stood up and, very slowly, began to undress.

Meir's memories had already lit his yetzer's fire, but watching Joheved take off her clothes turned it into an inferno. Any demons with designs on his virility never had a chance, and he proved that his earlier triumph was no accident.

Afterwards, he eagerly joined Joheved in the mealtime blessings. Now that one of his appetites was at least temporarily satisfied, he could turn his attention to the other. "Mm, capon, one of my favorite dishes."

"Didn't your mother say beef and onions was your favorite?" Joheved found herself enjoying how much he relished his food. This was going to be a truly joyous Shabbat, she could tell.

"Well, that's another one." He chuckled and scooped up some stewed vegetables with a large slice of bread. "When I'm hungry nearly every dish is my favorite food . . . except maybe lamb."

"You don't like lamb, even though your father raises sheep?" She couldn't help but laugh too; his happiness was contagious.

"When you've eaten as much lamb as I have, you'll find that you prefer almost anything else," he replied. "Which reminds me, where are the little fried fishes? Did the Notzrim buy them all at the market today?" Small fish coated in flour and fried in olive oil were a traditional Shabbat evening dish, but since Christians were forbidden to eat meat on Friday, there was much competition to buy fish that day.

"Oh, they're eating some downstairs." Joheved had refused to take any for herself; it would be rude to eat something in front of Meir that he couldn't. "Your mother said you should wait before eating fried foods again."

"Very well, I'm content to eat capon tonight. After all, that's what we ate at our betrothal."

Joheved handed him one of the dessert pastries. "I didn't know my talmid chacham had such a good memory for anything besides his studies." She was both surprised and flattered that Meir remembered that afternoon so well. She doubted that she could have told him what had been on the menu.

"I recall that you were wearing a blue dress, the exact same color as your eyes." Meir tilted up her chin so they were looking into each other's eyes, and Joheved felt a surge of heat between her thighs at the intensity of his gaze. He ended their conversation with a kiss.

As the company below filled the air with the joyous sounds of Sabbath table songs, Meir proceeded to make his wife rejoice as they fulfilled their obligation to perform the holy deed on Shabbat. Later, as he drifted off to sleep, Joheved already snoring softly in his arms, he decided that tonight had been even better than their wedding night.

The autumn leaves put on a brilliant show, but Meir didn't get to see them. Being bedridden for over six weeks had taken its toll, and when he tried to stand up, his legs were as weak as a newborn lamb's. It was weeks before he could get around on his own, and that required the help of Grandmama Leah's old cane.

As the Cold Fair grew closer, Meir was determined to build up his strength so he could walk to synagogue and study with the mature scholars. But for now, he was housebound. He didn't know if it was the result of his illness, but the weather seemed cooler than it ought to be in late October. Even bundled in furs, a short trip to the privy left him shivering.

Thus he found himself at home late one Friday afternoon while the rest of the household was at services. Rivka had delegated the Shabbat lamp lighting to Joheved, and Meir was finishing his own prayers when he noticed his wife kindling the flame. A wave of nostalgia washed over him as he realized that he hadn't seen a woman lighting the Sabbath lamp since he was a little boy watching his mother. Once he was old enough, he accompanied his father to synagogue to welcome the Sabbath there, returning home to find the lamp already lit.

Watching Joheved, he fondly imagined the identical scene with a couple of small children at her side. Then his eyes widened in surprise. She was praying as she kindled the light, but he couldn't make out the words. His mother hadn't said anything, and he knew he'd never seen any such blessing in the Talmud. He forced himself to wait quietly until Joheved finished.

"Joheved," he tried not to sound particularly curious, "what were you saying just now when you lit the Sabbath lamp?"

She tilted her head and squinted at him. "I was saying the blessing. What else would I be saying?"

"I don't know; that's why I asked you." He couldn't believe it. She was acting as though he had asked what color snow was. "My mother doesn't say anything when she lights the Sabbath lamp."

"She doesn't?" It was Joheved's turn to be surprised. "Since you asked, I say what my grandmother taught me: Baruch ata Adonai, . . . Who commands us to kindle the Sabbath lights."

That made sense—the same blessing as Hanukkah except she says Sabbath lights instead of Hanukkah lights. But where did it come from? "I know you've studied Tractate Berachot, and some of Tractate Shabbat as well," Meir said. "Haven't you wondered why the Sages never mention this blessing?"

"I never thought about it. I assumed it came from someplace else in the Talmud." Her jaw dropped as she realized what his question implied. "You mean this blessing isn't in the Talmud?"

He nodded and quickly added, "But I haven't studied every page yet—we can always ask your father."

Later that night, they did. Salomon was familiar with the blessing; after all, it was his own mother who said it. But he admitted that he had not seen it written anywhere in the Talmud and that there was no Jewish law that mandated it. It was obviously derived from the Hanukkah blessing, but he had no idea how universal the practice was. Rivka wasn't much help. She'd also learned the blessing from Leah.

Baruch weighed in that Shemiah had occasionally left him to light the Shabbat lamp, yet he'd never told him to make a special blessing. Now Salomon's curiosity was piqued, and he declared that he would question every foreign scholar at the Cold Fair about the practice.

This proved no easy task. Many merchants had no idea what their wives said at home, and some were not sure what their mothers had done. Yet Salomon persevered, and the following Shabbat he announced that German women made the blessing, those from Provence or Sepharad did not, and the Parisians might go either way. Joheved and Meir found the whole thing fascinating; it had never occurred to either of them that other Jewish women didn't do the same thing their mothers did.

Once the Cold Fair opened, Meir found it wasn't just him—everyone was complaining about the weather. It had never been so cold this early in the season. Joheved kept the windows in the wine cellar tightly closed and hoped that the temperature wouldn't drop low enough to halt fermentation prematurely. Thank goodness Hanukkah came early this year; wine dealers were eager to buy and be on their way before heavy snow made traveling more difficult than usual.

Meir's yetzer hara remained strong, and Joheved eagerly accommodated him. Before the demon bound him, Meir had felt it necessary to restrain himself and not burden Joheved with his needs. But now that his wife made it plain that her need was as great as his, he indulged her (and his) every desire. Besides, it was the husband's duty to "cause his wife to rejoice," which the Sages said he must accomplish by means of the holy deed. Salomon made a point of criticizing those who incorrectly translated this passage in Deuteronomy to read, "rejoice *with* his wife," which valued the husband's pleasure instead of his wife's.

So when Joheved insisted on keeping the lamp lit at night for fear of demons, he didn't argue. Meir had fleeting feelings of guilt for allowing his yetzer hara such license, but if his wife wanted him to make up for six months of deprivation as soon as possible, wasn't he obliged to do so? And they had plenty of opportunity; it was the season of long nights.

While she enjoyed her husband's attentions, Joheved didn't encourage him solely for her own pleasure's sake. She'd neglected to ask Ben Yochai how long she should continue to strengthen Meir's yetzer once it was freed. And when should she remove the mirror from under the bed, if ever? Since he hadn't told her, she decided to take no chances and just keep doing what she was doing. At least she knew it worked, even if she was becoming more exhausted every day.

It was only when Joheved threw up one morning that Meir left her undisturbed in bed. But she developed no fever, and though her nausea returned the next day, she felt no worse and was able to go about her business as usual. After a week of vomiting each morning, Joheved was desperately trying to recall when she'd last visited the mikvah. She knew she hadn't immersed since Meir's health had returned, but had she gone before Sukkot or after?

No matter. It had been nearly two months, and even allowing for her usual irregularity, that was too long. She had to be pregnant. Yet she continued to check herself for blood twice a day, as the Sages recommended. Best to fool the demons as long as possible. Meir came to the identical conclusion, but he wasn't about to tempt the Evil Eye and say anything either.

Hanukkah came and went, and with it departed a good deal of Salomon's wine. Snow was falling heavily, and Joheved worried about Samson's absence. Last year he'd arrived with plenty of time to contract with the wine dealers. Even more disappointing, last year Samson had brought an excellent selection of furs from Russia. And if there was any year when furs were likely to be in demand, this was going to be the one.

In the weeks that followed, it snowed nearly every day. Powerful north winds exacerbated the low temperatures, and Meir, determined to regain his strength, helped Baruch chop wood. He also tried to ride to Ramerupt when the weather cleared, not only because he and his horse needed the exercise but also because it cheered his mother immensely to see him.

Joheved volunteered to brave the snow and buy the morning's bread, a chore Anna was only too glad to relinquish. The brief walk to the bakery and back took just enough time to settle Joheved's stomach, yet never chilled her more than a short stint in front of the hearth could fix. She couldn't complain—near the bakery there were always beggars, and they looked to be in far worse shape than merely uncomfortable.

Most of the baker's customers ignored them. Many agreed with him that handing out bread only encouraged beggars to frequent the bakery and interfere with his customers. Some intimated that the so-called paupers were frauds trying to avoid an honest day's work, but Joheved took pity on a few women and shared her bread with them.

She remembered the story about giving charity that Grandmama Leah had often told her and Miriam. It was about Rabbi Akiva's daughter, who the stars foretold would die on her wedding night. Akiva kept his knowledge secret and arranged her marriage with a heavy heart. Then, the next morning, Akiva hurried to visit his daughter. He was overjoyed to see her unharmed, staring in shock at a poisonous snake, now quite dead, pierced through the eye and fixed to the wall with a large hair pin.

During the night, Akiva's daughter had removed her hairpin and, intending to stick it in the wall for safekeeping, thus impaled the snake. Akiva told her what he'd foreseen and questioned her about what had saved her. She replied that at the marriage feast she had noticed a poor, hungry, old man standing near the door, and since the servants were occupied, she gave him food from her own plate. "Now I see that 'Charity saves from death,'" Akiva cried joyously, and he went out to teach this lesson from Proverbs to his disciples.

Joheved smiled to herself at the memory of seeing this same tale in Tractate Shabbat, and recalled how delighted she and Miriam had been to find their familiar childhood story in the Talmud. But as she surveyed the paupers crouching against the wall, trying their best to stay out of the icy wind, her smile disappeared. She was approaching the dangerous time of childbirth, and maybe giving just one beggar some bread would make the difference when her life hung in the balance.

One particularly freezing morning, the wind was howling so loudly that both Rivka and Salomon urged her to stay home. But the stifling air inside only increased Joheved's nausea, and she couldn't help but think of the poor beggars who had spent a night like this outdoors. Wrapped in Meir's fur-lined cloak, crossing the courtyard wasn't too bad, but once on the street, the snowy gusts almost forced her to return.

"*Bonjour,* Mistress," came a muffled voice from the road. It was the dung collector, whose usual unsavory occupation had been augmented by the even more unpleasant job of removing from public streets the bodies of those unfortunate enough to have frozen to death the previous night. His cart seemed more full than usual.

"*Bonjour* to you," Joheved replied. "If you stop by later, there will be some leftover trenchers and warm stirabout for you." Mama made sure there was always food available for the dung collector, who reciprocated in the spring by delivering fertilizer to the vineyard.

Joheved hurried to the bakery, motivated less by the cold than by the desire to maximize the distance between her and the odious cart. There she collected her bread and prepared to leave, putting all the loaves except two into her bag. Thus ready to distribute her charity, Joheved stepped into the frigid outdoors. Several of the beggars recognized her and held out their hands in petition.

"Alms for the poor, Mistress."

"Just a little bread, Mistress. I haven't eaten since this hour yesterday."

"Have mercy on me and my hungry children."

"A small piece of bread, please. Remember that charity delivers from death."

Joheved's senses, dulled by the scene of misery before her, snapped to attention at that last plea. The woman's voice was familiar, but how could anyone Joheved knew have sunk to such depths? She looked carefully at the beggars, most of them extending hands thinner than Meir's at his worst last fall.

"Catharina—is that you?"

twenty-six

Troyes
Winter 4837 (1076–77 C.E.)

he parchment maker's daughter stared up at Joheved with sunken eyes. Joheved didn't stop to think; she hauled Catharina under her furs and hustled them home. Her friend's slender body was hot with fever. Once inside the courtyard, Joheved decided she'd better take Catharina to Aunt Sarah's house. After all, the woman was a known prostitute and not even Jewish.

Sarah wasn't happy with the unexpected guest, but Joheved and Miriam's tearful pleas persuaded her to let Catharina convalesce under her roof. Over the next few days, the two sisters extracted her sad story.

"My bad luck started when a customer beat me up and stole my money," she told them. "Then I got too sick to work and my landlord evicted me."

Catharina paused as a chill shook her. "Like a fool, I begged for help at the church. But the priests, who knew very well I was a harlot because many of them had shared my company, would only aid me if I agreed to enter a convent," she said with disgust. "Finally, I stationed myself at the bakery the Jews frequented and prayed that somebody would share their bread. And Le Bon Dieu answered my prayer." She smiled up at Joheved.

But Sarah was not so sympathetic. One afternoon about a week later, she took Miriam aside, and it was obvious that the midwife was barely controlling her temper. "I know your sister meant well in bringing this common woman to my house, but there is a problem," Sarah said with a grimace. "Your friend is pregnant."

At first Miriam didn't know what to say. "Does she know?"

"She suspected, and when I confirmed it, she had the nerve to ask me to help her lose the baby." Sarah's voice shook with rage. "She has no idea how dangerous the situation is—and that's just for her. I hate to think what would happen if the authorities found out I was responsible for ending an Edomite's pregnancy."

"I'm sorry, Aunt Sarah, I guess I told her you were a midwife a long time ago." Her aunt's fury was justified, but Miriam felt a duty towards the woman who had been her and Joheved's only childhood companion. "Please, can't we help her? Catharina's life has been so difficult." Miriam was trying hard not to cry. "I'm sure she won't tell anyone."

Miriam had always been tenderhearted, the one who rescued kittens stuck in the apple tree, who tried to save baby birds that had fallen from their nests. Sarah found it difficult to refuse her teary-eyed niece. "Let me think about it."

For the next several days, Miriam and Joheved prayed that their aunt would relent. But when she did, it was with firm conditions. First of all, Catharina must give up her disgraceful profession. Even a hint of dalliances with the yeshiva students and she would be out, no matter how foul the weather. Second, she'd continue to live in Sarah's house as a maidservant, in payment for Sarah's kindness. Third, Sarah herself would do nothing to end the pregnancy other than provide Miriam with the necessary herbs and directions on how to use them. It was something Miriam needed to learn eventually.

They waited until Catharina's fever was gone. After her friend fasted for a day, Miriam carefully measured out the dittany root, pennyroyal leaves, and iris flowers, then dropped them all into a pot of boiling water. Next she crushed juniper berries and mixed them in a cup of wine. She tried to appear calm, but she trembled slightly as she handed Catharina the cups of tea and wine, and once her patient got into bed, her hand shook so hard she could barely insert the pessary made of artemisia and myrrh.

Two days later, with Catharina moaning that she felt worse than after she'd been beaten, her womb was empty. After a week, she was able to perform some light tasks in Sarah's service, but she hesitated to go outdoors, and not just because of the snow.

"What about the yeshiva students? Suppose one of them recognizes me?" Catharina had no intention of resuming her former occupation. After what she'd just experienced, if she never lay with a man again it would be too soon.

Miriam remembered Benjamin and Asher going to watch the rams rut. "You'll keep your hair covered and try to avoid them."

The cold weather made it easy for Catharina to keep herself well covered and avoid almost everyone in Salomon's household. Her duties at Sarah's kept her busy during the week, and when the other Edomite servants went out on Shabbat, she preferred to stay home. Thus she began a tentative friendship with Anna, who seemed equally eager to avoid strange men.

Salomon's wines had been officially tasted at Hanukkah, but with Passover approaching, Joheved needed to judge the contents of the remaining casks in order to price them accordingly. But when she tasted them, she discovered that some of the barrels hadn't completed their fermentation. Joheved's first inclination was to dump the bubbly stuff out. But the wine didn't appear spoiled, so she called Miriam down to the cellar to see what she thought.

"It's different, but it doesn't taste bad." Miriam actually liked the bubbles in the wine, but she wanted to hear Joheved's judgment before sharing her opinion.

"Not bad, not bad at all." Joheved took another, longer drink. "The bubbles may even improve the flavor." She downed the entire cup, let out a small burp and noticed that her indigestion had lessened considerably.

Miriam quickly finished her cup. "Do you suppose anyone will want to buy it? And if so, do we charge them more or less than for the regular wine?"

"We'd better ask Papa."

Salomon recalled that his mother had occasionally produced an odd vintage like this. He was quick to agree that, while there wasn't much color to the wine, it was, in fact, rather tasty.

"Why isn't this wine red?" Joheved asked. It wasn't clear, like water, but more of a pale pink.

"Of course you wouldn't know—you were so busy taking care of Meir that you missed the wine harvest entirely," he replied. "We didn't have enough people to tread the grapes until all the color leached from their skins. So I drew off the juice from Robert's grapes early."

The rest of the household began to notice that something interesting was happening in the cellar, and soon everyone was sampling the strange, pale, bubbling wine.

"I like it, Papa," Rachel declared. "It tickles my nose when I drink it."

"My father has wine come out like this sometimes," Benjamin said, already on his second cup. "They call it *vin diable,* the devil's wine, and he always charges extra for it. He wishes he could make it come out bubbly all the time."

Then he started to chuckle. "But you can't transport it hardly any distance at all. Papa sold a cask to the Archbishop of Rheims, and when they opened it, an entire roomful of priests got sprayed." Benjamin was laughing so hard he could barely get the story out. "They certainly considered it the devil's wine."

By now it was quite a jolly group of people in the cellar. Rivka brought down some bread and cheese, and several of the students got into a belching contest. Meir was standing close to Joheved, and the way they were gazing at each other, it appeared that they would be leaving the impromptu party early.

Miriam still had wits enough to ask her father, "But Papa, if it's dangerous to move this wine around, how can we sell it?"

"Well, I suppose we could limit sales to local customers, who can carry it home in their own vessels," he said. "Or maybe, if there's not very much, we can just keep it for ourselves." The festive atmosphere was contagious, prompting Salomon to whisper, "Maybe we should see this as the Holy One's blessing, and save it for the *brit* (circumcision)."

"Joheved said she hasn't told anyone." Miriam couldn't help but notice that her sister threw up almost every morning before they put on tefillin and prayed together. "How did you know?"

"A man congratulated me the other night at synagogue." Salomon frowned with distaste. "He pointed out that we'd been studying Talmud every night for two months during the Cold Fair, and not once during that time did my oldest daughter—may the Holy One protect her—visit the mikvah."

Miriam was appalled. "I hope you rebuked him strongly." It was considered extremely bad taste for anyone to discuss a woman's mikvah attendance. But then Miriam had another thought. "If we serve this wine at the *brit,* you can't call it *vin diable.* That would be tempting Satan."

"I suppose you're right." Salomon stroked his beard. "I know, we'll call it Vin Champagne instead."

As springtime drew closer and snow continued to fall, Samson's failure to appear caused increasing anxiety. Not only did they fear for his safety, but how was Salomon's wine going to get to Paris in time for Passover?

Jewish wine shipped without a Jew accompanying it lost its kosher status, without which it wasn't worth shipping. Wine was a necessity at Passover, but once the festival was over, its price would drop significantly.

Just when it seemed that some alternative arrangement would have to be made, Samson walked into the courtyard. And he wasn't alone. Clinging tightly to his mantle was a small, red-haired boy, perhaps five or six years old. He watched wide-eyed as Samson hugged Anna and Baruch and then shook Salomon's hand, all the while never losing his grip on the tall man's cloak.

"I would like you all to meet my son, also named Nicolae, but now called Jacob, after my old master." Samson spoke in Hebrew, and it was obvious that the boy understood him. "We would have been here sooner except that his circumcision took a long time to heal, and we were forced to remain in Mayence all winter."

"Your son?" Anna stared at him in disbelief. "Since when have you had a son?"

"I didn't know I had a son either," he replied with a wink. "Finding you made me wonder if somebody else from our family might still be alive back home, so I decided to go see."

Anna took a deep breath and asked, "What did you find there?"

"There was nobody left." Samson struggled to keep his sorrow under control. "Our village had been rebuilt, but everyone living there was a stranger. I asked and asked, and finally somebody directed me to a cousin who had little Nicolae."

"When I brought him back to Mayence, the Jews there warned me to have him circumcised right away. They said if a crazy Edomite caught me with him first, I'd be accused of kidnapping one of their children for some devilish purpose." He shook his head in exasperation. "Well, I'm here, better late than never."

When it came time for Samson to leave for Paris, Anna begged him to leave the boy with her, but he refused. During the entire week he had been in Troyes, the child had not left his side.

"But you can't have him travel around with you like a dog," she scolded him. "A Jewish boy has to go to school."

"They start studying Torah so young?" he asked.

The concerned look on his face was enough to convince Anna that this problem had not occurred to him. "Like it or not, Uncle, you're going to have to settle down. I'm surprised you've managed to stay unmarried so long. Jews usually like everyone all matched up, like in Noah's ark."

"Oh, my old master tries to marry me off, but I barely make enough money to support myself, let alone a family. And who'd want to marry me anyway?"

"Don't tell me that you don't make enough money." She wagged her finger at him. "Everyone says that a Jew who can't get rich these days is either lazy or stupid, and I know you're neither. As for where you'd find a bride, that's not difficult. There are lots more women converts than men."

That was true; women converts had only to immerse themselves in the mikvah, while men had to undergo circumcision, a formidable obstacle. Anna knew that only a convert would marry a man with as little learning as Samson, but the odds were still in his favor.

"Very well, Anna, you win," Samson said with a sigh. She was right; he needed a wife to help take care of Jacob. "I'll see about it when I get back to Mayence."

But he never did get back to Mayence that year. He quickly conducted his business in Paris and returned to Troyes in time for Passover. After the seder, Baruch insisted that Samson remain in Troyes so Jacob could begin his education immediately.

"Here in Troyes, Anna can look after the boy when you're away, and with all the Champagne fairs, you'll find plenty of business opportunities."

Anna pressed his point. "And wouldn't it be nice for little Pesach to have a cousin living nearby? Then, once you find a bride, you can move back to Mayence or not, whatever suits you."

Samson was no match for their arguments, and as it turned out, living in Troyes wasn't much different from living in Mayence. During the fairs it was simple to make the same type of arrangements with merchants that he had previously made in the Rhineland. And as long as he was there, he'd get to know Sarah's new maidservant better; experience had taught him that the young women who worked for the Jews were not always so chaste as they appeared.

For Joheved, May and June were delightful months. After six months of snow, the weather finally warmed, her nausea and tiredness were gone and she felt extraordinarily well. The baby was kicking vigorously, and nothing enthralled Meir more than lying in bed with his hand on her swollen belly, waiting to feel his child move within. Salomon had agreed to study Tractate Shabbat, and they soon reached the second chapter, which contained the Mishnah about women dying in childbirth.

Miriam and Joheved made no attempt to hide their interest in the discussion, and for Salomon's pupils, his pregnant daughter's presence brought immediacy to their Talmud studies. Joheved felt an urge to participate in the lesson herself, something she had never done before, and her throat tightened in anxiety. This was ridiculous—Papa and Meir both knew she studied Talmud. Why should she be tongue-tied in front of their students? The Mishnah began as she remembered it:

> For three transgressions women die in childbirth. Because they neglect *niddah, challah,* kindling the (Sabbath) light.

Salomon immediately asked why these three laws were singled out; why not other transgressions?

Joheved knew the answer and was trying to find the courage to speak when Benjamin beat her to it. "Because women are the ones primarily responsible for observing them," he said. "Niddah obviously depends on her. And since she makes the family bread, she has the opportunity to take challah. Finally, she is the one at home, rather than in synagogue, when Shabbat begins, so lighting the Shabbat lamp also falls to her."

"These are also mitzvot that men must trust women to perform correctly," Miriam whispered to Joheved. "If a woman neglects niddah or taking challah, her husband transgresses as well when he sleeps with her or eats the untithed bread."

"I'm sure whatever you told your sister is something we would all find of value," Salomon admonished her.

Miriam blushingly repeated her comment aloud and added, "And if she forgets to light the Shabbat lamp in time, her family will have to sit in darkness."

Salomon held up his hand to get his students attention. "I want to dispel the notion that death in childbirth is retribution for the woman who has sinned in one of these three ways." He surveyed the room as if daring anyone to contradict him. "Childbirth is so dangerous that a woman may need benevolence from the Merciful One in order to survive. Even if she has sufficient merit to preserve her in ordinary circumstances, it may not give her the extra protection necessary to save her when she is in the throes of childbirth."

His audience sat rapt with attention, and several students raised hands, but he dismissed them by stating, "Please save your questions until we've read the Gemara, which may answer them."

The Gemara continued with the biblical verses that supported the importance of the three obligations for which women were responsible.

> It was taught before Rav Hisda that the Holy One, Blessed be He, said: I gave you life-blood and I commanded you concerning blood. I called you "the first" and I commanded you concerning "the first." The soul that I put within you is called "a light" and I commanded you concerning lights. If you fulfill these, all is well; but if not, I will take back your souls.

Salomon saw some blank looks, and asked for someone to quote the appropriate verses and explain how they supported the Gemara. None of the students looked like they wanted to answer him, and Meir was just about to when Joheved began speaking. The entire class stared at her in amazement.

Her voice quavered at first, then grew steady. "The prophet Jeremiah calls Israel holy to God, the 'first' among His grain, and in Numbers the challah tithe is called the 'first' of our kneading. In Proverbs it states: The light of God is man's soul."

Now Joheved addressed the room with authority. "Thus Rav Hisda means that if you neglect the mitzvot of blood, challah and light, The Holy One will: Take back your blood, revoke your designation as 'first,' and extinguish your 'light,' your soul." She was gratified to see that none of the students looked confused now, and that Meir was smiling at her with pride.

But there was another explanation, one from Midrash Bereshit Rabbah, and Meir needed to hear Salomon resolve the difference between them. "But what about Rav Yehoshua's words?"

"Ah oui." Salomon frowned. "I suppose we must discuss them now that you've brought up the subject." He turned to the students and said, "There is also a *midrash* on this subject—it goes as follows:

> Because Eve spilled the blood of Adam, the first of men, women were given the mitzvah of niddah. Because she spoiled Adam, the first pure dough of the world, women were given the mitzvah of challah. And because she extinguished the light of Adam's soul, women were given the mitzvah of Shabbat lights.

Salomon paused to let his students digest what they'd just heard, and then asked them, "What is the difficulty with Rav Yehoshua's *midrash?*"

This time Joheved spoke up immediately and her voice was angry. "The Creator gave us mitzvot to make us holy, not as a punishment. Why else would we bless Him whenever we perform one?"

"I agree," Meir said loudly, eager to support his wife's reasoning. "Certainly no other mitzvot were given as punishment."

"The mitzvah of lighting the Shabbat lamp isn't only for women," Asher said. "My father lights it when he travels; all Jewish merchants do."

"And all Jewish bakers take challah," Miriam added, "whether they're men or women."

"Enough." Salomon's voice was adamant. "Our Sages knew this *midrash* and they rejected it. Rav Yehoshua's teaching is not recorded in the Gemara, not even as a dissent. Our Sages also reject Rav Yehoshua's notion that Eve was responsible for Adam's death."

Again Salomon stared around the room, daring anyone to challenge him. "They were driven from Eden because of Adam's ingratitude, his shameful act of trying to shift the blame onto Eve, whom the Holy One had given him as a gift."

Salomon glanced down at the text. "Let's return to the Gemara. It now asks the question,

> 'Why does punishment come at their time of childbirth? Mar Ukva said: When the shepherd is lame and the goats are running, there is rebuke at the pen's gate and judgment at the corral door.'"

Salomon smiled at the silent classroom. As he expected, nobody volunteered to explain this cryptic passage. It was a reminder of why it was impossible to study Talmud without a teacher, one who has learned its meanings from his own teacher. Salomon worried that this knowledge was too vast for one man to recall, which is why he labored over his kuntres.

"What Mar Ukva means is that when the goats are penned in and cannot escape, even a crippled shepherd can catch up with them and discipline them," he explained. "So too a healthy woman needs only a little merit to see her through the small pitfalls of life. But a woman in childbirth may be in such grave danger that it takes a miracle to save her, and then she will either be rebuked or judged worthy of such a miracle."

Joheved and Meir exchanged anxious glances. Poor Hannah, only a miracle could have saved her. Meir offered a prayer that Joheved would be deserving of such a miracle, while Joheved prayed that her childbirth would be so easy that no miracles were needed. And to prove the point that men also need the Merciful One's benevolence in order to survive danger, the Gemara now asked:

> And men, when are they searched for misdeeds? Reish Lakish said: When they cross over a bridge. Only over a bridge and no more? Rav would not travel on a ferry upon which an idolater rode. Rav Zeira would not walk between palm trees when the severe south wind blew. Rav Yitzchak said: If a man becomes ill, the Heavenly Tribunal asks for his merit before they free him.

"So we see that a man too is vulnerable in dangerous situations," Salomon explained. "And like a woman, as long as he is in good health, he does not need any special worthiness to remain in this state. But if he takes ill, the burden of proof is shifted to his shoulders."

Again Meir worried about Joheved and the baby; his store of good deeds had surely been used up when he was so terribly sick last autumn. How much weight would his prayers carry now at the Heavenly Tribunal?

Salomon worried about Joheved as well. When she saved her husband from the demons, had she made herself their target instead? Still, even if his daughter were deserving of death for some sin of her own, his own piety might protect her.

As for Joheved, she tried to think about childbirth as little as possible. She busied herself in the vineyard—the fresh spring air smelled so good. She made sure the wine accounts were current and arranged for the collection of any payments due at the conclusion of the Hot Fair—in case, heaven forbid, that Papa or Miriam had to deal with them. She didn't dare mention her fear of childbirth to Meir, but after their studies, she did respond honestly when Miriam brought up the subject.

"Joheved," her sister asked one morning as they put away their tefillin, "now that we've studied the Gemara about women dying in childbirth, are you more or less worried than before?"

"I don't know." Joheved was almost relieved that Miriam had broached the subject. "After what happened with Hannah, of course I'm scared. But if that fate has been decreed for me . . ."

"You're one of the most devout women in Troyes." Miriam took her sister's hand and squeezed it. "The Merciful One has gotten them through childbirth safely; surely He will protect you too."

"So I'm more learned, that's no guarantee. The Holy One may hold me to a higher standard." Joheved remembered how Meir had grabbed her while she was still niddah, that night when he'd had a nightmare. Would that count as neglecting the mitzvot?

"After the baby is born, I want you to tell me exactly how it felt," Miriam said. "Leave out no detail."

"What?" Joheved sensed that Miriam was worried and tried to lighten their discussion. "Do you want to know if it's really as painful as it sounds, or if women just scream to make their husbands feel guilty?"

"Actually I intend to scream just for the fun of it when my turn comes," Miriam replied in turn. "When else are you allowed to yell your head off and everybody thinks it's normal?"

Joheved turned serious again. "Well, I hope I don't have to scream much. It's going to be difficult enough for Meir." But if she were screaming, he'd know she was still alive. "Now that you've asked, I'm more worried about the pain than dying."

Miriam squeezed Joheved's hand again and smiled. "No matter how much a woman moans or curses, it seems like she always forgets the pain as soon as she holds her baby."

Joheved remained silent. How much was it going to hurt her? Papa taught that the reason it was ordained in Leviticus for women to bring a "sin" offering to the temple after childbirth was that, during the travail of labor, they swear that they will never lie with their husbands again. Would she suffer such agony that she would sooner give up using the bed than endure childbirth again?

It made her blood freeze just thinking about it. But she couldn't share those fears. Miriam was still a maiden—how could she appreciate how precious marriage's physical pleasures were, especially to one the demons had stolen them from?

"Don't worry," Miriam said, sure it took more than fear of pain to quiet her sister. "You can't die in childbirth after saving poor Catharina's life. She would have frozen to death if not for you."

"I don't see how saving an Edomite prostitute's life will impress the Heavenly Tribunal." Joheved scowled. She deserved no reward for saving Catharina. Mitzvot should be performed for their own sake, not in order to receive a reward.

"But she's not a prostitute any more." Miriam lowered her voice to a whisper. "And I'm not sure she's going to be an Edomite much longer either. Anna told me that Catharina has been asking her about conversion."

Joheved gasped. "Oh non. Doesn't she understand how dangerous it is?"

"How would Anna know? She was a pagan in the east when she converted. She has no idea how the Church views such things."

Though the Church tolerated the Jews in its midst and rarely interfered with how they practiced their own religion, Jews were forbidden to proselytize among its flock. The Jew caught trying to convert a Christian, if he was lucky enough to escape with his life, could count on being beaten and expelled from town along with his family. His friends would disassociate themselves from him in order to spare themselves the same fate, and who knows how far he might have to travel to escape the long arm of the Church?

The lot of the new convert, if discovered, was worse. The Church recognized no possibility of undoing baptism. Converts were considered heretics, subject to every persuasion the Church could muster in order to force them back to the "true faith."

When Joheved and Miriam asked Anna to discourage Catharina from this perilous path, they discovered that they were too late. At first, Catharina had intended only to remain in Aunt Sarah's service until she had paid off her debt to the midwife. As soon as good traveling weather came, she would return to Provins, where she hoped to find some savings still being kept for her.

But it was still snowing in April, and life in Sarah's household was better than Catharina expected. Sarah had her help Miriam collect and prepare their store of medicinal herbs, a task she found fascinating. Then there was the exciting night when two women were in labor at the same time, so Catharina was conscripted to assist Sarah with the more difficult birth, while Miriam handled the routine one alone.

Miriam's delivery went well, but the woman Sarah attended gave birth to a stillborn. It was then that Catharina learned of a difference between Judaism and Christianity that affected her profoundly. When Catharina began to cry over the dead infant, forever tainted by original sin and consigned to hell by its lack of baptism, Sarah gently informed her that Jews had no such belief.

Jewish Law declared that infants younger than thirty days old had not yet acquired a soul, so if they died, their ordained soul remained with the Creator. Even older babies who died went straight to the Garden of Eden—what sins could they possibly have committed in such a short life?

Catharina had never thought about the theological differences between Jews and Christians. She had learned that, in their stubbornness, Jews didn't accept Jesus as Savior, for which they were eternally damned, but that in time they would see the error of their ways. She had also been taught that they were a greedy, wretched people, abandoned by God to live in crowded, miserable hovels in the worst part of town.

But Catharina saw no evidence of misery in Sarah or Miriam's households, and inside, they were finely furnished. The Jews didn't think that God had abandoned them, and in fact, believed quite the opposite. They appeared to be perfectly content with their own religion and its rituals, and it was obvious to all that Miriam's father was a good and pious man.

The longer Catharina resided with Sarah, the more impressed she was with how the Jews lived. She was awed by the discovery that every Jewish male knew how to read and write, as did many of the women. In the Christian world, only the wealthy educated their sons, and even they rarely schooled more than one.

Catharina's conversations with Anna also forced her to see Christianity in a less appealing light. Anna knew only paganism before she converted, and she was curious about this religion the Jews viewed with such hostility. She never dared to question the other servants, but one morning when they were doing laundry together, Catharina seemed approachable.

First they filled the large wooden washing trough with hot water, then added wood ashes and caustic soda. Chemises were always laundered first, while the wash water was fresh, the bed and table linens later. The two women were stirring the clothes around when Anna brought up the touchy subject.

"So who exactly is Jesus and what did he do?" Anna asked. She knew that he had to be somebody important for the Notzrim, mainly because the Jews vilified him so much.

"Jesus is the Messiah, the Son of God." Catharina scrubbed at a stubborn stain with some mutton fat soap. "He lived a long time ago, died for our sins, and if you believe in him, you go to heaven."

"The Messiah? The hero who's supposed to bring peace to the world and take the Jews back to the Holy Land?" Anna knew what the word meant; the Jews prayed every day for the Messiah to come. But if he had lived so long ago, then why was there still war and how come Jews still lived in France and Allemagne?

Catharina examined the chemise for any remaining stains, and finding none, rinsed it out and hung it up to dry. "Jesus will do that when he comes back again. He just came the first time to be crucified, resurrected and be our Savior."

Catharina could see that Anna looked confused. Maybe she didn't know what "crucified" meant. "When they crucified him, what they did was to nail him to a cross and leave him there until he died. That's why the cross is our symbol."

Anna noticed a chemise with loose embroidery and put it aside for mending. Now she understood why the Jews referred to the Notzrim as "those who worshipped the Hanged One." She couldn't imagine praying to a corpse, and she tried to think of something else to ask about while she went inside to get more hot water.

"You said Jesus was the Son of God. Who was his mother?" Anna had overheard merchants telling stories about Jesus' mother. One version said she was seduced by a wicked neighbor while her husband was away studying at the yeshiva, thereby making her son, the product of adultery, a bastard. Another version improved on this tale by also making his mother niddah when the stranger lay with her, thus adding an additional sin to Jesus' conception.

Catharina threw a handful of chicken feathers into the washtub and dumped in the dirty table linens; chicken feathers and hot water were particularly good for removing grease stains. "His mother was the Blessed

Virgin Mary, a mortal woman, who is now at her son's side in heaven. If you pray to her, she can influence him to be merciful and help you." She hoped Anna didn't ask about the immaculate conception, a concept that only the most learned clergy understood.

"Oh, I see." Anna had grown up with the Roman gods, who regularly impregnated human females.

The two women silently scrubbed the soiled tablecloths and napkins, pausing occasionally to pour some green grape verjuice cleaner on the worst stains. Anna was about to ask how Jesus' mother could be virgin, when Catharina asked if they could go to the bathhouse together the next time she went.

Catharina had never been to the stews until Sarah insisted that she bathe once she'd recovered from her illness. She'd gone with Miriam and Joheved the following Friday afternoon and discovered the nearest thing to heaven on earth. To relax in the warm water, surrounded by happy women looking forward to the Sabbath, was an unimaginable delight. And this was no rare occasion. Most Jewish women bathed at least monthly.

Even more amazing, when they started on the bed linens, Anna informed her that Jewish men were not allowed to lie with their wives whenever they felt like it, like animals did. "He must not even touch her during her flowers and for a week afterward," Anna explained. "At the end of that time, the woman bathes and then goes to the ritual bath. There she says a prayer, immerses and is again permitted to her husband."

"You mean that, if I were to become Jewish, there would be two weeks a month when no man could force his attentions on me?" Catharina turned around to face Anna, almost dropping the sheet she was trying to hang up, and Anna nodded emphatically.

"That's the most persuasive argument in favor of Judaism I've heard yet," Catharina said, her voice bitter.

Anna was convinced that men's mistreatment lay behind Catharina's sarcasm. As they folded the tablecloths and hung the rest of the bed linens to dry, Anna confided some of the details of her time as a barbarian captive, and how, when she immersed in the mikvah at her conversion, the pain and horror began to wash away in the pure water. And when she went to the mikvah again, after the product of her captor's rape had been expelled from her body, she emerged from the "living waters" a new woman, her trauma healed. Now those memories were little more than a dream.

That ritual immersion could cleanse Catharina too, and thereby remove the stains of her harlotry and subsequent abortion, was enough—she didn't need any more convincing. But unlike Anna, Catharina did realize the danger, and she wanted to wait until the time was right. One thing she did do was to accept Anna's offer to ask Samson to retrieve her possessions on his next trip to Provins. And to her relief, he did so without asking any questions.

He was an intriguing man, this tall, red-haired convert who had traveled so far to find his long-lost son, and she enjoyed watching them play together in the courtyard. She knew he admired her by the way he looked at her whenever she worked outside; he was almost as subtle at hiding his desire as the students were. But then it had been her business to notice such things.

twenty-seven

Summer 4837 (1077 C.E.)

It was late June, and with the Hot Fair approaching, Joheved was filled with conflicting emotions. Thank heaven her pregnancy had advanced to the point where the child would likely survive if she went into early labor. But once Papa began studying with the fair merchants, supervising the vineyard would fall to her, and walking any distance these days was so tiring. Even worse, there had been no rain for over a month, and if it didn't rain soon, the grape harvest would suffer. Then there was the dread she didn't dare think about, that of childbirth itself.

Papa and Mama hid their anxiety and acted eager for the birth of their first grandchild. Miriam worried too, but much of her attention was focused elsewhere; Papa had hinted that he would soon set her and Benjamin's wedding date. Only Meir viewed the future with complete trepidation. As advised in Tractate Berachot, he had spent three months praying that the babe not be stillborn, and now he diligently prayed for a safe delivery. But neither he nor Joheved could forget Hannah.

Count Thibault and his advisors were also worried. Besides the lack of rain, there was disturbing news from the east.

"Your Grace," Henri, the new seneschal, began his report. "Last winter, despite the heavy snow, King Henry managed to cross the Alps and meet with Pope Gregory. They say the king wore a penitent's smock and stood barefoot in the cold before the pope."

"I find it hard to believe that a monarch would debase himself so." Guy, the chamberlain, gazed at Henri with narrowed eyes. "Are you sure your information is accurate?"

Henri stared back at Guy. "Several people have confirmed it," he replied, his voice firm.

"What did King Henry give up?" Thibault asked anxiously.

"Nothing, Your Grace." Henri sounded puzzled. "There was no mention of lay investiture or selling of offices."

"Now all hell has broken loose," the seneschal continued. "The princes of Allemagne have chosen an antiking, Duke Rudolph of Swabia, and as soon as he was crowned, there was civil war. One side holds that no obedience is owed to an excommunicate, the other that a pope must not sit in judgment on kings."

Guy had heard enough from that pup, Henri. "I don't care what the pope and German kings do to each other, but their war is creating havoc for travelers." He stood up and began to pace the room. "Here it is, the first week of July . . . many merchants have been delayed and who knows how many will stay away altogether?"

"You are right to be concerned, Guy." Henri tried to mollify the older man. "The merchants' tempers flare when they finally do arrive in town, only to find others ensconced in their favorite stalls. My sergeants have been increasingly busy keeping order."

Thibault motioned his chamberlain to sit. "Don't worry. War usually means higher prices and greater profits, which ought to keep the merchants cordial." Neither he nor his men dared tempt fate and mention their real concern, the prospect of drought.

But not all merchants encountered delays. Hiyya ibn Ezra and others who traveled by ship avoided the battlefields and arrived on time, as did wool dealers from the north like Nissim. Yet there was no sign of Ben Yochai. Salomon tried to quell Joheved's anxiety by reminding her that Ben Yochai was very old; they couldn't expect him to keep making such an arduous trip forever. But she had to see him, to confront him over the cure that had nearly killed her husband.

As the Hot Fair entered an even hotter and drier second month, wheat prices rose so high that Thibault issued an edict that any speculator's grain would be confiscated. With any luck, word of the shortage would spread, and cartloads of wheat would arrive in time for the Cold Fair.

Thibault congratulated himself for strictly keeping his lands on a three-field system, thus insuring that they still had oats and barley from the spring harvest. Folks might have to eat more black bread than they liked, but it would take more than four months without rain before his Champagnois went hungry.

Wheat was not the only crop devastated by the dry weather. Vintners watched in dismay as their grapes withered on the vine. By filling empty casks in the Seine and forming a bucket brigade, Joheved managed to keep some of the vineyard irrigated. But this would produce only enough wine for local Jews, thus drastically reducing their income. Thank heaven she'd decided to sell the "Vin Champagne" at exorbitant prices rather than reduced ones.

Correspondence with Rheims confirmed a drought there as well. Reluctantly agreeing that neither one could afford a wedding until after next year's harvest, Salomon and Benjamin's father scheduled a tentative date for the following fall. Benjamin and Miriam consoled each other that at least their *nisuin* was arranged.

The hot, dry weather took its toll on Joheved. Now eight months pregnant, she'd never felt so uncomfortable in her life. Climbing stairs left her breathless, and for the first time, she prayed the afternoon service at home, only going to synagogue in the morning when it was not quite so stifling in the women's gallery. The women there smiled at her sympathetically, and a few told her that they prayed better when she was there to lead them. But the baby's vigorous movements cheered her, as did Aunt Sarah's pronouncement that all was going well.

Joheved had all but given up on seeing Ben Yochai again when Papa returned from afternoon services with some guests to share the evening meal. She was in the cellar, savoring its coolness while she took her time drawing a pitcher of wine, when he called to her. "Come up, ma fille; there's somebody here who especially wants to greet you."

The cellar steps were impossible to climb in her condition, especially carrying a pitcher of wine, so Joheved came in through the kitchen door. Her face lit up, and at first Meir thought she was smiling at him, not at the old man standing beside him who was searching his sleeves to find sugar almonds for Rachel.

"Shalom aleichem, Mistress Joheved." Ben Yochai's eyes widened at the sight of her swollen belly. He continued with obvious satisfaction, "I am so pleased to see you again. You are looking well indeed."

"Aleichem shalom, Ben Yochai, it's my pleasure to greet you," she replied in turn. He looked even more wizened than she remembered. "I hope your health is good."

"My health is in the Merciful One's hands," he answered. "But your health is another matter. If you come to my stall, I have a special protective amulet for you and your child."

Those few words were all they said to each other, but Meir sensed that more had been communicated between them. So when the elderly scholar rose to leave, and Joheved too eagerly volunteered to see him to the courtyard gate, Meir grew suspicious. Her poorly hidden distress when he suggested that they both walk their guest back to the synagogue only confirmed his misgivings.

Joheved said nothing as they strolled along, occasionally nodding at acquaintances they met on the way. While the fair was in session, Count Thibault kept torches burning to light Troyes' streets at night, and many people were outdoors taking advantage of the cool evening air. She wasn't happy about going to the fairgrounds to meet Ben Yochai, but she had to speak to him alone.

Meir must have read her thoughts. "Ben Yochai," he said, "I don't think it's good for my wife to be wandering around the marketplace in her condition. Can't you bring the amulets here?"

The old scholar heard more than concern for Joheved's propriety in the young man's voice. The cure had obviously been successful; secrecy was unnecessary now.

"Meir, if you allow me a few moments of private conversation with your wife, I will answer all your questions on our way to synagogue." When Ben Yochai saw the way Meir's expression hardened in response, he knew he was right.

It would be impolite to deny their guest's request, so Meir stalked off ahead of them. His wife and Ben Yochai were up to something, and the sorcerer's explanation had better be a good one.

"Just one question," Joheved spoke hurriedly. The longer she kept Meir waiting, the more upset he'd be. "When should I take the mirror out from under the bed? It's still there." She wanted to ask about Meir's illness, but that would take too much time.

"You can remove it now; its work is done." He glanced at Meir, leaning against a wall and tapping his foot while waiting for them to finish. "Does your husband know anything?"

Joheved shook her head and Ben Yochai continued, "Then I think it is best for us to tell him." He motioned for Meir to rejoin them.

"Ahem, Meir." The old man cleared his throat. "Last summer your wife consulted me about a very delicate matter."

Meir caught the scholar's drift, and a red flush began creeping up his face. Joheved kept her eyes cast down as Ben Yochai continued, "It was manifest to me that we were dealing with a dangerous and powerful demon. So I gave your wife two weapons to fight it, which apparently have been effective. Oui?"

Meir could only nod; he was so embarrassed that this stranger should be privy to such intimate information. Then he remembered the man's reputation and his curiosity won out. "Is it permitted, Master, for you to explain what these weapons were?"

Ben Yochai waited for the people nearby to walk on. "One was a potion to weaken the demon and the other was an amulet for strengthening your yetzer hara. I can't divulge the potion's ingredients, but I can tell you that the amulet consisted of a plain silver mirror . . ." He explained Joheved's part in their battle plan.

"But, Master," Joheved couldn't let Ben Yochai continue under false pretenses. "I tried for several weeks, but I couldn't find any dogs mating in time for the new moon. Then I remembered that Meir's family raises sheep, so I captured reflections of them." Not wanting to see either man's expression, she kept her eyes fixed firmly on the ground.

Ben Yochai erupted with a startled exclamation in some foreign language and then immediately apologized. "You procured images of rams and ewes? That's far too much power for such a small mirror. May the Merciful One protect us all; it's a miracle your husband is still alive."

Joheved's worst fears were confirmed. She had tampered with the amulet's spell and only narrowly averted tragedy. "But he did nearly die!" she said, tears welling in her eyes.

Meir put a comforting arm around her shoulders. "It's all right, Joheved, don't cry."

Now he understood her mysterious absences. Nobody had asked him, but if they had, he would have considered death an acceptable risk.

Besides, he had not only survived, he was better than ever. He turned and addressed Ben Yochai, "There's no damage done, is there?"

"You would know if there was, young man." The sorcerer's wrinkled face took on an expression somewhere between a bemused smirk and a lecherous grin. "You are a very lucky fellow, or perhaps I should say that your wife is a very lucky woman."

Ben Yochai chortled to himself and continued, "You two will have sons such as were unknown even in the generation of Moses." He bid Meir see his wife home; they'd meet later at the study session. They left him shaking his head in amazement and muttering, "Sheep, I can't believe she used sheep."

"Meir, please forgive me," Joheved burst out. "I was only trying to cure you, to expel the demon. I knew it might be dangerous, but I never thought you'd get so sick. And I couldn't tell you—Ben Yochai said the demon had to be taken by surprise."

"There's nothing to forgive, but I forgive you anyway." He wrinkled his nose in pretend disgust and gave her another hug. "I much prefer the yetzer of a ram to that of a dog."

So did she. Then she remembered what the old scholar had said before he left. "Meir, what did Ben Yochai mean about us having sons such as were unknown even in the generation of Moses? He said it as though he expected you to know."

"I guess you haven't studied Tractate Eruvin yet," he replied. "I know it's in the tenth chapter. Give me a moment to remember it properly and I'll quote it for you . . ."

> Rav Shmuel said in the name of Rabbi Yohanan: Any man whose wife solicits him for the holy deed will have children such as were unknown even in Moses' generation.

Meir waited for her face to redden and wasn't disappointed.

> For regarding Moses' generation it says, "Get yourself intelligent, wise and renowned men." Then it is written, "And I took as tribal heads, renowned and intelligent men." He could not find "wise men."

"So Moses found intelligent and renowned men, but not wise ones," she repeated, trying to understand the passage from Deuteronomy. "Go on."

> But regarding Leah it is written: Leah went out to him (her husband Jacob) and said, "You shall sleep with me tonight, for I have hired you"; and it then says, "The children of Issachar (the son conceived by that union) were acquainted with wisdom."

"Because she solicited her husband, Jacob, to lie with her, Leah begat Issachar, whose wise descendants were even greater than the men of Moses' time," Joheved said uncertainly.

Women were supposed to behave modestly with their husbands, and this was the first time Joheved heard it was admirable to openly initiate relations. But hadn't she been doing something like that last autumn? She needed to see the whole Talmud text, not just these few lines. They reached the courtyard gate, and Meir leaned down to kiss her before he returned to the synagogue.

"Are you sure you're not angry with me?" she asked.

"Of course I'm not." How could she understand that a young man might consider death preferable to impotence? "Joheved, if you hadn't expelled the demon, divorce would have been inevitable. And I would rather die than see you married to another man!" His vehement devotion startled her, and he tried to lighten his tone. "Just think of all the wonderful sons we're going to have now."

She wanted to return his obvious affection. "That reminds me, I think I'll study Tractate Eruvin with Miriam tonight while you're with the scholars. That way I'll still be awake when you get home." The invitation in her voice was unmistakable.

As she watched her husband walk back down the street, Joheved wondered if Ben Yochai would be right, at least the part about having sons. Well, she'd know soon enough. Then she began to smile; she had a feeling Miriam would be as intrigued by that passage in Tractate Eruvin as she was.

It took some searching before they located the provocative text in their father's kuntres. The section began with a Baraita that interpreted a verse from Proverbs.

> "He who acts impetuously with his feet is a sinner" refers to one who performs the marital act and then repeats it.

Joheved knew that scripture often used euphemisms, and sure enough, Papa's commentary explained that the word "feet" implied a reference to the reproductive organs. "Papa says such behavior is sinful because it badgers the woman. But see here, the Gemara immediately offers a challenge:

> Is this so? Rava said—One who wants to have male children should perform the holy deed and then repeat it.

"Look at this, Joheved. Papa's kuntres on this text is longer than the verse." Miriam eagerly read it to her. "Her desire having been aroused by the first act, the woman will climax and issue her seed before the man does during the second act. Whenever a woman conceives as a result of discharging her seed before her husband, the resulting child will be male."

Joheved continued this train of thought aloud. "Since the aroused woman desires the second act, her situation is different from the Baraita, which claims that it bothers her."

Miriam giggled and couldn't resist teasing her sister. "Are you speaking theoretically or from personal experience?"

The blush on Joheved's face as she tried to avert her eyes from her sister's gave her away.

Miriam continued with the text about Rav Shmuel, and the reward for the wife who solicits her husband for his marital obligation. Joheved was pleased to see that Meir had quoted it accurately. But the Gemara raised an objection, and the text, which had been amusingly risqué, suddenly took a serious turn.

> Is this so? Eve was cursed (for eating from the Tree of Knowledge), as it is written: To the woman He said "I will make severe . . . your suffering"—this refers to the sorrow of raising children, . . . "And your childbearing"—this refers to the distress of pregnancy . . . "And in pain you shall bear children"—this is to be understood literally. "Your desire shall be for your husband and he shall rule over you"—this teaches that a woman asks for satisfaction in her heart, and a man with his mouth. And this is decreed a fine thing among women.

The sisters sat quietly for a few moments. The curses of Eve would fall on them too. Joheved thought of Marona mourning her daughter's death, what she'd said about the whole village losing children in a smallpox epidemic—the sorrow of raising children. So far the distress of pregnancy had been bearable, but she would soon know firsthand the pain of childbirth. Her throat tightened in fear.

"I think this section is almost done; let's finish it." Joheved wanted to think about anything but the pain of childbirth.

> When is it praiseworthy for a woman to request her desire? When she does so (silently) by making herself attractive before her husband.

This Papa described as approaching him indirectly with affection and charm, but he wrote nothing else about silent petitioning being admirable except that it contradicted what Rav Shmuel had said earlier.

Joheved smiled to herself as she thought of the ways she was able to silently encourage Meir these days. A long and lingering kiss or her fingers playing gently on his thigh under the table during souper. At least the last curse didn't apply to her; she had no difficulty making her needs known to Meir. But not last summer, she reminded herself.

"Joheved," Miriam said cautiously, interrupting her sister's thoughts. "What made you want to study this particular text tonight?"

Maybe it was the intimacy of having studied together, or maybe because Meir now knew everything, but Joheved confided the entire saga of Meir's impotence and Ben Yochai's cure. Miriam was impressed with her sister's fortitude and expressed disappointment only when Joheved admitted that she had no idea what was in the antidemonic potion.

"I bet Ben Yochai's right about your sons," Miriam said with a giggle. "You must have spent months soliciting your husband." And with the yetzer of a ram, Meir probably had no difficulty repeating the holy deed.

"We'll see." Joheved wasn't sure. Maybe her behavior, while silent, was still too brazen. Yet Leah had blatantly told Jacob that he must sleep with her and she was rewarded. Maybe she should ask Meir about it. She yawned widely and wondered what was keeping him. Mama and Rachel had gone to bed ages ago.

What was keeping Meir was that which often detours men during an evening with good company, especially when the weather is hot and dry. Salomon and his students had lingered at a local tavern. Salomon was in a particularly good mood; he had discovered a fine new student, slightly younger than Meir, who had previously studied in Allemagne. The young man had come to Troyes to marry a wealthy merchant's daughter, with the understanding that he would continue his studies here at his father-in-law's expense. His name was Shemayah, and Salomon was looking forward to teaching such an excellent pupil.

When Salomon and his students finally arrived home, somewhat less sober than when they had left, they found Joheved and Miriam sitting at the dining table, bent over a volume of Talmud. Seeing his daughters deep in study of the holy text filled Salomon's heart with pride and affection, and he warmly asked them what they were learning.

"Tractate Eruvin, Papa, the tenth chapter," Miriam replied with a yawn. "It has an interesting section about women and childbirth in it, and your kuntres explains it very well."

"And what made you choose that tractate?" He kept his voice neutral, not wanting to alarm her. Even with his commentary as a guide, it wasn't appropriate for his daughters to study Arayot on their own.

Miriam had no idea why she and Joheved should not study this part of Tractate Eruvin, and replied innocently, "Ben Yochai quoted some of it to Joheved and Meir, about how wise their sons were going to be, and Meir told her where to find the passage."

The words were already out of her mouth before she realized what her comment implied about her sister and brother-in-law's intimate relations. Luckily the students were still making a good deal of noise with their chatter, and Miriam hoped that Papa would be the only one to hear and understand what she'd said.

"Hush!" Joheved whispered. Now the more discerning students would think she brazenly demanded marital relations from Meir.

When Joheved said, "Hush," her voice somehow carried across the room. The salon quieted, except for the new student, Shemayah. He had been too poor to frequent taverns in Allemagne, but now, with coins in his purse and comrades to spend them with, he had consumed far more ale than he should have.

He had both heard and understood Miriam, and was whispering a quote from Tractate Sotah to Asher,

> Rabbi Eliezer said: Whoever teaches his daughter Torah, teaches her "*tiflut!*"

Tiflut can be translated as nonsense, but Shemayah intended its usual meaning, lewdness or lechery. Unfortunately for the newcomer, his words seemed to echo through the otherwise silent room. He found himself standing alone, adrift in a sea of animosity. Even those students who didn't recognize his quote knew that such a saying would infuriate their teacher, and they watched with trepidation as, indeed, Salomon struggled to control his temper.

It was all Asher could do to restrain Benjamin from physically assaulting the stranger who had just insulted his fiancée. Frenchmen were notoriously sensitive when it came to defending their women's honor, and in this regard, French Jews were no different than their non-Jewish compatriots.

Meir was angry too, but he knew he had to prevent Salomon from losing his infamous temper. He turned to the new student and said, as coldly as he could, "Shemayah, I'd like to introduce you to my wife, Joheved, and her sister, Miriam, Rabbenu Salomon's daughters." Then Meir watched with guilty pleasure while the color drained from Shemayah's face as the extent of his iniquity dawned on him.

Shemayah had only just arrived in Troyes and had never been to Salomon's house before. His intellect dulled by drink, how was he to know who these two women were? He swallowed hard, vowing to never drink ale again.

Thump! The room was shaken by the sudden crack of Salomon's fist hitting the dining table. Joheved and Miriam grabbed at their book to keep it from flying off the table, but a ceramic flask crashed to the floor. As the other students slunk back, the terrified new pupil did the only thing he could think of, and humbly introduced himself in return to Joheved and Miriam. It was all he could do to keep from stammering.

Miriam, who wasn't sure what *tiflut* meant, started feeling sorry for the miserable-looking fellow. She could see that if Benjamin got his hands on him, tonight's woe would be nothing in comparison. So she acknowledged his greeting with a polite nod and set about cleaning up the broken crockery. Joheved, also eager to defuse her father's fury, stood up and welcomed him to their home.

Shemayah groaned inwardly when he saw her hugely pregnant form; it was strictly prohibited to mention any sins that a woman approaching childbirth might have committed. Heaven forbid anyone should give the Heavenly Tribunal information about her misdeeds. Undoubtedly her husband and father would be feeling even more protective of her than usual.

He quailed when Meir, looking down at his hands and appearing annoyed to find that he had no gloves to take off, addressed Salomon, "Rabbenu, I think I need to teach Shemayah some manners."

Mon Dieu, thought poor Shemayah, who had never learned to use a sword. Meir was going to challenge him to a duel.

By this time, the painful throbbing in Salomon's hand had enabled him to regain control of himself, and he saw that things had gone far enough. He rubbed his aching palm and sighed. "Meir, I think that my new student needs to learn discretion rather than manners. From now on, perhaps you ought to be his study partner?"

Meir's study partner? What about her? Joheved shot her father a hurt look and he responded by patting his belly and gently shaking his head. He was right, she thought sadly. Everything would be different once the baby came, for both her and Meir. Then she brightened as she felt a kick from the infant within. The child, she would be the one to teach him . . . or her.

Meir, who had never intended to fight Shemayah, took this piece of information with equanimity. He enjoyed going over texts with Joheved, but he missed studying with a regular partner, like Benjamin and Asher did. Each fair he studied with a different merchant, some more learned than others, but it was frustrating having to start anew each season. And there was no denying that Shemayah was very smart.

Meir wanted to make his agreement public. "Very well, and I intend to teach him all the texts about learned women." Meir tried to make his smile to Shemayah as warm as he had been cold before. But there was something else he needed to say.

He chose his words carefully, trying to sum up what he had heard Salomon maintain before. "I have been taught that a man must teach his daughters the mitzvot. As to those that say, 'He who teaches his daughter Torah teaches her *tiflut,*' this refers to the deepest learning, the mysteries of the Torah, which we do not teach to women or to children. But Torah he must teach her, for if she does not know the laws of Shabbat, how can she keep them? And the same goes for all the commandments, in order that she be careful in their performance."

Meir's defense filled Salomon with pride, and he added to his son-in-law's words. "I read in a manuscript where advice was given to a wise woman on this very question. 'The statement about *tiflut* refers to a father teaching a young daughter, who like most girls, is lightheaded, spending her time on nonsense. But women whose hearts have drawn them to approach the Holy One—surely they may ascend the mountain of the Eternal. Scholars should treat them with honor and encourage them in their venture.'"

The tension in the salon dissipated, and the students began to bid one another "*bonne nuit.*" When they'd all left, Salomon climbed upstairs with his tired children and whispered to Meir, "Go over Tractate Eruvin with Joheved and make sure she understands it properly. Then she can do the same with her sister."

Alone in their room, Joheved was effusive in praise of her husband. Meir let her gush, until finally, sure that his swelled head would explode if he heard any more, he changed the subject. "By the way, I'd like to see this wonderful mirror of yours."

Joheved took a step back. "Well, I guess it would be all right," she said as she rummaged around under the mattress. She pulled out the amulet and handed it to him.

Meir looked down at the plain, silver mirror. The words, "Meir ben Samuel" were etched around the edge in small Hebrew letters. His own visage stared intently back at him, and disconcerted, he quickly returned the mirror to Joheved.

"It doesn't look like anything special."

"Ben Yochai says it's just an ordinary mirror now." She started to put it away, but Meir stayed her hand.

"Let's leave it where it was," he said. "It can't hurt."

"All right," she replied. His hand was still holding hers and she squeezed it. "We can always take it out again if we need to look in a mirror."

His free hand tilted her head up and she returned his kisses enthusiastically. So far she continued to welcome his attentions, although they no longer had relations with him on top.

He was glad he had thought to show her the Baraita in Tractate Niddah that taught:

> During the last months of pregnancy, marital relations benefit both the woman and the child, because on account of it the child becomes well-formed and strong.

Of course Joheved wanted to know why this was so, and anticipating a student's question, Salomon had written in his kuntres, "The semen acts to clean the fluid surrounding the fetus by removing any impurities." As for why relations should be beneficial for the woman, Salomon wrote that he didn't know.

After what happened tonight, Meir decided he had better teach Joheved all the Arayot texts, not just Tractate Eruvin. Otherwise she might attempt to study them on her own or with her sister. But then his wife's embrace began to cloud his mind, and he forgot about everything except the effect her sweet caresses were having on his body. He blew out the lamp.

twenty-eight

Troyes

Late Summer 4837 (1077 C.E.)

Another late night, two months later, and Joheved had never felt so exhausted in her life. Yet it was impossible to follow Aunt Sarah's advice and relax between contractions. No sooner did one pain recede than the next crescendo began, and it was all Joheved could do to keep her moans from turning into screams. But she would not cry out, just as she refused to curse her husband or her Creator.

Aunt Sarah assured her that all was well. In fact, Miriam whispered to her—unwilling to provoke the Evil Eye—her progress was quite typical. When Joheved had gotten up that morning, she'd felt nothing unusual. But after using the chamber pot, she discovered liquid still dripping down her legs.

Miriam, and then Sarah, confirmed that her water had broken. Joheved insisted that she felt fine, but they sent her back to bed without breakfast. Then the household sprang into action, except for her. Baruch rode to Ramerupt to get Meir's mother, Salomon hurried to the synagogue to bring home a Torah scroll, and the yeshiva students prepared for a day, or days, of prayers on her behalf.

Meir carefully hung his tefillin at the head of the bed, and then, to Joheved's chagrin, he went out and returned with her own tefillin, which he silently arranged next to his.

"How long have you known?" she asked, too ashamed to look at him. No wonder he'd been so suspicious last summer.

"Oh, quite some time," he replied nonchalantly. He didn't want her to worry, not now. "Rachel doesn't always close the door behind her when she comes down in the morning."

"You don't mind?" she asked anxiously, unable to accept what his actions implied.

"Of course not; every mitzvah you perform is to your credit." Couldn't he say something more reassuring than that? Mon Dieu, this might be the last conversation he'd ever have with her. *Stop thinking like that! Don't give Satan, the Accuser, an opening.*

Meir fought to overcome his panic, and when he felt calmer, he took his wife's hand and gazed into those incredibly blue eyes. "Joheved, I am proud to be married to such a righteous woman.

Once Salomon's tefillin joined the other two pairs, Rivka ushered her son-in-law out. Then she unwrapped Ben Yochai's birth amulet. It was a small scroll, inscribed with the names Sanvi, Sansanvi and Semangelaf, the three angels dispatched to capture Lillit. The three were urged to protect, help, deliver, save and rescue Joheved, daughter of Rivka, from all who seek her harm. This was followed by Psalm 126:

> Adonai will do great things for us and we shall rejoice.
> Restore our fortunes, Adonai, like the rivers of the Negev.
> They who sow in tears shall reap with songs of joy.
> Though he goes along weeping, carrying a seed-bag
> He shall come back with songs of joy, carrying his sheaves.

Rivka attached the amulet to the footboard, while Rachel drew a circle in chalk around the bed. Then, with great concentration, Rachel chalked the magical inscription, "Sanvi, Sansanvi and Semangelaf, Adam and Eve, barring Lillit," on the door and walls, rubbing out and meticulously redrawing any word that didn't meet her standards. By the time she was done, Joheved was feeling occasional mild cramps, but nothing that justified the fuss everyone was making.

Still, she let them dress her in one of Meir's chemises, to share his strength, and his sword, normally stored inside his chest near the bed, now lay on top, ready for battle. She drank Aunt Sarah's medicinal teas and inhaled the sweet herbs burning on the brazier. Surrounded by her female relatives, all babbling excitedly, it was rather like a party.

But that had been hours ago and now it was nearly midnight. Joheved, her hair loose and disheveled, sweat dripping down her body in the warm room, prayed that she would never have to suffer like this again. Everyone agreed that the first child's birth hurt the most. If she could endure this one, the others would be easier. She tensed and clutched Rivka's hand as the next contraction gripped her, but the pain was accompanied by a new feeling, an urge to push so strong that she was forced to obey it.

"Rachel, go tell Meir that the child is nearly ready to be born." At Joheved's insistence, Aunt Sarah sent Rachel downstairs regularly with reports. "All right, Joheved, let's get you onto the birthing stool."

The bottomless chair was not particularly comfortable, and with the next urge to push, Joheved was unpleasantly reminded of using the privy, only worse. Her labor pains became unremitting; every push was torture, made bearable only by the knowledge that each one brought her suffering closer to its finish. Finally there was a burst of agony, and Joheved pushed with a strength so great that it seemed to come from outside her.

"Keep pushing, keep pushing," Miriam urged her on, her voice high with excitement. "The head is coming now, I see dark hair."

Joheved felt as though her bones were breaking, and the scream she had struggled so long to suppress tore from her throat. Then suddenly, it was over. Another urge to push came, but the pain was nothing compared to her previous effort.

"The head is out now; we're almost there," Aunt Sarah said, standing behind Miriam and letting her apprentice handle this so far uneventful birth. "Here come the shoulders."

Joheved could feel the baby being pulled from her and then the joyous cacophony began. "It's a boy! A boy! You have a son! Mazel Tov!" The baby let out a cry and the room was again filled with happy chatter; Rivka was sobbing and smiling simultaneously.

The new mother opened her eyes just wide enough to view her naked, squirming child, loudly protesting against being evicted from his warm abode, then she sank back against the stool. The pain was gone; the bone-wrenching agony was finally over. Joheved could barely speak, but she managed to make the blessing, "Baruch ata Adonai . . . Who is good and does good."

She could hear Rachel shouting the news to those below, and she wished she could be there to enjoy her husband's reactions, to hear him make the same blessing a parent traditionally makes at the birth of a son.

She wanted to lie down again, but she wasn't done. Another two pushes for the afterbirth, and then she felt gentle hands applying a soothing balm to the mouth of her womb.

Aunt Sarah had been more than amazed when Marona arrived with the alkanet salve in addition to an armful of ferns. "It's a miracle," she said, giving the woman a grateful hug. "I'd given up hope of ever finding alkanet bushes around here."

"We have some growing near our manor," Marona explained. "There's nothing better for healing the inevitable wounds of childbirth, especially a woman's first childbirth." She smiled fondly at Joheved.

Downstairs, Meir and Salomon were being enthusiastically congratulated. Both shed tears and Meir found it difficult to finish the blessing without choking up. When Joheved screamed, he'd jumped up and started towards the stairs, but then he'd stopped, terrified, at the bottom step. For an interminable instant he was convinced the worst had happened, but then there was Rachel, grinning widely, yelling that he had a son. Before he knew it, he'd picked her up and was swinging her around the room. Then Salomon did the same.

Now, after what seemed like an eternity, Rivka was leading him upstairs to see his wife and new son. He took a deep breath outside the door and, recalling his sister, nervously stepped inside. All the women had gone except his mother, who was arranging fern fronds on the floor. She gave him a fierce hug and then joined Rivka in bidding him good night.

The scene before him could not have been more different from his last visit to a lying-in room. Joheved, her hair neatly braided, was sitting up in their bed, surrounded by cushions. At her breast, propped up by one of those cushions, was their new son, quietly enjoying his first meal.

Meir could feel the tears running down his cheeks. He tried to absorb everything before him, so he could keep this memory like a treasure, to take out and cherish whenever he wanted.

"Oh, Meir, isn't he beautiful?" Joheved welcomed him. "Your mother says he looks just like you did when you were born."

Meir approached slowly, reluctant to disturb the baby's contentment. Nearly covered with swaddling, only the infant's small face and a shock of black hair could be seen. "I think you look beautiful," he replied, emphasizing the "you."

He sat down just as the bells of Matins begin to chime. Tonight and every night until the boy's circumcision, Meir was determined to stay up studying Torah in this room. A healthy birth by no means ended the need for protection from the forces of evil; for the seven days preceding the *brit,* mother and child were in great danger. From this moment on, until the boy entered into the covenant of Abraham, neither he nor Joheved would be left alone.

"Are you all right? I mean are you in pain or do you need anything?" Meir had heard her scream in agony not so long ago, yet she looked perfectly fine now.

"I'm mostly tired, that's all." It was odd, but even though Joheved knew she had been in terrible pain earlier, now it was only a vague memory, something she knew had happened to her but could no longer feel. "The baby's stopped sucking; would you like to hold him?" She gently offered Meir the sleeping form.

He gingerly picked up his new son. The child was so small, he fit perfectly between his father's palm and elbow. Meir was marveling at the miracle in his arms when there was a soft knock on the door. Meir didn't want to say anything for fear of waking the baby, but Joheved called out for the visitor to enter.

Salomon walked quickly to where Meir sat, his eyes not leaving the babe for an instant. "I don't want to disturb you, but I can't sleep until I've seen my grandson."

With practiced ease Salomon lifted the child and held him up to the light. "Baruch ata Adonai . . . Shehecheyanu, . . . Who has kept us alive, sustained us, and brought us to this season." He slowly recited the traditional prayer of thanksgiving, his voice choked with emotion.

Then he handed the bundle back to Joheved and kissed her hand. "Thank you for this precious gift. I'll be back before dawn, Meir, so you can get some sleep."

Joheved watched her father close the door behind him, and her happiness faded. He hadn't asked about her at all; he had eyes only for his new grandson. Well, what did she expect? How many years had he been waiting for a male offspring?

But then she felt Meir staring at her, and when their eyes met, she knew that she was uppermost in his thoughts. His loving expression warmed her like a ray of sunshine that suddenly breaks through a cloudy sky.

"Shall we name him Salomon?" Meir whispered. A boy was named publicly at his circumcision, and even his parents never mentioned the chosen name until then. If Lillit, heaven forbid, should come looking for the child, he would be harder to find without a name.

"How about Samuel?" Joheved countered, reluctant to admit that she'd rather not use the name Salomon.

"My sister's little boy is named Samuel." Meir shook his head; the thought of a baby named Samuel prompted too many painful memories. "Besides, I think we should use a name from your side of the family. He is your parents' first grandchild."

"All right then, what do you think of Isaac?" She looked down at the baby and smiled. "That was my grandfather's name." Isaac was also the name of Grandmama Leah's father; it would be a way to remember and honor her too.

"Maybe." Meir nodded his approval, not wanting to say the chosen name out loud. Then he grinned at her. She was alive, the baby was alive—it was a miracle! "Then again, we could call him Issachar." She returned his smile and closed her eyes.

For a while Meir sat there, watching her and the baby, asleep together in the large bed. Then he remembered he had work to do. He picked up his text and began to study.

The next six days passed uneventfully. Joheved's milk came in, her bleeding tapered off and she remained free from fever. The baby sucked well and dirtied what seemed an inordinate amount of wool swaddling as a result. Downstairs, the kitchen was the hub of tremendous activity, the air saturated with the most delectable odors as Rivka prepared for the feast they were giving that evening in anticipation of her grandson's Brit Milah.

Upstairs, Salomon sat by his daughter's bed and worked on his kuntres. Mother and son were at their most vulnerable the day before the *brit,* but tomorrow the danger would pass. Right now Salomon needed to relieve himself. Meir, who should have been back already, had fallen asleep downstairs while listening to his students recite their lessons, and they had left him undisturbed. Salomon finally called Rivka upstairs so he could use the privy.

On his way back to the house, Sarah accosted him. "Brother, I need to talk with you," she said soberly. "We have a problem."

The look of alarm on Salomon's face revealed that he had misunderstood her. "Don't worry, Joheved and the child are fine," she added. "This concerns another matter."

"Can't it wait until after the *brit?*" he asked, annoyance replacing relief. Rivka wouldn't like being kept away from the kitchen.

"No, it can't." She leaned towards him and lowered her voice. "And we need to speak privately."

"Very well, let's go down to the cellar."

Sarah followed him downstairs, where, to his consternation, they were soon joined by Baruch, Anna, Miriam, and the parchment maker's daughter, now Sarah's new maidservant.

"I thought you wanted to speak privately?" he said.

If Salomon was peeved now, it was nothing compared to how he felt once Sarah explained that her maidservant, Catharina, had grown disillusioned with worshipping the hanged one and wanted to convert. He had no idea why all these people had to be here with her, but he suspected rightly that they had chosen this moment to tell him because they hoped he'd be too happily occupied with his grandson's Brit Milah to refuse.

He gazed from one serious face to another and asked, "Do you understand the consequences of this act?"

Salomon had expected Sarah to answer him and was taken aback when Catharina replied solemnly, "I know that I shall be a Jew and not a Christian, and that at the New Year, God will judge me, and if I am worthy, forgive my sins."

He turned and warned her, "If I do this, you cannot remain in Troyes—it would be too dangerous, both for you and for us."

"Nothing would please me more than to leave this city." She spoke with unusual vehemence. "And the sooner, the better."

"There's not really any hurry," Miriam interrupted Catharina by taking her arm. No one should think this had been a hasty decision. "When Papa hears us out, I'm sure he will agree."

"Hears us out?" Salomon looked around the room and scowled. "Does everyone here have something to say?"

Baruch explained how Catharina had become friends with Anna, how their talks had caused her to reject her old religion. Sarah then verified that her maidservant knew the things a Jewish woman needed to know. But Anna made the clinching argument.

"I have spoken with Uncle Samson," she announced proudly. "If Catharina converts, he will marry her and take her to live in Mayence. Nobody could possibly know her there."

"I see you have given this much thought," Salomon said slowly, stroking his beard. It was a perilous decision, but he could not deny a conversion to someone who truly desired to become a Jew, just because it entailed risk.

"Please, Papa," Miriam beseeched him. "I know Catharina is sincere. And she will make a good mother for little Jacob."

"Here is my ruling," he said. "Until Yom Kippur is over, no one speaks of this matter to anyone but our family. Catharina remains one of the Notzrim in every way. The servants must suspect nothing." He stared sternly at the group surrounding him. "Then, if Catharina still wishes to join the Children of Israel at Sukkot, I will convert her and perform the marriage. Afterwards, she and Samson must leave the city. Do you agree?"

Catharina nodded, too overcome to speak.

"Merci, Papa." Miriam hugged him. She couldn't wait to tell Joheved the wonderful news.

Baruch clasped his hand warmly. "Merci, Master, on behalf of my wife's uncle as well."

"Merci, Brother," Sarah said teasingly. "At least you let me keep my maidservant until Sukkot."

The next morning saw Salomon's household in the kind of joyous tumult they hadn't experienced since Joheved's wedding. The previous night, Joheved had stayed indoors with Rivka and an ever-changing group of women visitors while everyone else feasted in the courtyard and drank the *vin diable,* now called Vin Champagne. But today, after the ceremony, Meir and his father would host another banquet, and she would finally be free to go outside and celebrate with the others.

Joheved and Meir wore their nuptial finery, and she was relieved to see that she could still buckle the matching girdle. Even the baby was dressed in sumptuous garments. Rivka had saved a small amount of fabric from Joheved's wedding bliaut, hoping to use it for just such an occasion, and her first grandson now wore a fine linen chemise, a blue silk mantle and a tiny ornamented hat.

The occupants of the synagogue's women's gallery could not restrain their delight at their community's newest member, clothed like a miniature bridegroom. But all their enthusiastic chatter couldn't take Joheved's mind off the fact that very soon, her precious baby would have his blood shed in front of her very eyes.

Suddenly it was time. With great reluctance Joheved made her way downstairs, where Meir was waiting for her. Recently there had been complaints that it was not appropriate for a beautifully dressed young woman to sit among the men, but most people considered it cruel to remove the newborn from his mother's arms at a time when he would most need her comfort. Salomon saw no reason to change things. Baby boys in Troyes had been circumcised on their mother's laps for as long as anyone could remember, and that's the way it would remain.

Meir assisted his wife to the center of the main floor, where two thrones were covered with fine cloth. One was for Elijah the Prophet, whose legend said he'd been rewarded for his zealous defense of circumcision with the promise that he would attend every one. The other was for Joheved, who would sit there holding her son while the ritual was performed.

The congregation stood as she carried him in. "Blessed be he who enters," they recited, although nobody was sure whether they meant the baby or Elijah.

Meir took his son while Joheved sat down. Once she was comfortable, he pronounced the father's customary invocation, that he was ready to perform the mitzvah of Brit Milah. When he handed the baby back to her, her hands were trembling. As proud as she was to have given Meir a son, at that moment Joheved wished she could be anywhere except where she was. She grasped her son's legs firmly, shut her eyes tight, and took a deep breath. She felt Meir's hand squeeze her shoulder reassuringly. She dare not move a muscle.

Things happened very quickly at this point. The *mohel,* the ritual circumciser, made his blessing, "Baruch ata Adonai . . . Who commands us concerning circumcision," and immediately, the baby gave out a howl. Joheved let out her breath and every man in the congregation relaxed his clenched thighs—it was done.

As the *mohel* bandaged the wound with a cloth smeared with olive oil and healing herbs, Meir made the father's traditional blessing, "Baruch ata Adonai . . . Who commands us to bring our sons into the covenant of Abraham our father." The *mohel* gave Joheved a wine-soaked cloth for the now-swaddled baby to suck on, which quieted him enough for the rest of the blessings to be heard.

Now Salomon joined them. Just as it had been his responsibility, representing the mother's family, to host the first banquet, it was his privilege to chant the Brit Milah benedictions. First came the one over wine, and Salomon waited until a cup of the bubbly stuff found Joheved's hand before he began. Then there were prayers of healing, one for the baby and one for Joheved. These were followed by the *gomel* blessing for Joheved, for her having survived childbirth, *gomel* being the special prayer of thanksgiving said at one's first synagogue visit after escaping from great danger.

Meir added his "Amen" and shook his head in amazement. Had it only been ten months earlier that he'd recited the *gomel* blessing himself after his illness? Back then he'd barely been strong enough to climb up to the *bimah*.

Joheved, her terror beginning to dissipate, clutched the precious bundle that was her child to her shoulder and whispered soothing words. The cry of her son, so helpless and unable to pacify himself at her bosom, had produced an unexpected flood of milk from her breasts. Thank heaven for Johanna, who had handed her some absorbent material to place under her chemise and protect her beautiful silk bliaut from stains. Joheved also gave thanks that, unlike her rescuer, mother of twin boys, she had to endure only one Brit Milah at a time.

Surprisingly, her son seemed content with the wine-soaked cloth, so she turned to watch the ceremony's conclusion. Salomon was on the last blessing now, the one announcing his grandson's name. Joheved, indeed the entire congregation, waited with bated breath as Meir slowly leaned forward to whisper the boy's chosen name in his ear. Her father's tears began to flow immediately, and Joheved couldn't help but cry herself as she watched him struggle to control his emotions and finish the benediction.

Salomon gave Meir a long hug and then cleared his throat. "May this child, named in the House of Israel, Isaac ben Meir, become great. Even as he has entered into the covenant, so may he enter into Torah, into the marriage canopy, and into the practice of good deeds."

The congregation responded heartily, "Amen." ❋

afterword

ONE OF THE FIRST QUESTIONS people ask me when they finish reading *Rashi's Daughters* is: What is real and what is fiction?

Rashi (Salomon ben Isaac, 1040–1105) is, of course, a real person, as are his mother, Leah, and his daughters, Joheved, Miriam and Rachel. He refers to his wife only twice, once in his kuntres, complaining how she threw the keys at him when she was niddah, and the other time in a responsum, when she interrupted him at afternoon services because a non-Jew was bringing them a gift of bread and cake before the end of Passover. Rashi doesn't mention her name, but legends about him call his wife Rivka.

Rashi's teachers in Germany included Isaac ben Judah, whom he calls brother. Since I knew Rashi had no siblings, I decided that this Isaac ben Judah was his brother-in-law. Rivka's sister, Sarah, however, is completely imaginary, as is Miriam's profession as a midwife.

Isaac, the Parnas of Troyes, appears in several responsa, and Rashi's first two students were indeed his grandsons, Joseph's sons. Joseph's wife was, of course, nameless, as was Meir ben Samuel's mother, so I invented other woman's names, Johanna and Marona, for them. Marona wasn't a complete invention; one of Meir's granddaughters bore that name.

According to one of his sons' commentary to the Talmud, Meir's livelihood came from viticulture and raising sheep in Ramerupt. Both these occupations required a good deal of land, which implied that his father was a feudal lord. As seen in many responsa dealing with land transactions, other Jews held estates as vassals as well.

Jews were also involved in the slave trade that transported pagans captured in the Slavic lands to Muslim Spain and North Africa. While there is no direct evidence that Rashi owned Jewish slaves, other French Jews of his time did, and it seemed a likely explanation for how he managed to find Jewish servants to assist with his winemaking.

The great Champagne fairs were famous throughout Europe, and while there is some debate over when they began, we know they were held in Troyes during Rashi's time because we have responsa that discuss them. Count Thibault, his wife Adelaide de Bar, and his advisors are historical figures, and Pope Gregory's controversial reform of the Catholic Church is well documented. The great famine of 1030–33 killed much of the population of northern France, and the winter of 1076–77 was called the coldest in 100 years, with snow falling from November through April.

Many of the foods I describe appear in Rashi's kuntres, and the clothing Jews wore are detailed both there and in *Machzor Vitry,* an 800-page anthology of Jewish law, liturgy and customs whose primary author was Simcha ben Samuel of Vitry (Meir's brother-in-law). In fact, *Machzor Vitry* was my primary source for knowledge of how Rashi's community observed Jewish holidays and life-cycle events. The chapters on marriage and Brit Milah were particularly illuminating, as were those describing Sukkot and Passover. All the magical and medical remedies I used in *Rashi's Daughters,* as well as the demonology, were culled from medieval sources; I could never have invented such bizarre stuff.

Many of Rashi's responsa are known today, including Rashi's angry response to his teachers and his private letter to Meir over kosher slaughtering. Rashi's students wrote of their surprise when he ignored tradition and mourned for a little girl during a festival, causing some historians to speculate that she was his daughter. Leah's petition, protesting taxes on her vineyard, is a rare example of a Jewish medieval woman's actual words, and I couldn't resist including it.

At this time there was a great controversy over whether a woman should say a blessing over the Sabbath lights, which was settled only after Rashi's death when one of his granddaughters wrote responsa explaining how the ritual was performed in her mother's home.

This brings up a touchy subject. Nearly every biography of Rashi states that his daughters were learned women who reputedly prayed with tefillin, and I wouldn't have had much of a book unless I presented them that way. But is there evidence of this?

Besides the Shabbat lights responsa, there is another one, written late in Rashi's life, that begins by stating that the reader will not recognize his handwriting because, due to his incapacity, it is being written by his daughter. Thus at least one daughter was learned enough to compose legal responsa in erudite Hebrew, and probably the others were too.

The evidence for Joheved wearing tefillin is less clear. In the Tosefot to Tractate Rosh Hashanah 33a, Rabbenu Tam (Jacob ben Meir) mentions that Michal, King Saul's daughter, wore tefillin. He then states that in his time, women not only performed these time-bound mitzvot, but when they did so, they said the blessing (thanking God for the commandment). But tefillin were not worn outside the home, so Jacob could know only that women said the blessing over them from watching his mother, Joheved, or perhaps his older sisters. In any case, because I am writing fiction, I can draw whatever conclusion I like.

Speaking of tractates, some of the Talmud passages quoted in *Rashi's Daughters* are Berachot 60a (ch.2), Pesachim 112a (ch.4), Ber 57b (ch.6), Bava Metzia 65a (ch.7), Shabbat 21b (ch.9), Pes 116a (ch 10), Ber 20b (ch.11), Ketubot 62b (ch.12), Yevamot 63b (ch. 12), Pes 114a (ch.13), Shab 140b (ch.17), Rosh Hashanah 33a (ch.20), Ber 18b (ch.24), Shab 31b (ch.26), and Eruvin 100b (ch.27).

For those readers who are interested, a partial bibliography is located on my Web site, www.rashisdaughters.com. For those who are very interested, I can provide a complete bibliography of my over 250 sources.

glossary

Allemagne Germany

Angleterre England

Bavel Babylon

Bet Din Jewish court

Bimah pulpit, raised platform in synagogue where Torah is read

Bliaut tunic, outer garment worn over a chemise by men and women

Brit Milah ritual circumcision, performed when a baby boy is eight days old

Chacham Jewish scholar

Challah special bread eaten on the Sabbath, also that portion of dough that belongs to the priests and is burnt outside of Israel

Compline last of the seven canonical hours, approximately 9 p.m.

Denier silver penny; a chicken costs four deniers

Disner midday meal, usually the largest meal of the day

Edomite European non-Jews (Talmudic term for Roman)

Erusin formal betrothal that cannot be annulled without a divorce but does not allow the couple to live together

Havdalah Saturday evening ceremony that marks the end of the Sabbath

Kapparah ceremony performed the day before Yom Kippur where a fowl is waved over a person's head and his/her sins are passed on to the bird

Ketubah Jewish marriage contract given by the groom to the bride specifying his obligations during the marriage and in the event of divorce or his death

Kuntres notes and commentary explaining the Talmudic text

Lillit demon responsible for killing newborn babies and women in childbirth, Adam's first wife

Livre one pound, unit of money equal to 240 deniers

Matins first canonical hour, midnight

Matzah unleavened bread eaten during Passover

Mazikim demon, evil spirit

Midrash genre of rabbinic commentary that expands and explains the biblical text, generally used to refer to nonlegal material

Mikvah ritual bath used for purification, particularly by a woman when she is no longer niddah

Minim heretics

Mitzvah (plural **mitzvot**) divine commandment, also a good deed

Mohel man who performs the ritual circumcision

Niddah menstruating woman

Notzrim polite Jewish word for Christians, literally those who worship the one from Nazareth

Nisuin ceremony that completes a marriage, followed by cohabitation

Parnas leader, or mayor, of Jewish community

Potach demon of forgetfulness

Seder ceremony and ritual meal observed in a Jewish home on the first two nights of Passover

Selichot prayers for forgiveness

Sepharad Spain

Sext noon

Shiva seven days of mourning following the death of a relative

Shofar ram's horn sounded on Rosh Hashanah

Sotah married woman suspected of adultery by her husband

Souper supper, evening meal

Sukkah booth in which Jews dwell during the harvest festival of Sukkot

Taharah preparation of a corpse for burial

Talmid Chacham great Jewish scholar

Tefillin phylacteries, small leather cases containing passages from scripture worn by Jewish men while reciting morning prayers

Trencher piece of day-old bread used to hold meat (instead of a plate)

Vespers sixth of the seven canonical hours, approximately 6 p.m.

Yeshiva Talmud academy

Yetzer Hara evil inclination, usually refers to the sexual urge

Experience the lives and loves of the three daughters of the great Talmud scholar...

ISBN 978-0-452-28862-1

ISBN 978-0-452-28863-8

Look for

Rashi's Daughters, Book III: Rachel

Coming soon

www.rashisdaughters.com

Available wherever books are sold.

Plume
A member of Penguin Group (USA) Inc.
www.penguin.com